BAREFOOT OVER STONES

Liz Lyons

TRANSWORLD IRELAND

TRANSWORLD IRELAND
an imprint of The Random House Group Limited
20 Vauxhall Bridge Road, London SW1V 2SA
www.rbooks.co.uk

First published in Great Britain
in 2009 by Transworld Ireland
an imprint of Transworld Publishers

A CIP catalogue record for this book
is available from the British Library.

ISBN 9781848270534

Addresses for Random House Group Ltd companies outside the UK
can be found at: www.randomhouse.co.uk
The Random House Group Ltd Reg. No. 954009

The Random House Group Limited supports The Forest Stewardship
Council (FSC), the leading international forest-certification organization.
All our titles that are printed on Greenpeace-approved FSC-certified
paper carry the FSC logo. Our paper procurement policy can be
found at www.rbooks.co.uk/environment

Typeset in 11½/15pt Sabon by
Kestrel Data, Exeter, Devon.
Printed in the UK by
CPI Mackays, Chatham, ME5 8TD.

2 4 6 8 10 9 7 5 3 1

For Noel, Eva, Amy and Robert

Part One

You may not always shine as you go
Barefoot over stone
You might be so long together
Or you might walk alone
And you won't find that love comes easy
But that love is always right
So even when the dark clouds gather
You will be the light

'Never Be The Sun', Donagh Long

Michaelmas House, Caharoe, Co. Cork
2005

Today I buried Dan. I wore a blue dress that he always liked and I was careful with my hair, curling it softly around my face to cover the hollowness I knew it showed. I shook every offered hand and murmured in appreciation at the slow river of kind and sympathetic words. My eyes were red and sore, bitten by three days of constant tears. The harrowing spectre of grief has come to settle like a silent friend at my side.

I felt the heartbreaking shudders of my daughter's body against me as her dad's coffin first bobbed and then disappeared out of sight. I held her tightly as she stood overwhelmed by the flood of unexpected loss. Mam and Dad flew home to be with us within hours of hearing the news. They stand at either side of me. They fear I will fall under the weight of this. All three of us united in a parent's instinct to take the part of our suffering child, to stop the pain before it enters the heart of our cherished charge.

It is more than a decade since the summer it all began. I knew in my heart you would not come. But I still scanned the crowd for your face and looked back one last time to the deserted grave before we were driven back to Michaelmas, to the house that has always been home.

Even tonight if I close my eyes I can take myself back to those evenings on the beach at Aughasallagh. I could not believe it when you turned up at the cottage there. I hadn't even told you exactly where we were going. His uncle's place somewhere in Kerry was all I said. But in truth I didn't know myself. I left all that to Dan. I was in the kitchen drinking tea, still half asleep and lulled by the soft low voice of the morning radio. Dan's textbooks and notes were strewn across the breakfast table and his abandoned cigarette was smoking itself out on an overflowing ashtray. You bustled into the kitchen ahead of Dan as if you owned the place. Your ancient purple knapsack was slung over your shoulder and you had a plastic carrier bag struggling to contain the shuddering cackle of a few bottles of cheap wine.

Dan was furious when he followed you through to the tiny kitchen. A week to his final exams and you, of all people, had arrived on the doorstep of his hideaway. He blamed me for inviting you even though I absolutely hadn't. I put it down to the fact that you guessed I would be lonely while Dan studied day and night and you had made it your business to ask around and find out exactly where we were. You always knew the right thing to do; one of the reasons you had me in your thrall. As much as I loved Dan and wanted to be with him, sitting with him as he smoked and cursed about how much study he had left to do had not exactly been the holiday of a lifetime. Then you arrived, filling the house with chatter and gossip and driving Dan up the wall. His face wrinkled in unspoken anger and I knew we had better get out of the house before he blew a fuse.

The weather was glorious and we headed giddily to the beach every day of that week. We swam lengths together along the line of the strand, both terrified of the rough currents of the Atlantic and their merciless strength. From the depths of your backpack you would produce some mangled and dog-eared bodice ripper and in full dramatic voice read out the more jaw-dropping passionate encounters. I collapsed in heaps of helpless laughter. We got disapproving looks from the locals with whom we shared the beach but that merely egged you on, your delivery gaining confidence with every aggressive sigh.

We walked the mile or so to Daly's shop when hunger struck and made makeshift lunches with their fresh white bread and hunks of cheese and ham. I made sure that we bought enough so that I could make a supper for Dan when he arrived pale-faced and exhausted from hours of study. He would devour every last scrap of food and then produce slabs of Dairy Milk chocolate from our cottage stash. When you thought the time was right you would wordlessly nudge a picnic mug of wine in his direction and he would drink it greedily; our three-way harmony thankfully restored.

And I picture now the three of us sitting there preserved in the treasure box of returning memory. The punishing heat of the sun has long since subsided. The taste of the too-sweet wine is on my lips. Sand is gritty between my toes and the excited shrieks of children in the water beyond can be heard like grace notes to our idle chatter. Dan's head is cradled on my lap. The wine is taking hold in all of us and I am becoming quieter while you two are just getting started, as usual. That night, like many others, the topic was the state of the nation.

'Charlie Haughey was a gangster and he nearly ran this country into the ground. Sure even Gay Byrne said this morning on the radio that it will take years to undo all the mistakes of the last decade.' Your face crumples in disdain at Dan's wine-fuelled righteousness and I know that you revel in fanning the flames.

'That man talks through his hole, Dan, and you'd want to catch yourself on 'cause you are beginning to sound a bit like him.'

Dan rises gleefully to the bait and on you both go until the incoming tide drives us back reluctantly to the darkness of the cottage.

I think now that it is always like this. All is clear and certain the moment before our world changes. A day, an evening or maybe just a single hour when we think we can see for ever.

Tell me, Ciara, can you remember it too?

Chapter One

Dublin 1990

The Daisy May on Camden Street had definitely seen better days. The paintwork was scuffed and the windows were permanently steamed up. The menus looked as if they had survived the trauma of decades. But the café had its fans and a steady trade of coffee-slugging students who seemed to hold its comfortable shabbiness in real affection. Alison had fallen for the Daisy May during her first weeks in Dublin. She had clung to its friendly warmth between lectures on days when there was much to read and little to keep her in Mrs Duggan's miserable digs.

It was Rose, whose name and life she would later learn, who served her the first of many milky coffees and toasted cheese sandwiches and gave her enough part-time hours so that she could escape the clutches of the unbearably nosy Bea Duggan and her smelly little box room. Within weeks of starting work in the Daisy May she had found a flat to share with another girl on the first floor of a house in Ranelagh. The landlady, who lived on the ground floor, seemed cheerfully oblivious to their existence except for every second Friday when she accepted their rent money.

'Oh, is today Friday?' she would enquire with feigned innocence as she grasped the notes out of their hands with poorly concealed glee. The gin bottles that sprawled around the black plastic bin on weekend mornings gave the girls some indication of their key role in Jean McDermott's household budget. Alison was gone from Mrs Duggan's two weeks before her father discovered that she had left.

'What do you mean you have moved?' Richard Shepherd was prone to sudden flashes of temper that subsided nearly as quickly as they rose. Alison stayed silent, hoping that if she didn't aggravate him any further, this one conversation might be the end of it. She had told her mother as soon as she had found the flat and needed the deposit of a month's rent. Cathy Shepherd had been terrified of her only daughter being lonely at Mrs Duggan's and was in favour of the move if it meant she had company of her own age. She had promised to break the news to Richard the next time Alison came home for the weekend.

Here they were now at the kitchen table after Sunday dinner and he looked as if his switch had tripped and his entire fuse-board had blown. 'But it took us ages to find those digs,' he spluttered, looking to his wife for solidarity. 'Talk to her, Cathy, for God's sake talk to her!'

'Richard, you know Alison has a good head on her shoulders. I think she deserves our trust, don't you? She has found a part-time job so it will actually end up costing us less than the digs. Besides, think of the company she will have.'

Cathy's voice was soft like honey and Richard's deflation was more or less immediate under its gentle pressure. He muttered something about square meals and all-night parties while he rolled the newspapers furiously into an impossibly tight bundle. Alison pictured the last Spam and canned pineapple concoction that Mrs Duggan had allegedly 'cooked' and barely stifled a laugh. Her mother flashed Alison a conspiratorial grin as her father turned and went to the living room to read the paper. As the custard congealed on his untouched bread pudding Alison knew that the matter was over, for the moment at least.

An hour or so later she reheated his dessert for him over a pan of boiling water. In the living room the papers were strewn around him, tossed in untidy heaps. He accepted his daughter's peace offering with an indulgent smile. 'You will mind yourself, Alison, won't you? You are there to study, not to carouse. Remember where you come from. Be careful who you hang around with.'

Alison interrupted him in mid flow before he started reminding her not to take sweets from strangers. 'Dad, of course I will. I'm older now and I can take care of myself.'

His tears welled up but Richard forced a smile for this ever-so-grown-up girl that his daughter had become while he had been looking elsewhere. Years had passed, becoming a decade, with a second one now close on the heels of the first. It seemed to him like no time at all.

'There must be loads of fine-looking men in that college of yours,' Rose chirped on Alison's second or third week at the Daisy May.

Alison pictured some of the earnest and dreary faces that had turned up to the tutorial on the Crusades that morning. 'Do you know what, Rose, I think the entire history department is sorely lacking a decent-looking man. I thought secondary school was bad but this is ridiculous.' She felt very free, being able to indulge in this kind of talk, and relished the anonymity of her existence in Dublin. Nobody yet knew her past or what she had been like growing up. Rose didn't know, as they chatted about men, that Alison had been painfully shy at Caharoe secondary school and had never so much as gone out with a boy, let alone discussed them in such a casual fashion with anyone. Up to now her love interests had been a painful mess of crushes and awkwardness.

'Well, Alison, you will just have to look further afield to find a nice young man with prospects.'

'I'm only eighteen. I think I would settle for the good looks and hang the prospects for the moment.'

Rose eyed her and was charmed by a familiar innocence. She too had had high hopes once but they had crumbled under the strain of experience. 'I was married when I was barely older than you are now. I loved my Frank but cursed money was always scarce and there's feck all romance in scrimping. Remember that.'

Alison thought for a second that Rose was going to cry and she wasn't sure how she was going to comfort this grown woman whom she barely knew. Sensing the girl's awkwardness, Rose's face broke into her familiar grin.

'Here's one for you now,' she said, flashing a smile at a gangly but gorgeous man who had just walked in. Alison was frying bread for a full Irish that had been ordered by a couple of builder's labourers at a corner table. Typical, she thought. Here she was covered in grease, wearing a hairnet and an oversized cook's jacket in a shade of tired and insipid grey. 'The usual is it, Dan?' she heard Rose say. The fried bread needed to be rescued before it smouldered to the same colour as the pan but Alison was putting off any movement that wasn't strictly necessary. She did not dare attempt to move because she feared nerves rooted her to the spot. Rose moved behind her to butter a mound of toast.

'It's a fry they were wanting not a cremation,' she said in a low-enough whisper, giving Alison an encouraging nudge of her elbow. Rose delivered the toast to the counter in front of Dan with a mug of steaming coffee as Alison finally plucked the bread from the pan. 'Oh, you haven't met my new girl, have you, Dan?' she said, giving Alison an animated wink. Alison turned her flushed face to meet the gleam of piercing green eyes as Rose introduced them. 'Dan Abernethy, meet Alison. Alison Shepherd.'

Chapter Two

Jean McDermott was dragging a dustbin to the front gate when Alison arrived home from the Daisy May. It was a run-of-the-mill household task apart from the clatter of glass bottles betraying the drunken secrets within. 'Ah, there you are, Mary. Cold, isn't it?'

It was pointless correcting her. Alison and Ciara had tried, in the first few days, to get her to call them by their real names but were now convinced that Jean had let the flat to them in a drunken stupor and probably thought that she had just one tenant, a nice wee girl called Mary, quite possibly from Dungloe.

In the hallway Alison found Ciara fiddling with the electricity meter. 'Keep watch there for our esteemed landlady, will you, Alison? This could save us a bloody fortune.' Alison looked on as Ciara inserted a fifty-pence piece and deftly wound the meter until the coin was just about to drop and then quickly wound it back again. Each rotation brought the gauge up higher and when the meter was up to the maximum Ciara wound all the way and let the coin click into the box. 'Electricity for the week for a very reasonable fifty pence!' Ciara was chuffed with herself.

'Where did you learn to do that?' asked a genuinely impressed Alison.

'Oh, I have my sources and this particular one is a total honey from Waterford.'

Although Ciara had only been in college for a matter of months, she already seemed to know every haunt and was never short of someone with whom to strike up a conversation. They were the same age but Alison couldn't help feeling that Ciara belonged to the crowd that seemed to have been running around places like Trinity and UCD since they could toddle. By comparison Alison was definitely relegated to the novice hurdles. She felt genuinely lucky to have hooked up with Ciara. She hoped that if she hid how gormless and out of her depth she always felt she could somehow pull off this whole college thing by observing closely the skills that seemed to serve her flatmate so well.

Alison had noticed Ciara in the first week of term. Well, to be more precise, she had noticed her clothes. How could you not? In a bland sea of jeans and sweatshirts she certainly stood out. Sailing up and down the interminable corridors of the history department, she was a spectacular foil to the muted decor. Her unruly auburn hair was the crowning glory for a seemingly endless array of prim Victorian blouses, shawls and floor-skimming skirts. Months later Alison would experience first hand where Ciara found all her clothes when she was taken on a whistle-stop tour of the charity shops around Rathmines and Camden Street. It would never have occurred to Alison that normal people might shop for clothes in charity shops. The Shepherds donated lots of old clothes to the St Vincent de Paul but Alison thought it was strictly for the poor and the very hard-up. She wasn't so sure about the smell either. Ciara swore to her that every item was laundered before being put on sale but why then did all the shops smell like a packed and sweaty number 13A bus on a wet Monday evening? Whatever her reservations about their source, Alison would never tire of looking at Ciara modelling her latest finds. Ciara's look was pure theatre and Alison found her sense of glamour utterly captivating. In the early weeks of term they shared some tutorials and when she first heard Ciara speak Alison was genuinely surprised to hear a country accent fairly similar to her own. Kerry, she guessed, or maybe Tipperary. Somehow Ciara looked more exotic than Alison had imagined anyone from the country could manage to be.

Before one tutorial Ciara announced to the assembled group that she was moving out of the place she had rented on Leeson Street. 'I took on a family of squatting mice and I am ashamed to say they have beaten me. The little shaggers are popping out of everywhere. Anyone know of a room going? Preferably a vermin-free zone!'

'I need to move out of my place,' Alison piped up to her own astonishment. 'Maybe we could find a place for two? My folks fixed me up with a nightmare landlady,' she said as coolly as she could while her insides churned. Before Alison had time to change her mind, Ciara fell on her offer enthusiastically.

'Jesus, that would be great, Alison! But I have to warn you I'm on a bit of a tight budget. Forty quid a week max.'

Dr Fitzgerald bustled through the room carrying a pile of paperwork. Alison spent the tutorial somewhat panic-stricken at the thought of telling her parents what she had just agreed. But by the end of an hour on Cromwell and the massacre in Drogheda, of which she had only heard a scant word or two, she had decided that sharing a flat with Ciara was the answer to all her prayers. She would find a way to break the news at home. She told herself firmly that they would understand. Get it first and tell them later. Alison surprised herself with her talent for deceit when she spoke to her parents from Bea Duggan's front hallway that night. No news. No news at all. Everything fine here.

A few copies of the *Evening Herald* and some visits to truly appalling flats later had brought them to Jean McDermott's doorstep. And here she was now, waddling back from the gate, a little unsteady on her feet. She eyed Ciara and Alison suspiciously as they stood in the small shared hallway. Her eyes squinted at them as if startled by their presence. After what seemed an eternity she spoke: 'Make sure to put on the Chubb lock, Mary.' Then she disappeared, with the swish of rancid plastic raincoat, into the downstairs flat.

'Mad as a fucking March hare,' Ciara said rather too loudly as they climbed the staircase. 'Come on, wee Mary, you have an essay to write on the bleeding Crusades and I have an essay belonging to you to creatively paraphrase.'

Alison smiled. Today was a good day. Not even an essay on the Crusades was going to spoil tonight. His name ran around her head. In her mind she heard Rose say it again. Dan Abernethy. Suddenly the Daisy May, her comfort blanket, had become the most exotic place in Dublin. Two days to her next shift and Alison thought it was quite possible she might burst in anticipation.

Her mood was somewhat punctured by the filthy state of the kitchen and living room. Dirty dishes rose in a tower from the sink and clothes lay strewn everywhere. Alison loved her new-found freedom with Ciara but someone was going to have to take the place in hand. Her mam and dad were bound to come and see the place she had decided was better than their original choice of Bea Duggan's house. They would have a freak attack if they saw it as it was now.

Even the most rudimentary skills of housekeeping escaped Ciara's attention. She really did appear oblivious as she swept from room to room. When she had found herself in the flat in Leeson Street at the beginning of term she waited until every item of crockery had been used and had pitched its tent in the kitchen sink. Then she extracted the least soiled items: a water tumbler or a plate that had held yesterday's toast, which could easily put in a second day's service without so much as a glance at running water. After one week she had deleted Weetabix from her mental shopping list. Having never soaked a cereal bowl after eating from it she deemed it a food that conspired to glue itself to her bowls and render them out of action. Cornflakes were definitely better, less like wallpaper paste after a day and a half. After two weeks there were fumes coming from the sink, which made Ciara think she might have to clear it soon. But in the name of God how? In her waking hours her mother Aggie maintained her stance at the kitchen sink at home in Leachlara looking out at the cattle grazing in the fields. Neither Ciara nor her brother or sister ever offered to do the washing-up, as her mother seemed to enjoy being lost in contemplation of the world beyond her windows. Ciara's lack of experience was telling in the smelly realm of her Leeson Street flat.

The water in the tap was never more than lukewarm. She had no sponge: she had flung the one that was in the sink when she arrived into the bin. The smell of it had reminded her of a dead mouse that she had had a whiff of in another flat to let in Rathmines. Washing-up or no washing-up, it had to go. After one enquiring visit too many by her slimy landlord she had decided to tell him to shove the flat up his arse, or words to that effect. She'd taken a sly satisfaction in leaving him a sink full of dirty dishes and maybe inconveniencing his next letting somewhat. She'd sworn that next time she would find a place to live herself and keep her father from hooking her up with another of the Leachlara mafia with their swathes of property in Dublin.

Alison now handed Ciara a list of cleaning materials that she had compiled as a means of opening the awkward conversation. Ciara didn't know whether to laugh or cry. Alison was eyeing her so seriously that she knew she had to respond, with sincerity if possible. The list was half a refill page long: toilet cleaner, Jif, bleach, fabric softener and washing powder. It went on and on. God, they might as well go to Dunnes and do a trolley dash through the cleaning products aisle.

'Do you think maybe this is a bit over the top, Alison? Maybe we could start small and build it up over the year?'

'That's kind of a basic kit that any house would need, Ciara. I asked my mam to help me with it at the weekend.'

'Right, I suppose if you think we need it. My budget is a bit tight so we will have to buy it over a few weeks if that's all right.'

'Well, Mam sorted me out with a few extra bob when I was at home so I can just get it all this week and you can get me back whenever you have it. Mam tried her best to buy the stuff in Caharoe at the weekend. I had a hard job stopping her until I reminded her that I couldn't carry it all the way back here on my own. Besides, I told her that you would probably want to come with me to get it.'

'If you want me to, yeah, I suppose I could, but I wouldn't know what most of these things were if they came up and slapped me on the face.' Ciara was doing her best to show interest but she was failing miserably. 'I mean, forgive my ignorance, but what in the fuck is bicarbonate of soda?'

'It's for baking really but Mam says it's great for stain removal and would be handy for soaking dishcloths and dusters.'

'A few hundred packets of it might sort out this vomit-inducing swirl we like to call a carpet,' Ciara said, hoping that humour might lighten the atmosphere a little. Alison looked at the dreary browns and yellows patched together with indeterminate stains. It looked a bit like the compost heap that rotted and heaved at the back of the garden at Michaelmas.

'It is shockingly bad, isn't it?'

'Woeful, Alison, woeful, but sure we will just have to make the most of it.'

Alison motioned to the corner of the room, which they rather grandly referred to as the kitchen. In reality it was a counter top masking a grim line of yellow melamine units. 'Would a cup of tea and a biscuit help, do you think?'

'Jesus, I thought you'd never ask. My head is fucking wrecked from Toilet Duck and Mr Sheen. Whatever happened to a sink full of hot water and where the hell was I when life got so bloody complicated?'

Chapter Three

'Jesus Christ, that fucking hurts.' Hurtling towards the shrill ring of the phone in the hallway, Alison had stubbed her toe on the saddle of her bedroom door. She had been in a deep sleep, dreaming of Dan Abernethy, but the persistent ringing had forced her to rouse herself and abandon his delicious face at the counter of the Daisy May. She fumbled for the landing switch. When she finally reached it the light flickered for a second and gave a little tinkle before the bulb blew. Still the phone kept ringing and still there was not a sign of life from Ciara's room. 'Don't worry, I'll get it!' Alison said a touch savagely as she hobbled past Ciara's door on the way down the stairs.

'Is that you, Ciara?' a girl's voice whispered urgently when Alison picked up the receiver.

'No, this is Ciara's flatmate, Alison. I'll get her for you now. Who will I say is looking for her?'

'This is Leda.' Ciara's sister's voice was barely audible and Alison felt instinctively that she was in some sort of trouble. A loud knock on Ciara's door brought no response. Eventually, after much hammering, a dishevelled Ciara in outrageously loud pink satin pyjamas emerged looking viciously sulky.

'Someone better be on fire. That's all I am saying. What fucking time is it anyway?'

'About three, I think. It's Leda. She seems a bit upset.'

'It's the middle of the shagging night. I'm a bit upset myself.'

The pink apparition disappeared down the stairs and Alison rolled back into her still mercifully warm bed to resume an imaginary romance with Dan. She fell asleep to the lull of conversation from the hallway.

A short note in Ciara's handwriting had been left tagged to the kettle next morning when Alison got up to make breakfast. 'Have to sort something out at home so getting the seven o'clock from Busáras. Will be back Sunday night, sorry about the weekend, Ciara x.'

Waves of panic washed over Alison. She and Ciara had decided to stay in Dublin for the weekend to go to the cinema, visit the national gallery and generally act like first-year students delighted to be away from home. It had been Ciara's idea. In fairness, nearly everything was. Alison had broken the news to her mother at the bus stop in Caharoe the Sunday night before.

'Ciara and I are thinking of staying in Dublin this weekend, Mam – you know, to get a few of the long essays started. Is that all right? I'll be home the following Friday.'

Cathy Shepherd hesitated and Alison knew her mother was steeling herself to say the right thing. Her dearest wish was that going to college would make Alison grow in confidence and even though the thought of her only child being away for two whole weeks made her fit to faint she pulled herself together.

'Of course, love. You'll be careful, won't you? You will need extra money.' Cathy started to delve in her cavernous handbag and produced a carefully folded twenty-pound note from a zipped pocket. 'Ring if you think you are going to run out and I'll send you some more in the post.'

'I'll be grand, Mam, honestly. I have wages from the Daisy May coming to me on Friday so I won't be short.'

Watching her mother watching her was driving Alison mad and ever closer to tears. Trying to pretend to be brave was hard on the nerves and the last thing she wanted to do was start getting weepy in front of her mother, who was looking decidedly shaky herself. God, how she wished the bus driver would actually let them on the bus instead of leaving them to stand there in the freezing November cold. Eventually the bus did pull away from the pavement and Alison breathed a sigh of relief. Two buses and a train journey and she would be back in the flat in Ranelagh and in Ciara's uplifting company. She had Rose and her shifts in the Daisy May. Her college work was hard but not by any means beyond her. Thanks to her dad's GP practice there was enough money for all her college needs, so she didn't feel short of anything. She was on talking terms with a good few people in her class, owing in no small measure to Ciara, who had the knack for chat and in whose company Alison tried mostly to stay. Somehow if Alison could join up the scattered dots of her Dublin existence she might manage to have a life outside Caharoe.

Faced a few days later with Ciara's note, Alison momentarily thought about phoning home with the change of plan. Her mother would be delighted. She was halfway down the stairs when she pulled herself back from the safety net into which she was about to plunge headlong. 'Come on, Alison, don't be such a chicken,' she chided herself. How hard could it be? It was Wednesday. Four nights and Ciara would be back to the flat. In the meantime she could actually catch up on study. There was no law against going to see a film on your own, was there? The time would fly by if she kept herself busy. 'Pull yourself together,' she tutored herself, with only a shard of confidence, before quickly retreating up the stairs.

Cathy Shepherd had stood on the Main Street in Caharoe until the bus carrying Alison back to Dublin disappeared from her view. Only then did she start the short walk to Michaelmas House on the edge of the town square. Her woollen coat was buttoned up right to the collar to protect against the bitter wind and maybe also against a rising loneliness that threatened to engulf her.

Michaelmas was one of a quartet of grand houses standing like imposing sentry keepers around the green in Caharoe. It had been their home for twenty years and Cathy thoroughly loved it. The grand navy front door with its glistening brass fittings reminded her of the week of their wedding when she had lovingly painted it, covering her hands with specks of gloss paint that were murder to clean off.

When Richard had first shown her the house out of which he operated his fledgling GP practice she had been thoroughly shocked by its near-derelict state. The waiting room and surgery, which Richard had allegedly decorated, were the only rooms that were remotely habitable. Even that was a pretty impossible stretch of the imagination. Richard slept on a couch in a room at the back of the house with at least three layers of bedding to defeat the cold. It was there, in that spartan room, that they had first wrapped up in the delicious warmth of each other's bodies under a sea of shabby quilts. It was there also, one evening a few months after they had first met, that Richard had asked her to marry him and live with him in Caharoe.

'Here? In this dive?' Cathy had asked in mock incredulity. It was worth it to see his face but the look of total joy on her face told him the only answer he wanted to hear. 'Yes, I will marry you, Richard, but this place needs a serious shake-up. I love you but you live in a hovel.'

'It's not great, is it?' Richard had said, looking at the wall opposite them from where the hideous flock wallpaper hung precariously, planning its path of descent.

'You keep treating the sick people of Caharoe and I will make sure they don't vomit at the sight of the house. Is that not a fair deal, Dr Shepherd?'

'Deal.' Richard grinned before pulling her beneath the quilts again.

Hugh Lalor, the solicitor who lived in one of the other corner houses of the square, had recommended a builder to Richard when he had first bought the house. Richard had transcribed the details diligently, meaning to do something some day, before filing the information with all the legal papers regarding the sale. Cathy soon unearthed them and so began her transformation of the 'barn', as she had taken to calling Richard's house. She approached Lovett's Hotel across the square and asked if Richard's surgery could move there temporarily while its permanent home was being refurbished. Tadhg Lovett was delighted by the prospect. His lounge, ordinarily empty during the day, would become a flurry of tea-drinking and ham-sandwich-eating and his handful of hotel rooms, usually only inhabited by the odd returning emigrant, would have a purpose.

'Business is business wherever it comes from,' he said, shaking Cathy's hand to seal the deal. 'And tell me now, miss, are you the doctor's housekeeper or secretary? It's just that I have a bad knee that I have been meaning to get checked.'

Cathy imbued her smile with a friendship she was finding hard to muster. 'I am Richard's fiancée, Mr Lovett, and I am sure he would be happy to look at your knee if you can make it across to us. Otherwise he does house calls, whatever best suits the patient's needs.'

'Ah, sure I'll wait until he moves over here for the few weeks. He can have a look at my knee in passing, in between jobs. I should get a discount really, seeing as he will be my lodger.'

'Richard won't see you suffer with your knee, Mr Lovett.' Cathy took herself back to the barn before she said something smart. Caharoe was a small place and it was better to keep on the right side of everyone. God, this doctor's wife thing was shaping up to be great fun altogether.

Tadhg watched her tall, sweeping figure cross the street. 'Fiancée, if you don't mind. Did you ever hear the like of it?' he said to no one in particular, but he was already plotting the sliced-pan order for the sandwiches required for the makeshift surgery and its hungry patients.

The builders took down the partition walls that a previous owner had erected, restoring the original proportions of the house. When all the months of structural work had been completed Cathy took to the decorating with feverish intent. She and her younger brother Donal came most evenings that summer to paint, sand and varnish every surface. Richard supplied the money for the restoration work and brought roughly made picnics to the workers. He was totally useless but he sat keeping them company. If a song he loved came on the battered paint-stained radio he would release Cathy from her vice-like grip on the paintbrush and waltz her around the room. Donal would turn scarlet and look away embarrassed, painting even faster while his sister and Richard danced. When exhaustion overtook them they would sit on a bare floor sipping bottled beer and eating egg sandwiches followed by slices of jam sponge or cream rolls from the bakery on Earl Street.

It took all of that summer to get the house and surgery completed but Cathy enjoyed every minute of it. Tadhg Lovett sold a mountain of sandwiches and had his knee fixed into the bargain. Cathy barely had time to get ready for their wedding, which was set for 29 September, Michaelmas Day. She chose a simple shift dress to the knee in the softest shade of ivory. She wore no veil and her long dark hair hung loose around her shoulders. She carried a clutch of fiery orange-blossomed crocosmia picked for her by her mother. Not for the first time Richard stood captivated by Cathy's radiance. That day he was sure he was the luckiest man alive.

As a wedding present for them both, Cathy got a brass name-plate made for their barn. She read it now twenty years later surrounded as it was by the climbing bark of mature wisteria and clematis.

Michaelmas House
Caharoe
Dr Richard Shepherd
General Practitioner

First Richard, this house and then Alison had been the focus of her life.

She stood hesitating before she put her key in the front door. Her heart was breaking with loneliness for Alison and tears welled in her eyes. Richard was across at Lovett's knocking back whiskey as he always was on a Sunday night. When exactly had it happened? When had her life shrunk to such a small, predictable package of care and duty? As she turned the key on an empty Michaelmas House Cathy Shepherd decided to go easy on herself. She was lonely, that's all, and it was best not to dwell on things that could not easily be changed.

Throughout the week a small part of her hoped Alison would change her mind and come home for the weekend. She was not ready to think of her stint in Dublin as anything other than a temporary arrangement. Alison phoned on the usual days and her form was very good. Cathy managed not to ask her to change her mind. 'It will be good for her, help her to find her feet,' she told a very dubious Richard. If she said it often enough she might just convince them both, she hoped.

Cathy held it together until the following Saturday, comforted by the routine at the surgery. All the regulars, of whom the practice had scores, dragging in their dead legs and arthritic joints on a weekly basis, enquired after Alison. How was she doing in Dublin? Was she living far from the college? Cathy found herself delivering confident assertions that Alison was doing just fine. She had moved in with a lovely girl, Ciara, from Tipperary, and was doing well at her course. All true, she reminded herself if her certainty wavered even for a moment.

She and Richard shared a bottle of red wine on the Friday night and when he admitted that he too was missing Alison that made Cathy feel less pathetic.

'Maybe we could visit her in Dublin some weekend, see the den of vice and squalor she has landed herself in?'

'Ah, show a bit of faith, Richard! I'm sure Alison found a grand flat and to be honest I wasn't as keen as you were on Bea Duggan. She seemed terribly sour.'

'You see, Cathy, that's exactly what I liked about her. She looked stubborn, looked like she wouldn't tolerate any late hours or bad company. Sour can be a good trait in a landlady.'

'God, you can sound like a right old misery guts when you want to.'

'I'm entitled to be miserable when I have had Tadhg Lovett's septic toe presented to me on three separate occasions this week, only one of which happened in the privacy of my surgery. Honestly, I am dreading the moment and the hour when he discovers a boil on his backside, because I won't be able to get a drink in this town without offering to lance it first.'

Cathy collapsed in fits of laughter at the unbearable mental image and felt light-hearted for the first time in days. It could be the wine gone to her head but she didn't really care. Midnight came and went while they chatted and cuddled together in front of the open fire, still alive with the vivid colours of the shrinking turf.

Saturday was shaping up well enough too. She had planned to see an art exhibition in the Jenkin Gallery in Cork with Rena Lalor. Cathy knew in her heart that Rena would humour her with about ten minutes at the gallery before her insatiable thirst for the city boutiques and department stores would overcome her and have to be quenched by an empowering excursion down Patrick Street. And so it was. Rena smooched with the gallery owner while gasping in a seemingly new-found appreciation of the artist's vision. She was particularly taken by the red planet at the bottom of a painting of warring lovers. It was, she thought (aloud, naturally), symbolic of their love transcending this world. Neither Cathy nor the gallery owner pointed out to her that it was just a sticker marking the painting sold. Cathy didn't because she couldn't bear to burst her friend's exuberance and the gallery owner refrained because he was already mentally lodging the cheque from what he expected was a certain sale. When Rena found out that her warring lovers were sold she picked out another close to it which Cathy was sure she had not even given a second glance. With the painting bought and promptly forgotten Rena was ready to move on to her sartorial prey.

Being in Rena's company was like being in a tidal wave of consumerism. She always needed an outfit for a forthcoming occasion. She and Hugh were on a continual round of race meetings, charity socials and fund-raising dinner dances. The Lalor legal practice was thriving and was drawing clients from all over the southwest. 'You have to entertain the clients,' was Hugh's mantra after one or two swiftly downed tumblers of the doctor's whiskey. 'They expect it and they expect to see my Rena in a new rig-out.' He would stare at Rena in between gulps and his gaze consisted of one part devotion to several parts lechery. Cathy could just about tolerate Hugh Lalor when he was sober but his drink-fuelled playboy act threatened to make her stomach turn. Richard would often give her a good-humoured wink as if to implore that she turn a blind eye to Hugh's antics. She knew Richard was very fond of him and for her husband's and Rena's sake she usually held her tongue. She knew her friend relied on shopping to fill lonely hours when her husband and son had no time to talk, so busy were they with professional lives that required her inclusion only on an intermittent basis. Shopping for the social calendar had become her salvation and consequently her chief topic of conversation. Last year's dress for the Galway Races could do Tralee Races at a push but it could never go back to Galway and would not have been stylish enough for Punchestown or Fairyhouse in the first place. There was an etiquette involved in dressing for these outings and through these shopping trips Cathy was getting a master class, even though she was not remotely interested in ever going to such places.

The shopping today was proving a welcome distraction when she would normally have spent the day with Alison while Richard was at the golf club. She was standing in the middle of the Winthrop boutique waiting for Rena to release a flurry of shop assistants from active service when a midnight-blue-coloured silk skirt caught her eye. It was ages since she had bought anything for herself. She had lots of clothes, expensive and well-tailored items that suited her job as the practice manager and the doctor's wife but something about the frivolity of buying something gorgeous because she loved the look of it appealed to her. It was a size ten. It should fit, but she invaded Rena's kingdom in the dressing rooms just to make sure. It fitted beautifully, showing off her slender waist.

'My God, that is fabulous on you,' shrieked Rena when she spotted Cathy twirling happily, almost decadently, in front of the mirror. Rena was taken aback. Cathy has the figure, she thought to herself a bit sourly, but she wouldn't allow jealousy to fester. Everyone deserves to look well, she lectured herself silently while deciding to take the blouse she was trying on in all three colours. ('It's well cut,' she would find herself telling the shop girls as if she was selling the merchandise herself.)

'You have to buy it, Cathy, you just have to,' Rena went on. 'It's calling for a touch of flamboyance though, if you don't mind me saying so. A nice blazer and a hat maybe. The right match would set it off to a T.'

They emerged from the changing room. Cathy carried the blue skirt and three girls struggled under Rena's assorted purchases.

'You know what, Rena, I will buy it but I don't need a hat. Remember we don't move in the same social circle as you and Hugh. The odd GP conference is the stellar point of our social calendar and hats don't really get a look in there.'

'Well, it's not for the want of asking you. I am sick, sore and sorry of trying to drag you both along to the races or the charity balls. We would always find you a spot at our table. You would enjoy it, you know, if you just gave it a chance.'

'Ah, you never know, maybe we will,' Cathy said good-humouredly, but she was quite sure that hell would freeze and possibly thaw again first.

It wasn't until the bell for seven o'clock mass was ringing that Cathy pulled her car into the driveway of Michaelmas House. Rena had left most of her bags in Cathy's car. It helped Rena to bring home her shopping piecemeal because that way she would not have to acknowledge the sight of the complete haul. The guilt of that had often outweighed the retail therapy itself. She would collect them during the week when Hugh was tucked away in his office at the back of the house. It wasn't that he minded her spending, she had to admit. If it bothered him he never said as much. It was more that sometimes her capacity for spending money shocked even herself. The painting had been an extravagance. She would look out for the next bank statement and bin it. Maybe she would even give the painting to Cathy. Cathy loved that arty-farty racket. Well, she'd only bought it because she was in Cathy's company, hadn't she? It was her fault really. That conclusion comforted her somewhat. She wasn't sure that nude ladies had a place in the home of a prominent solicitor. What in the name of God had she been thinking of?

There was always a flurry of traffic around Caharoe in the run-up to mass and then a slow drift afterwards as the street emptied into the pubs. The lights of Lovett's Hotel were reflected in the low-lit windows of Michaelmas. Soon the languorous hum of conversation and laughter would grow steadily louder and Cathy and Richard would hear it as they prepared and ate dinner. He would tell her anything he had heard at the golf club, snippets of local gossip that Hugh Lalor never seemed to be without. She would fill him in on the art exhibition that she had seen and all of the exploits with Rena. They would talk lightly of Alison, trying to be positive, trying not to be lonely.

After the ritual dash to the television for the headlines Richard would say, 'I will knock across to Lovett's for one.' Some drink, Cathy often thought, as he was rarely home before midnight. Tonight, she had decided, would be different.

'Wait for me, I will come too,' Cathy announced. Richard looked a bit stunned but a little bit delighted too, she thought. Mostly stunned though, it had to be said.

Alison rang at ten when she got home from an early showing at the Savoy. The phone rang out as she pictured the hall table at Michaelmas and the carpeted steps of the stairs where her mother sat when she settled in for a long conversation with Rena or one of her sisters. The table lamp, always lit from nightfall, would cast her in a soft and flattering light. Her shoes would be kicked off and her long legs would be curled under the folds of her skirt. As the phone rang Alison thought that she must persuade her mother to buy some new clothes for herself. Maybe she would come shopping to Dublin some Saturday when Dad was playing golf? She would suggest it if her mother ever answered the blasted phone. When Cathy didn't pick up Alison had nobody to tell that she had just seen possibly the worst film ever made.

Chapter Four

The kitty would never stretch to the amount of HobNobs that Leda Clancy was putting away on a daily basis. Alison thought she'd have been able to handle it if the constant mugs of tea and biscuits improved her appearance or her mood in the slightest bit. But no. Leda still looked like the perished kitten that had lurked on Jean McDermott's landing the previous Sunday night.

Alison had nipped down to the corner shop at the end of their road for supplies at around nine o'clock when she expected Ciara to be home. She had planned that they would catch up over mugs of tea and biscuits. Ciara would have hated *Ghost*, the film that Alison had gone to see the evening before. She would have judged it way too soppy and not worthy of her money or her time. When Alison had admitted that *Dirty Dancing* was her favourite film of all time Ciara had started to gag so she knew she was in for a slagging but she was relishing the thought of her friend's company. She had really missed her.

Ciara was dragging her bags up the stairs when Alison arrived back from the shop.

'Hi there, welcome back. It was quiet without you.'

'It is good to be back, I can tell you that. Such crap that I have had to listen to over the past few days.'

'Is everything all right at home? Is Leda OK?'

'Nothing is right at home, Alison. In fact we would get the bloody Oscar for nothing ever being right. Maybe there is a grant from Europe for being the biggest fuck-up of a family ever to exist. Free therapy maybe for the rest of our natural lives. As for my darling sister Leda, well, you can ask her yourself.' She nodded upwards to where Leda stood on the landing. She was much taller than her sister but they shared the same slender silhouette. Her big blue eyes seemed bloodshot from tears or lack of sleep or both. Long, dark, wavy hair framed a heart-shaped face. She looked as if she was there against her will but there was no denying her incredible beauty, even if she seemed to do her best to conceal it with a surly expression.

'Hi, Leda,' Alison chirped, making a real effort to be friendly. 'Go on in to the kitchen there and stick on the kettle.' Leda didn't move.

'Move it, Leda!' Ciara said with vehemence and Leda disappeared into the kitchen at her sister's sudden command. Alison dropped the groceries in the hallway to give Ciara a hand with the heaviest of the bags.

'Ciara, have you lifted the contents of your folks' place or what? This bag weighs a bloody ton.'

'I'll tell you all in a minute. I just don't want Jean McDermott to spot me bringing in Leda or her stuff.' She nodded at their landlady's door but they need not have worried about being caught. Jean had bought the Sunday newspapers, chiefly to camouflage a litre bottle of gin that she had also purchased and since consumed. She had passed out at about teatime, her spittle pooling a lonesome dribble on the *Times* review pages. Going on previous form, she was unlikely to wake before the oil-thirsty brakes of morning buses began their relentless chorus outside her door.

Leda ate the first packet of biscuits from where she had perched them on her lap. Mindlessly, laconically, she munched away, unwilling or unable to make the slightest effort at conversation. She was barely conscious, it seemed, but incredibly hungry for all that.

It was a tight fit but Ciara managed to squeeze a makeshift bed for Leda between her own bed and the wall. Alison and herself took the cushions from the mottled brown couch in the living room. Alison donated a pillow and spare blankets to the cause. Ciara barely had enough for her own bed while Cathy Shepherd had sent Alison to Dublin with a bedding bale that would furnish an entire dormitory. It was a relief to see some of the surplus getting used. Leda sat on the only remaining cushion on the couch while the effort to accommodate her proceeded at efficient pace. She didn't look particularly upset, Alison thought, and because there was little chance that Leda would exert herself to overhear their conversation she decided to tackle Ciara.

'When are you going to tell me what's going on and why you've dragged your sixteen-year-old sister to Dublin with you?'

'Seventeen actually.'

'What?'

'Leda is seventeen. Her birthday was last month.'

'There is not much difference, Ciara, she is still too young. Are your parents not going to be out of their brains with worry? Mine would.'

'Your folks, Alison, sound like they are a bit different to my crew, to say the very least of it. They weren't that bothered when I suggested it, to be honest, but then Mam is on happy pills just to get through the day and Dad is mostly getting over the last drink or thirsting for the next one.'

'I don't believe what you're saying. Look, I know something pretty crap must have happened but how do you think we are going to look after Leda? We are at college all day; at least we're supposed to be. She should be at home with your parents. She should be in school, for God's sake.'

'Look, I haven't thought it through. I just knew I had to get her out of there before she got in deeper with this slimeball that's sniffing around her. Home is just about the last place she should be. I mean my stupid father probably thinks it's all right because your man is rich and stands him reams of drink in the pub. Thinks it's some sort of privilege that an upstart politician would be interested in bedding his teenage daughter. Never mind the fact that he is fifty-bloody-seven and married with a son older than us. That is why I went home. Leda is telling me she is in love with him and my folks can see no harm. It's sick, Alison, it's absolutely sick and I don't fucking know what to do!'

Alison was dumbfounded. Ciara was on the verge of tears and her features were etched with a vitriolic temper that she hadn't known her friend possessed. Alison had thought of a few possible reasons for Leda's sudden appearance. Maybe she had been dossing school, had fallen in with the wrong crowd or she was sneaking drink at the bar where she was lounge girl. These were all plausible: similar small dramas had played out in the school in Caharoe every week. Things like these were commonplace among teenagers. Leda's predicament was anything but. Alison thought of Ciara's mother. Even before tonight Ciara had made no secret of her mother's battle with depression, but Alison was sure that she would still want to keep her daughter safe from harm.

'What about your mam, Ciara. Would she not step in even if your father won't and sort this mess out? Warn your man off or tell his wife if she had to?'

'My mam is on Valium, antidepressants and sleeping tablets and probably a lot more besides. It started after Leda was born. I think she had postnatal depression and it just didn't get diagnosed. Come to think of it, postmarital depression might be more apt after discovering that she married an absolute dickhead.'

Ciara collapsed on the bed, exhausted by the physical effort of dragging her sister halfway up the country and now not having the first clue what to do with her. 'The story is that Mam's been on serious medication for the guts of sixteen years. So, no, she wouldn't be able to sort this out. She barely sorts getting out of bed in the morning. I love her to bits, Alison, but she is useless when it comes to life in general, not to mind a crisis, and by God she has had plenty of practice watching them unfold being married to my dad.'

Alison nodded towards the sitting room. 'And Leda, what does Leda think about your man? She seems to be awful calm. She looks like this whole thing is going over her head – or is she just too upset to talk? She hasn't said one word to me, not even hello.'

'Oh, she threw the head when I told her I was bringing her back with me. I got the whole angst bit that nobody understands her. That she is in love and I am too bitter to understand. The whole nine yards. Sure he gave her a gold watch for her birthday so she is taking that as proof that he really cares. So I bribed her with a pint of Heineken in Shanahan's while we were waiting for the bus and I crumbled three of Mammy's Valium into it while she was in the loo. Haven't heard a peep since but I bet you she will register on the Richter scale tomorrow morning when it wears off. I have the box of pills with me by the way, so don't be short!' Ciara's attempt at a joke did nothing to placate Alison who thought she might pass out.

'Jesus! You can't do that. What about your mam? Won't she need the pills? Dad always says how dangerous it is to suddenly stop taking drugs like that if your system is dependent on them. You have to tell her you have taken them. Ring her now.'

'Listen, Alison, I'm sure your dad is a fantastic doctor and never repeats prescriptions without seeing the patient first but Mam could power the whole of Leachlara with the amount of pills and prescriptions she has in that bathroom cabinet. She could rival the national grid. Anyway, I had to get Leda away from that house, the pub and that sleazeball. I admit it was a bit drastic but I wasn't exactly thinking straight. I'll flush the pills, I promise. To tell you the truth, the guy owned the place on Leeson Street that I had the flat in. That's why I wanted to move. It wasn't so much the vermin within as having that dirty rat Abernethy as a landlord. I could not have anything to do with him. Calling around on a Thursday looking for his rent and God knows what else he thought might be on offer.'

The familiarity of the surname jolted Alison out of her concerned-citizen reverie. A coincidence, she convinced herself firmly, listening from her room as Ciara directed a lacklustre Leda to her bed. The crease of light under the doorway blackened when Ciara put out the lights in the living room. Only the orange glow of the street lamp through the curtains lit the room. Alison lay awake in the utterly quiet house. No banging from Jean McDermott. No mysterious thuds to punctuate the hours to daylight. The street outside was almost at rest. The lovely fantasy that she had been building in the past few weeks with the exotic-sounding Dan Abernethy was inexplicably ruined by the presence of his slimy namesake in Leachlara, over a hundred miles away.

Ciara lay awake in the quiet blackness of her room, alongside a peacefully sleeping Leda. Alison was right, of course. Bringing Leda to Dublin with her was a totally daft and reckless move and she knew that her sister would probably be back in Leachlara before the end of the week. A few days in Dublin and a precious couple of days off school and Leda would want to go back home. Ciara knew she could not and would not stop her. She had adopted the role of parent but lacked all the necessary skills. Mind you, that had been no deterrent to Ted or Aggie Clancy.

As she lay now, willing her body to warm the cold sheets, she allowed her mind to wander back to nights spent rigid with fear in her bedroom in Leachlara. Her mother normally knew enough to be out of the way when Ted Clancy came home from the pub but sometimes sleep failed her and she would come to the kitchen to make tea or to sit staring at the TV. From her bed Ciara would hear the tirade of abuse that would start when her father returned with a belly full of drink. If he had suffered a slight, real or imagined, from any of his drinking buddies he had a perfect target in his defenceless wife. He would criticize her shabby appearance, telling her that it was a good job she never left the house because she was a disgrace to herself and to him. Aggie's vacant expression, her old dressing gown and her greasy hair that tended to mat did little to refute her husband's worst insults. He would start making himself something to eat, complaining that she was a useless excuse for a wife. The sound of banging pans and the smell of burning fat would fill the night air, creeping under doors and stealing any chance of sleep.

Being the eldest, Ciara felt responsible for making sure that her brother and sister were not frightened by their parents' quarrelling. If she found either of them awake she would climb into the bed with them, pulling the blankets snugly around. The presence of their sister brought them much-needed security and, soothed, they would fall asleep again. Ted always stopped short of hitting his wife and though Ciara felt she should have been grateful for that she had long since realized that words and fear brought their own bruises, not visible to the eye but slow to heal, nonetheless. Eventually her mother would go to bed and her father, having lost his easy target, would put his voice away for the night. Alone again he would feel comfortable going to the cupboard and to the whiskey that might yet numb the hour before exhaustion would overtake him.

The few months Ciara had lived in Dublin had made her less and less tolerant of the situation at home. When she was in school she dreamed that college and city life would whisk her away from the dysfunction of her family. She would do her best to help her siblings but the best she could hope for was that they too would walk away just as she herself had done.

By Wednesday Leda was restless and by Thursday she was gone, together with the contents of the kitty and one of her sister's favourite skirts. She was due to work a shift in Shanahan's and didn't intend to miss the opportunity to meet Con Abernethy, who would be home from another week in the Dáil. There was no explanatory note when Ciara came back to the flat to find her sister's things gone but she knew before she even rang home that it was there she would find her.

The skirt she had stolen from Ciara fitted Leda like a glove and as she swung her neat hips around to get a good view of herself in the mirror of her bedroom she decided that it looked better on her than it ever had on her sister. She didn't usually get dressed up that much for her work at Shanahan's – God knew she got plenty of attention from the crew that drank there without so much as a smear of lipstick or a hint of jewellery – but she had hatched a plan while she was in Dublin for the previous few days. It involved some fast-tracking of an idea that she had been brewing for a while without much success. In the midst of all the men that fancied their chances with Paddy Shanahan's new lounge girl was Con Abernethy the TD, but much as she had encouraged his attention something was holding him back. She couldn't work out what. He was unwilling to cross the line despite Leda's none-too-subtle invitations to do so. True, he had given her a watch but that was only because her birthday had coincided with the school trip to the Dáil a few weeks before. Leda had got her friends to mention it during the lunch he had bought for them so he had been cornered into that purchase. She had even seen Columbo Connors ducking inside a crappy little jewellery shop near Busáras and emerging with the bag that Con presented to her before the class boarded the bus home. She knew it was done to impress the school group and the teachers but she made a big deal of it to Ciara anyway. Gold, she had told her, but it was the type that cost thirty pounds as she saw from the receipt that Columbo had neglected to remove from the bag. Her sister was easy to wind up, she discovered, and the mention of Con Abernethy's name was a sure bet to set her off on one. One phone call had Ciara rushing home to save her honour.

Leda had decided to up her efforts a little. She wasn't averse to the idea of sleeping with him if that's what it took for him to start parting with some money. He wasn't bad looking for a man in his late fifties and no matter how much he drank he still looked good in a suit. He smelt rich when a lot of other men around Leachlara seemed to smell of fags or cow dung or old sweat. Worse still, they were spotty and poor like lads of her age. Sex with him would be fine, she concluded, and maybe he wouldn't take her seriously for anything less. Everyone knew his wife was a total bitch so he must be gagging for it, she reasoned to herself. She fancied a job up in Dublin with him, well paid, and maybe a nice apartment. These were the things that she wanted and Con Abernethy was, as far as she could see, her only means of getting them.

Being in the company of Ciara and her dreary flatmate for the past few days had made up her mind. Her big sister had always dreamed of getting away from Leachlara and college was her chosen method. All very well if you had the brains for school or the patience and Leda realized that she had rather limited stocks of both. The principal never tired of comparing Leda's average exam results with those of her sister. It seemed a stunning Leaving Cert. results sheet had divinely erased all of Ciara's transgressions in secondary school. Leda knew it would take a miracle for her to emulate her sister's achievements. Besides, after watching Ciara and Alison slog at essays and seeing the dismal place they lived in she was fairly certain that it wasn't worth the effort. It took some skill for Ciara to flee the house where her alcoholic father held court only to end up paying money to stay in a horrible flat with an alcoholic landlady into the bargain. There was an easier way. She would just have to flesh out the bones of her plan and get Con Abernethy to make a move. If anyone from her class enquired where she had been and why she had been absent from school for the past week she planned on telling them that Con had taken her to Dublin for a few days. No harm in a few white lies to get the ball rolling.

Aggie Clancy was fixing dinner when Leda came into the kitchen dressed up and ready for her shift at Shanahan's.

'I thought you would stay a bit longer with Ciara. She rang a while ago to check if you had made it back home all right.'

'Well, I thought I had missed too much school already, Mammy, and besides I have work tonight, remember?' Leda was happy to play the good daughter, conscientious about her schoolwork, as long as it kept her mother on an even keel.

'Ciara has done so well and she is happy in Dublin. Lovely flatmate. Alice, I think Ciara said her name was, but of course you met her,' her mother added vaguely, stirring the dinner that smelt as if it was slowly but surely sticking to the bottom of the pan.

'Yeah, she's a dote, Mammy. Ciara and herself are like two peas in a pod . . . Boring as fucking hell too,' she added more quietly but not bothering to disguise the sarcasm. It was over Aggie Clancy's head. Most things were.

'Call in your brother there, Leda. He must be starving, because he never takes a lunch to school as far as I can see.'

Leda pushed open the back door, which led into a filthy concrete yard littered with broken bits of farm machinery and household rubbish. The hum of the milking machine and their father roaring and cursing at the cows in his charge filled the evening air. Her brother was kicking a ball incessantly at the back wall of the house, which was littered with marks: the legacy of his past target practice.

'Mammy has dinner ready, Michael. Come in.'

'In a while. I'm not hungry.'

'Look, none of us are hungry for Mammy's food but at the rate he is roaring at those poor cows' – she nodded at the cow shed – 'he will let half of them out without milking them at all. So it depends if you want to get the dinner thing over before he comes in like a bear. I know I do.'

Michael took one more pop at the wall with a resounding kick that missed his bedroom window by a hair's breadth. Inside they pushed the stew around the plate. It wasn't their mother's worst offering but they had both learned that a packet of crisps and a bar of chocolate from the tuck shop at lunchtime would best serve as the main meal of the day. Aggie rarely ate dinners at the family table. She preferred to munch on crackers or raisins at an open cupboard, leaning on the kitchen counter for support. Michael and Leda heard the milking machine stop and they got immediately to their feet and cleared their plates into the bin. Aggie was already filling the sink with hot soapy water to do the washing-up.

'I've homework to finish, Ma,' Michael murmured before he left for his room.

'And I'm off to Shanahan's. I told Paddy I would get in early to help him,' Leda lied with the greatest of ease.

In his room Michael found a plastic bag filled with chocolate and crisps and a bottle of Coke that Leda had deemed was his share of the stolen kitty money. He managed his first smile of the day.

Con made Shanahan's for last orders as he habitually did on a Thursday night. Leda made sure that she was out from behind the counter so he could get a good look at what he had hitherto resisted. Fair play to Ciara's skirt, it seemed to be doing the trick. By the time the pub closed Con was making no secret of the fact that he couldn't keep his eyes off her and when she asked him for a lift home she was sure he was about to oblige until Columbo, his sidekick, put his spoke in and said he would make the trip to save Con the trouble.

'Another time,' Con said to a disappointed Leda.

'I hope you are the type of man to keep your promises,' she said, loosening her dark curls from where she had pinned them back for work.

'You can count on that,' Con said, drinking in one last look at her as she walked out of the door behind Columbo.

Chapter Five

'I know I can't return the invitation so I can't accept it.' Ciara was touched by the kindness of Alison and she did appreciate being asked to spend the weekend in Caharoe in Alison's parents' house. But she wouldn't go, of course; couldn't go in fact. Since the minute that she had left Leachlara for the first week of term she had decided that her life was now going to be in Dublin and beyond. Having her new-found friend expecting visits to her parents' house was not part of the plan. She hadn't, however, counted on Alison's determination.

'Oh, Ciara, I would just love you to come. My folks would relax a bit if they saw that I hadn't shacked up with a total floozy. My dad is having a tough time coping with the fact that I am not in digs being overseen by an adult at all times.'

'Look, I feel bad, Ali, 'cause my crowd are nuts and I would rather die than take you home.'

'Oh, would you forget about asking me back? Just say you'll come. Please?'

'Well, OK, I suppose I could turn on the charm to your dad, make him realize the smart move you made landing Ciara Clancy as a flatmate.'

'Brilliant! I'll tell my mam. She will start piling high the buns and the brown bread. She goes a bit into overdrive when anyone visits. I think running a guesthouse would suit her a lot better than running my dad's surgery. Do you want to check with your folks first to see if it's all right?'

'I'll give them a call on Friday just to say I won't be home. It's no big deal at all.'

Alison was a bit puzzled. She would never forget her mother's reaction the first time she told her she was going to stay away for the weekend. Her going to college in Dublin was firmly based on the contract that she would return home at the weekends to Caharoe. Things were very different in the Clancy house. Ciara seemed to think they didn't care one way or the other, which couldn't really be true, Alison decided. Her friend sometimes tried to be too cool for her own good.

Ciara was caught off balance by an unusual wave of quietness when they were making their way from the bus stop to the square in Caharoe. She had literally not shut up all the way to Heuston station and then on the long journey on a packed Friday train she had kept Alison entertained with wild accounts of her school days in Leachlara. In five years in secondary school she had been suspended twice. The first time was for vociferously challenging the principal, Sister Agatha, that she owed it to the women's movement to promote the existence of a female deity or, failing that, at least to entertain the idea. That she was a young lady who didn't know her place in the school or in God's holy universe was Sister Agatha's reason for the suspension cited in a letter to the Clancy parents, which winged its way from Ciara's schoolbag straight to the bin in the Abbey corridor toilets. The second suspension was for sharing a cigarette and a kiss with a fifth-year boy in the trees behind the school canteen. Ciara's parents remained similarly unaware of that transgression. 'He turned out to be an absolute louser though, not worth getting suspended for. Told all his friends that I was mad for him, spotty little upstart.'

Alison had never so much as received a detention or a note home in her six years in the community school in Caharoe and she had to admit that bringing Ciara home to Caharoe was the first step in showing everybody how sophisticated her life was in Dublin.

'Holy fuck, is this your house? It's huge!' Ciara was stunned when Alison headed in the direction of one of the grandest houses, at the north edge of the square. Nobody she knew lived in a house this size. It looked unbelievably posh and she was dying to have a look inside.

'It's not that big really. Dad's surgery takes up the entire front half of the house so we kind of live in the back bit and the basement,' Alison explained. She didn't want her friend to be put off by the size of the house.

'Oh, let me guess: do the butler and the housekeeper have their quarters down there?'

'Don't be daft, Ciara!'

Before Alison got a chance to turn the key in the front door, Cathy Shepherd had opened it. She stood there beaming at her daughter and her friend. It had taken a fantastic feat of willpower for her not to walk to the bus stop to meet Alison but she had watched the girls' relaxed saunter from Richard's surgery window, pouncing on the Chubb lock at the moment she knew they would be standing there.

Alison had not been joking about her mother's propensity for over-catering. Everywhere Ciara looked there was something good to eat. Scones with cream and raspberry jam, apple crumbles and brown bread, not to mention a delicious smell of dinner coming from the range, roast chicken maybe and garlic definitely. Whatever it was made her mouth water with hunger. The last thing she had eaten was a slice of chocolate biscuit cake in the arts block café before her twelve o'clock lecture. It hadn't exactly filled the gap and she was thoroughly ravenous now.

'You girls must be starving,' Cathy Shepherd announced as if reading Ciara's mind. 'Alison will take your coat, Ciara. Pull up a chair and I will make us a pot of tea. You do drink tea, don't you?'

'We drink pots of it, don't we, Alison?'

'Yeah, loads, it's an excuse for us to stop studying for a bit and meet up in what we rather grandly refer to as the sitting room. Where's Dad anyway, Mam?'

'He had a house call, love, but hopefully it won't take too long. It's Mrs Langton. She has taken a turn for the worse this last while I am afraid and she can't make it to the surgery any more. He is dying to see you, and you too, Ciara, to find out what you are made of!'

Alison was in total awe of the performance Ciara put on for her parents. She was completely charming, funny and so opinionated on current affairs that for once Richard Shepherd had to take a back seat at his own dinner table. His normally razor-sharp critical faculties seemed to be totally suspended and Alison thought she might pass out when he suggested that they head over the road to Lovett's for an after-dinner drink. Alison had only ever been to Lovett's for the odd Sunday lunch with her parents and she could not recall a time when her mother had accompanied her father on his routine Friday-night saunter across to the hotel. She was fairly sure that her dad thought his teenage charges were thirsting for a nice Fanta or 7up and a bag of crisps. His face was a total picture when Ciara coolly requested a pint of Heineken without pausing to register a shred of her host's discomfort. In fairness, he recovered his composure eventually and made sure Ciara was introduced to the Lalors and anyone else they knew in the pub.

Alison was happy to see her mother looking so relaxed. She looked beautiful and seemed to have bought some new clothes.

Maybe the shopping trips with Rena Lalor were not such a dead loss after all, though the lady herself resembled a burst sofa at a table opposite. She must give advice on fashion better than she takes it, Alison decided. In her own moments of loneliness, when Dublin threatened to overwhelm her, she worried that her mother might be finding her absence difficult to cope with. They had, after all, been inseparable for as long as she could remember. Tonight was definitely putting her mind at ease.

Two Heinekens for a teenage girl was the limit of Richard Shepherd's tolerance and they were back at Michaelmas by eleven, drinking tea and eating biscuits by the dilapidated open fire in the living room.

Cathy had put Ciara in the spare bed in Alison's room and they chatted late into the night. Alison found herself confiding about the customer in the Daisy May that she had only met twice but fancied like mad.

'Jesus, girl, you sound like you have it bad. Take it from someone who has had experience of a few: they are all arseholes. None of them are ever as nice as they pretend to be the first time you meet them.'

'I don't know why you are trying to set me against men – you do a fair bit of window-shopping yourself around Trinity! What about Eoin from Waterford in our American history tutorial? Don't tell me you don't see a bit of romantic potential there?'

'I suppose there are a few exceptions to my rule and little hotpot Eoin may indeed prove to be one of them, but a lot of lads our age are total eejits.'

'Dan *is* older than us though, a good few years I'd say. He just seems really clever and nice. Did I say that Rose told me he was studying medicine?'

'Oh, Dr Dan, is it now? Oh, sure that makes all the difference. A doctor's daughter, sure of course you would be on the lookout for a medical student! And it follows that I will be trying to track down a big brawny lump of a farmer like Daddy dearest. Not.'

'Ah, don't be so cynical, Ciara! I didn't even find out he was a medical student until yesterday. I think Rose is getting a bit of fun out of torturing me.'

'What do you mean?'

'Well, she is drip-feeding the information about him very slowly. She's known him for ages, says he has been coming in and out of the Daisy May as long as she has been working there. She has sort of guessed I fancy him even though I haven't said anything.'

'Well, I'd say going puce every time the poor chap shows his face is a bit of a dead giveaway. If you want my opinion, the direct route is always the best. Tell Rose. If she is anyway decent at all she will put in a good word for you with the delectable Dr Dan!'

'Oh, I don't know. I can barely look at him when he comes in at the moment and that's with Rose knowing nothing for sure. I think if I told her out straight I'd have to run out the back if he ever darkened the door again.'

Ciara sat up in the bed. She was going to have to seriously motivate Alison. 'No point in letting this fella think he is God's gift. You are a gorgeous-looking girl and you'd better start realizing it. You are just lacking a bit of gumption, that's all. I'll call in some day to you at the Daisy May and see what I can find out from your one Rose. Give me the facts again. Dr Dan—'

'Will you stop calling him Dr Dan, for God's sake, he is a medical student not one of your Mills and Boon favourites.'

'Actually, now that you say it, *The Ravishing Doctor Dan* would make a cracking title for my first oeuvre in the romantic genre.'

Alison lobbed a cushion from her luxuriantly plumped bed and caught Ciara in the side of the head.

'OK, cool it. Plain old Dan it is then. Medical student. Any idea where he's from?'

'No idea but he sounds a bit posh. Could be from Dublin. Certainly not from somewhere like here anyway.'

'Jesus, Caharoe is a grand spot. Want to see a backwater? Take yourself off to Leachlara in the arse end of Tipperary. This house is totally amazing and your folks are cool. This house has a name, for God's sake. How posh is that? Our place is called the new bungalow and it's been there for twenty years! This is a jammy set-up you have going here, Alison!'

'I do love the house and my folks are sound. I'm just not all that keen on Caharoe, that's all. The whole doctor's daughter thing got a bit annoying very early on. I always thought people treated me differently, the teachers in school and that. To tell you the truth I wasn't great at the whole making-friends thing in school. I was never in the gang – always standing outside looking on. Too good for my own good, if you know what I mean.'

'Well, you are in my gang now and I am very glad to have you. So I'll say it again. You are a lucky wench, Alison Shepherd!'

They spent Sunday helping Cathy sort the Christmas decorations, bringing them down from the attic and deciding what should go in each room. Ciara was stunned by the amount and quality of the decorations. There was no cheap tinsel here and the fairy lights were all tasteful white. When bulbs blew Richard had a stash of spares so nothing would spoil the beautiful display. All of Michaelmas's windows were to have pillar candles surrounded by holly and ivy and, as a finishing touch, on the front door would hang a beautiful and imposing wreath finished with a burgundy-ribbon bow.

A week later Ciara went back to Leachlara for the Christmas holidays. She unpacked the small parcel of decorations that were kept on the top shelf of the wardrobe in the box room. Tinsel, baubles, old Christmas cards and a horrible-looking plug-in candle were the best of what she found. Well, it might not be Michaelmas, she thought, but they could surely do better than this. A trip to the discount shop on the main street of Leachlara and two bags later she was ready to bring some semblance of Christmas to her family.

Leda was waiting to puncture her sister's attempts at festive spirit.

'Jesus, Ciara, why would you bother? Christmas in this house is a lost cause. Dad will have started on the whiskey before breakfast and it will all crash and burn around dinnertime. More tinsel is not going to help the situation.'

'The place could do with a buck-up, that's all, and you could get off your backside and help me put these up,' Ciara said, handing her sister one end of a silver garland.

'I can give you ten minutes before I have to get ready for my shift in the pub,' she offered miserably.

Ciara tried to ignore Leda's negativity about Clancy family Christmases but in her heart she knew that while decorations were a start they wouldn't be enough. Ted Clancy had won an enormous twenty-pound turkey in Shanahan's Christmas raffle. (He had bought books of tickets so in reality had shelled out for an entire flock.) Proud as punch, he warned Aggie to make proper stuffing for the fine bird he had provided for the Christmas dinner. He hauled it home after closing time on Christmas Eve but he never thought to put it in the fridge. When Ciara and Aggie got up on Christmas morning it had dripped its juice down the front of the kitchen cupboards and all over the kitchen floor. Ciara cleaned up the mess and set about helping her mother peeling spuds and carrots. Aggie had made plenty of stuffing and for a while that morning Ciara thought things might be different that year. The turkey would only fit into the gas oven if they cut off the legs and squashed it into the one battered roasting tray the kitchen possessed. After an hour a smell of gas filled the kitchen instead of the smell of roasting meat that Ciara had expected. Her mother had gone to lie down on Ciara's bed and her father hadn't surfaced yet so she sent Michael to the shed looking for a spare bottle of gas that she knew in her heart he would not find. The Clancys had always made scant provision for the future. Leda sat at the corner of the table munching on a bowl of breakfast cereal. She brought her empty bowl to the sink, all the while smirking at her sister's disappointment.

'Well, all we need now is for a fairy godmother to appear with a bottle of gas under her wing. I did tell you that all the decorations in the world wouldn't change this house, Ciara. Christmas here is always a fuck-up, made worse by the fact that it's the one day Dad can't disappear to the pub and give us all a break.'

Ciara knew Leda was right but a stubborn streak wouldn't allow her to give up just yet. As far as she knew, the microwave still worked. She took the still-mostly-raw bird from the oven and, using the blunt carving knife, she hacked lumps of meat from the carcass and laid it out on plates. She would nuke it at dinnertime and hope for the best. Pot noodles and gravy would only need the addition of boiling water from the electric kettle. Vegetables they could live without.

Her mother cried when she found out what had happened. 'I gave money to your father to pay for briquettes and gas at Murtagh's. I rang when they didn't deliver during the week but they said the bill was still outstanding and we were not to have anything else on credit. I just hoped the bottle of gas would last. He will be so cross, Ciara.'

Ted Clancy was as sour as a pig when he finally emerged from bed to do some work on the farm at midday. 'The finest specimen of a turkey this house has ever seen and you had to fuck it up,' he roared at Aggie, who looked miserable and cold as she leaned against the kitchen counter.

Ciara was not about to allow him to get away with blaming her mother. 'Well, if you had paid the bill at Murtagh's with the money that Mammy gave you instead of drinking it at Shanahan's they might not have left us without gas to cook the shagging turkey. Now go and feed the cattle before they go down to the neighbours' looking for something to eat. Dinner will be at two.'

Ted cursed his way to the cow shed. His head was sore and his stomach heaved from drink and no food to undo its poison. He kicked his loyal cattle dog in the shins when it ran in front of him, welcoming him to their morning's work.

The turkey was tough and a bit charred after ten minutes in the microwave. The noodles and gravy tasted as they should but the food was nothing like a real Christmas dinner and the lack of conversation around the table made the meal almost unbearable. Ciara had bought a box of Christmas crackers but they could stay under her bed for another year. Even she hadn't the stomach for that. Michael and Leda milled through the jelly and ice cream that Ciara doled out in big bowlfuls in an attempt to make amends for the lousy first course they had endured. Ted threw savage looks at his wife but Aggie had taken herself off to another world with the help of a couple of her pills and didn't notice.

As dusk fell Ciara went to the kettle to make herself a hot drink. The house was cold and she thought about draining a bit of whiskey from Ted's stash to add to her coffee. He was out in the yard, most likely having a swig from some bottle he had hidden out there, so he would hardly notice. Leda and Michael were stretched out watching the TV and Ciara offered up a quick word of gratitude that at least the electricity hadn't been cut off. From the kitchen window she could see her mother doling out the still-meat-rich carcass of the turkey to the dogs and cats that lined up in grateful appreciation at their unexpected good fortune. Well, at least the animals are having a good day, Ciara thought as she took her drink to her room and lost herself in a book Alison had given her for Christmas.

Chapter Six

A balding waddle of a man shuffled down the bustling corridor that led to the St James and Pious wing of the Mercy Hospital. His voluminous bolster of belly flesh operated the swing entrance doors so he didn't have to raise his hands to the job. They remained firmly buried in the pockets of his trench coat. He had young Abernethy pegged the moment he spotted a crowd of white-coated junior doctors subserviently tailing a consultant down the length of the corridor, disappearing and reappearing from the wards like a string of performing puppets. Dan Abernethy stood a good half a foot taller than any of his cohorts and so was plainly visible even to the somewhat shortsighted advancing pensioner. Had Dan not been paying such rapt attention to the teaching consultant he would have seen Johnny Columbo Connors making for him with frightening intent.

His father's right-hand man in the constituency had stood with Con Abernethy at every rain-sodden commemoration. He had canvassed at doors without number and remained resolutely cheerful when they slammed in his face. He attended funerals of people he had never heard of and made sure his candidate knew the name of the bereaved spouse and any children's names so he would appear heartfelt in his sympathy. Columbo wore out three pairs of shoes at every general election campaign making sure that Con would be returned to his Dáil seat. His job was to serve the party and the party deemed Con Abernethy to be the right man to represent them. Columbo did not appear to possess any latent ambition ever to be the candidate himself or, if he did, its concealment was impeccable.

Con Abernethy was never seen anywhere without his faithful servant close by ready to shake a hand, pass on a request or stand a drink to grease a palm.

Columbo's constant presence meant that Dan had been slagged endlessly by lads in his class in Leachlara Community School. In the run-up to any election the ribbing became ever more vigorous.

'So tell us, Dan, how does your mam feel when she wakes up to find your dad and Columbo in the bed with her talking quotas and strategy?'

'Does Columbo eat the dinner with you all or does he have a dog bowl at the foot of the table?'

'Will it be your mother or Columbo that gets the first passionate snog the night of the election count?'

On and on it went and Dan coped by laughing the loudest of all. He could have swung a languid punch and knocked any of the smart alecs on the side of their cocky jaw. As the tallest of all his classmates, one punch might have been enough to silence a multitude. He decided early on that the relaxed approach was the best one. Leachlara had plenty to say about the Abernethys without hotheadedness from Dan giving them further ammunition.

As an only child Dan relished the company of the lads in school. He found the quietness and order at home stifling. His father even ran his TD clinics from Shanahan's pub on Main Street because his wife would not allow the great unwashed of

Leachlara to step on her carpets or put their car keys on her French-polished furniture. In truth the dog-bowl-for-Columbo jibe was not too far off the mark. There was a green mug that he always got his tea in when he called to see Con. Columbo took it as an honour that he was so much part of the family he had his own mug. In truth Mary Abernethy did not want Columbo's dentures, and the filth she imagined they carried, defiling the china. She mostly discouraged Con from bringing him further than the back door and certainly no further than the kitchen table, where the tiles could cope better than her carpets with anything that might fall from his shoes. Columbo felt he had a seat at the heart of Con's home and that was an honour in itself. As for the trench coat that had earned him his nickname, well, she tried not to think where that had been and how long it had travelled without so much as a whistle of dry cleaning. She had made Con give Columbo a generous voucher for Harty's Gentleman's Outfitters in Tipperary when he topped the poll at the last election, in the hope that he would get a new overcoat. A pair of brand-new wellington boots for the ploughing championships seemed to be the only purchase so far and possibly some fabulously loud neckties which were whipped out with overwhelming pride for party functions, especially the odd nights in the Dáil bar when Con brought the faithful to the city to reward their hard and relentless work on his behalf.

'Tell him to buy himself a decent coat, Con. He is no addition to you dressed like that.'

Dan watched his mother vigorously clean the chair that Columbo had just vacated with a small lake of disinfectant. His father eyed his mother dismissively. 'Columbo is not responsible for most of the foul smells around here.'

Mary Abernethy, oblivious it seemed to her husband's sharp dig, cleaned on like a woman whose very existence depended on the polishing cloth.

Dan did wince inside when the mockery moved to speculating about Columbo sharing his parents' marital bed. He could not remember a time when his parents had slept in the same room. As far back as his memory could recall his mother's room had been at the top of the landing while Con Abernethy slept in the back of the house in a room that doubled as his office. While the Dáil sat he stayed in Dublin in the apartment he had bought near the Burlington.

Mary Abernethy travelled to Dublin on only very rare occasions, usually to show her face for the first day of parliamentary business after a general election or at the annual party conference. On these occasions she mostly stayed in the Gresham, in a room overlooking O'Connell Street. Con's apartment was small, she reasoned, and there was always bound to be some hanger-on from home wanting to pitch themselves in the TD's place, anxious for a sniff at the pot of power. She preferred to hold court in Leachlara while her husband attended to business elsewhere. Her only son was her favourite project. He would turn out perfectly, she would see to that.

Dan felt the pressure of his mother's ambition for him but he did not allow it to weigh heavily on his shoulders. He loved his mother, or at least he thought he must, but his father was his real companion in the house. He looked forward to him coming home from Dublin on a Thursday night because his presence made the shipshape house a shade unpredictable. The phone would start to ring checking that Con was back and party workers would troop to the kitchen table (through the back door, that was understood) to hear the gossip from Dublin and share any snippets of local news or dissent that Con would find useful before his Saturday-morning clinic in Shanahan's lounge. Dan loved to join in these kitchen-table conferences and his presence was respected and encouraged by his father's troupe of workers. Who knew? They could be looking at a future candidate. No one wanted to start off on the wrong foot with someone they might well be championing in the future. Whatever their reasons for tolerating him in their grown man's world, Dan was grateful, not least because his father's job and Dan's access to his coterie of supporters gave him some sense of the world that lay beyond Leachlara, a world he planned to escape to at the first available opportunity.

So it was with a mixture of affection and utter bemusement that Dan turned in the direction of the familiar booming voice that had interrupted Consultant Mackey's lecture. Columbo was no stranger to the loudhailer style of delivery and had neglected to turn down the volume in the hushed surroundings of a corridor in a teaching hospital.

'Heartiest apologies for interrupting the serious work at hand, sir, but I need a quick word with young Dr Abernethy here on urgent personal business.'

Dan flushed. Columbo had awarded him his medical qualification about a year prematurely. He shot a glance at Consultant Mackey and he could see the look of withering disdain building behind the forbidding spectacles.

'Well, it is most irregular to have a teaching slot interrupted but I suppose, *Mr* Abernethy, if your personal business is more important than my time then so be it.' Then, beckoning to Dan's fellow students, he said haughtily, 'Further training, for those of you that remain interested, will take place in the Alphonsos Ward.'

As if in one of the less eventful episodes of *One Man and His Dog*, the medical students set off in sheeplike formation in Consultant Mackey's wake, leaving Dan and Columbo alone in the freshly deserted corridor.

'Jesus, Columbo, what's this all about? What are you doing here?'

'Sorry, Dan, but I had to come and talk to you. It's your father. Well, it's your mother really that's posing the problem but I suppose you could say that your father started it.'

'What in the name of God are you talking about?'

'They're fighting again. At each other's throats this time.'

'For God's sake, they are always fighting. They can't fucking stand each other. So what's new that has you hunting me down in Dublin about it?'

Columbo seemed winded and Dan motioned to a bench at the end of the corridor. After Columbo had downed his considerable bulk on the low bench there was barely enough room for Dan. Impatience was rising within him, but it was directed at his absent parents so he decided to spare Columbo his more barbed thoughts.

'It's a bit delicate but I suppose you see a lot in your line of work. Makes you cope with the unpalatable.'

'Has my mam taken a swipe at him or what? For God's sake, Columbo, spit it out!'

'Jesus, no, it's nothing like that. She has only upped and taken into her head that your father is having a fling, and I'll tell you this much it's making the woman mighty sour. She looks like she is about to blow. She's talking newspapers, *Liveline*, the lot.'

'An affair? Who with, for God's sake?'

'Dan, a bit of faith in your father, please. There isn't a more decent man in the town of Leachlara.'

'Well, who does she *think* he is having the affair with so, or are you saying my mother is making it up?'

'It's a shocking misunderstanding really, nothing to it at all. There's a girl, Leda Clancy, that does the odd night behind the bar at Shanahan's. You know her, I'd say. She would be a daughter to Ted Clancy, a farmer from Briartullog above the town.'

Dan nodded. He was beginning to suspect where this was going and his gut knotted at the sickening prospect. The Clancy girls were younger than he was. He thought one of them might have been living in one of his father's houses on Leeson Street.

He was there the night that her father arranged the flat for her with his dad.

'Well, she has taken a bit of a shine to your father and your father has been very nice to her – like he is to everyone else in the town, I may say.' Columbo's indignation was rising with each snippet of the drip feed to Dan. His master was under fire and arms were to the ready for his staunch defence. 'He even brought her to the Dáil outing that last time we came. Very important to get the young vote, you know, and your father never forgets the young. You know that, Dan.'

Columbo could see that Dan was struggling with the news. No response was forthcoming so he gamely continued. No point in letting silence fester. Dr Abernethy here was going to be part of the solution, not part of the problem.

'She is a grand girl really but I suppose you could say that she has had her head turned by your father. Some louser is after making a note into a hymn for your mother and between the jigs and the reels she has put one and two together and come up with the atomic bomb. I tell you this much, if I got my hands on the fucker that's spreading this slurry about an innocent man—'

'What makes you so sure it's not true?' Dan's voice was no louder than a whisper.

'Jesus, am I not after telling you that there's nothing to it? Only some little wily weasel getting to your mother and trying to spoil all your father's hard work? No civil word is coming from your mother's direction. If this blows your father is a goner. The girl is still in school and there is no way it's going to look good. The thing is, Dan, they need you home. Now. Today.'

'I can't. This is my life right here. This hospital, lectures, being a doctor. I can't just head off home to Leachlara to sort this mess out. If it's a misunderstanding they will get over it without my being there.' Dan was saying the words but he knew in his heart and soul that before the evening was out he would be asking his tutor to sign him off ward duty and picking the right moment to tell Consultant Mackey that his private business was indeed more important than his medical training, for a few days at least.

Columbo retreated up the corridor of St James and Pious Wing having extracted a promise from Dan that he would be at Leeson Street Bridge at nine o'clock, ready to accept a lift to Leachlara. His belly hit the cold air first and he dragged the edges of his coat together to barricade himself against the slicing wind. Business done he ambled his way to the hospital car park and onwards to the bar of Buswell's where he would while away the hours until night fell. There was always someone there that he could tap for information and see if word of the trouble for Deputy Abernethy had seeped outside Leachlara. If they moved fast he hoped that the whole sorry mess could be contained, a blip in an otherwise smack-smooth year. In these circumstances, Columbo firmly believed that it was an excellent idea to be seen keeping the bright side out, just in case someone was watching and sniffing a touch of scandal.

Chapter Seven

The Naas road was hospitably and unusually clear of heavy traffic. Not even the wet glare of the damp roads was doing anything to delay Columbo as he cruised his way to Leachlara with Dan in absolutely reluctant tow. He might as well have been mute, not in a sullen way but totally preoccupied, so Columbo had decided to leave him be. He had of course made some valiant attempts at conversation, but Dan was having none of it. Faced with a wall of silence unwilling to crumble, Columbo turned up the radio and concentrated on getting to Leachlara as soon as possible. He adhered to the speed limit erratically and mostly unintentionally. A frivolity such as a speed sign was not going to obstruct important business; besides, he did happen to know a few people who could quash a summons if the need arose.

At teatime he had rung the Abernethy house to have a quick word with Con. He felt triumphant that he had snared Dan and was bringing him home to ease the pressure on Con and defuse a nasty situation for the party. His boss was edgy on the phone and didn't seem half as grateful as Columbo felt was his due. Maybe Mary was in the vicinity and causing tension, he reasoned to himself through his disappointment. The conversation was brief, with Columbo blaming a bad line so that the awkwardness between them would not have to be acknowledged. A thaw set in on his passenger as they covered the last miles to Leachlara.

'I'm not sure what you all think I can do, you know. When Mam goes off the deep end she generally has to make the return trip all by herself. If Dad has tried and failed – well, then I'm not sure I have a hope in hell. It's a mistake me coming down. Sure neither of them listens to me.'

Columbo waited, not wanting to interrupt Dan's sudden bout of loquaciousness, but Dan just as quickly fell silent again. Columbo dived in with rousing encouragement.

'Good God, Dan, they idolize you! Don't you see that is why I am bringing you home? You are Exhibit A. You are the reason that this tripe your mother is peddling will never leave the four walls. You are the bomb-disposal unit of the Abernethy house. Your mother would never risk your future or embarrassment no matter how pissed she is with your father.'

'Columbo, when you came to the hospital today you said it was all a horrible misunderstanding, that Mam was blowing things all out of proportion. Can I take it that you are now admitting that something actually happened between my father and Leda Clancy?'

Columbo didn't answer. He was getting angry with a cautious driver in front who was pedantic about being in the thirty-miles-an-hour zone, but mostly he was just buying time. Con Abernethy's house was only five minutes away and he had to deliver Dan in the best possible form, ready to put his shoulder to the job of calming Mary Abernethy down.

Dan knew what his silence meant and he reacted as if he had been kicked in the gut. 'For Jesus' sake, Columbo, there is no point lying to me. Why didn't you just tell me what you knew about this rather than bringing me here like some kind of blindfolded social worker to iron this shit out? If my dad is shagging a schoolgirl don't you think I might need to know the truth?'

The Abernethy house was coming into their view, fully illuminated in a copse of trees and set back from the main road. It had been a rector's house originally and had now been owned by the Abernethy family for two generations. The copper and russet tones of a beech hedge lined the curling avenue and the bare bark of a Virginia creeper clad the elegant walls with its branches framing the imposing entrance. Columbo slowed the pace to a respectful limit as he proceeded up the avenue. He brought the car to a halt in the yard that ran round the side of the house and led to the back door. When the car was silent, save for the radio, he turned to give Dan one more shot of adrenalin before he left the cocoon of the car.

'Look, your father is a good man. If he has slipped and made a mistake – and I am not saying for sure that he has, mind – but if he has, then it's one slip-up in a glorious and unblemished life.'

'You'll be nominating him for canonization next and we both know, whatever he is, my father is certainly no saint.'

Columbo allowed himself a small sigh of relief at Dan's stab at humour. Maybe all was not lost. 'All I am saying is talk to them. Bring your mother down from the roof where she has perched herself. She will give herself heart failure and we don't want that.'

Dan wasn't so sure Columbo felt that benignly about his mother: a bout of ill health for her would probably be utterly convenient because it would put the genie back in the bottle and harmony would be restored, temporarily at least. Still, there was no point in blaming Columbo, the party, or Leda Clancy for that matter. The Abernethys had brought this crap on themselves and it looked as if he had been appointed mediator supreme. He grabbed his holdall from the back seat where he had flung it when he had got in at Leeson Street Bridge. 'I take it you are not coming in then?' he said, trying to get a rise out of Columbo. He knew that tonight of all nights his father's apostle would offer to swim laps of Lough Derg instead.

'Ah no, Dan, it's late and you will need your own time to sort this out. I'll talk to your father in the morning. Maybe call round even. To tell you the truth, I'm hoping to make Shanahan's before they close because I told a fellow I'd meet him there.'

Lucky bastard, Dan thought as he ambled his way to the back porch. The outside light was on and a gleeful array of moths flirted in the brightness. With a heavy heart he turned his key in the back door and went inside to see who and what was still up.

Chapter Eight

The family silver was laid out carefully on the dining-room table. Goblets, platters, butter dishes, a cream and jam set, teapots and milk jugs lay in glistening array before Mary Abernethy's satisfied eyes. She had been collecting pieces for years in auction rooms around the county, adding to what her in-laws had left in the house when they died. It was a handsome collection by any standards, though grudgingly she had to admit that her husband's public life had garnered its own fair share of silverware. If it had not been spoiled by the engraving of his name and that of the blasted party she might have the same regard for it as she did for the pieces she had squirrelled herself.

The entire collection was taken down from the mahogany sideboards on the first day of each season and Mary Abernethy applied herself with relish to the task of polishing it. When the job was finished she would turn on the crystal chandelier in the centre of the room in order to admire her glittering handiwork. She was on the last piece when she heard the latch on the back door. Presuming it was Con, back from Shanahan's or wherever he had taken himself off to, she polished the handle of the silver tray while bile rose within her. The door opened behind her and the lights from the hallway flooded in. If he has come back with a bellyful of drink and he feels like a fight he has come to the right place, she thought. Her son's voice startled her.

'Hi, Mam. Still taking excellent care of my inheritance, I see.'

'Jesus, Mary and Joseph, what are you doing here, Dan? Is there something wrong?'

'Well, you tell me. According to Columbo, who more or less kidnapped me in the hospital, you and Dad are about to kill one another. Some misunderstanding, he said?'

Dan thought it best to keep the whole thing low key, pretending that Columbo had only given him the bare bones of the story and not all the grisly details. There was still an outside chance that the normal and manageable level of hostility native to his parents' relationship could be satisfactorily restored.

'That lousy runt! I cannot believe he dragged you away from your studies. Do you know the night before last I caught him coming up the stairs to talk to me with his sweaty hands on my banisters and his ignorant boots traipsing across my carpets?

'Your father and I will sort this out – or more to the point your father will. That little sneak Columbo had no right—'

Dan cut across her. He had listened to her berate his father and Columbo for as long as he could remember. It was doubtful that it would get them anywhere useful.

'Just what exactly is going on, Mam? I couldn't get a straight word out of Columbo. First it was nothing at all and then you were going to the papers to blow the whistle on him. Will you just fill me in, for God's sake?'

Mary Abernethy put down the silver platter, irritated a little by the fact that she had not given it her full attention but irritated more by the fact that Columbo, obviously acting on Con's instructions, had the temerity to drag Dan into all of this. There were it seemed no depths to which her husband would not stoop and no limit to how far his cronies, particularly his brainless sidekick, would go to pull him out of the firing line.

'We had better make tea, Dan. You must be gasping for a cup. I know I am.'

Dan followed his mother into the kitchen. It looked as if Columbo had overstated the case a little bit. His mother was undoubtedly irritated with Con but on balance she seemed calm enough. So much for having to talk her down from the roof! He would have a word or two for Columbo before he headed back to Dublin in the morning. It would take some time to bring Consultant Mackey back on side and all for what?

Mary Abernethy brewed a pot of tea, one bag apiece and one for the pot. When the china mugs were out and the tea ready to pour she allowed herself to tell her side of the story. She felt bad for burdening Dan but it was lovely to have him home and she had not confided in anyone else, fearing their judgement but above all not wanting their pity.

'Your father has been lying to me. The lying is nothing new but this time he has taken it too far. His latest stunt is just a bit sicker than I thought even he was capable of.'

Dan's heart began to sink. It obviously was just as bad as Columbo had intimated. Mary Abernethy was on a roll now and she paused only to take a restorative sip from her tea.

'Your father has been messing around with a young girl from the area. I'm not sure to what extent but there have been trips to the apartment in Dublin and dinners out. Leda Clancy is her name. You probably know the family. They live out in Briartullog, the townland that runs above the graveyard?'

'I know who she is. She works in Shanahan's as a lounge girl.'

'Well, that she is the kind of girl that would be working in a pub when she should be attending to her homework does not surprise me. Your father spends enough time in that drinking pit to pick up some fluff on the way out. She must be a bit simple really. I mean, your father was never exactly a playboy but at fifty-seven and balding the girl must be a bit lacking if she thinks he is a catch.'

'I know Dad has done some dodgy stuff businesswise and hasn't always been up front with you about money and that, but this, Mam, this is different. Is there any chance that you could be reading too much into something innocent?'

'Your father wouldn't know innocent if it walked up and struck him on the face. I would never have dragged you into it, but seeing as he sent his lackey for you the least I can do is to tell you the truth. It's a disappointment to you, I can see that in your face, but I am well used to the disappointment that comes with being Mrs Con Abernethy. I have supported his career even when I didn't feel like it and he repays me with the disrespect of picking up a teenager and risking making us the laughing stock of Leachlara. He won't get away with this.'

'Well, are you going to go public and if you are what do you think that will achieve? If you are worried about people knowing, surely we should keep a lid on things. The whole thing is mortifying. Is there no end to the trouble that you two can create for yourselves?'

'I would never do anything to jeopardize your future or your career, Dan, but I had to make some sort of threat to get his attention. I wanted him to think about how long it would take for his ministerial ambitions to evaporate under the scrutiny of a few journalists with the scent of a scandal. He has a responsibility to be discreet and not show me up in Leachlara. This is my home more than it is his now. I am the one that's here to face the people.'

'So you are just playing games? You don't even care if he is really sleeping with her, do you? It's just the scandal, the way it looks to people. Everything is just about appearances with you both. Can't we sort it out in this house between ourselves without having everyone laughing at us?'

'Oh, the squirming and the worried looks have been enjoyable. That little rancid sidekick of his has sweated more than an Alsatian in heat in the last week and it has been worth it for that alone!'

'So how long are you going to dangle him before you put him out of his misery? The stress of the whole thing could bring on a heart attack.'

'I wouldn't worry about your father's heart, Dan. I doubt his body devotes much time to its upkeep.'

'Please stop talking about him like that. I wouldn't let him say ugly things about you so—'

'Look, I'm sorry. It wasn't my choice to involve you, but maybe you can be a go-between as I can't look at that man now.'

'Charming. Stuck in the middle of this fucking mess. Go on, let me have it. What do you need to bring this to an end?'

'I want that Leda girl out of Leachlara, as far away as she can manage.'

'She is only sixteen or seventeen, Mam. I think she had better stay with her family.' Dan pleaded for common sense. Mary Abernethy wasn't listening, so in thrall was she to her own grand plan.

'Then I want a renewal of our marriage vows ceremony in Leachlara and a second honeymoon, in Rome maybe – although I haven't decided if that is the most desirable destination yet. The travel agent in Tipperary did say that Rome was being replaced by Venice and Florence as the most popular place. Anyway, somewhere in Italy definitely.'

'You are joking, aren't you, Mam? I wasn't aware that the first honeymoon was such a roaring success that you would want to relive the experience. You can't stand the man – why on earth would you want to go to Rome with him?'

'He doesn't even have to get on the same plane. Just as long as he doesn't show his face in Leachlara or in the Dáil bar for the duration I will be happy. He can go to his brother's place in Aughasallagh. That would keep him nicely out of harm's way. In fact, now that you mention it, your father would be the ruination of Rome. Hanging around with the party yes men for all these years has done nothing for his conversation skills. And you can tell him in no uncertain terms that he got off lightly because, of all things, I would not upset you, Dan.'

'God, I think it's a bit late in the day to be worrying about my feelings. It never stopped you pulling each other to ribbons before.'

'Don't be cross with me. I could not bear that.' Mary Abernethy had adopted her wheedling tone accompanied by the little-girl eyes that made her son embarrassed even to look her straight in the eye.

'I'm not cross. It's fine. I will talk to him, although I imagine he will faint laughing at your little revenge drama.'

'You are the best thing I have done, Dan Abernethy, and you are the sole reason I stay with your father.'

Dan muttered under his breath that sometimes he wished she didn't bother but his mother was not listening. She busied herself putting the milk jug into the fridge and washing her mug. Dan looked at the mottled skin that the milk had formed on his untouched tea. No matter how many times he felt he was making good his escape from this house and all the unpleasant memories it held it could always draw him back and threaten to sink him. He had been in the house less than an hour after nearly two months' absence and already he felt he was suffocating in a swell of negativity and small-mindedness. This house may have reared him but more than that it had filled him with an instinct to flee for his own good.

Mary continued her fastidious clean-up oblivious to her son's discomfort. It was so nice to have him home, especially tonight, when he was not monopolized by his father. She went to bed deciding that she would make a habit of visiting Dan in Dublin. She missed him and she knew he missed her too. He was just too proud to show it. As she fell asleep she congratulated herself on rearing him well – and rearing him mostly alone.

Dan spotted his father's car was pulled on to the grass verge just inside the entrance gates. He had waited up until well past midnight hoping to talk to him but there had been no sign of Con Abernethy. His mother didn't know where her husband had gone. She wasn't, she reminded Dan, privy to that sort of information. The phone in the hallway had remained resolutely silent, so Dan concluded that his father must be with his party workers at a meeting or more likely at a lock-in at Shanahan's or Power's. In fact, Dan thought Columbo had probably been going straight to meet him when he had left himself off at the house to defuse his mother. Now out on a stroll before bed to clear his head and to stop a headache in its tracks, he could make out his father's Mercedes with the headlights dimmed. He walked towards it, afraid of what he might find but compelled to look nonetheless. Surely, he thought, he hasn't brought Leda Clancy here? But what else could he be doing, hiding like a thief in the grounds of his own home in the early hours of the morning? His pace quickened. His heart pounded in his chest, echoing the gravel crunching beneath his feet. He reached the navy Mercedes ready for anything at all except perhaps for what he found. Con Abernethy's head was tilted back against the soft pillow of the headrest. His eyes were closed and tears were streaming down his face.

Chapter Nine

'I'm no ogre, Dan, no matter what she will have you believe.'

Con had fumbled for a handkerchief from his jacket pocket to dry the tears when his son knocked on the passenger window. He was thoroughly embarrassed that Dan had seen him crying. He wasn't sure what had come over him really because he was usually good when under pressure. There was not a meeting, a speech or an election campaign that had ever fazed him. He was, everyone thought (including himself), born for the exhausting slog of public life, but today was different. Today he would think nothing of running away and never looking back.

Dan had been close to turning and running too when he saw the sorry sight of his father weeping uncontrollably in the car but he decided there was nothing to be gained from putting off this conversation for another day. He sat beside his father and waited for any explanation that might make sense. He wasn't interested in hearing how his mother got it all so wrong, he just wanted to hear how Con Abernethy was going to set it straight.

'Look, Dad, I'm not a fool. I don't need anyone to tell me

how bad this whole thing is. You and Leda? For God's sake, she's only a schoolgirl. What do you think you are playing at?'

'I promise I will explain, but not here. Let's go back to the house. It's cold and, besides, your mother will be in bed by now.'

'Is that what made you stop here? Waiting until Mam went to bed so you can sneak into your own house?'

'It's not my style to run scared and you know that. I can normally face her no matter what kind of order she is in but tonight it was just beyond me. I have stupidly brought trouble on myself but it is unnatural the pleasure your mother finds in my misfortune.'

'I don't think that's true. It's as plain as day that you two don't get on and shouldn't be married or living in the same house but Mam didn't create this for your discomfort. You seem capable of sinking yourself without any help from anyone else. Go on, drive up to the house. It's freezing here.'

Mary Abernethy's perpetually hungry cat wove under their feet as they made their way to the back door. A resounding kick from Con sent him simultaneously wailing and flying across the driveway and into a heather bed at the front of the house.

'Did Columbo tell you that he had dropped me here?'

'Yeah. He came into Shanahan's for the last few. He said you came to help and I'm thankful, Dan. I really am.'

He didn't talk again until he had half filled a tumbler of whiskey from the Paddy bottle. He topped it up a little with water from the cold tap. He raised the bottle in the direction of Dan. 'Fancy a drop?'

'No, I'm grand. I've hardly eaten so I'd be sick if I drank now.'

'Fair enough so but eat something, for heaven's sake. Your mother always has that fridge stocked with sun-dried tat and honking goat's cheese. You might find something edible if you look long and hard and have a strong nose.' Con took a huge gulp of whiskey and sat down across the table from his son. His face was blotched from the earlier tears but he seemed calmer now, relaxed even. 'Seeing as everyone else has had their say, maybe you will listen to me now.'

'Go ahead, Dad, I am all ears.'

'First and foremost there is nothing going on between Leda Clancy and myself. If you accept that then everything else I say to you will make perfect sense. I have known the Clancys all my life. I went to school with Leda's mother, Aggie. I put in a good word for Leda at Shanahan's because I knew the family were not exactly flush and the extra cash would come in handy. I see Ted every Thursday night in Shanahan's. My intentions in all of this were honourable. You have to believe me.'

'Why then is Columbo behaving like there has been a nuclear disaster and why did I just find you crying in your car afraid to come into your own house?'

Con bit his lip. 'Look, it won't come as a surprise to you that affection has been in short supply in my life for years. I admit it: I was flattered. Here was a beautiful girl who could have had her pick of any of the young bucks that are in and out of the pub and she got it into her head that I was more interesting than they were. My head was turned, Dan, and if that makes me seem weak and stupid then that's what I am – but that's *all* I am. I have done nothing wrong except encourage the attention of a schoolgirl with a crush. I thought she would get over it and in the meantime I decided to enjoy it. I didn't think it through and I had no idea that your mother would get up on her high horse about it. She's letting on she is jealous and her feelings are hurt. Well, both counts are laughable. If your mother has feelings for anything except you and what money can buy she has done a good job in hiding them for twenty years.'

'She says you have taken Leda out to dinner and taken her to the apartment in Dublin. Is she lying?'

'Leda was on a trip from the community school to Dublin.

I took the young people around government buildings and the Dáil and bought them lunch in a restaurant on Molesworth Street. I was never even on my own with her. She got the bus back to Thurles in the evening with all the rest of the group and I drove home as usual. Your mother is making things up to add fuel to her story. The only place I have ever spent any bit of time in Leda's company is in the lounge at Shanahan's after closing time. Paddy Shanahan is always there and there are always a few of my gang there too. I suppose my ego got stoked that such a lovely girl could fancy someone like me, an old fella heading for sixty years of age. I was taken in, Dan. I got a swelled head and I never really thought about the fact that I was leading her on. I assumed she would cop on to herself eventually and marvel at how she ever looked sideways at me.'

Dan was getting numb to the details. His father sounded as if he was telling the truth, but then Dan reminded himself that Con had often said that the mark of a good politician was someone who could appear sincere and interested when in fact he was neither. If he was delivering a performance Dan could not find it in himself to deliver the appropriate applause.

'What about her parents? Surely they have noticed that she has got the wrong idea about you?'

'The thing is the Clancys have always had it hard. Aggie has been suffering with her nerves for years and Ted never did a full day's work if he had the option of doing half a day instead. He has a fondness for the drink, too, so money is short for the family. I suppose Leda thought of me as a way out, a passport from everything at home. If I worked my brain at all I would have seen how vulnerable the girl was but I never stopped to think. She started telling her school friends there was something going on and maybe telling them we had been places when we hadn't and it got to your mother and here we are now. I mean, she asked me for lifts back home several nights and I knew how it would look so I made Columbo or one of the others go instead.

In fact I told Paddy Shanahan that a girl of her age shouldn't be trying to arrange lifts home with people she barely knew. I said it to Ted Clancy too but sure he can barely get himself home most nights so I was wasting my breath.'

'So why is Columbo acting as if he is concealing a grenade under his coat? He came storming into the hospital as if it was a matter of life and death. He even risked going up the stairs here to try and talk sense into Mam. The man has a death wish.'

'Look, I am very fond of Columbo but the thing is he presumes he always knows best. When I told him the bones of the story, as I have told you now, he didn't even listen. His modus operandi has always been to protect the party at any cost. If he suspects danger, even where there isn't any, he prides himself on being the first to head it off at the pass. He doesn't really care if I am telling the truth or not as long as the party comes through unscathed and he is seen to be doing his job. To Columbo I am irrelevant in all of this and if he feels that way about me you can be sure that Leda Clancy does not even register. It's a cruel game, this business, Dan. I am so glad you are doing something that could take you a million miles from here and you need never look back.'

They talked on until first light was breaking over the mountains at the back of the house. Dan told his father what his mother's demands were for a cessation of hostilities.

'A wedding and a trip to Rome? Sometimes I can't get over that woman. I'm not sure if she is bad or mad or both. What business would we have in Rome – the city of lovers and all that? We would be turned back at the airport.'

'To tell you the truth, Dad, I'm not sure your presence is required in anything but the most nominal sense. Will you do it?'

'Not if I can help it, no. My marriage has long been a disappointment to me and I don't really want anyone else shining a light where I won't dare to look myself. The wound is deep enough without adding salt.'

'What will you do so? She won't be happy, I can tell you that. She wants Leda out of the place too, which is just ridiculous. She's in school.'

'Well, between you and me, I am not sure that is the worst idea your mother has ever had. Things are bad at home for the Clancy children. The eldest girl is in college – fair play to her – and I am close enough to fixing up the young lad as a plumber's apprentice. Aggie isn't able and Ted is not a parent in any sense of the word. I could put Leda in the way of office work and such out of Leachlara. Give her a start so she gets her independence, a course maybe if that's what she wants. To be honest it's the least I can do to make amends. She feels let down and I reckon it's my responsibility even if it's not my fault.'

Dan looked at his father as he poured himself another generous measure of whiskey. He cupped the glass with both hands as if he depended on it for support. The bottle had gone from over half to a quarter full during the course of their conversation and Con was not bothering to dilute it any more. Not for the first time Dan was shocked at his father's capacity for drink. It seemed not to have any appreciable effect on him. He must have had a few in the pub too and still his words never slurred and his voice never faltered.

'So if you are not going to renew the vows or do the whole honeymoon thing, how do you expect this thing with Mam to be brought under control? She is looking for satisfaction and she won't rest without it.'

'Money, Dan. Most things with your mother come down to money in the end. After you there is nothing she cares about more. So I am guessing if I play willing, total up the cost of a suitably flashy renewal-of-wedding-vows party for a TD and the cost of a luxury trip to Rome, her mind will start racing at the thought of the things she could spend the money on.

She could get more silverware for the sideboard that no one sees and a replacement car for the one that nobody ever gets a lift in. I can see the list forming as we speak. Then if I round up the amount by a couple of grand and offer that to ease her pain and embarrassment this whole thing will be put behind us quietly and permanently. A cheque speaks volumes to your mother, always has done. It's the only way we converse any more. Her silence breaks only when she wants money or at least more money than she already has. She has even taken to leaving Post-its on the kettle with her account number on them – as if I needed reminding of my greatest money hole.'

Dan left his father and his whiskey at the kitchen table shortly before the clock on the wall began to ring for six o'clock. He had been up close to twenty-four hours and his body was succumbing to an enveloping exhaustion that rendered him almost speechless. He had done nothing to sort this mess out except listen to his mother's grandiose plans for retribution and then hear his father confidently assert he would outsmart her at the end with the power of his cheque book. He promised himself as he climbed into the bed in his old room that he would stay alone for ever rather than re-create a marriage like his parents': bound together by a child and mutual disdain. It was a horrible way to live. What struck him most about both his parents was their willingness to stay put for the sake of appearances, to endure any kind of misery as long as the set piece of their lives looked well to anyone looking on. Well, Dan had seen enough to know that he would not settle for the same life himself. It couldn't be that hard to better his parents' lousy attempt, he thought as he shifted uncomfortably in the bed. The sheets had had the heavy starch treatment so popular with his mother and he lay awake waiting for the bed to soften under him, enough for him to settle into overdue sleep.

The posters on the wall, dimly visible in the morning light, were the ones he had tacked up there a good few years before:

George Michael and Andrew Ridgeley togged out in matching white suits and their hair sprayed within an inch of its life. God, he couldn't imagine how he hadn't worked out that George Michael was gay. It was so obvious, yet Dan had been so unbelievably innocent. Besides, no one else in Leachlara Community School seemed to have worked it out either – or if they had they hadn't mentioned it.

Also there was the *St Elmo's Fire* cast poster that he had stolen from the Carlton foyer in Leachlara. He had a serious crush on Demi Moore for years after that film. Dan smiled to himself as he remembered how many times he had watched the video. God, she was gorgeous, but he wasn't sure about the really short hair in *Ghost*. It was as if she had taken a saucer from her potter's wheel and put it on her head. He definitely preferred her with long hair. As he finally drifted off to sleep he decided that he would definitely ask out Alison from Rose's café. She looked a bit like a very young Demi, he thought with a grin, and if she looked that good despite the shapeless chef's gear she always wore then she must be really beautiful. Thursday afternoon was when Rose said she would be in again. She had winked at him and his efforts at nonchalance had been lost in her uncontrollable ear-to-ear grin.

'Well, finally, Dan, I thought I was going to have to reach across there and check for a pulse. Yourself and Alison have been gazing at each other since well before Christmas. It's time you got a bloody move on!'

'Yes, Boss!' he had replied, more than a little surprised by the fact that his attraction to Alison had been so obvious when he thought he had been playing it cool. He had been rumbled – but what did it matter? A date with Alison Shepherd might just be what he needed to forget his family's misery and memories of all that had happened in Leachlara. He would ask her out on Thursday, he decided, then slept for ten straight hours.

Chapter Ten

Burnt onions were not a smell naturally conducive to romance. Alison could have killed Ciara for leaving the place in such a tip again. The kitchen units were strewn with vegetable peelings and utensils that had stirred a deep dark pit of something that was probably Ciara's attempt at Bolognese. A massive heap of congealed pasta nearby was a further clue to the recipe that had been attempted. Alison had encouraged her flatmate to start cooking dinners because for the first six weeks they lived together she seemed to eat nothing but toast and cereal. Alison had even written down some simple recipes. The remnants of this dinner did not bode well for Ciara's progress. Alison would have to spend the next half-hour cleaning up the mess before she could degrease herself after an afternoon at the Daisy May. In fairness she hadn't had a chance to tell Ciara that what she had been dreaming of for months had now finally come to pass. Dan Abernethy had asked her out and she was so proud that she hadn't collapsed before she managed to say yes. She had felt Rose's lurking presence behind them cleaning tables, taking ages to clear what she would normally have tidied in a few short minutes. It felt as if she was making space for something to happen but it wasn't until Dan clasped her hand in his as she set his mug of black coffee in front of him that she allowed herself to believe that this gorgeous, sophisticated man could be interested in her. His eyes were so intense that she felt her face fire up in a maddening blush when he spoke to her.

'Will you come out with me, Alison? To the pictures or to the pub or for a pizza, whichever one you fancy . . .' He punctuated the ensuing pause with a heartfelt, 'Please?'

She was finding it difficult to get the words out because all she could concentrate on was the fact that her hand was touching his and his eyes were fixed on her face waiting intently for her answer. Eventually her vocal cords managed to discharge their function.

'Yes, I'd love that. A drink would be nice.' What was she saying? She didn't even drink, but a film would be useless. She wanted to be able to look at him, listen to him, and a darkened cinema was not the place. Oh well, she would drink water all night if it meant finally spending time with Dan.

A customer at the other end of the counter slammed his mug on the countertop in a sullen unspoken demand for a refill. Alison darted to him with the coffee jug, relieved to have negotiated accepting the date without making a total idiot of herself by stumbling on her words or burning his hands with the scalding coffee or tripping over herself while trying to coolly move away.

With that Rose dropped her cleaning cloth and with it her long-drawn-out pretence of table polishing. She let out a dramatic sigh and approached Dan where he was seated at the counter with a massive smile on his face. 'Well, I do hope your future patients won't be as long waiting for a fecking blood transfusion or an amputation, Dan Abernethy, as I have been waiting for that little invitation of yours. It would be less painful to watch a snail crossing the street in heavy traffic. I'm going out for a cigarette, boy. My nerves are well and truly shot.'

Dan laughed. He was mad for Rose and very grateful to her that she had made herself scarce so he could talk to Alison alone.

Conlon's pub in Camden Street wasn't a popular student haunt and so was quieter on a Thursday night than most of the other pubs on the street. That was one of the reasons Dan had chosen it for his date with Alison. He wanted to be able to chat with her without any of the lads from his class butting in with their smart comments. It was a tradition to rag any couple on a date and Dan knew how merciless it all could be because he had been part of the good-natured taunting gang on several occasions. Alison was different to any of the girls he had been out with before. She was a bit mysterious and reserved and he wanted time to work her out for himself before anyone else had his or her say about her. He knew from Rose that she was from Cork, some smallish country town, though Rose couldn't remember the name of it. He knew like himself that she was an only child and that she was in first year Arts in Trinity. At twenty-four he was a good bit older but Alison – and he presumed their enthusiastic matchmaker Rose had filled her in about himself – didn't seem to mind. In fact she seemed delighted he had asked her out, if somewhat shell-shocked.

He had offered to pick her up at her flat in Ranelagh but she had insisted that she would meet him at Conlon's. The bus from Ranelagh stopped at the top of the street before it swung around on to Harcourt Street so at most it was only a few minutes' stroll. Dan arrived early, driven out from his flat off Leeson Street partly by nerves but mostly by his flatmate Anthony's liberal use of pound-shop aftershave, which he considered essential for a night on the pull. 'Captivate' was the latest brand adorning the toilet cistern in a frighteningly industrial-size can. Sparingly, Dan had told him, was the best way to impress a girl but Anthony continued to use quantities that would dip a flock of sheep and cure them of all their infestations. When he came to think of it, Dan decided sheep dip probably had the edge on any of Anthony's wooing scents.

'I think, Ant, the only captivating you will be doing tonight is if they fall at your feet overpowered by the whiff of your aerosol poison.'

'Control your jealousy, Abernethy, just because I have a line of hot babes waiting to succumb to my charms in pubs the length of Leeson Street and you, saddo, are taking yourself off to the cinema to munch your popcorn on your own. Why don't you come with me and watch the master at work? Pointers, my friend, that's what you need and I'm the very man to help you.'

'I wouldn't dream of cramping your style, Anthony. Talent like yours needs oxygen to breathe.'

'Well, enjoy the subtitles, and I will take care of the ladies,' Anthony replied before he swaggered out in search of his unsuspecting prey.

At the bar there was a row of Guinness-sipping heads, lined up like soldiers on their high stools silently admiring themselves in the gilt whiskey-label mirrors that lined the back of the bar. It seemed that real men in Conlon's sat at the bar because all the tables and chairs were vacant except for one in the corner, temporary home to a group of handbag-clutching, vodka-quaffing women who looked as if they were expecting the bingo numbers to roll any minute now.

'Did you say Leachlara?' Alison asked, knocked sideways by the coincidence that she had willed not to be the case ever since Ciara had disclosed to her the details of Leda's involvement with the dodgy politician in their home town.

'Yeah, I'm from Leachlara. Why, have you heard of it?' Dan was a bit taken aback. Anybody he had mentioned it to in Dublin had never heard of Leachlara, which didn't surprise him really. It was, after all, only a crooked miserable street with more pubs than it needed and precious little else. Columbo's battle cry was that Con Abernethy had put Leachlara on the map and it had struck Dan that it was a curiously pointless achievement – even if it were the case. Truly there was no point in going there unless you had the misfortune to call it home. Now it seemed to have followed him here and he didn't know how to react.

'My best friend is from Leachlara. She's my flatmate too.' Alison knew that he might be uncomfortable with the mention of her name but she thought it best to get it out of the way. Hopefully it would not scupper this thing with Dan before it even got started. She had to be honest. He was going to meet Ciara sooner rather than later and this whole thing would be better aired beforehand. 'I think you might know her. At least, she has spoken of a family of Abernethys from Leachlara. Ciara Clancy is her name.'

Dan was stunned. It couldn't get much worse than this. He had run from the mess that his father had created at home with Leda Clancy. He had sought refuge in his independent life in Dublin but it had followed him here like a bad smell and it could ruin the nicest thing that had happened to him in ages. Ciara Clancy was not likely to be impressed with her flatmate's choice of company.

Dan felt his throat tighten and his mouth dry but he forced himself to form some sort of an answer. 'I've heard of her. I mean, I know the Clancys and where they live. I don't think I have ever spoken to Ciara. She was at the same school but she was only starting when I was doing the Leaving.' Dan was rambling because he didn't know how much, if anything, Ciara might have told Alison about his father. There was no point in him blurting it all out to her if she was blissfully unaware. She would just think his dad was a creep, a point he might well have to concede, but he wasn't ready for her to think badly of himself too, not when they had only just met.

Anticipating how awfully this could turn out, Alison thought she had better rescue Dan from his obvious mortification. 'Look, Ciara has told me about your dad and her sister Leda and what's meant to be going on. But I am ready to hear your side if you want to tell me. Just because Ciara is my friend doesn't mean I don't want to get to know you. I'll understand though if you don't want to talk about it because we have only just met. It's none of my business, after all. I just figured that Abernethy is such an unusual name that there couldn't be too many families called that in a place the size of Leachlara.'

'No, there is only one lot of Abernethys. We punch above our weight though when it comes to shitty family stuff,' Dan said with as much humour as he could manage under the circumstances. The sensible thing to do would be to bolt for the door, but the longer he looked at Alison the more he wanted to stay. She had taken his breath away when she walked in. He'd known she was beautiful from watching her at the Daisy May but he was taken aback by just how gorgeous she looked. Her hair tumbled around her slightly made-up face and her petite frame was dressed in a slim-fitting red shirt and dark denims. He wanted to snog her there and then so there was no way he was going to let his father's foul-ups ruin his chances. 'If it's all right with you, Alison, maybe we could start off like this is a totally normal run-of-the-mill first date and I will get to the heavy stuff later. That's of course if you are still interested and you haven't decided to run for the hills.'

'I promise to stay until the end.' Alison was relieved. She would tell Ciara eventually but there was no need to tell her straight away.

They talked until after midnight when the barman at Conlon's downed tools and started to flick the lights in an effort to chase the handful of drinkers on to the street. They swapped stories about growing up, their respective schools and their university courses and agreed that it was nice to live in Dublin where people didn't know every ounce of your business.

'Well, at least I used to think that about Dublin until I asked out this beautiful, mysterious girl from the Daisy May and realized that she knew loads about me and all I knew about her was her name and that she was from Cork. Oh, and that she nearly always burns whatever is in the frying pan when I am drinking coffee at the counter. I'd say you owe poor Rose a brace of frying pans by now!'

Alison grinned. Talking to him was so easy; she felt she could say anything to him. No point then in ignoring the huge elephant sitting in the corner any longer. Con Abernethy might as well be sitting between them in Conlon's.

'Look, Ciara is just looking out for Leda. You can't blame her for that and she may have exaggerated the story a bit. I mean, I'm sure your dad wouldn't – didn't actually do anything. Did he?'

'To be honest, he says he didn't and I want to believe him but I can't be absolutely definite that this whole thing with Leda is entirely innocent. I'm just back from home now where all hell is breaking loose between my mam and dad. He seems remorseful that he might have led Leda on but he says that she made most of the story up to compensate for a pretty poor home life. I think he's telling the truth but he is a politician after all and his job is to make people believe him. He's good at that. As for my mam, she was never his biggest fan so she wants his guts for garters.'

'Well, I think he has a point about Ciara's parents. I've never met them but from what she says they are not with it at all. Ciara seems very glad to be away from home, says her dad is clueless and her mother has been depressed for a long time. So maybe Leda is just engineering a way out for herself too. She stayed with us for a couple of days in December. Ciara was trying to persuade her to stay longer but she hightailed it home without even telling us and took a week's kitty money with her. Ciara was livid but it made her realize that she can't force Leda to do anything. She might be Ciara's little sister but she has a mind of her own, that's for sure.'

'Does this mean that Ciara is going to be on your doorstep tonight ready to give me a whack on the side of the head with the mop and bucket when I walk you home?'

Alison looked at her watch. It was half past midnight. At this time Ciara would be in her bed with the loud hiss from her wonky radio stealing out from under her door. She had taken to leaving it on all night, liking the comfort of the voices. Silence made her think about all sorts of depressing things, she had told Alison, and that was a dodgy prospect if you needed your sleep. 'No, you're safe enough at this hour. Besides, if Ciara ever found the mop and bucket in the first place it would be a cause for celebration. She doesn't do housework. It's just as well she is great fun because she is a disaster when it comes to cleaning up. I can get a taxi anyway, you don't have to walk me home.'

'I am your taxi, Alison. I would love to walk you home if you'll let me.'

He wrapped his scarf around her neck to keep her warm and they took the route along Charlemont Street and over the Grand Canal still chatting under the orange glow of the street lights, strung like rough amber jewels across the night sky. Alison found out that Dan lived in a house owned by his father off Leeson Street. It was divided into a number of flats and he and Anthony Geoghan, another medical student, shared the roomiest one at the top of the house. Dan thought that his father owned a good few houses around Dublin but Con Abernethy kept specific information about his property portfolio close to his chest. He admitted that his mother hardly knew the ins and outs of his father's business dealings either, so anxious was he to keep it private. It seemed strange to Alison because she was so used to her mother and father discussing everything and working so closely together every day. Alison related the funny stories about Jean McDermott and her drinking habits and how she seemed to have forgotten that she had let out her upstairs flat to two students.

'She always seems fairly disoriented when she sees us and calls us both Mary. She never forgets the rent though. We are her passport to the off licences around the village. Well, our rent money and the sick pay that she seems to be getting from the civil service for work-related stress. The stress seems to have centred on actually having to turn up.'

'God, I am risking life and limb going to your front door tonight. First I have a gin-swilling landlady who thinks you are a trespasser and then a flatmate who would swing for me if she knew that I was an Abernethy from Leachlara.'

'Just as well I am worth the risk then, isn't it?' Alison chipped as they reached the picture-book gate and pathway of 9 Sycamore Street. It was a lesson in how deceiving appearances could be because the inside of Jean McDermott's house had little beautiful to recommend it.

Dan towered over her as he pulled her into a warm embrace. He kissed her softly on the lips, lingering and soaking in her taste. She thought she could happily melt into him. After the longest time he pulled away gently from her. 'I had better let you go inside. It's cold.'

Alison agreed though she felt no cold at all, just his arms around her and his face above her beaming down his gorgeous smile.

'Will you mind my scarf for me until I see you again?'

'Yes. I will take good care of it.' They kissed again and Dan waited until Alison turned the key in the Chubb lock and disappeared inside, first turning back to offer the favour of her smile and a wave.

He walked the length of Sycamore Street, turning left on to Ranelagh Road and heading for Leeson Street Bridge. His pace was energetic and his head buzzed with the excitement that Alison was truly nicer than he had dared to imagine. It was a good twenty-minute walk home. He hoped that it was a journey he would repeat until he knew all the strides of it by heart.

Chapter Eleven

'Two weeks, Alison, and I still haven't laid eyes on him. I'm beginning to think you're making up this whole Dr Dan business and that you're really sneaking out to see crap films in the Stella, ones you know I'd bawl you out for wanting to see.'

'Of course I'm not making him up! You will meet him soon, I promise.' Alison thought maybe now would be a good time to drop the bombshell that she knew more about the Abernethys of Leachlara than Ciara could possibly imagine.

'I'm not sure I think much of him if he lets you walk home from all these places that you meet him in. It's not very chivalrous, is it? Not exactly the bumper package of gentlemanly charisma that you had him down as, I am afraid.'

Ciara was enjoying having a tease at Alison's expense. She had been away with the birds for the last couple of weeks, out nearly every second night and she had been so tight-lipped about the romance. It seemed to Ciara that she was afraid to mention Dan in case he disappeared in a puff of smoke. Ciara firmly believed that men were not so scarce that they had to be handled so delicately but she also knew that she and Alison were about as different as it was possible to be and still get along, so they were not likely to agree on the cleverest way to pursue a romance. Still, she did think it was about time she met Dan, to see the altar that Alison insisted on worshipping at.

'Shows how observant you have been, Ciara. Dan has walked me home every single night that we have been out. He just hasn't ventured up to meet you yet, that's all.'

'What have you said, Alison Shepherd? That I would eat him without salt if he came up, or is it the bold Jean McDermott that would skull him with one of her empties for defiling onc of her precious lodgers?'

Alison steeled herself for the nuclear fallout. She had a skimpy ten minutes before Dan was due to call for her with the intention of meeting Ciara. She hoped to deliver her in relatively peaceful form but amiable was not a word that could ever capture the spirit of Ciara Clancy.

'Do you remember you said that the man that's carrying on with Leda, your old landlord, had a son our age or a bit older?'

'Yeah. He was well ahead of me in school. Why?'

'Well, Dan, my boyfriend, is Dan Abernethy from Leachlara, Con's son. A bit of a coincidence really, isn't it?' Alison trailed off, her confidence faltering in the face of Ciara's incredulous look.

'Hold on. The Daniel Abernethy I know went off to study law. His mother sickened everyone in Leachlara that would stop to listen to her that one day he would be Attorney General or Chief Justice, whichever paid the most. Whatever else he is he's not your doctor.'

'He started law in UCD but he didn't like it so he reapplied and got medicine, which is what he wanted to do in the first place.'

Ciara had fallen silent. She had even started to absent-mindedly sort the tray of cutlery that sat on the worktop, which was a sure sign she was not her usual relaxed self. Alison was afraid that she wouldn't speak before Dan arrived so she did her best to make light of the situation.

'Look, Ciara, I know it's a teensy bit awkward and everything but just give Dan a chance, please. He's sound, really down to earth, and even if his dad is a louser he can't be held responsible for that surely?'

'What do you mean "even if"? After all I've told you about him you should be in no doubt that he is indeed the biggest shit around, preying on my little sister while his wife lives it up like the Queen. That woman wouldn't clean her shoes with the Clancys and he just takes advantage of Leda because there is no one looking out for her at home.'

'I don't mean to sound like I doubt you, Ciara, because of course I don't, but I am asking you just to give Dan a chance, that's all. For me, because we are friends, please? He is not his father and can't be held accountable for him. I mean, it would be unfair if anyone thought you were the same as your folks, wouldn't it? Especially when you try so hard to be different. Give him the benefit of the doubt and see what he's made of. If you still hate his guts after talking to him then fair enough. I can't argue with that.'

'Jesus, Alison, of all the effing men in Dublin, why did you have to pick him? I could introduce you to forty lads in our year that are probably better looking, great fun and, crucially, are not Con Abernethy's son. You know I am hard-wired to hate him on sight because of his father. I think I'll go before he comes. I just can't think straight at the moment.' Ciara grabbed a lipstick from the pile that languished on the mantelpiece. It was her unofficial make-up counter. She complained that the lights in her bedroom were so crap that she looked like a ferociously ugly man in drag when she applied her make-up there. Now all her potions lived in the living room accompanied by a dinky little compact mirror, one of about five that she had in various places in the kitchen, on the landing and atop the electricity meter inside the front door. It was a habit she was in to check her face for flaws or blemishes as many times as she could before she left the house. She was a firm believer that opportunities flowed to those who made an effort and she was determined not to miss any that might come her way. She applied lipstick now with a practised ease as Alison desperately tried to think of a way of keeping her from deliberately avoiding Dan. It would make things so awkward between them and she didn't want that. Surely she shouldn't have to choose between having a friend or a boyfriend? There was no justice in that. Ciara, deliberately avoiding Alison's gaze, grabbed her coat, her latest charity-shop find, from where she had abandoned it on the sofa and had just fastened the first of the oversized buttons when the doorbell rang.

'I think Redmond's Lounge gets a bit crowded and it's a bit hard to talk. Will we try the Ivy Tree instead? I've never been but it might be OK.' Dan was doing his best to get things off to a good start with Ciara but first impressions were definitely not promising. It didn't help that Alison had looked crestfallen when she had opened the door to him. When they turned on to Ranelagh Road Ciara finally addressed Dan, although she didn't actually manage to look in his direction.

'The Ivy Tree is a shit hole, full of old fogeys back from the golf and puffing like windbags on their cigars. At least Redmond's has a bit of life.'

'Fair enough, Redmond's it is. That OK with you, Alison?' Dan squeezed her hand, trying to give her a bit of encouragement. Alison nodded silently. It seemed that it was highly likely that this was going to be an absolute disaster, worse in every respect than she had imagined. Not only was Ciara not going to let Dan off the hook, it seemed she was looking around to see a bigger, better barb that she might hang him from.

As they reached Redmond's, noise whistled out from behind

the heavy double doors. Ciara turned to Dan. 'You better be buying the drink. Some of us are on a grant, you know, and seeing as I wouldn't choose to have a drink with you in a million years then I at least should have the comfort of not having to pay for it. No doubt Daddy has set you up with an allowance.'

'Ciara, do you have to be so horrible?' Alison was appalled at the way she was treating Dan and it moved her to speak for the first time since they had left the house. 'I'll buy the bloody drink. If you find it so difficult to be in our company I am very sorry but you are not exactly sweetness and light yourself.'

Ciara was a bit ashamed. Her intention had never been to hurt Alison but she couldn't help feeling her family's pride was at stake and that she was letting Leda down by having anything to do with that scumbag's son. However, after two rounds of Heineken, bought by Dan because he insisted, she seemed to soften slightly. Her tone became a little less acerbic and her conversation developed a bit more flesh than the cut-and-dried remarks that had characterized the first hour. She had to admit that he was nice enough, charming if you were into that kind of malarkey – which she absolutely was not. Charm was someone scrambling to cover up the bad bits. Charm was someone intent on fooling you. Dan had filled out a good bit; he was unrecognizable as the lanky boy she half remembered. His shoulders were broader and if anything he seemed taller than the stalk from school. He was good-looking too and that irked her a bit because she had been expecting a junior Con Abernethy with the hair swept to one side, slimy and full of himself. She had to admit that being the son of a total creep obviously didn't mean that you had to turn out to be a creep too and for Alison's sake that had to be good news.

Across the table Alison's hopes began to rise. Nerves had made her drink three glasses of sparkling water very fast and she felt a bout of hiccups on the way. Dan was telling them about his exams that were coming up soon and his voice lulled her into a calmer, happier mood. Listening to him made her feel everything would be just fine and, seeing Ciara finally making a bit of an effort with him, Alison breathed a small sigh of relief. 'Will we stay for another one?' she ventured, rising to go to the bar and leaving them alone to sink or swim.

The Dáil never sat on a Friday and although the protracted session on amendments to the licensing regulations on Thursday had run late, Con Abernethy had still decided to make the trip back to Tipperary. He was being very diligent about turning up at committees and debates because there was an election due in the summer and it never hurt to show dedication when more eyes than usual were trained on the government backbenchers. Home-town followers didn't want you spending too much time away though; they reckoned your first priority should be their concerns and they expected you not to get carried away with your work in the Dáil or get too fond of your time in Dublin.

Politics was a hard station but he liked the glory of it, the excitement of the election count and the way he felt held in such esteem by the people of Leachlara and beyond. Still, people had short memories and favours would have to be done in the run-up to any election to guarantee the right result on the night. You were only as good as the last thing you had sorted for somebody and the loyalty of voters was seriously questionable. If you missed a funeral your slip-up could lose you a whole house and their extended family. It was no good sending Columbo or another representative either as they took that as a bigger slur than missing their big day altogether. He wasn't sure what else he would do with his life if he weren't a politician and the best thing about it was that it allowed him to live for the most part away from Mary, which was a very good thing indeed.

They should never have got married, he knew that now, but neither was willing to walk away, for plenty of reasons. Con did not want to be known as a divorced TD. In these matters the traditional way was always best, even if the personal price of that tradition was heavy beyond measure. Their match had made sense twenty-five years ago. He had inherited the Abernethy family home and a farm of land from his uncle and Mary was 'a laying hen', bringing money from the proceeds of the sale of her father's grocery business in Thurles. It might have worked but Con had been unprepared for Mary's coldness, which seemed to emerge the very second that she had called the house in Leachlara her own. She had withdrawn from their physical relationship the day she found out she was pregnant with Dan. She had taken to her bed by day and made it plain that he was not invited to join her by night. Con had got Eleanor Duffy, a friend of his late mother's from the town, to help with the housework. From her alleged sickbed Mary barked instructions about the running of the house and Con had taken to being out as much as he could because he found it embarrassing to listen to. He fixed Eleanor up with cigarettes and hot whiskeys at the end of each hard day to compensate for her treatment at the beck and call of Mary Abernethy and her wages far exceeded what she might have expected to earn. Con had been overjoyed when Dan finally arrived; he had craved a son so he could show him the things that Con's father had shown him, but also because he was the human embodiment of hope and trust in the future that had all but been extinguished by the barrier that had risen between him and his wife.

He thought that nobody in Leachlara, except his closest aides, knew that their marriage was a sham of false appearances and well-concealed disappointment and that was the way Con wanted it to stay. If your wife couldn't be a positive addition to your life, he took it as read that she should not be allowed to ruin your chances either. More or less friendless, Mary seemed not to have confided in anyone except Dan, who to Con's regret now knew that hatred and distrust had seeped into the cracks that love had failed miserably to fill. He counted on the fact that Dan knew his mother was a cold fish and the failure of the marriage rested mostly at her door. He had worked at having a warm and loving relationship with Dan and he was satisfied that that at least had been a success. His son talked to him, sought him out for advice and came to meet him in his apartment frequently while the Dáil was in session. Con wasn't much of a cook but there were any number of places whence you could order meals to be delivered and he would listen to all Dan's stories about his training while they ate the food and drank wine. He would leave the dirty dishes to one side because it was a novelty that he always relished not to have the plate taken out from under your chin by an overly zealous wife intent on clearing the evidence of any meal quicker than you had a chance to eat, never mind digest, it.

It took approximately ten minutes for Con Abernethy to get from the front door of Shanahan's lounge to the stool that Columbo had reserved for him at the bar. He was slapped on the back several times, words of gratitude were whispered quietly as if the favours alluded to might disappear if they were spoken of out loud, and new favours were mooted, their precise details to follow later at a weekend clinic. When Con finally reached the bar Columbo had a pint of Guinness and a double-shot chaser of whiskey waiting for him. He had ordered them from Leda and told her they were for Con so she was to pull a lovely pint because the man was thirsty. Leda did as she was told and Paddy Shanahan looked over her shoulder in case she would foul up the order. Con Abernethy was great for Paddy Shanahan's business. The minute he took a seat at the bar on a Thursday night the place got a second lease of life. People who had been ready to call it a night suddenly discovered a pocket of thirst in their beings that they had somehow overlooked. They shuffled closer to the bar. Given a while to relax, Con Abernethy would definitely stand a round to the house and it would pain them to miss it and have to hear about it the next day from someone who had been clever enough to wait on.

'Busy in here tonight, isn't it, Columbo?'

'Yerra. There was a match in the field and we lost. Again. So what better to do than ramble in here to soak up the disappointment? Speaking of winning matches, any word on the date for this godforsaken election?'

'No word yet. He is playing his cards close to his chest. I've heard from a few that have his ear that he wants to spring it on the other crowd so they won't get a chance to get constituency offices organized.'

'I'm all for stealing their thunder but in fairness, Con, it's hard to run a campaign when the fecker won't even tell his own team when he is going to throw in the ball.'

'You've always managed before, Columbo. Sure you love the challenge!'

Con knew that, for all Columbo's complaints, he lived for campaigning and was never as miserable as when the last of the ballot boxes were sealed on election night. After that normal life resumed and Columbo Connors didn't have a normal life to speak of. He farmed a bit, just enough to avail himself of every easy grant, and he did a bit of auctioneering, but his dedication and his appetite were for winning elections and for helping to carry Con shoulder high when the last of the votes were in. Con couldn't ask for a better campaign manager and it was fitting that he bought him an appreciative drink. He waited until Leda came closer, serving a customer to his left. She was wearing a tight black top and jeans and her long black hair was pulled back from a pale face that carried not a hint of make-up. There was no denying her beauty and there was also no concealing the fact that she was stealing glances at him from the corner of her eye. She left the ordered pint to settle and walked along the length of the bar to stand in front of Con, a smile teasing the corners of her mouth.

'Can I get you something, Con? Another drink maybe?'

What he wouldn't give for this bar to be empty now except for the two of them. Then he would tell her what he wanted. He forced himself to contain the thoughts rising within him and when he spoke his voice was low and gruff, thick with urges he could neither express nor admit. He was way beyond flirting now and he knew he was sliding into treacherous territory. Somehow the chat he had had with Dan a while back where he denied everything that Mary had insinuated about himself and Leda made him feel that the matter was closed. He had presented it as a harmless crush allowed to run too far and while the truth was that it had started that way, it was a shabby and incomplete description now. If it were innocent then Con Abernethy was beginning to realize that he had no intention of letting it remain so. Leda put a pint in front of him and winked at him as if she too knew that he was about to make his long-invited move.

Columbo scrutinized his political charge intently. There had been many things that could have mired Con Abernethy in scandal down through the years. His business dealings were shady in the extreme and, if he were pushed, Columbo would have to concede that Con was incapable of cutting a straight deal. There always had to be a little something extra for him, a pot of cash to sweeten the handshake. He had enough money stashed in foreign credit-card accounts to buy up most of the houses that snaked the length of the single street of Leachlara and he had a clutch of houses in Dublin all offering up their rent every week to bolster his already healthy finances. Con being fingered because of his crooked wheeling and dealing was always a live prospect for Columbo to deal with every day he stood as Con's main defender. Plenty of others had stumbled while trying to make hay while in public office. It was Columbo's job to stop Con falling through the cracks of his own making, but Leda Clancy and the disaster that might ensue if Con could not keep his ink dry was something that he felt at a loss to control. He would have to broach it and that was likely to go down like a lead balloon. Still, no man was bigger than the party and no man was big enough not to need reining in from time to time.

'You need to keep your nose clean, Con, between now and the election. Do nothing that you could not stand over if it were found out. Let your head do the thinking for you. Do you get my drift?'

Con shoved closer to Columbo, leaning his shoulder against the older man's considerable bulk. He didn't want anyone to hear what he was about to say but neither did he want Columbo to miss a word. 'You are a great man for the canvass, Columbo, and I don't know where I'd be without you, but anything else I do is none of your fucking business. I promise discretion but I owe the blasted lot of you nothing else. Now stand the house a drink for me and make sure you keep the receipt.'

A chastened Columbo did as he was told and when the drink was all delivered to gasping mouths Con made his way up to the top of the bar where Leda was waiting for him. The flip top of the counter was up in anticipation of his arrival. As glasses were raised to his health and generosity around the bar nobody, not even Ted Clancy, noticed that he had his hand on Leda's thigh, groping it roughly and hungrily, helping himself to her as if she were his own, something he might have paid for. She listened while he told her he had a flat and a job waiting for her in Dublin, a way out he said, away from Leachlara for good.

'You are eighteen now, aren't you?' Leda nodded. What difference did a year make when she had a chance like this? 'Leave everything to me, Leda, and you will never look back.'

It was the nicest thing anyone had ever said to her and Leda did not have to think twice about accepting his offer.

Con parked Columbo's car outside the church where he had told Leda he would meet her when she had cleared up at Shanahan's. He had told Columbo to take home some of the straggling drinkers in his Mercedes, a perk because of the hard work that was to come in the run-up to a possible election.

Columbo had wordlessly obliged. He had to admit that he liked having the boss's car parked outside his house from time to time. It said things to people, flagged how important he was to the preservation of power. Usually it was a status symbol, but tonight it seemed to him a symbol that his card had been marked. Limits had been drawn for him by Con, lines over which he was not to pass. Parking the car next to the path that ran the length of his terrace was a task that cored the very middle of him. Yes, he could tap into power and yes, he numbered many important people as his acquaintances, but tonight none of that made him feel any better. He clicked the key fob to lock the car and went to his front door without looking back. As he drifted into a fitful sleep he wished that his own car was parked outside and that Leda was safely home.

It was after one when Leda finally finished work and got into Columbo's car. She had had lifts in it many times before and Columbo had always made sure that the front door was opened and the hall light switched on before he would swing the car round in the rough avenue and make his way home. Con drove swiftly to the disused quarry halfway between Leachlara and Briartullog. The Clancys had played there as children, climbing the face of the quarry, kicking the shale with their worn-out shoes and writing their names with sticks in the sand. Leda knew what was going to happen next. She had invited it but her lack of experience bothered her. What if he knew she was clueless: would he lose interest?

He was hungry for her, grinding into her, artlessly and wordlessly taking his own pleasure. It had been such a long time. He didn't look at her face and it seemed not to occur to him that it was her first time. Tonight was about him and no one else, nobody's business but his. He slumped back against his seat, breathing heavily but otherwise silent. For her part Leda was glad the first time was over and that it hadn't really hurt. Con would keep his promise to her. She would see to that. He smelt of cigarettes mingled with expensive aftershave and recently gulped whiskey. Leda had smelt of perfume, soap and the fresh sweat of a hard evening's work but afterwards she smelt only of him.

Chapter Twelve

The applications for the J1 visa to America seemed straightforward enough and Ciara picked up two. She would persuade Alison to come with her. It would be the best time, swishing around Boston or Cape Cod with money in their pockets and the sun high in the sky. They could pretend that they were Oscar Wilde's or James Joyce's grand-nieces or great-grand-nieces. She would work out which one would be chronologically plausible, obviously. The Americans loved the young Irish, but they were fairly well up on their heroes too so there was no point in trying to tell a blatant lie. Sure they would walk into good jobs, preferably not on the burger line of some highway fast-food place. She could do without the monotony of that and she was certain that Alison would prefer a change from a café job too. Now that Dan Abernethy was snared the shifts at the Daisy May had surely fulfilled their purpose. She could see him any time now and not just when he fancied a coffee. No, a job in an art gallery or museum or in one of those massive American bookshops with coffee houses and four-piece jazz bands playing in the basement would do nicely. Good sociable hours so they could get out every night and meet anyone worth meeting and spend their money. Ciara raced home, skipping her Tuesday-evening lecture such was her excitement.

'What do you mean you don't want to go? Are you off your head? This is one of the main reasons I came to college, the chance to spend the summer abroad. We can spend the summer in Dublin next year or any time at all but we would be raving mad to pass up on this.' Ciara shook the treasured visa applications in disbelief. Sometimes Alison needed a good boot.

'I wasn't actually planning on spending the summer anywhere but at home in Caharoe. I kind of promised Mam and Dad that as soon as the exams were over I would head for home. They want me to work at the surgery because Maggie is going on maternity leave.' Alison was surprised that Ciara had presumed she would be keen on going. Sure they had talked about it, but in general terms only, saying that it would be great to do it some time.

'They could get anyone to do that job instead of you. A temping agency would supply someone at short notice. They are probably only obliging you by giving you the job when they could easily get someone else. I bet you if you were to ring them now they would tell you to go and not to be daft. Look, if I can scrape the money together you have no excuse. Better still, I will ring your dad now and tell him that you would love to go to America but are worried about letting him down. I would have the whole thing sorted in a few minutes. Sure Dick Shepherd and myself are drinking buddies. I could charm him in an instant.'

Alison was in a panic; the last thing she wanted was Ciara taking up the reins to fight a battle on her behalf that she didn't want to win. 'Look, Ciara, I don't want to go. I want to go home. My folks miss me and I miss them and I would like to spend the summer there. Besides . . .'

'Besides what, Alison? Dan Abernethy is here and that's why you want to stay, like a gillie at his beck and call? I should have known it would boil down to proximity to Dan. Don't you trust him? Don't you trust that he would still be here waiting for you when you came back? It's pathetic, Alison. He would go if he were in your shoes, make no mistake about that. He wouldn't be afraid to leave your side. He's the first guy you have ever gone out with. Don't you think you need a bit of perspective? There could be a bigger, better, sexier doctor or lawyer in Boston or New York just waiting to sweep you off your feet but you will never know because you are too bloody timid to find out.' Ciara flung the visa-application papers at the fireplace in disgust before collapsing on the couch exhausted by her own rage.

'Are you finished your rant?' Alison asked, her voice a total contrast in tone to her flatmate's. When Ciara refused to answer Alison took it as permission to speak without interruption or heckling from a temper out of control. 'I have promised my folks to go home for the summer and I don't think there is anything timid about that. They pay for everything for me and the least I can do is to keep my tiny side of the bargain. I do miss them. For as long as I remember it's been just them and me and I have found being away from home for weeks at a time fairly hard to get used to. Whereas you seem happy enough to give the odd phone call and skip the visits entirely. I would like to go to the US but not this summer, Ciara. Maybe next year or the year after.'

'You have made your point, Alison, but don't tell me it has nothing to do with Dan because I won't believe you.'

'Yes I am looking forward to seeing Dan during the summer, but he is staying in Dublin on a placement so I won't exactly be in his pocket clinging on for dear life. Thanks for pointing out that he is my first boyfriend, as if that makes me some sort of a freak. I know it might not last but I don't think there is anything wrong with hoping that it might or enjoying it while it does.'

'You are just doing the typical girl thing, putting your life on hold for someone whom you have just built up in your head as Mr Perfect. It pisses me off!'

'Only a few weeks ago you were singing Paul Crampton's praises, saying he was sound, sexy and funny. The list went on and on. I bet you wouldn't be going to America if it had worked out with him and we wouldn't be sitting here fighting like cats.'

'He was just a little dickhead like all the rest of them. I should have added big-headed, pretentious and spineless to the list. It would have made it a touch more accurate.'

'Jesus, that bad, was he?' Ciara hadn't really told Alison the ins and outs of how they had broken up, just that it was finished and that his name was a pile of dung to be stepped over in conversation. 'What exactly happened, or do you not want to talk about it?'

'I went to the loo in Harty's the night after that stupid rugby match that he persuaded me to go to. I overheard a friend of his telling Paul that I didn't seem like his type. Well, I waited for Paul's answer to put him in his place. He didn't realize I was standing behind him and he told this little upstart that there was room for all types of fillies in his stable while he waited for his thoroughbred and no better man to put them all through their paces.'

'My God! You poor thing, what did you say?' Alison was incredulous. What kind of a horrible person would talk like that about Ciara? Paul had seemed so sweet too.

'Oh, talking is too good for a prick like that. I landed a pint of warm Smithwick's on top of his head and while he was struggling to see through that I kneed him in the groin to make his insignificant little willy shrivel like a three-day-old sausage dipped in vinegar. It felt good, even if I did get some beer on my green slingbacks. A small price to pay, I suppose.'

'I am so sorry. Why didn't you tell me before now? You shouldn't have had to go through that alone.'

'I fully meant to tell you. I called to an off licence on the way home and got the bottle of rosé that's sitting in the fridge, but you and Dan were here cuddled up on the couch looking like Tracy and Hepburn before they did the dirty deed so I took myself off to bed. There was no point in ruining your night too.'

'I could have told Dan to go. He would have understood. And seeing as you're fishing for information, no, we have not done the dirty deed, as you so charmingly put it.' Alison blushed. It was no good. She could never carry off talk like this and keep her composure.

'I should bloody hope not. A girl has to have standards. You will have to wait at least a year so he respects you.'

'Would you cop on with your standards, Ciara Clancy, seeing as you have no intention of ever adhering to your own rules of engagement? You wouldn't have even waited this long!'

'You cheeky wagon! I will thank you not to take pot shots at my virtue. I have the highest of standards: I just haven't met any man who even comes close to deserving my good behaviour. Trust me, Ali, they are all plonkers really, even the delectable Dr Dan. Now crack open that bottle of rosé. I am parched.'

Alison got two glasses. She would have just a little taste to keep Ciara company for a bit instead of letting her drink alone. She hadn't really liked the taste of wine any time she had tried it. She found the bottle opener buried deep in the utensil drawer and looked at the bottle without a clue what to do next.

Ciara got to her feet. 'It's a screw top, honey, just like Paul Crampton's brain.' She poured two generous glasses. Alison nearly fainted at the measure. She had never even drunk a fraction of that.

'That's a bit much for me, Ciara. You know I don't really drink.'

'Oh, this stuff is like TK Lemonade. It's barely alcoholic. Besides, if I can't bring you to America with me, the least I can do is show you how to drink a glass of wine without losing the run of yourself entirely. Call it part of your education. The off-syllabus parts are my speciality.'

Alison took a little sip. It wasn't very strong, she had to admit. Maybe it was even a bit pleasant.

'To a good life,' Ciara toasted.

'To good men!' Alison ventured.

'To a life without arseholes or at least to having damn fine shoes to step over them,' Ciara countered as they clinked their glasses.

Chapter Thirteen

Leda wasn't sure exactly what kind of flat she had been expecting but she knew that this definitely wasn't it. The basement flat of a dilapidated house off Leeson Street that Con had given her the keys to was a huge disappointment. She had imagined somewhere that Con would want to come to relax, somewhere to unwind with her at the end of a stressful day. She couldn't picture him here at all, but maybe somewhere simple was what he craved. Everyone said that the bag he was married to took it very badly if you walked on her carpets after they had been vacuumed so he could probably do with a rest from that. If she was honest with herself, she had listened to him talking about the apartment he lived in near the Burlington when he was attending the Dáil and it was something along those lines she had been looking forward to. Obviously she knew she could not actually stay there. Con had been adamant about the need for discretion. No one would understand their feelings for one another, he had explained, and what they had was so special that it needed to be protected from prying eyes. She had to hand it to him, he was an expert at talking the talk. She had been hoping to hide out in his apartment for a little while to get used to being away from home but he hadn't even shown it to her, insisting that she move in straight away to the flat he had earmarked for her.

Although she was terrified at the thought of living alone, she didn't admit that to Con. Her mother had always been at the house at home so she seldom had to use her key to get in late at night. Aggie Clancy had long since learned that Ted would sooner break glass and knock down the door than put his hands in his pockets to find a key when he was drunk. An unlocked door was now something of pure terror to Leda and the first nights in the flat she slept fitfully with the keys clenched to her chest. Every noise was cause for utter panic, outside the banging of a car door, the sounds of dustbin lids clanging, and within the rustle of old pipes creaking and faceless voices from other layers of the house muffled and whispering behind strangers' doors. Leda was determined that she wouldn't run home scared but it took every ounce of spirit that she had to stay.

Every day she expected a visit from Con. He was, after all, the reason she was here, but the first evenings passed and she only had the bare, stained walls for company. Ciara was in Dublin, of course, only about two miles away, but Leda couldn't face meeting her yet. She would be first with the lecture and her little sister knew she could not deal with that right now. Nagging, and Ciara was a champion nagger, was not going to improve anything at all. She had heard Ciara complaining about the flat that she had rented in one of Con Abernethy's houses in the same area. To be honest, knowing how much Ciara detested him, she had more or less decided that if he had presented Ciara with the keys to the Mansion House her sister would likely have said it was not fit for human habitation. Ciara hadn't even wanted to stay there in the first place, but their father had been adamant that Con had done her a huge favour and anyone from the country looking for a flat would give their eye-teeth to be set up without having to trudge the streets looking for a place themselves. Ciara relented and accepted the flat but, as with most things, she got her own way in the end.

Leda had bought flowers from a stand outside a newsagent's on Leeson Street, thinking that a few blooms might brighten the place up. Looking at them now on the kitchen counter rammed into a pint glass, the only thing resembling a vase in the place, she had to admit that flowers weren't going to fix the smell or the damp patches that leered from every wall or the depressing glow of the bare bulbs that hung like fractured limbs from the ceilings. The toilet bowl was stained and smelt as if it had been lifted from the toilets at Shanahan's after a particularly late and drunken night. There was much to be depressed about when she looked around but Leda was not about to complain. She had just worked a whole week at a job that Con had fixed her up with in a solicitor's office. The lawyer looked after a lot of Con's property dealings and had made it plain to Leda that as long as Con kept his business with the office her job was as safe as houses. The money was good too and not a penny of it had to go towards rent, so for the first time in her life Leda could see independence looming and that made her very pleased indeed. Con told her father about her move to Dublin and explained why there was no reason she should stay in school to do her Leaving. Leda had been loading the glasses into the pub dishwasher and wondering what her mam would actually do if she ever got one to free her from the interminable washing-up when she overheard Con's flood of conviction that swayed her father.

'Sure that girl there has brains to burn, Ted. She doesn't need a slip of paper to prove that to anyone. She will be in a job, a well-paying job at that mind, the Monday morning after she gets to Dublin.' That conversation had ended with her father clapping Con Abernethy on the back and insisting on buying him a drink to thank him for looking out for yet another of his daughters.

'I wouldn't doubt you, Con Abernethy. I won't forget this for you and I'll make sure my girls will never forget it either.'

She had expected her mother to barely register that she was going but for some reason Aggie Clancy seemed more with it than normal when Leda told her of her plans to give up school and head for Dublin.

'Leda, would you not wait? Another twelve months and you would have your Leaving behind you. Who knows, you might get to college like Ciara? It makes me so happy to think of Ciara making choices for herself and opening up the world. I want the same for you. Leda, for me, will you please stay and do your exams?'

Leda was surprised. She couldn't remember the last time her mother had mentioned her schoolwork or plans for her future. Couldn't remember maybe because it had never happened. Well, she wasn't about to let this belated bout of parental concern trip her up now.

'Look, Mam, I know you mean well but don't you see this is my chance? I'm never going to college. Let's face it, Ciara got the brains when they were dishing them out. Maybe Michael will end up going too, but I think that if he got to score a few goals for Leachlara, that's all he wants.' Michael was a shy teenager, overwhelmed by the powerful disinterest of his father. Leda worried about him, the same way, she realized, that Ciara had worried about her, but not enough to stay and change her plans, any more than Ciara would have stayed for Leda's benefit. When she told her mother she was definitely going, her mother wished her luck and pressed some folded notes into her palm.

'You need this, Mam, more than I do. Keep it, for God's sake. I will be grand.' Leda was not about to fleece her mother for money on the way out of the door, knowing how tight things were, but Aggie was insistent.

'I will gladly take it back if you never have call to use it.

It's safer in your hands than in this house. It would last your father a few foolish nights in Shanahan's standing drink to people who could buy a brewery and not notice a wrinkle in their wallet.'

Leda put the money in her jeans pocket, vowing not to spend a penny of it and to return with it and more besides. She hugged her mother for the first time in ages and noticed how small and frail she felt. Her plumpness had disappeared and her bones stood proud of her meagre flesh. Aggie pulled away from her daughter's embrace. There was something else she had to say.

'You will mind yourself from Con, won't you?'

'What do you mean? Mind myself? Sure if it wasn't for Con none of this would be happening for me.'

'I know he means well, Leda love, but he has had a hard life with Mary. I can see it in him. He is not the gentle sort of man now that I remember when we were younger. He is bitter, feels hard done by and let down by life, and sometimes that makes people do things they shouldn't. Just remember you owe him nothing but to do well with the opportunities he has given you. Everything else you must keep for yourself.'

Con's visits fell into a pattern that Leda came to depend on to salve the loneliness she felt in the flat. He never came before 11 p.m. and he would ring just as he was at the end of the road, presumably so he wouldn't have to stand around at the door waiting to be let in. He sometimes brought a takeaway, Chinese or Indian, food that Leda rarely touched. He always brought alcohol and usually drank most of what he brought before he began to fondle Leda and, from that moment until he rolled off her on to the quilt she had laid out on the sitting-room floor, she knew it would be about half an hour before he left. He never spent the night and he never carried her to her bed, feeling more comfortable with the sex he could have quickly and casually on a floor lit by the harsh oranges and reds of the miserable gas fire. She would hear the rustle of his clothes as he put them back on, the hard click of his belt buckle, his shirt being tucked in and finally the clanking of his keys in his pocket, a signal that it was time for him to be at home. He would drain his glass of wine, lean down and kiss her on the forehead, and always his final words were: 'Night, pet.' When the door closed after him she would pick herself and the quilt up from the floor and go to the door to push over the shooting bolt. From there she would go to the cold sheets of her bed and will herself to sleep a mercifully dreamless sleep.

About a month after she arrived in Dublin she was walking up Kildare Street on her way home from work. She saw Con dart in through the gates of Leinster House with another suited man whom she didn't recognize. She called out his name but he seemed not to hear her. If he had time maybe they could have dinner, out somewhere this time, somewhere swanky and not in her flat, which she was thoroughly sick of. Through the black railings she shouted after him. 'Con, wait up! Con, it's me. Con!'

He stopped and looked in her direction but her smile was not returned. He curtailed his conversation with the other man and when he nodded in Leda's direction they both laughed. He made his way back to the gate, saluting the security man on duty at the cabin. When he finally addressed Leda his tone was cold and cutting. 'What the hell are you doing here?'

'I was just passing on my way from work. I saw you and I wanted to say hello. I just thought that we might go for something to eat or a drink maybe if you are at a loose end.'

'Well, I am very glad that I got you such a cushy job that you are finished work at teatime, but I have another few hours to go before I can call my day even half finished, so take yourself off home and don't ever bother me at work again.'

'Con, I was only passing—'

'Well, don't pass this way again. This is serious shit, Leda, and you have no business meddling where I don't want you. I'll say it one more time. Go home and make sure to stay away from here. Don't ruin everything when it is going so well.'

'Will I see you later?' she asked, although she regretted immediately how weak she sounded.

'I have loads on this evening. I can't say for sure.'

'Well, if you do get finished early . . .' Leda countered, attempting a casual tone.

'I know where to find you.' He headed back in the direction of the Dáil with a vigorous stride.

Leda turned away from the railing eventually, several minutes after Con had disappeared inside. She changed her route home and vowed never to pass that way again. As she walked the streets that led to the flat she gave herself a serious lecture. She had become clingy and dependent on Con because she had found it miserable being away from home, however unlikely an eventuality that had seemed the day she left her parents' house in Leachlara. The prospect of freedom and independence had intoxicated her and she chided herself now for being unable to handle what she had craved for so long. Well, from now on things would change. She would go out more for a start. There were a few girls at the solicitor's office who seemed up for a laugh. They had asked her out for drinks a few times and she had always declined, wanting to be at the flat in case Con would choose those nights to visit. There was going to be no more of that kind of stupidity. It would shake him up a bit if she was not always at his beck and call. He might even hurry up and set up that credit-card account that he had been promising her since she arrived. She looked forward to spending his money because Dublin had a lot of shops that were currently out of her league. Definitely time to renegotiate, she decided. What's more, if she met a cute man there was nothing to stop her doing whatever she liked with him. It's not as if sex with Con was actually all that pleasant. She always felt grotty afterwards. If there was better on offer Leda Clancy was going to have it. Buoyed with renewed determination, she walked down the steps leading to her basement flat only to spot Ciara sitting on the stoop waiting for her return.

'To what do I owe the pleasure, Ciara?' Leda asked sharply, although she was glad she had pulled herself together on the way home. No point in Ciara knowing she'd had a wobble of confidence.

'Just thought I would check out where he had you holed up. Good God, I thought the place he gave me to rent was bad but Con obviously had worse to offer. Mammy keeps saying that you are going to visit me but you have no intention, have you?' Ciara was doing her best to scrutinize how Leda was doing and she had to admit she looked as if she had come to no harm. She had lost a bit of weight that she could not afford to lose, but otherwise she looked pretty good. She was smartly dressed in what was definitely a new coat that made her look more grown up than she was.

'I have a lot on, Ciara, and running around to see you and your little flatmate has not been top of my agenda. I doubt much has changed in your set-up anyway.'

'Alison and I are doing grand. Standing on our own two feet, not that you would know anything about that while you insist on attaching yourself to Con. How in the name of God can you stick it, stick him touching you?'

'I have a job earning good money. You should try it yourself. Oh, I forgot it would be about another three years before you have a bob to your name. As for Con, he is treating me well and you would not understand.' She reached for the keys in her pocket, brushing past Ciara to put them in the lock.

'Well, make me a cup of tea and explain it to me because you are right I don't understand. I think you should go home. Do your Leaving and stop making an eejit of yourself over a scumbag like Con. Please listen to me,' Ciara implored.

There was no way Leda was letting Ciara into the flat because she knew what she would say about it and worse still it would be the truth. The flat was temporary: she would see to that too. In the meantime her sister was definitely not coming inside to pass judgement.

'You go home, Ciara, back to Alison and your lush of a landlady. I'm happy and I am staying right here. Pick someone else to save because I am doing just fine.' With that she banged the door behind her and left Ciara looking at the rotting woodwork.

Chapter Fourteen

The restaurant was picked with some care by Con. He believed the occasion was going to require all his charm and skill to carry off properly. He didn't want to have to worry about the food or the service and so he decided that the Liffey Bar and Grill would be just perfect for the job. He had had the pleasure of several lunches there over the previous months and he had never been anything but impressed by the place. It was pricey, of course, but it most definitely wasn't the time for penny-pinching. It wasn't every day that your only son came to you and said he wanted you to meet his girlfriend. Con was sure that Dan had been out with loads of girls since he began his degree. He had wheedled some information out of him but Dan tended towards discretion and was not the type to brag – well, not to his father anyway. Obviously Alison Shepherd from Caharoe had struck a chord with his son that other girls had not and so an introductory lunch had been arranged with Dan's consent. The only downside, and Con considered it a fairly steep descent indeed, was that Dan had insisted that his mother be invited also.

'Ah why, Dan? You know what she is like. She will be picking fault with the food, with me, with your girlfriend even. Would you not let me meet Alison first and when we have built up a bit of a rapport we can bring your mother into the proceedings?'

'Look, I would really appreciate it if we could act like a normal family for a couple of hours. She knows things aren't great between you and Mam so she is not expecting sweetness and light but it's important to me that you both meet her. She is lovely and smart and I am mad about her. Please, Dad, for me? I will talk to Mam too and make sure she is on best behaviour. I will tell her that she has to be nice to you for my sake.'

Con laughed. 'Jesus, you better shake the holy water and take a rub of a relic because I cannot remember the last time your mother was nice to me. For you and this Alison of yours I promise to turn myself inside out and I can't do better than that.'

'Thanks. Um, there is just one other thing.'

'Don't worry, I will pick one of the best restaurants in Dublin—'

'No, it's not that. Any restaurant will be grand, we are not fussy at all. The thing is, Alison's flatmate is Ciara Clancy from Leachlara. As in Leda Clancy's sister?'

Dan looked for revelatory shock in his father's face but he seemed relaxed and unperturbed by the news. 'I know who she is. Sure, I rented her a flat last autumn. She hightailed it without so much as a by your leave. I take it Alison won't be mentioning her in the course of conversation? You must tell her that it is a delicate situation and likely to make your mother blow a gasket.'

'No, she knows that Mam doesn't relish the Clancys so she won't say a thing. I just thought that you should know, that's all.'

'That would be the wisest move all right. We may have to start block-booking the fire brigade if she gets wind that your new girlfriend could be contaminated by riff-raff from Leachlara.'

Con was a little shocked. He wasn't sure if Leda was on speaking or confiding terms with her sister but if she was she wouldn't have been painting a pretty picture, based on his shabby treatment of her recently. He decided that Leda must be staying quiet about their little arrangement. The fact that she was prepared to protect him by her silence made him a bit guilty for the way he had begun to ignore her a little more and like her a little less. He had begun to think that landing her in dangerous proximity to his highflying Dublin life had been a serious error of judgement. He had underestimated how many people he knew in Dublin and he didn't want the gossipmongers who dealt in the abundant details of who was sleeping with whom ever turning their forensic attention on him. Still, besides turning up at the railings of Leinster House shouting his name like an imbecile, he couldn't say she had put a foot wrong. Even then he had passed the girl at the gate off as a young constituent who was a little star-struck and a few slices short of a full loaf. His solicitor said she was a demon of a worker who would turn her hand to anything and seemed very mature in comparison to some of the other girls who worked in the office.

Con decided he would make an effort to call at the flat more often, take her some of that chocolate she liked and maybe slip her a bit of money for new clothes to show his appreciation for her patience and her silence. With an election campaign looming he wanted everything in order and he had to admit that sleeping with Leda made him feel young again. Six months ago he had felt depressed that his life was winding down to an inexorable miserable end. He wasn't sure if his seat would be safe in the next election nor whether he had the bottle to fight for every last vote to make it so; and if he didn't win, the thought of an open-ended retirement in Leachlara sank his mood further. All that had changed the night he had taken his life by the scruff of the neck and decided to think just of himself and put his own pleasure first for a change. Leda was getting her pay-off and he was getting his. He felt alive and ready for anything and everything that might come his way.

The prawns were tough and the sauce was watery and under-seasoned. Mary Abernethy was not impressed by her husband's choice of restaurant. She could think of at least half a dozen places in nearby streets that could top his choice but lack of taste and poor judgement were traits she depended on in her husband. In fact she found it comforting that he so often got so much wrong. Still, it was lovely to see Dan and she had to admit that his little slip of a girlfriend seemed sweet and was very attractive. Her features were delicate. She was well groomed in a way that pleased Mary Abernethy. Her long dark hair was swept back from her face in a chic pleat, her fingernails were polished and her dress, though a little on the low-cut side for Mary's liking, was elegant and looked expensive. Dan had chosen well but then again she expected nothing less. She had taught him to recognize class when he saw it. Dan seemed very proud of Alison. He scarcely took his eyes off her and in the interests of keeping her son happy Mary decided that she would do her best not to show how much she detested her husband. She would try to conceal how her skin prickled with disdain when he opened his mouth. It was only right that young people should believe in love and believe that another person could make you happy. She had believed in all that once too, believed that Con Abernethy would never let her down. She ate the turgid prawns as her way of committing to an acceptably pleasant afternoon.

Alison had ordered the prawns too and thought they were delicious. She had never been to any place quite so posh and was doing her best not to show how overwhelmed she felt by the occasion and the restaurant. Caharoe didn't really run to smart places to eat. Lovett's was the mainstay of the Sunday-lunch crowd and apart from a sandwich bar and a small coffee shop and bakery at the end of Earl Street there was nowhere else. She wondered what Rose, probably now up to her neck in chip fat at the Daisy May, would make of the Liffey Bar and Grill. She might take her the single-sheet daily-specials menu as a souvenir. If Ciara were there she would more than likely lift the salt cellar, a few napkin rings or maybe a light fitting, but Alison had none of her bravery or lack of fear.

Ciara had sent her with the express purpose of finding out exactly what Mary Abernethy was like. She maintained that she knew all she needed to know about Con. All of Leachlara thought his wife was a stuck-up cow and nothing that Alison was witnessing was giving her much cause to disagree. Mary was cold and formal with her husband, hardly willing to look his way or wait for him to finish a point before interrupting him. She was different with Dan but her adoring gazes and acquiescent nods seemed overplayed and somewhat fake. The lack of natural warmth between them was quite startling. Dan behaved with her as if he was in the company of an ageing aunt who had to be indulged and tolerated. In contrast Dan and Con were a comfortable double act and Alison was finding it very hard to reconcile the idea of his father that she had garnered from Ciara's damning reports with the man who sat opposite her making every effort to put her at her ease.

'So, Alison, I promise not to hold it against you, but do you reckon your folks vote with my lot or do they line up with the chancers on the other side?' Con winked at her so she knew he really didn't give two hoots what way her parents voted.

Before she had a chance to reply Mary was in like a shot. 'For God's sake, Con, will you let the girl alone? Do you really think she cares one iota about politics? A young girl has other things on her mind and, just in case you think the fame of Con Abernethy has reached our neighbouring counties, I doubt very much if Mr and Mrs Shepherd have ever heard of you. You might think you are a sniff away from the cabinet table but you are just a big fish in a small pond. Now, if you will excuse me, Alison and Dan, I must go to the bathroom.'

When she left the table the air of tension that had settled around them like a coiled spring relented and Alison knew that in this dynamic she would always feel more at home with the Abernethy men. Ciara was right. Mary was a stuck-up cow and she felt sad for Dan that every time his mother opened her mouth he seemed to freeze in anticipation of another bitter comment to follow on from the last. Con chatted to her about Caharoe; he had worked there straight after he left school but she thought the business he spoke of must no longer exist because its name didn't ring a bell. She told him about her father's practice and how her mother looked after all the practicalities of running it so her father could concentrate on the patients. As she talked to Con she could feel Dan watching her with admiring warmth, adding in details which she had forgotten and making sure the flow of conversation continued. She felt she was doing OK, giving a good account of herself as Rose had urged her to do in her pep talk the day before. By the time Mary came back from the bathroom Con had gone ahead and ordered desserts. He was due back at the Daíl for an important vote for which he had no pairing and so could not linger with them. In her absence he ordered crème brûlée for his wife. 'It's her favourite,' he explained to Alison, 'or used to be anyway,' he added a touch wistfully.

Mary didn't lift a spoon to her dessert. 'Far too warm a day to think of eating sweet things,' she said, though no one at the table, devouring their delicious desserts, was sure what exactly that was supposed to mean.

Con kissed Alison on the cheek, said how delighted he was to meet her and thanked her for making Dan look so happy. Dan hugged his father warmly and watched with practised resignation as his mother refused to catch his father's eye as he left the restaurant. Mary settled a little when Con had left and she seemed to make a renewed effort to be pleasant and engaging.

'I hope you will come to see us in Leachlara now, Alison. We are quite convenient to the town, so you and Dan could go out although quite what there is to do in Leachlara of a night remains a mystery to me. Still, we would love to see you. Let's arrange it soon, Dan.'

'Yeah, Mam, but we both have exams coming up so it might be the summer before we can get down.'

'Right, well, whatever you say, pet. Anyway, I have to make the three-thirty from Heuston. Would you ever be an angel and get them to call a taxi for me?'

With his mother packed off to the train Dan led Alison for a meandering stroll through Stephen's Green. He was subdued and when pressed he admitted that he had found his parents' brittle behaviour and the resulting awkwardness difficult to bear because he had wanted it to be easy for Alison.

'It wasn't that bad, Dan. They both made an effort, especially your dad. I thought he was quite sweet, to be honest, and I wasn't really expecting that. I thought he would have at least one pair of horns and a tail to swing.'

'It's Mam who always makes things difficult. I know he isn't always right but she could bear a grudge for an entire continent. Anyway, thanks for meeting them. You were absolutely brilliant. Promise me one thing though.'

'Anything.'

'Really? Anything at all? Well, I know the very thing that would make me blissfully happy but seeing as you are blushing now we can negotiate that later.' He touched her face gently with his hand, feeling the soft lushness of her skin. Alison was willing her face not to redden any more.

'What do you want me to promise, Dan?' she asked as coolly as she could manage.

'That we will never end up like them and that even if it's the last place on earth we will never live in Leachlara. I will live anywhere else as long as I am with you. I might even risk life and limb and chance a stint in Cork,' he added with a wink.

'I promise.'

Thcy found a seat by the duck pond and Alison cuddled into him to share another of their gorgeous kisses. She was grateful that he wasn't putting pressure on her to sleep with him but if she were truthful she would admit that she wanted to more than anything. Everything about Dan made her want to get in deeper and to know him better. She trusted her judgement and she trusted him. She kissed him passionately and as the April afternoon sun slipped from the sky she knew she was in love and that life could not possibly offer anything else that would make her happier.

Chapter Fifteen

It wasn't the best timing in the world but Alison was not about to reject her parents' offer of a visit. She and Ciara had piles of revision to do but her dad had said on the phone that it was going to be a flying trip to Dublin. They had a two-day conference with a reception and dinner on the first night that they were going to skip in order to spend the evening with Alison. She hadn't been home in two weekends because of exam preparation and they were missing her and wanted to make sure she was looking after herself. Their main concern, if they were honest, was that Alison had a boyfriend of a few months' standing and Richard Shepherd wanted to make sure that no unsuitable type was lurking around his daughter and maybe interfering with her college work. He had told Alison that she was to invite her boyfriend along to meet him and her mother. No decent young man would decline that offer, he reasoned to himself. If he wouldn't show up Richard was more than happy to draw his own conclusions about him.

His wife, on the other hand, was anxious to get a look at this Dan Abernethy who seemed to have knocked her normally unflappable daughter sideways. Alison wasn't being totally secretive about him but she was being reticent in a way that was new in her dealings with her mother. Cathy Shepherd's curiosity was spiked by this change in Alison but ultimately she trusted her daughter's judgement, which was more than could be said for her husband, who was just short of practising his stale boxing skills.

The flat was in its usual jumble-sale state but Alison felt that she would be able to make it look fairly presentable with a few hours' work. Just as long as her parents didn't look into any cupboards or pull out any drawers where she was planning on storing all the paraphernalia that she and Ciara (mostly Ciara, it had to be said) had left hanging around the living room. She had told Dan that they wanted to see him and had been delighted at his positive response.

'Well, they can't be any more dysfunctional than the Leachlara division. Actually it will be quite something to observe a married couple that actually like each other. I would come for that alone. Will Ciara be there?'

'She says she might make herself scarce but I have told her that she is totally welcome to stay for dinner, whatever that's going to be. The gas cooker is so bloody temperamental that I haven't a bog's notion what I'll give them to eat. At the moment a few cartons of Pot Noodle from Spar seems like the most viable option.'

'Look, my dad keeps filling the freezer with hunks of meat that Tony and myself are never likely to get through, especially now that Tony has become a vegetarian to impress the ladies. I have stacks of steaks and everything so I will bring over a few of those and grill them. We will make some salad and stick on a few spuds to bake. It will be better than anything they would get at that conference dinner. I will bring over plenty in case Ciara decides to grace us with her presence.'

'God, Dan, that is just brilliant. I can't believe you would do all that for me. Thanks a million.' Alison clasped her arms about him in gratitude for how relaxed he was being about everything but also because she couldn't keep her hands off him.

'Listen, it's the least I can do after putting you through that crappy lunch with my folks. I owe you and I am looking forward to showing your dad that I am not the low life he suspects I am.'

'Why would he think you're a low life? He hardly knows anything about you – I have been keeping your details to myself.'

Dan smirked. 'It's a father's main function in life to think that whoever is hanging around his daughter is up to no good. Anyway, I will turn on the charm and see if I can distract him from the urge to throttle me on sight.'

Alison set about the cleaning of the apartment with as much energy as she could muster. It was not going to be a root-and-branch clean that her mother would approve of but, coupled with a blast of air freshener, hopefully it would do the trick.

'Dan cooking steaks?' Ciara was thoroughly amused at the prospect of seeing him get into a sweat over their temperamental grill while the Shepherds looked on.

'What's so funny about that? I think he is absolutely wonderful to help out because I was beginning to panic about what I could give them to eat. Dad is a proper-dinner man so one of our toasted ham and cheese specials was not going to be enough.'

'Do you know what? I think I am going to have to stay to witness this, Alison. Will he bring a steak for me or will I have to fend for myself?'

'Of course he will, Ciara. We are hardly going to sit there eating a big dinner while you eat beans out of the tin. Now, seeing as you are no good at cleaning, would you go down to the shop and get an apple tart and a block of vanilla ice cream please?'

Ciara wouldn't take any money from Alison. 'Let this be my

contribution to the war effort. Never let it be said that I refused to break bread with an Abernethy. I don't even like steak, but for this I would eat the cow's head.'

Much to Ciara's disappointment, Dan didn't burn the steaks or fill the flat with smoke and fumes. In fact he seemed like an old hand at the cooking game and it was clear that the Shepherds were well impressed with Alison's boyfriend. Richard did his best to play hardball in the beginning but Dan's charm had won him over within the first hour. He proclaimed the steak to be the best he had eaten in a long time. They didn't even seem to mind that they were balancing their dinners precariously on their laps because Jean McDermott had neglected to provide the flat with a table. Cathy murmured her appreciation of the food and smiled so agreeably at everything Dan said that Ciara thought she was in real danger of puking at the love-in she was witnessing. Alison, who had been in floods of nerves all day at the prospect of her boyfriend meeting her parents, began to relax as the dinner progressed.

Dan had brought two bottles of wine, as had the Shepherds, so Ciara decided that there was nothing else for it but to start laying into the red in order to render her system immune to the display of happy families. She might have stayed there sipping her red wine, adding an odd superfluous comment to the conversation and helping herself to a second bowl of ice cream, but she was stopped in her tracks when Richard Shepherd started speculating about the future political career of Con Abernethy and the possibility of a ministerial portfolio. She listened as Dan commended his father and praised his ability and his patience in dealing with his constituents' problems at every hour of the day and night. Ciara was deeply unsettled by the whitewash hypocrisy of the conversation and the way Alison sat there agog as if she had never heard a word that Ciara had said about Dan's low-life father. In her eyes Con Abernethy was nothing more than a jumped-up stroke puller, a big fish in the murky pond of Leachlara, but most of all she thought of him as the pervert who was shamelessly tailing her teenage sister. It annoyed her to the very core that Con was being hailed as a politician awaiting his big break, a local hero about to grace the national stage.

Ciara topped up her wine glass from the bottle that sat on the hearth without offering to top up anyone else's diminishing glass. Richard Shepherd looked at her and thought, yet again, that she drank a lot for a teenage girl and was most likely not the best influence for Alison. Unaware, Ciara continued to knock back the wine, willing it to work some of its relaxation magic. Her heart thumped in her chest with anger and although she had promised herself she would not say anything she could feel the threads of that promise unravel within her.

It was Cathy Shepherd who unwittingly snipped the final thread. 'Your mother must be so proud of him, Dan. Did she ever think about running herself as a candidate?'

'Ah, politics doesn't really interest my mam, to be honest. She lets that side of things to my dad. It's his strong point.' Dan got up to make coffee, struggling with the awkward turn the conversation had taken. He wished he didn't clam up every time he had to talk about his mother or his parents' marriage, but worse was still to come. Ciara cleared her throat.

'The pressure of politics is pretty terrible on families, isn't it, Dan? I was reading an article in the *Independent* last week that said there was worldwide research to prove that politicians had the unhappiest marriages of any profession and that they were ten times more likely to have affairs than, say, doctors, solicitors or teachers. All that time away from home would I guess take its toll and give them plenty of opportunity.' She took another satisfied gulp of her red wine and looked around to see the effect that she was having.

Richard sat staring at her. He was stunned that she would raise a topic that was so unsuitable. Too much alcohol did terrible things to people. Alison thought she might choke. What in the name of God did Ciara think she was doing? Her mother seemed embarrassed that Ciara was talking about affairs and was anxious to say something that would assuage the discomfort that she thought Dan must feel.

'Well, that's very interesting, Ciara, but I'm sure they were talking about foreign politicians and not about Irish ones. Ireland is too small for people in the public eye to get away with that sort of thing.' Dan smiled at her to show his gratitude for her interjection, but it was premature, because Ciara had just climbed to the top of the roller coaster where, it turned out, she was totally comfortable.

'Well, that is what you would think, Mrs Shepherd, but the article made specific reference to one rural Irish politician. They couldn't give his name, obviously, as politicians are notoriously litigious. He is screwing around on his wife with a schoolgirl, by all accounts.'

She paused to take satisfactory note of Richard Shepherd's slack jaw, his mouth gaping in disbelief. Either he had scalded himself with the hot apple tart or the word 'screwing' was not common currency in the salubrious streets of Caharoe or the genteel rooms of the Shepherd household.

'Picked her up in the local pub where she is a lounge girl and now he has moved her up to Dublin to one of his flats so he can carry on with her on the quiet. I was stunned, I have to say. You just wouldn't think things like that would be happening in the places we come from, would you?'

Alison's father cut in before she had a chance to muddy the evening any further with her indelicate talk. 'No, indeed you would not. You know, Ciara, some of these newspapers thrive on the salacious and when it's not there they make it up. I'm sure you have been told by someone before now not to believe everything you read.' Richard had adopted a teacher-like tone. He would not tolerate Ciara's sort of talk in front of his daughter or his wife and he wouldn't have Dan embarrassed either, because he had to admit that Dan seemed like a fine sort of a man indeed. To break up the conversation he asked a pale-faced Dan to help him bring in from his car a desk that he had picked up at an auction for Alison. She had told him that she did her work at the kitchen worktop because it was the only flat surface, other than her bed, where she could lay out her books, so he felt she needed a desk, especially for the upcoming exams. Cathy told her husband to mind his back lifting the desk and excused herself to go to the dismal bathroom on the landing, leaving Alison and Ciara to face each other in the living room.

'What the hell do you think you are doing, Ciara, bringing all that shit up? I could have swung for you, honestly. You had no right embarrassing Dan like that.'

'What I was doing was injecting a slight dose of reality into the Walton-family glucose that you are all peddling. How many times do I have to explain to you that Con Abernethy is a shit, an absolute bastard? You still won't take it seriously because of Dan. Do you realize how sickening it is for me to listen to all that talk of your father's about the wonderful public servant that he is and how lucky rural Ireland is to have people like him? And to see Dan agreeing, even though he knows he is shagging my little sister and you sitting there like you have lost your tongue? That's if you ever had one to speak of.'

Alison heard her mother flush the toilet and knew they had only a moment or two before she would be back in the room. She was hardly likely to linger there, as mould clung stubbornly to every surface. 'We will talk about it again when they have gone.'

'Oh, spare me that fucking fob-off. I cannot stick this hypocritical balderdash for one more minute.' Hurtling down the stairwell, she squeezed past Alison's father and Dan struggling with the awkward desk.

'Where are you off to, young lady?' Richard looked at his

watch and was surprised that she would think of going out walking alone at such an hour.

'I'm going for fresh air. It's in short supply up there.' She slammed the gate after her and was quickly hidden by the pavement-side hedges of the neighbouring houses. Dan looked at Richard, searching for something intelligent to say, but all words failed him.

'I think that young girl has a tiny bit of a problem with the drink and with her temper. Drink makes her sour and her talk random. She drank a whole bottle of red bar the one glass that Cathy had.'

'She's worried about her exams coming up, I think,' Dan said, ridiculously grateful that Richard had not made the connection between Ciara's rant and his father.

When they finally managed to negotiate the route into Alison's room, Dan moved her books from the bed and put them in a neat pile on the new desk. 'She will be delighted with this, Dr Shepherd.'

'Call me Richard, please. The doctor title is pleasing for about a week after you qualify but you get sick of it, as you will find out for yourself.'

'OK, Richard it is then.'

In the living room Cathy Shepherd was listening to her daughter explaining that Ciara was very stressed about the exams because she had not done enough during the year and that she would never have meant to offend anyone. Her daughter's upper lip was twitching, as it always did when she was nervous. Cathy nodded as if she bought the story, but in her mind she resolved to find out a little more about Con Abernethy. It did seem that Ciara was making very personal digs and she was, after all, from Leachlara so maybe she knew something that Alison didn't. Cathy decided to talk to Rena Lalor. Between them, Rena and Hugh knew everyone in Munster. Con Abernethy was doubtless not beyond their radar. Meanwhile, she would comfort herself with the fact that whatever the truth was about his father, Dan Abernethy was a very attractive and personable young man who seemed to really care for Alison.

After her parents had gone Dan helped Alison to wash up and put the stuff back in the cupboards. He washed the plates silently, scrubbing off every remnant of food with the dishcloth.

'Ciara really does know how to put the cat among the pigeons, but I think the dinner went off really well, don't you?' Alison offered as cheerfully as she could. Dan smiled at her gratefully but he was utterly crestfallen. He had put thoughts of his father and Leda Clancy as far out of his head as possible, because it was such a disgusting prospect, but Ciara was so adamant that they were having sex that it was no longer feasible to deny it to himself. His father had lied to him and treated him like a fool and Dan felt it like a kick in the stomach.

'I really didn't think it was true, Ali. I believed him when he said it was all made up. He must think I am a right dunce. As for this stuff about moving her up to Dublin, what's that all about? Leda is still in school in Leachlara. She must have just thrown that in for effect.'

Alison ventured information that she had deliberately withheld until now. 'Well actually, I don't think she is making it up. Ciara told me a few weeks ago that Leda had packed in school in Leachlara and taken a job up here in a solicitor's firm, a job arranged by your dad. I didn't say anything because you get so upset every time her name is mentioned. I am sorry, Dan. I should have said something.'

He pulled her to him, needing her touch, needing to feel her in his arms. 'Well, it looks like Mam was right about him all along. I really thought I could trust him. Why hasn't Ciara gone for me about the whole thing?'

'She likes you, Dan, realizes that you can't control what he does, any more than she can get Leda to do a single thing she says. She went to her flat and tried to tell her to go home and that she was making a fool of herself but Leda wouldn't even let her in. She told her she was perfectly happy and that Ciara would not understand.'

'Let me guess. She lives in one of my dad's houses on Leeson Street?'

Alison nodded.

'Oh, excellent. I have a teenage neighbour that my father is sleeping with. Yes, my life is practically complete. All I need now is for my mam to shack up with one of the lads from school.' He bowed his head.

Alison hated to see him so distressed. She squeezed his hand. 'Will you stay with me tonight, Dan, please?'

'You mean stay here in the flat?'

'Will you stay in my bed with me?'

Dan let her lead him to her cramped bedroom. They undressed in between feverish kissing and fondling. Dan flung his shirt and trousers on top of the desk, not stopping to think what Richard Shepherd would do to him if he caught him now. They climbed underneath the covers shivering and grasping each other for warmth and closeness. 'Are you sure?' Dan asked as he ran his hands along her slender limbs and cupped the rounded softness of her breasts and bottom. She kissed him firmly on the lips before she answered.

'I am certain. I want this. I want you.'

As he rolled around the heat of her body and moved within, exploring her soft wetness, he felt consumed by utter desire and happiness. He had never wanted anyone so badly, never wanted anyone to need him more.

Afterwards they fell into a deep contented sleep, clinging together in the comically narrow bed. Not even the after-midnight thuds of Jean McDermott as she ransacked her house looking for an emergency bottle of gin or Ciara as she slammed the front door in the early hours could wake them from where they were.

Chapter Sixteen

Dublin, Leachlara and Aughasallagh
1994

Con refused to be carried away by rumours or tip-offs. He knew his colleagues lied all the time, layering untruths around a fragment of news in order to advance their own cause. However, the inkling of a cabinet reshuffle had come from so many sources that he allowed himself to believe in it a little. He would usually have told Columbo to keep his ambitions reined in but this time he couldn't help thinking that he might well be in the running for a top job. Even a junior ministry would be a start, although being a junior anything when he was sixty years of age seemed a touch ridiculous. Still, he would not of course knock it back if the offer came. Better to make his mark while he still had a chance, even if Columbo had sworn not to down tools until he had placed his man in the top slot. The Taoiseach was not a man Con could claim to know well: he had of course, as a long-serving deputy, been in his company countless times, but there was no way he was within a sniff of the inner circle. A certain crew had that sewn up. Even at parliamentary party meetings it was a small number of senior party figures that controlled the agenda, and backbenchers were expected to toe the appropriate line. You obeyed the whip if you knew what was good for you. Never was a phrase so apt in politics, and it seemed to Con that democracy was an ideal only barely tolerated within the parliamentary party. Mavericks didn't get very far in the long run. Con Abernethy had shown himself willing to champion the party on local radio and in the newspapers and had proven to be a top-class vote-getter. He had topped the poll for the first time in the last election and he knew it was because he had never been hungrier for the contest, chasing every vote down to the last minute of the eve of polling day. He had to admit that his constituency team had worked for him harder than ever before and he liked to think that his spectacular personal-vote tally had elevated him somewhat in the eyes of the top people.

Mary's illness had played a part too, though he knew that fact probably galled her more than the discovery of the cancer itself. He had gone on Tipptalk FM to champion the cause of breast-cancer treatment and the need for Breast Check to roll out to the regions, tearfully, if not wholly sincerely, detailing how the tragedy of his wife's illness had rocked his family to its foundations. In reality breast cancer was little more than a footnote in the disaster of their marriage. Mary had been incandescent with rage, but the short radio piece had brought him requests for further interviews from two national newspapers and this had heightened his profile more than any of his hitherto, admittedly local, political achievements. Someone from Marian Finucane's morning radio programme had been on to his office, but it hadn't come to anything and Con didn't want to be seen pursuing it. He could not appear to be crassly capitalizing on his wife's illness even if that was his true intent. He had been coping with Mary's rage for most of his life and now he shouldered the burden of its redoubling without noticing the extra weight. After a nurse in the Mater had shown the heart-rending interview in the *Independent* to her, Mary had rung to tell him, again, in no uncertain terms, he was she thought of him. He held the receiver away from his ear while she told him he was a worthless piece of shit and waited for her anger to deplete its oxygen supply.

'I spoke to your consultant. He says you are responding very well to your chemo. Certainly hasn't exhausted you any, that's for sure.'

'You have no business talking to my consultant. He is my doctor and—'

Con cut her off because this was one line of attack he would not let her get away with. 'You are in Dublin, Mary, because everyone told me that the best oncology services are there. For the considerable amount of money I am paying out I will ring your consultant to check the answer to nine across in the *Irish Times* crossword if I want to.'

'You are despicable,' was all she could manage, rendered inarticulate by her own fury.

The words rang in his ears. If he had any residual feelings to be hurt by his wife the words would have been like sand-paper rubbed on open wounds but Con had long since gated that avenue of pain. Nobody – except Dan – knew him better and nobody hated him more, but as long as he had his son he knew he could face anything. So every evening he pulled his car into an empty bay in the visitors' car park. He took a ticket from the attendant in the shelter cabin and listened as the closing time of the car park was recited again. He bought flowers when he judged that the last lot had been disposed of and he always brought magazines and chocolate. He sat beside Mary's bed every night alongside Dan, and sometimes Alison, who had become a permanent fixture in his son's life, saying what spouses say and doing what they do when they know their children are watching. Mary concealed her distaste for him as best she could, remaining mostly impassive when he spoke, and although his presence irritated her he knew that she would be infinitely more irritated if he were true to them both and never came at all.

After a double mastectomy and more than four months' worth of chemotherapy Mary was declared to be in remission. She resumed her life in the shadow of the three-monthly appointments that punctuate the cancer patient's calendar. Each day survived was an achievement in itself but also brought the next hospital appointment and its attendant dangers even closer. If anything, Con would think to himself afterwards, cancer had mellowed his wife, blunting the rough corners of her anger. The truth was that Mary Abernethy was thinking of other things: an unsatisfactory life half lived and the stack of its remaining days possibly numbered and steadily petering out.

She took a call from the Taoiseach's wife in the hall of their house in Leachlara and Con listened, panicked at first and then stunned at how easily she detailed how supportive he had been at her time of greatest need, how he had done everything to make her time in hospital bearable, how she would certainly be lost without him. Her facility for deceit impressed him and when she put down the phone crisply he smiled in gratitude for a performance well delivered. In that moment he recognized that a mutual pragmatism had bound them together in a way that love and respect had never done. Con's future success would keep him out of her house and out of her life and this marriage that they had long ago decided to cling to, not for better but definitely for worse, would remain a testament to endurance and proof that love need not mean a thing.

Dan had taken his mother's illness badly. Of course he didn't want his mother to be sick but neither did he want to partake in the charade of family unity that had ensued since she had been diagnosed. He was ashamed when he admitted to Alison that the nightly visiting sessions at the hospital drained him so much that he often pretended that his work had delayed him and managed only ten minutes at the end of visiting time to sit and witness his parents enact their elaborate masquerade. He could tell Alison anything and consequently told her everything, depending on her warmth and normality to curb how awkward his own flesh and blood made him feel.

'If anything, Ali, you would think that my mam's cancer would bring either or both of them to their senses, but the tension in the room is unbearable. I love it when you come because they pull out all the stops when you are there.'

Alison hugged him tightly to her. She had spent almost four years with Dan Abernethy and every day made her look forward to another. Two peas in a pod, Rose had said to her the day she shut up the Daisy May for the last time, its lease too expensive for her modest operation. 'Don't ever forget that you and Dan are meant to be together. Whatever comes your way, stick it out. Romance isn't worth a flake unless it steels you for the tough times.' Then, weary of doling out sound advice, she had added, 'By the way, if I find out that you got married and you didn't invite me I will come from whatever point on the planet I am on and will haunt you for the rest of your days.' Alison guaranteed Rose an invitation to the big day when and if it happened and she took heed of her friend's advice. In years of working shifts at the Daisy May she had never tired of listening to Rose's take on life. By any measure she had had a fairly dismal run in life but here she was in her late fifties thinking of heading off on a trip to some far-flung corner of the world to see if she could wring something worthwhile from the second half. Beneath her sarcasm, and there was much of it to wade through, she retained her sense of humour and she was convinced that Dan and Alison were meant for each other. It was a sentiment that Alison never tired of agreeing with, daring to hope it was true. She loved having Dan in her life and could not imagine a single thing that their love could not overcome.

They fought, of course, but their arguments flared and died out almost in the same breath. They squabbled about who would pay for things, and they argued about Ciara who had remained Alison's flatmate throughout their time at college, but neither was afraid to tell the other what they thought.

Ciara's disapproval of Dan ebbed and flowed but Alison demanded respect for the other from both of them. It would be totally unfair if they made her choose between them, she chided, and mostly they complied and tolerated one another. Tensions flared when Ciara had time on her hands in between a steady procession of boyfriends and her conscience about Leda would lead her to throw a few daggers in Dan's direction. Yet even Ciara had to admit that Leda seemed to have settled for her limited role in Con's life, amounting to little more than convenient sex. She was willing to tolerate the bad treatment in between as long as she could live rent free, in a flashier apartment now than in the beginning, and with money in her pocket. She returned home to Leachlara at Christmastime only and she kept her mouth shut about Con when she was there, as he had instructed her to do, while flaunting what his money had bought her. Ciara finally understood that it was all about the pay-off for Leda and had never really been about Con at all. He was merely a means to her chosen end. Leda was no longer a teenager and if Con's twenty-one-year-old lover had agreed to abide by his dodgy morals then Ciara had grudgingly decided to let her, and consequently Dan, be.

Con Abernethy's hand shook now as he put the phone down in his Leinster House office. It was a cramped room that he shared with a backbench colleague from Kerry. Two desks, two phones and some random constituency and party promotion leaflets and little more filled the limited space. Anything personal or of value he kept in the house at Leachlara. The rumours, it seemed, had been spot on. He had received a call from the party secretary to attend the Taoiseach's office at

7 p.m. sharp. It could only mean one thing. He straightened his already straight tie and smoothed down the lapels of his immaculate Louis Copeland suit, congratulating himself for deciding to wear it this very day, then made a call to Dan at the hospital staffroom. Would he and Alison meet him outside Leinster House around nine? He had some good news that he would share with them over dinner. If his gut feelings about his impending promotion were correct then Dan and Alison would be there to flank him as he talked to the political correspondent on the nine o'clock news. He could have told Columbo about the summons to the Taoiseach's office and no doubt Columbo would have broken every speed limit from Leachlara to Kildare Street in an effort to be there to witness the proud moment, but Con decided against it. He had waited much too long for this moment, and he wanted to savour it as a personal achievement before it was swallowed up by the party workers as a group success or analysed by the media as merely a strategic stroke by a political leader responding to trouble in the polls. He would tell Mary too of course when it had been confirmed. She would not be interested in hearing from him now when he was merely anticipating the good news. She would dismiss him for ill-advised presumption before the fact. Mary only dealt in cold facts, so he would make that call on his return from his seven o'clock appointment. Bereft of congratulation, as he knew it would be, it should take no more than thirty seconds. Leda might hear it on the news, although admittedly that was unlikely, as he had never once heard a voice on that radio of hers, just thumping dance music that she thankfully knew to turn off when he came in. He would see how things went with Dan and Alison, how long they would spend with him and maybe he would call over to Leda afterwards.

He kept a bottle of Jameson whiskey in the top drawer of his desk and he found himself thinking more and more of it as the clock seemed to crawl from six-thirty. Every minute seemed to drag, wilfully torturing him. With ten minutes to go he gulped greedily from the bottle and chewed a mint on his way down the corridors to meet with the future. It had taken longer than he had planned, but it was welcome all the same.

Chapter Seventeen

Stress was bound to have played a part. Dan knew this from his experience in the hospital and since his mother had had a recurrence of her cancer he had made it his business to talk to every consultant that would give him the time of day about her setback and treatment possibilities. He wanted to be doing something practical but the resulting prognoses were bringing him no relief. He knew by looking at her scans that it was easier now to point out the pockets of her body that the cancer had not visited, so rampant had been its spread. He entered the bright foyer of the Mater to visit his mother knowing that soon she would have to be moved from there to a hospice or back home, though home seemed an unlikely prospect now. Every ounce of fight she possessed seemed to have evaporated amidst the scandal that had unfolded around his father.

Dan got a coffee in the restaurant and sat for a while before he took the lift to see his mother, who appeared to be disappearing before his eyes. A table at the back was his best bet. He wanted to tuck himself away from faces he might recognize and well-meant enquiries about his mother that he didn't have the heart to answer. He thought back to the night that his father's junior ministerial position had been announced and to the day this nightmare had begun in earnest.

Dan and Alison had made their way to Leinster House, arriving before 9 p.m. There had been some speculation on 'Five Seven Live' and on news bulletins throughout the day that a major shake-up of the cabinet was in the offing, and Dan had told Alison that although his father had said very little in the phone call he presumed that he was about to be promoted. By the time they arrived there was a media circus around the steps, reflecting the fact that there had been six changes to the cabinet team: four moves, two drops and two promotions, of which Con was one. His dad had handled the media very well considering his relative lack of experience and watching him made Dan incredibly proud. He borrowed his father's new mobile phone, a recent acquisition, to phone his mother, feeling that she should be included in the excitement of the night. She had seen the news and wished them all a good night. When Dan said it was a pity she wasn't here, she said there would be time enough for celebrations and, just briefly, Dan allowed himself to think that things might well improve between his parents from now on. She seemed a little proud, not very mind you, but just a little.

Con had booked a table for them at a nearby restaurant, but what started as a private celebration inevitably expanded into a huge party, with every stray party hack coming to the table to congratulate Con and stay for a drink. Columbo docked with a coterie of party workers from Tipperary. The remains of his thinning hair were doused with Brylcreem and his ample face shone alarmingly with delight when he spotted Con. He was kitted out in a new overcoat (Mary Abernethy would approve) and when he lunged at the new Junior Minister for a hug Alison remarked to Dan that she thought he was going to cry or collapse with excitement or both.

'I think Columbo has a bit of a crush on your dad, Dan. That reaction is just a little bit over the top, isn't it?'

'Very little about Columbo could be described as normal but in fairness he has put as much work into tonight as my dad, possibly even more. The man doesn't really have a life outside politics.'

When Columbo finally released Con from his suffocating clasp he practically knocked down the maître d' asking for drink for the table. Dan knew it was going to be a big night and he motioned to Alison that now might be a good time to escape. Con thanked them for coming and said he would be in touch in the morning. It might have stayed just that, a big night for a provincial politician and his team, had Con not decided to set up a tab at the bar, which he would settle in the morning, and take a midnight drive to see Leda. He was well on his way to triple the legal alcohol limit when he knocked down a female pedestrian dashing for a late bus at the corner of Stephen's Green. At exactly 12.15 a.m. Garda Paul Crampton was taking a cigarette break on Stephen's Green East. He had parked on a double yellow line in front of an emergency access lane because, frankly, who was going to stop him? He would testify that he noticed a black Mercedes being driven erratically in the direction of Leeson Street Bridge. He would further give evidence that it took several minutes for Con Abernethy to pull his vehicle to the side of the road. It appeared, Paul Crampton would say, that the Junior Minister (because he was one at the time of the accident, albeit for a historically brief tenure) was oblivious to the police siren instructing him to pull over. Two witnesses to the hit and run on Stephen's Green would link the black Mercedes to the scene and if that were not enough strands of the injured girl's hair and fibres from her clothing were found on the damaged wing of Con Abernethy's car.

The Taoiseach, who had hoped to wake to positive media coverage for his cabinet revamp, was instead woken in the early hours by a phone call from a party aide whose presence had been requested by a rapidly sobering Con when he found himself at Harcourt Street Garda station without a leg to stand on. The Taoiseach visited the injured girl in hospital and breathed a small sigh of relief when she was finally declared out of danger. Con was only allowed to visit the girl and her family privately. Senior party figures did not want pictures of him to grace the front pages of the dailies with another series of inevitably unbecoming headlines.

At seven o'clock that morning Ciara Clancy was buttering what might well have been her tenth slice of toast after a particularly bad night's sleep in the flat she shared with Alison just a few streets away from where they had first rented from Jean McDermott. Ranelagh had charmed them with its opportunity to live alongside people who had rakes more money and status, and there were plenty of places because houses were still better rented than sold. She idly turned on Alison's stereo. Whatever was worth anything in the flat belonged to Alison, bought for her by her folks or sometimes by Dan. Ciara was hoping that situation might change any day now. She could practically smell her first real pay packet for something other than petty bits of shop work or waiting on tables, the inherent servitude of which she disdained. Alison had the fecking stereo tuned to Radio 1 again. My God, some things about that girl were proving impossible to change. She fiddled with the dial but not before she had heard Con Abernethy's name in the headlines. She spat out her toast and rapidly turned the dial back to where she had found it.

Dan kind of knew he was oversleeping but he was reluctant to leave the warmth of Alison's bed. He had to be at the hospital at eight and he knew he had to rouse himself within a few minutes. He pulled the quilt over their heads to enjoy one last snuggle. Ciara didn't wait for an answer when she knocked on her flatmate's door. No show of good manners would change the news. She burst in and when they sat up in the bed, the covers clenched to their naked bodies, she blurted out, 'Jesus, Dan, your father has well and truly fucked it all up now.'

His performance at the previous general election had been extinguished by his carelessness and the long road to ministerial responsibility destroyed by an instant of irresponsibility. Mary Abernethy would say that the news broke her heart and Con would say with as much black humour as he could manage that, if she had one, she had kept it well hidden all these years.

The Mater café was getting busy with evening meals and Dan knew that the waitress who cleared his stone-cold coffee cup would rather he move so people who were buying meals could sit down. His mother was in good form when he got to her room and had been visited by a palliative-care consultant from St Matthew's Hospice. She told Dan, as she had told his father earlier in the day, that she would move there once a place became available.

'You are being very brave, Mam. I'm very proud of the way you are handling all of this and I know Dad is too, even though he might not say so.'

She looked at him sceptically but there was a glimmer of softness where he had expected none. 'Your father is love-bombing me with visits. He has a lot of time on his hands now that he has put the kibosh on his career. It's funny the way no one wants to deal with someone who has been disgraced, as if they think they might catch something. I think that Clancy trollop has even decided that it's contagious and has made herself scarce.'

'I guess it's too late for you two to forgive each other all the slurs and the harsh words. But it would be good if something positive came from all this – for everyone's sake.'

Her breathing was laboured and the almost violent rising and falling of her chest, protected now only by a sliver of flesh, was painful for Dan to watch.

'Oh, Dan, I know you have suffered and I know we gave you no example of how to live. I regret that, I really do. You see, I withdrew from the marriage early on, withdrew my company and my friendship and – you know – other stuff. I turned myself into a commodity that I was unwilling to trade.' Mary seemed uncomfortable at the mere reference to sexual relations and much as he wanted to listen to his mother, Dan was relieved that embarrassment might save them both having to contemplate her deepest regrets in graphic detail. Having regained her composure, Mary continued. 'The trouble was I never knew how to try again with our relationship. In the early years your father might well have forgiven me but I just could not find the way back. Pride, I suppose, but inexperience too. I never made it easy for him, and you have to make the effort for the other person or they lose the will to try. He had his career and he treated that like it was much more important than I was, and I suppose it saved him from madness or loneliness or both. I had you and the house and I had money to do what I liked. Mostly that was enough. Plenty of people have less than that to be going on with. For ages I felt lucky, not blessed but lucky.'

'Do you think things could have been different? Do you think you could have been happy together? I just remember you fighting. I don't remember a good time, but maybe there was and I just don't recall it.' Dan hadn't expected his mother to open up and he couldn't stem his flood of questions. They broke like waves on the surface of the conversation, looking for answers to calm them.

'Who knows what way life plays out? But we could have been happy enough. I would settle for that, I know that now but it's too late, of course. My cancer and your father's spectacular disgrace have taken the energy from our little feud. It's not right to hate each other any more; hardly seems worth the effort when everything else has gone wrong. Every cloud has a silver lining and all that. Mind you, I am not sure that your father would willingly trade what he has lost for our modest silver lining. The state car that never was, the perks he never claimed. He took all that as a huge blow, you must realize.'

Dan took his mother's hand. It was frail now and her finger too small for the mocking wedding band that swamped it like a child's plaything. He squeezed it, willing her to understand that he forgave her and that he knew she had done her best even if that was not very good at all.

Con appeared at the door with another bunch of flowers. He looked as if he suspected they might have been talking about him but he didn't mind.

'Con Abernethy, I've told you not to buy me another single flower. The nurses are cursing me because all the vases for the entire floor are in this room.'

'Ah, sure the florist down below knows me now. I couldn't pass without buying something. He would think it bad form. Besides, it's amazing the admiring glances you get when you are carrying a bit of a bouquet.'

Dan looked at his parents nearly grinning at each other and knew that this probably was as good as it got. He decided to be thankful before it was too late.

Chapter Eighteen

'I see you made it for the barbecue too, sis.' Leda waltzed into Shanahan's lounge on the day of Mary Abernethy's funeral, ignoring the admiring and lust-filled gazes that followed her to the counter from every corner of the bar. She was hoping to have a few quiet words with Con and had been momentarily nonplussed to see her sister standing cheek by jowl with Dan and his friends at the counter. She didn't think her sister's mystifyingly close friendship with Dan's glucose pop of a girlfriend would run to her presence at his mother's funeral, but it seemed her loyalty was boundless.

'I think you will find that the more common term is cremation, Leda, and for your information there was a change of plan. She was buried instead. Would you not stay away today of all days?' Ciara had moved to greet Leda a little away from Dan because he was having a tough enough day without seeing his father's on–off girlfriend hanging around. Leda's timing was, as ever, brutal.

'Where is the Rose of Tralee herself? Up making tea at the house, I suppose, preparing to be the new and improved Mrs Abernethy, though that shouldn't be too hard.'

'Listen, Leda, keep your poisonous rant to yourself. Alison has a job interview in Cork this evening and Dan insisted she go ahead with it. She asked me to stay here with Dan. We are getting the train in the morning when all this is over.'

'God, you two must be as tight as thieves that she trusts you with him. He is a fucking ride. I know what I would do if she left him in my care. I'd show him what a real woman could do for him. After Con he would most definitely be on my target list but I do prefer the more mature man. They are grateful for any attention and the cash is stacked higher. Dan is probably still getting pocket money from Con. Something like twenty years to qualify as a doctor, isn't it? Still though, Ciara, you could do a lot worse.' As she said this Leda was scanning the lounge to see if she could see any sign of Con. She saw her father all right, looking as if he had had a fair few already, and she raised her hand to him in salute.

Ted Clancy was mighty proud that his two daughters knew enough to turn up at the funeral to show their gratitude for everything Con had done for them over the years. He had taught them well and as he took another slug from his pint that thought was some consolation for the fact that neither was showing any sign of coming over to talk to him.

Ciara's face had turned scarlet with rage. How dare Leda presume to know anything about the way she felt about Dan – and was it really that obvious that she fancied him? More than she would even admit to herself? 'You are unbelievable. You shouldn't judge the rest of us by your own lousy standards. Alison is my friend and Dan is her boyfriend. End of story.'

'Yeah, yeah, I believe you. Not. Anyway, where is the man of the moment? I feel he could do with some company at a time like this. You know, a shoulder to lean on, a bridge over troubled water, etc.'

Dan was coming towards them and Ciara knew she had only

a few seconds to bring this conversation to an end. Leda didn't know where to stop. She was likely to say anything.

'He's up at the house. Said he might come down later. For what it's worth I think you should have the decency to leave him alone. He's with friends and relatives and you, Leda Clancy, are neither.'

'Thanks for the information, sis.' Appraising the approaching Dan, Leda added, 'Don't do anything I wouldn't do.'

Dan tapped Ciara on the shoulder. 'You OK?' He eyeballed Leda, knowing that her presence meant only trouble. His father could not be relied on to do the right thing when she was around. She flattered his ego and he lost any iota of self-restraint he possessed. Leda smirked at him and turned with a flourish and left.

'As OK as I can manage when my wrecking ball of a sister comes to town. She's looking for your dad. Told her I didn't know where he was but she is determined to find him. Said she would try the house.'

'Oh, great! The relations will love that. I suppose he can pass her off as just another constituent; the place was coming down with callers all last night and this morning so she won't look too much out of place. I was going to suggest we head off after this one but I think I will get us another drink. I don't think I could stomach Leda this evening and I can't depend on my father to act properly. He is totally brain dead when she is around. No offence, but she should have known better than to come.'

'I think she feels I have no business here either, thinks I am being hypocritical after all I have said and I suppose she is right.'

Dan took Ciara's hand in his and she hoped that the wave of weakness she felt at his touch didn't show on her face. 'I know we have had our differences, Ciara, and I know it took a lot for you to overcome your blanket hatred of the Abernethys to let me in. I appreciate it very much and I know that Alison does too, because she never tires of telling me how grateful to you I should be – and I am. I truly am. It's nice to have you here this evening. It would be hard otherwise, and I would be lonesome for Alison even with every sodding relation I never knew I had and all the old crowd from school.' He waved to the gang of young people he had left at the bar who had come to show their friendship to Dan by paying their respects to a woman they didn't really know.

The mention of Alison's name brought Ciara back to the reality from which she had allowed herself to drift. Of course, that's why she was here. She was an inadequate substitute for his real girlfriend and Dan knew her place even if she had momentarily forgotten it. Some crazy mix of pity – for him, for herself and her own miserable selection of men – and discomfort at being back in Leachlara had messed with her mind. Thank God she hadn't made a fool of herself by saying or, worse still, doing anything. Leda's presence had been her unlikely saviour. There was always a first time for everything, she supposed.

'Well, seeing as neither of us has any real home to go to at the minute maybe we should have a drink. I know I said I wouldn't because of the day that's in it and all, but I am gasping. And Shanahan's without a drink in your hand is hard on the spirit.'

'A pint?' Dan ventured.

'I would mow you down for one.' She followed him as he strode back to the bar and as she watched him weave with ease into his childhood company she warned herself nothing beyond friendship and sympathy was appropriate. He had just lost his mother. His girlfriend was her best friend. It was all pretty clear if you managed to stop and think about it.

It was close to midnight and the perennial deadline of last orders when Con Abernethy made it to the door of Shanahan's. He had company. Columbo had not left his side in the last few days and some other party workers had stood their ground too. His wife's death seemed to have ameliorated some of the smell of defeat that had lingered after the road accident and the promotion that had rapidly transformed into a shameful demotion. He had shaken off the last of the relatives who had clung to the house like glue over the preceding days. He told them he would need their company far more in the lonesome weeks that stretched ahead and he said he was worried about Dan. He should go out and find him and bring him home. They left unwillingly, feeling their work wasn't done, and Columbo had got rid of the last of the stragglers. Con wasn't sure what he had said to them, but it had worked and that was the main thing. There were advantages to this bereavement process; being too upset to talk for long was chief amongst them.

Leda left a decent amount of time before she followed Con to the pub. He had been shocked to see her at the house because he had most decidedly kept as much distance as he could manage from her over the past months while Mary's health had deteriorated. Mary had at least that much respect due to her and to Leda's credit she hadn't made a fuss. He showed her to the room that he used as his home office and told her to wait there until he got rid of everyone downstairs. Before he left with Columbo he gave her his car keys and told her to meet him at Shanahan's in a little while. He wasn't sure what he would do about her but he felt sure that their sharing a drink could not do any harm. Tonight he could hardly do any wrong.

Dan knew his father would turn up at the pub eventually. The place had been his living room all his life. He knew that there would be loads of people who would use his mother's death to pick up the thread of a conversation that had paused with his father's dismissal from the cabinet. Dan would not be surprised by that hypocrisy because he had spent the last few days on the receiving end of the same sort of heavy but well-meant sentiment. He had planned to go over and talk to his father and see how he was doing, but something about the way

Leda slithered in so easily to stand alongside his father made his stomach turn. He knew he had had too much to drink long before the barman came to offer himself and his friends a round of drinks from Con, who had taken up his usual position at the snug corner of the lounge. As alcohol penetrated the inner reaches of the company the noise got louder, smoke clouds filled the space above their heads and any air of bereavement evaporated with every pull and slug.

'Tell him to keep his money and his drink,' he told the puzzled barman and then he turned to Ciara. 'I'm off home. I'm knackered. I'm getting the seven-thirty train in the morning. I need not to be here any more watching him not giving a shit.'

'Here, I'll come with you. Can I be cheeky and stay the night in your house? It's just I don't fancy sharing a room with Leda at home tonight. Please?'

'Whatever, Ciara, but I wouldn't be too sure that you won't be seeing her over toast in my house. Take a look at them.'

'He wouldn't take her to your house, would he?'

'With Mam gone anything is possible. That's why the less I see of him at the moment the better.'

Ciara turned to look for her sister before she left the pub. Leda was leaning in towards Con, enjoying a joke. Apart from the sombre suit, Con looked nothing like the grieving widower. He was in his element, at the centre of a crowd who once again hung on his every word. He did not notice that his son was gone until Paddy Shanahan, having suffered two Garda raids in quick succession, got cranky about closing time and his duty to observe it. At that stage Ciara and Dan, with hunger born of huge amounts of alcohol, were milling through the platters of sandwiches left over from the funeral that littered every surface of the Abernethys' kitchen. Dirty cups filled the sink and Dan knew his mother would never have stood for this level of disarray, nor would Con have allowed it to happen in her temporary absence. Except now she wouldn't be arriving back to bawl them out about it.

'God, if Mam could see this mess now she would freak out. She asked him to have the house private, you know, and instead of that he got the caterers in and let anyone from miles around through the place.'

'Do you mind? About the people coming here for the past few days?'

'It's not my house, Ciara. I don't give a shit except for her. I think he could have done his best to do things the way she would have wanted them done but there are more votes in a prolonged Irish wake than in what she had in mind. Last wishes and all that. They should mean something, shouldn't they?' Dan did his best to hold back the tears but they ran down his face in spite or maybe because of his efforts to contain them.

Ciara had been sitting opposite him at the kitchen table. She didn't have to think twice about going to comfort him. 'Oh Dan,' she murmured as she crouched down on her knees by his seat, taking his hand in hers, hoping her touch would bring him comfort or pleasure or perhaps both. 'I'm sure he was trying to do the right thing and maybe he needed loads of people around him to cope with all this.'

The shock of hearing Ciara saying something almost positive about his father gave Dan enough of a jolt to control his tears. 'God, don't get carried away now. This is my father we are talking about. You know, the biggest rat in Leachlara, evil incarnate and all that. Surely you haven't forgotten what you think of him.'

'I don't even believe myself. Sorry, I am crap when people break down. I say anything to pull them back together.'

Dan laughed and pulled her into an embrace. 'It's good that you are here. I'm glad I am not alone.'

Afterwards Ciara would know exactly what he meant. She would know that the house felt strange and empty and that company eased the loneliness he was feeling in a house that was home but felt anything but. She would know that when he hugged her the right thing to do would have been to accept his gratitude and move away. But they had both drunk oceans during the course of the evening and reason and straight thinking were in short supply. When he tentatively offered his kisses to her she took them shyly at first and when he pulled back, shocked by what they were doing, Ciara's lips found his hungrily, confident her touch could erase everything that had been wrong with this most difficult of days. She relished the feel of his hands, burning through her flimsy clothes to her skin. She unbuttoned her shirt and placed his hand on the soft rise of her breast and she pulled at his shirt buttons to reach his smooth skin beneath. When he rose from the chair she thought she had prompted him to take control of what she had started and that his initial shyness had dissipated. She closed her eyes ready for him to decide what happened next to her and to them.

Suddenly sobering and with a rising sense of disgust at her and at himself, Dan pushed her away as if he had been stung. Ciara stumbled across the kitchen, reeling from desire and rejection bundled together in the same split second.

'I think you'd better go home, Ciara. We have had too much to drink. This is insane. What about Alison?' Dan was dishevelled and shaken and he clung to the kitchen doorframe as if he might collapse but for its support.

'Fuck Alison, she is not even here. Her job interview was more important than you or your blasted mother. Besides, don't blame her for starting what you couldn't finish. At least your father is man enough to do the deed when he gets the chance. Obviously he has all the red blood in this family.'

'Go home. I have a phone number for Leachlara Cabs. I'll ring them.'

'Stuff your cab up your hole, Dan. I'd rather walk to Dublin than spend another second here.'

He pleaded with her to have common sense but she was already walking away, struggling with her coat in drunken awkwardness and embarrassment. He ran after her but she ran faster, her heels crunching the gravel in mortified anger. Dan stood for a while shell shocked as she disappeared from view. He returned to the kitchen, locking the door behind him, and went to climb the stairs to bed. The red light was flashing on the answering machine. He heard Alison's voice telling him that she loved him and hoped the day hadn't been too hard after she had left. The interview had gone well. She would talk to him in the morning. She loved him, but she had said that already, hadn't she? He went to bed with her voice whispering in his head and the salted memory of what had just happened with Ciara waiting for him and taunting him on every step of the stairs.

Ciara made it on foot back to the middle of Leachlara, rapidly sobering with every passing minute. Her feet were killing her and the remnants of make-up, so carefully applied earlier in the day, streaked down her face, mingling with her embarrassed tears. She felt more stupid than she had ever felt in her whole life and her head spun every time she allowed herself to think about what had just happened. She didn't see Columbo where he stood next to his car outside Shanahan's. He had spotted her the moment she had started to walk up the main street illuminated by the harsh orange of the street lights.

'Are you stuck for a lift, Ciara?' he enquired kindly when she was close enough to hear him.

'I am, yeah,' she answered, startled to hear her name but relieved that it was only Columbo and not anyone else she knew.

'Get in and I will run you home. If you were here ten minutes ago you could have shared a lift with your sister. I am just back from dropping her home.'

'I am surprised she didn't stay until the bitter end,' Ciara said, nodding at the door of Shanahan's.

'There's a bit of a lock-in going on all right, it being the night that's in it, but Leda had no real interest in staying. Your father on the other hand will be there until the last drop is drained from the last bottle. I've never met a better man to drink.'

'It's enough to make a daughter burst with pride,' was the last bit of conversation that Ciara managed before she closed her eyes in shame.

Leda was in the kitchen munching on biscuits when Ciara turned up. She had hoped her sister would be asleep and that she would be able to straighten herself up before having to face anyone, but no such luck.

'Good God, what happened to you? Don't tell me young Dan had his wicked way with you? I saw you both leaving together looking cosy as anything.'

'I thought you would still be at the pub with Con, wiping away his tears.'

'Oh, it never hurts to leave them when they still want more. Besides, Dad was there being obnoxious and looking for drink so I thought it best to get out. Well, are you going to tell me what happened to you then? You look rough as hell.'

Ciara sat down on one of the battered kitchen chairs. She ached all over. Maybe it would help to tell someone, even if that person was Leda. She didn't think it through before she opened her mouth and told her sister what had happened. Leda couldn't believe her ears. She barely managed to stifle a grin while her big sister wept uncontrollably.

Chapter Nineteen

The last of the patients had been seen at Michaelmas GP practice in Caharoe and Cathy was extremely glad to be going to lock the surgery door. She had found the last few days exhausting and she was delighted that it was Friday and that the weekend beckoned. The week had started on a great note with the news that Alison had got a job teaching in her old secondary school in Caharoe. The contract was for a year only but both Cathy and Richard were hoping that their daughter might impress the board of management enough that if funds were to become available her post might become permanent. They knew that Alison was not convinced that she wanted to stay in Caharoe permanently but they also knew that a good deal of her indecision was due to her relationship with Dan. They were so thoroughly in love with each other that Cathy understood that they would have to be in the same place, knowing through experience that the pull of love would not tolerate anything else. She was working on a plan for that also and she had nearly convinced Richard of its merits.

They had always wanted to take some time off from the surgery, travel a little and rest from the humdrum routine of nearly twenty-five years of running a practice, a relentless schedule that had exhausted them. They were way off wanting to retire fully but desire for a change and a chance to live a little had crept into many conversations since Alison had left for college. Dan was just about to finish his GP training and would be shortly looking for his first post. It seemed thoroughly obvious to Cathy, and increasingly to Richard (although he was slow to agree fully to the plan), that they should offer Dan a post at the practice in Caharoe. His presence would keep Alison near home and Dan could find his feet as a family doctor, benefiting from Richard's decades of experience. If it all worked out she hoped maybe Dan and Alison could stay in Caharoe for good. It was at that point in her happy families reverie that Cathy reined in her overactive imagination. Just having Alison at home for another year would be bliss.

She went downstairs, where Richard was ferreting for a corkscrew to open a bottle of white. A glass of wine was just what she felt like. 'I am totally wiped. Would a Chinese takeout be OK for dinner?'

'I've rung them already. I ordered your favourite. They will deliver around seven.'

'Thanks, Richard. I just couldn't face making a dinner tonight,' Cathy said, accepting a drink gratefully. They clinked glasses and Richard kissed her forehead.

'For what it's worth, I think you are right about Dan. He has the makings of a good GP and I think we should give him a chance for our sakes as well as for Alison. Mind you, with his mother dying he may not be in any position to make a decision. I will leave the timing up to you, see when you think is best to mention it.'

'Well, they are in his uncle's place in Aughasallagh until Sunday. Alison is coming back here for a few days and Dan is going on to Dublin to sit his last exams. Maybe we will run it by Alison when she comes home in case she hates the idea but I doubt she will. She just wants to be with Dan.'

'That's a good idea, love. You know, I was talking to Hugh Lalor today and our friend Con Abernethy's name came down in conversation. Seems he hasn't wasted much time since Dan's mother died in helping himself to some female company. According to Hugh, and his sources are normally fairly reliable, Ciara's younger sister is back on the scene and a few others are beating a path to the house as well. Would you not think that he could let Mary be dead a decent amount of time before he starts that racket again?'

'Well, you know I don't think an awful lot of Con Abernethy. I know the Lalors say he is lovely but, honestly, have you ever heard the pair of them say a bad word about someone who has influence, power or rakes of money? Sure Rena made excuses for him having a teenage girlfriend when I quizzed her about what Ciara had said about him. Apparently it was his wife's entire fault for being difficult. He ticks all the Lalor boxes but not any of mine. I really don't know where Dan was got at all because Mary *was* a bit of an old boot and Dan is so nice and thoughtful and treats Alison like a queen. She was lucky to meet him.'

'Well, I think he was the lucky one actually. Sure our Alison is the best in the world!'

'You are a big old softie, Richard.'

'Ah, sure I know but where is the harm in that? She's my daughter and I'll never stop looking out for her.'

Dan was struggling with revising for his last set of exams. His mother was dead barely a month and he just couldn't seem to get his head round anything. At his mother's funeral he had met his uncle Jack, who had offered him his cottage near a beach in Kerry for studying or for holidays. Dan had thanked him but he had no intention of taking up the offer. The flat in Dublin was where he intended to do the last of his preparation, close to the libraries for last-minute dashes, close to friends for support and, crucially, a couple of miles from Alison who had decided to stay on in her own flat for a couple of weeks after her own exams to keep him company until his were finished. That had been the plan until he and Ciara had stupidly messed around in the kitchen in Leachlara. His head had been silently imploding with pressure every day since. He was sure Alison would notice the change in him soon but that was probably his own guilty conscience. Alison was as she always was, it was he who couldn't see past the possibility that Ciara would tell Alison what had happened and that she might assume him guilty because he hadn't had the guts to confess to a stupid drunken mistake.

Ciara had got herself a summer job as a tour guide in Trinity and so there seemed no possibility that she would just go off for the summer and leave them alone. Any time they had met Dan had made an effort to act normally but when Alison was busy or popped out of the room to get something Dan found himself on the receiving end of Ciara's derisory smirks. She was enjoying torturing him, loving the fact that with one word to Alison she could rattle their world. He thought about talking to her but realized that it was Alison he should speak to and that he couldn't face right now. Uncle Jack's cottage in Aughasallagh for a week or ten days occurred to him then as a useful stopgap. He would ring his uncle and tell him to leave the key at Daly's pub for him. He would persuade Alison to come with him. They could take the train to Leachlara and pick up his mother's car from the house. It had been one of a few specific bequests to him along with her beloved silverware and nearly thirty thousand pounds, secreted from a very surprised Con, in a bank account in Thurles. From there it would be two hours' drive at most to Aughasallagh. He would lose a full day's studying in the process but it was better than failing the exams and that was what would happen if he stayed in Dublin waiting for Ciara to open her mouth. The cottage would be quiet enough to do some worthwhile study and Alison could be with him and away from Ciara until he had finished his exams. Then he could talk to her. He would make her understand that the sight of his father with Leda the night of his mother's funeral coupled with too much drink had made him do something stupid, but that it really didn't mean a thing. It was just a kiss and a drunken fumble, he told himself when doubt swelled from the pit of his stomach and threatened to strangle his ability to breathe. He hoped that all the years they had spent together would count for something against a stupid slip-up – even if his slip-up involved Alison's closest friend.

The cottage in Aughasallagh was in tiptop shape and that at least gave Alison some slight comfort, because she had been looking forward to a couple of relaxing weeks in Dublin before she had to start looking seriously for a teaching post. There had been the offer of a temporary job in her old school in Caharoe and she would decide shortly if she should take it or not. She knew by her parents' behaviour on the phone when they opened the letter and told her the news that they were gasping for her to accept the job, but she had another couple of days to work it all out. Besides, a lot would depend on where Dan would end up and he was in no mood for discussing life beyond the exams at the moment.

She had been taken aback when he had suggested the trip but he seemed set on it and, to be honest, his form was so shaky since his mother had died that she was willing to go along with anything if she thought she would get the old Dan back. Her parents had advised her that Dan would need a lot of support: grieving for a dead parent on top of the extreme pressure of final exams was potentially too much to bear. She was willing to do everything possible for him and that included hiding out in the wilds of Kerry with no company except a doddery radio, a stack of books that she congratulated herself for packing and a chain-smoking boyfriend who was so lost in his own thoughts that he talked only infrequently and rarely sounded at all like he used to. She had mentioned it to Ciara only to be given a rough fob-off. 'For God's sake, his mother has just croaked it. Cut the boy some slack.' Ciara's reluctant ceasefire on Dan that had started in the last while looked set to continue and that at least was a good thing. The two of them getting on as well as they did would have looked like a miracle to her in the first few months after they had met. If that could happen, anything was possible, she thought.

Dan discovered that anything was indeed possible when an early morning doorbell ring at the cottage found him staring at Ciara on the front doorstep. Her hair was tousled by the boisterous sea wind and she wore a bright blue T-shirt under a pair of incredibly worn and baggy dungarees. She carried a small knapsack on her back with a jacket rolled up in the straps at its base. She had hitched here, must have, he reasoned, because there was no such thing as public transport in this or any other rural corner of the county. Ciara smiled at Dan but he could not return the favour. She sensed rage and exasperation from him. He rubbed his forehead with the heel of his hand as he always did when he was utterly flummoxed.

'What the hell are you doing here, Ciara? How dare you follow us and how in the name of God did you find us?'

'Calm down, Dan. You'll have a heart attack and, seeing as you are the doctor and I'm forbidden to do mouth-to-mouth resuscitation on you, it might be better if you didn't. I came to see Alison. You know, my best friend. Your girlfriend – remember?'

'Who told you where to find us?'

'Well, I have to say I have never given your father the credit he deserves for being an outstanding public representative. One phone call was all it took to get the address out of him. He was in such a hurry to get me off the phone, to attend to other constituents no doubt, that I didn't get a chance to thank him properly.' Ciara was enjoying Dan's discomfort and she paused a while to take in all its glory before brushing past him and heading down the hallway to find Alison listening to bloody Radio 1 again. She, at least, was ecstatic to see her. Dan's guilty conscience was obviously preventing him from being much in the way of company at the moment.

Ciara wasn't quite sure why she had to come to Aughasallagh, but she had been compelled to do so. She wasn't sure if it was just to see Alison or to tell her friend the truth of what had happened the night of Mary Abernethy's funeral and take the consequences, whatever they might be. Ciara was reluctant to admit to herself that at some level she wanted to see Dan more than she wanted to see Alison. That fact was proving difficult to get her head around and all the way from Dublin, hitching lifts and making conversations with strangers she would not ordinarily give the time of day to, she tried not to think too much about what she had wanted to happen with Dan and how he had rejected her.

She was in no hurry to get back to Dublin because she had packed in the tour-guide job in Trinity. She was absolutely not cut out to deal with tourists. They were all so shagging happy, thinking Ireland was the dearest, sweetest country, all looking for a long-lost great-granny whom their forbears had said goodbye to at the open fire where she sat stirring a pot of stew or pummelling a lump of brown soda dough into submission. She couldn't be satisfying their need for nostalgia or telling them with a straight face that of course their tour-bus driver was right, there were still a few leprechauns left if you knew where to look. She had more or less decided to head to France or Spain, maybe to teach English, a short course, so she could be out of Dublin, for a while anyway but maybe for good. There was no way she was heading back to Leachlara. That house seemed to shrink any time she went back there, with her parents still living the same excuse for a life. Her father was only happy when he was drunk and her mother was never happy at all but not driven enough to raise so much as a protesting murmur. Her brother was gone now as well. St Con had set him up as an apprentice with a building firm in Galway and the whiff of freedom had seduced him. She couldn't spend any more time in Dublin looking at Dan and Alison either, their closeness mocking all her failures with men. She had made a move on Dan because she had begun to find him incredibly attractive but maybe also to prove to herself that no one was perfect, Dan and Alison included, and that not even they had it all. Space between herself and Alison after years in each other's pockets would be no bad thing anyway. She convinced herself that she would have arrived at this conclusion even if she had never touched or wanted to touch Dan. Still, there was no harm in one last long visit, a week together before she hightailed somewhere, anywhere that Dan Abernethy was just a memory, and a new life could begin.

The weather was balmy and beautiful on the Friday night and they stayed on the beach long past dusk, huddled at a high corner where the lapping tide could not reach. Dan had brought a bottle of wine, crisps and cheese from the house. It was a sure sign that he was planning to wrench as much freedom from the night as possible. He had managed to chill out a bit, relaxing a little because he was finally getting to grips with his exam preparation and with every passing day it seemed less and less likely that Ciara had come to spill the beans. Their normal topics of conversation resumed: animated banter about politics, films they had seen and books they had read, and when Alison rose to go for a walk along the peace of the darkening strand to clear her head she left them engaged in a heated debate from which she had long tuned out, her head made fuzzy by the free-flowing wine. Even though she loved the sea the sound of its lost whispers at night always made her a little maudlin. She moved to the far side of the beach, intending to climb up and walk back along the rough grass-topped dunes that lined the strand where it met the green lushness of the fields. Darkness began to fall a little quicker than she had expected so she quickened her pace. She could hear the rise and fall of their voices below her, a familiar sound but the details unintelligible. She moved stealthily, wanting to make them jump out of their skin by appearing from where they would not expect. Moving closer, their words became clearer, but their tone was so serious she felt she was eavesdropping and her heart pounded a little. Bewildered, she stood rooted to the spot.

'I thought you were coming to make trouble between me and Alison.' Dan had thought it better to clear the air once and for all between himself and Ciara.

'Oh, I thought about it, believe me, but she won't hear it from my lips. I know Alison. She wouldn't forgive or forget. You're getting off the hook because I couldn't face hurting her. You should tell her that you messed around with someone though. Just don't say it was me, for God's sake, or she would have our guts for garters!' She laughed but clearly Dan did not enjoy the joke.

'What happened between us that night was just a drunken mistake and it meant nothing. It was just stupid. We were drunk, so let's forget it.'

'Well, thanks for dismissing it out of hand, but don't forget, Dan Abernethy, it was you who made the first move the night of your mother's funeral. You kissed me, remember? And what's more you seemed to enjoy it, or are you trying to block that bit out to salve your conscience?' Ciara's ire was rising at Dan's guilty attempt to wipe the slate clean but it was tempered with a resurgent desire to reach across and touch him. Fumbling with the straps of her sundress, Ciara did her best to reason with herself. She was not going to do something reckless here just because she had the chance, but the harder she tried the more she found she could not take her eyes off him, stretched out just inches away from her and oblivious to the effect he was having.

Dan's discomfort at Ciara's unwillingness to make light of the incident and move on was evident. He was conscious that Alison would not be much longer, as darkness was well and truly falling and she would be thinking of going home. He had to bring the conversation to a halt. 'I don't remember the details, Ciara,' he said dismissively. He got up on his knees to gather their things in preparation for returning to the cottage.

'Well, maybe I should remind you,' Ciara said as she moved close enough to touch him. She put her hands on his waist and stretched up to her full height to kiss him passionately on the lips, arching her body against the length of his.

Dan jerked away, wiping his mouth and pushing her hands off. His expression was one of pure disgust mixed with disbelief at her stupidity. 'God's sake, are you mad in the head? Get the message, will you, I don't fancy you! Never have and never will. Now get the hell away from me. Ali will be back any minute and she doesn't need to hear a word of this shit!'

He hadn't noticed Alison standing above them on the high dunes, her slight frame blending into the newly settled darkness. She was shaking but her voice was steady when she spoke. 'Too late for that, Dan, I am already here.'

They went back to the cottage separately, Dan doing his best to catch up with Alison, who didn't know which one of them she wanted to hit harder or if she was ever going to stop crying. She could hear Dan pleading with her to wait up, that he could explain and that it was all a big mistake, but she ran as if her life depended on it. Ciara lingered at the beach, collecting the enamel cups that they had drunk the wine from and emptying the remains of the bottle on the sand. She bagged their rubbish carefully and picked up Alison's jacket from where she had left it. Daly's had rooms above the shop and she decided to call there on the way to the cottage and see if she could arrange one at short notice. Someone in the bar would help her, because she absolutely could not stay in the same house as Dan and Alison tonight. While she was there she decided to have a pint to steady her nerves and give them a chance to talk.

When she reached the cottage she thought seriously about not going in, but she knew she would have to face Alison sooner rather than later. They could sort it out. She would understand, eventually. Dan was right. Stupid things happened when you were too drunk to know what you were doing. No matter how many times she repeated it to herself on the way back to the cottage, though, it never quite rang true.

'Your bag is packed. There are places you can stay up in the town. I think you should go. Now.' Alison was standing at the kitchen table, her arms folded defiantly. Her eyes were raw and her face blotchy from the tears she had shed. Dan sat on the couch, his head buried in his hands.

'Look, Alison, it was just a stupid pissed thing we did, a kiss that shouldn't have happened. That's *all*. We can work this out. We're best friends, for God's sake.'

Alison shook her head, unimpressed by Ciara's beseeching expression. 'Best friends don't do this to each other. I asked you to mind Dan that night in Leachlara because I couldn't be there. I didn't ask you to lunge at him and try to sleep with him. I know you have had plenty of practice but this is a bit lousy even for you, don't you think? Once wasn't even enough – you had to try it on again tonight while my back was turned. You are a shameless bitch and I don't want to see you again, do you understand?'

'I didn't lunge at him. Dan, tell her it wasn't like that!' Ciara implored.

Dan looked at her, but before he had a chance to say anything Alison grabbed Ciara's knapsack and thrust it in her direction.

It collapsed at her feet. 'Get out. This is between me and Dan now and you have no place being here.'

'Alison, please . . .' Ciara wasn't ready to leave without sorting something out. Her friend would need time to calm down, but surely then it could be worked out?

Dan rose from the sofa, his long limbs untangling themselves to their full height. He stood near to Alison, careful not to touch her, as unnatural as that felt, because he was fearful his touch would be rejected. He nodded at the packed bag and then to the door.

'You should go, Ciara. Alison is right: we need to talk. They have rooms in Daly's or the guesthouse across the street from there.'

Ciara grabbed the knapsack and her coat from the arm of a nearby chair. She didn't look at either of them as she left, stifling the desire for a backward glance. Her face was reddening with an anger and distress that she wanted neither of them to witness.

Alison dropped her head to her chest when the door closed, knowing instinctively that nothing would ever be the same again.

Part Two

You'll never be the sun
Turning in the sky
And you won't be the moon above us
On a moonlit night
And you won't be the stars in heaven
Although they burn so bright
But even on the deepest ocean
You will be the light

'Never Be The Sun', Donagh Long

Chapter Twenty

Caharoe 2005

The postcards from Cathy and Richard Shepherd wallpapered the fridge, so frequent was their arrival, and the very sight of them made Alison smile. Dan and she had packed them off to France six months before and it seemed as if they had taken to their semi-retirement with gusto. They were working their way through the picturesque villages of Brittany but poor weather, much the same as they had hoped to leave behind them in Caharoe, had persuaded them that further south, where sunshine was guaranteed, might well be where they would buy a place.

Her father had worried about the surgery and leaving Dan to handle a huge patient list on his own. After so many years at the helm of his own practice he was finding it immeasurably more difficult than Cathy to make the break. Freedom for herself and her husband to relax more and see a different life, and freedom for Dan and Alison to turn Michaelmas into truly their own: these were the things that she had craved and had, with remarkable determination, finally brought to fruition.

'For God's sake, Richard, that's what locum agencies are for and if you get fairly comfortable sitting out on the deck and tasting all that wine sure we can look at hiring someone permanently and letting you and Cathy relax a bit more.' Dan had reassured Richard over and over again that everything would be perfectly fine in his absence but he knew his father-in-law would still need to be shoved out the door of Michaelmas the morning they were due to depart for France.

If truth be told Dan was relishing getting the practice to himself and giving it a big overhaul. It was over a decade since he had taken up the junior GP post at his father-in-law's practice and although Richard had been incredibly supportive (he and Cathy had even moved out to a smaller house on Earl Street so Alison and Dan could make Michaelmas House their own after they got married) he had a niggling feeling that he would always be the minor partner while Richard was still coming in every day. Alison agreed that her parents needed a break from the surgery and that Michaelmas might need a respite from their vigilant supervision too.

'The place could do with a good shake-up. Some of those *House and Home* magazines in the waiting room are probably fit to move on to the museum in Cork. You should make it your own, Dan, because you have served your time long enough.'

In the end Richard's common sense prevailed and he agreed with the temporary move to France on a trial basis. Cathy Shepherd's threat to divorce him if he didn't get on the ferry probably played a substantial part also.

Con Abernethy visited his son and his family intermittently because Dan resolutely refused to make the trip to Leachlara under any circumstances. He had not been back since the night of his mother's funeral: nothing had tempted him in the intervening years, not even Con Abernethy's hangdog expression every time he met him in Dublin or in Caharoe or beyond. He was on such a visit now and the usual whining had begun.

'I'm getting old, you know, Dan. Soon I won't be able to travel and you will have to come to me.'

'Listen, Dad, you might have resigned from the Daíl but you're hale and hearty enough to zip it around to football matches and race meetings with Columbo and the lads, putting down bets and knocking back the drink. I'd say there's years of life in the old dog yet!'

'And what about when I can't make it to see you and Alison and young Lucy? Will you just leave me in Leachlara to rot away in my old age?'

'I am tired of telling you to sell that blasted house. We both hate it and it has no sentimental value whatsoever. Sell it and enjoy the money. Some big shot from Dublin would fall on it if it were put up for sale. You could buy a smaller place somewhere closer to us. Alison has even said there is space for you to move in here. We could convert some of the basement into a granddad flat but to be honest my wife's goodwill runs away with her at times. I can't really see you up at the Caharoe Senior Citizens' lunch days or whiling away the hours playing whist at Lovett's but there are lots of worse places than Caharoe and Leachlara tops that list in my mind.'

'Your wife, Dan Abernethy, and I hope you know it, is the sweetest woman I have ever met. Imagine her thinking of me moving in here? But I couldn't leave Leachlara. It's too late for big changes for me now.'

'You are right about Ali. She is an absolute treasure and, don't worry, I remember every day when I open my eyes that she is the best thing that ever happened to me.'

'You didn't turn out bad, Dan, do you know that?'

Dan smirked at his father, who was silently congratulating himself for a son well raised. 'It must have been all those parenting courses you and Mam went on that put me on the right track.'

'Impertinence is an awful trait in anyone.' Con did his best to pretend he was annoyed but there was no mistaking the wry smile that played along his lips.

Later, when Alison hauled back the supermarket shopping, Con appeared from the living room, where he had spent the afternoon speculating on racing form, to greet his daughter-in-law back from teaching at the secondary school in Caharoe and his beloved granddaughter home from the primary school on the road out of town where Caharoe drifted into the farmland beyond.

Alison gave him a big hug. Trailing her was a beaming seven-year-old Lucy, helping herself to a punnett of strawberries, her lips and cheeks stained red from her impromptu snack. She offered her granddad the remnants of a few squashed berries from the bottom of the tray along with a welcoming kiss.

'Yerra, pet, you're grand. I will keep my appetite for the gorgeous dinner that I know your mother will be putting together for us.' He winked at Lucy conspiratorially. 'Have you any idea what she's making for us, do you?'

'She's making enchiladas. She says you probably won't like it. She says you will say it's foreign muck and that no one knows how to cook plain food well any more.'

'Lucy Abernethy, I said no such a thing!' Alison was mortified and she looked plaintively at Con in an effort to appease him, but his mirthful expression persuaded her he had taken no offence.

'But you did, Mammy! That's what you said in the supermarket.'

Con did his best to stop laughing. He adored Lucy and how outspoken she was and how it embarrassed her mother.

'Maybe you should scoot up to the living room, Lucy, to do your homework and stop getting me into trouble with your grandfather.'

'OK, but call me when the enchiladas are ready. I'm starving.'

And with that she was gone down the corridor, singing to herself.

'God, that one would hang you out to dry, Con. Anyway, I am very glad Dan persuaded you to stay for dinner, foreign muck or not.'

'Well, it wasn't that hard to persuade me, to be honest. I have something troubling me and I was hoping you and Dan could see a way out of it that I am not managing to see.'

'Sounds ominous. Are you in difficulty? Don't tell me you have lost your shirt at the races.'

'No, nothing like that, and I will thank you to have a little more confidence in my ability to place a clever bet.'

'What is it then that has you so rattled?' Alison was chopping vegetables absent-mindedly, imagining that Con had fallen out with someone in the local in Leachlara or some other little insignificant drama that he could easily be counselled about. After a lifetime of frantic activity she often thought that the burden of time on his hands, to think or be idle, was proving difficult for him to bear. In his case she felt that the gifts that retirement had brought had been mostly unwelcome.

'Do you remember Leda Clancy?'

Alison's knife stilled over the waiting peppers on the chopping board. 'How could I forget her? The Clancys are hard to forget, believe me. They leave a long shadow. Please don't tell me that you have wound yourself up with her again and for God's sake don't tell Dan because he will lose the rag.'

'Look, I haven't seen the girl in almost five years. When I made it plain that I wasn't funding any more extravagances or paying any more of her bills she lost whatever interest she once had. The thing is I have had a threatening phone call from her. She rang the house in Leachlara yesterday, but from a blocked number, so I don't even know from whereabouts she is hurling her little threats. I came here to see if you two could help me deal with her. She has incriminating evidence about my financial affairs that could ruin me. She says it's her insurance policy and that she is calling it in before I croak it. Whatever charm the girl once had, I have to tell you I am failing to see even a fragment of it at the moment and that's for sure.'

'What sort of incriminating evidence? I know you will never be confused with Snow White, but what could Leda know that's so damning and how does she know something that you haven't even told Dan or me about?' Alison had put the knife down on the chopping board and turned her full bristling attention to Con. Her father-in-law had always kept his financial affairs to himself and had never felt compelled to divulge any of the longwinded details to them before now.

'Years ago I bragged to her, like the fecking eejit I was, that I had money loaded up in foreign credit-card accounts. They have been fairly untraceable up until now as anyone looking would presume they would be showing a debit instead of a credit and would not be considered in any list of assets. The thing is the Revenue is smartening up a bit about this sort of thing so I was looking to clean up my affairs a little bit, put them beyond question. Leda has all the credit-card numbers, the banks they were issued from and the countries in which they are held. That's what she now says is her insurance policy. She says there will be some wing of some tribunal interested in my tucked-away money and she's dead right, Alison. They would be down on me like a ton of bricks. It wouldn't matter that I am finished with politics either, it would still be news. I didn't do anything that most of the rest of them weren't doing, you know. You could fit the truly straight crowd in Leinster House into a phone box, but I am unfortunate enough to have Leda ready, willing and able to blow the whistle.'

'Have you told Dan any of this?'

'No. He will be furious because he warned me about Leda. You both did but to be honest I had no idea that she knew specific details about my accounts.'

'How did she get the information? How could she know stuff that you wouldn't confide to your own son?'

'It's not that I wouldn't confide in Dan but he has always acted like he didn't want to know any of the details of my business. He feels, and he is probably right, that money caused untold damage between his mother and myself. You must realize that it's all for Dan's and your benefit in the end. Every penny of it will go to you both and little Lucy to do with what you will.'

'Oh, Con, I'm not asking after your money, for God's sake. It's just that I know that Leda takes advantage of people, that's all, and I wish you hadn't allowed her to do that to you. We'll have to tell Dan the minute he finishes upstairs at the surgery.'

For all her annoyance with Con for his foolishness Alison would have to admit that he was right about Dan's lack of interest in his money or his business affairs. Dan hated to think about it and whatever relationship he had with his father was based on very limited knowledge of what he imagined were reams of crooked dealings. Money had poisoned his parents' marriage, seeping into the very veins of it, suffocating all other forms of communication. Dan had decided to quench it as a subject open for discussion between himself and his father. Without its influence he felt more comfortable in their relationship. Alison had respected that wish until now, when Leda Clancy had come calling for what was not hers.

Con was sitting on one of her mother's old kitchen chairs with his tall frame hunched over, deeply preoccupied. Looking at him, his daughter-in-law could still honestly say that he would pass for a man at least ten years younger. He was as sharp-suited as ever. His love of good tailoring had endured and the fact that middle age had not added an ounce to his lean frame meant that the bespoke suits he had invested in for his political career still fitted and gave him the air of someone on important business.

Alison left the dinner preparation aside and poured them two coffees from the jug that Dan had brewed at lunchtime. He was her husband's father and she loved him. He deserved a little dose of pity with the interrogation she had subjected him to and she felt remiss for being so harsh on him.

'Have a drink of that, Con, and get it all off your chest.' Dinner could wait.

Con took the mug from her and smiled gratefully. 'I was only saying to Dan earlier that you are the best in the world.'

'Oh, I remind him of that fact frequently, don't worry. Can't have him taking me for granted. Now switch off the charm and turn on the facts until I see what we are really dealing with.'

'After Mary died I gave Leda the run of the house in Leachlara. I gave her a key too so she could let herself in if I wasn't around. You and Dan never came to visit after the funeral so I suppose I didn't see the harm. Otherwise I would be rattling around the place meeting ghosts around corners. She used to call there when she was home from Dublin, said it was more comfortable than going home to the Clancys' place, and now that wouldn't be hard.'

'I bet the little wagon couldn't believe her luck.' Alison's derisory tone increased Con's discomfort by several notches. To think he had decided that telling her before Dan would soften the blow. He continued because talking gave him some respite from feeling like an old fool, a feeling that had consumed him since he had spoken to Leda the day before.

'Anyway, while she was there it seems she took the opportunity to photocopy anything in my office that she thought might be incriminating and she opened post I had left lying around. The upshot of it now is that she has me in a vice grip. If I give in to her demands I am a hundred grand down straight off, more maybe if she gets greedy. If I don't I could lose the lot when the big guns come snooping. To top it all I really don't trust her to keep her mouth shut even if she gets the money . . .' Con tailed off, knowing from Alison's bewildered expression that she was taken aback by the depth and breadth of his stupidity.

'What do you think he should do?' Alison and Dan were at the kitchen sink putting the last of the dinner dishes into the dishwasher and clearing the kitchen worktops. Con had repaired to the living room to watch the news, thinking it was better to let them discuss him and his crisis alone. Dan had listened silently to his father's account of his misfortune, with Alison filling in any details that the older man forgot or hadn't the stomach to mention. Now Alison was trying to get to the bottom of how her husband felt about Con's little bombshell.

'I think he should find out exactly how much she wants to keep her quiet for good, add a bit and then hopefully a cheque will do the trick.'

'I don't know, Dan. Honestly, it's blackmail and she shouldn't be allowed to get away with it.' Alison, in pleading for a little bit of common sense, was hoping to engender a bit of fight in her husband. After all, Leda Clancy had already gained enough from her liaison with Con Abernethy. She should not be allowed to clean him out, silently and secretly, without anyone showing any resistance. Alison would not even admit to herself that she might be yet feeling the slight of another Clancy who tried to take what was not rightfully hers and had never paid the price.

'Oh, it looks like he has money salted away here, there and everywhere. It's not like he needs it and, as he says, he will lose the lot of it anyway if Leda tips off the Revenue. As far as I'm concerned she is the sort that money talks to so he should give it to her and send her packing. The last thing he needs is this all going public. About all he has left now is the respect of the locals in Leachlara and around there. I think he should suffer the loss of the money to keep safe what matters to him most. I will talk to Hugh or Robert Lalor and see if we can look into putting his affairs on a proper footing. Maybe they could arrange a settlement with Revenue that would see it all sorted for good.'

'Do you not care that it's your family money? That eventually some of it might come to Lucy and that Leda Clancy will be spending what was rightfully your daughter's inheritance? Does any of that bother you?' Alison did her best to keep her tone calm and even. She hated fighting with Dan but his craving for peace at all costs exasperated her.

'Lucy won't need any of my father's money. We will see that she has plenty. She won't need to call on a cent from Leachlara.'

'That's not the point! It would be like someone laying claim to Michaelmas. You or I would not allow that because it belongs to our family. I can't see why you don't want to protect what is rightfully yours from a parasite like Leda.'

'Michaelmas is different, Ali. Your father and mother built this place from scratch. They invested years of themselves and their hard-earned money in the place, just as you and I are doing now. Michaelmas is a source of pride for all of us and I hope Lucy feels that way too when she is older. Whatever my father has accumulated over the years has been done under the cover of dishonesty and abuse of a system whose weaknesses he knew inside out. It's money, and that's all it is, and if it takes a sizeable chunk of it to shut Leda Clancy up then fair enough. If you think about it she paid a fairly high price for hanging out with my father. It's not as if her life blossomed while she was with him.'

Dan put the kettle on to boil and set out the tray with three mugs and a pot for tea. He knew his father would be paying scant attention to the evening news, waiting for their discussion of him to end and the problem-solving to begin.

'What makes you think she will stop at one bite of the cherry? What if she comes back for more and more until it's all gone? I'd say Con will be fairly miserable then, wouldn't you?'

'Maybe you're right, but my instinct about Leda is that she will take the money and run, and run is exactly what I want her to do. The last thing I want is the Clancys back in our lives. I'll see what I can find out about her circumstances. I'll talk to a few people in Leachlara and I will speak to Hugh Lalor. There aren't that many people he can't get the inside track on and I won't have to tell him why I need the information. That's the advantage about being a doctor, people take it that you mean well. Go with me on this one, Alison, please. I will try to sort it out as neatly and as cleanly as possible for all our sakes.'

'OK, whatever you think, but I don't have your faith that this is the last we will hear of her.'

Alison watched him as he left the kitchen. She knew his distaste for conflict would always lead him away from the fray if given half a chance. She wasn't surprised that he wasn't up for a fight. His desire to smooth the waters was one of the strong points of his character but a part of Alison wished that Leda had to deal with someone less honourable than her husband.

Chapter Twenty-One

Colm Lifford cursed the postman every time he arrived at the front door of his solicitor's practice on Bridge Street, Caharoe. Reams of important documents and correspondence were bent, folded and scrunched before being jammed unceremoniously through the letterbox. Their tail end stuck out for the whole street to admire. Colm had tried to talk to Paddy about the state the post was in when it was delivered.

'Any chance, Paddy, you could feed the letters in a few at a time? There's important stuff in there, you know.'

The postman had looked at him sarcastically. 'Do you see these hands, Mr Lifford? Up since half five sorting the post of Caharoe and these feet out since eight delivering it hail, rain and shine. It's not in Dublin you are now, you know. This is a one-man operation and I am heartily sorry if it's not entirely to your satisfaction.'

He walked off with his head in the air leaving Colm standing on the street slightly stunned. There were one or two mornings following that conversation when Paddy obliged, but this morning was typical. Colm crouched on the floor picking up the scattered correspondence and Betty Linehan, the practice secretary, almost fell on top of him as she turned up for work.

'Oh, I see Paddy's been.' She laughed. 'Give it here to me and I will see what can be salvaged.'

'Thanks, Betty, you are a star.'

'Show me you mean it with a big mug of tea.'

'No problem.' Colm smiled and retreated down the gloomy hallway to his office to drop his coat and onward to the kitchen to fuel Betty. As the kettle began to sing he could hear Betty launching into a show tune that would be the soundtrack to their day if Colm could not block it out with the radio. It was a good thing that she was an excellent worker because her singing was next door to unbearable. In it, as in everything else, Betty Linehan was wildly enthusiastic but it took a certain skill to miss *all* the notes. The rising note of the electric kettle did not have a chance against her vocal onslaught. Standing at a miniscule five feet nothing with her cropped head of blond highlights Betty actually looked like Caharoe's answer to Elaine Paige – only bereft of the voice. Colm sugared his tea but left Betty's plain. The woman was high enough.

'You are up at the courthouse all morning and then back here at midday for your appointment with Dan Abernethy,' she breezed, interrupting the singing for one blissful moment.

Colm had moved to Caharoe because it was a growing commuter town and had plenty of new houses and new people who needed legal advice and representation. It offered business potential but crucially it had seemed like a place that was better than any other he knew to raise Tom. His mother had spent summers here as a child and when Colm took it into his head to move from Dublin she had suggested that he consider Caharoe. She came with him and when she saw that the house on the banks of the Bracken River that her family had rented some fifty years before was for sale she thought it a sign from God.

Colm was far less likely to believe that God had taken an

active interest in his decision to move to the country. Lantern Lodge won him over without any divine intervention at all. It was a beautifully renovated farmhouse that nestled with its back to a gentle hill above the river that wound its way with lazy inefficiency through Caharoe. It came with an orchard to the back of the house and two fields that ran along the path of the river. With proper fencing Colm imagined that Tom might like to have a pony there or have friends over to play football. He was looking for a future for them both and Lantern Lodge seemed as if it would suit their needs down to the ground. What was more, his mother was happy with his decision and Iris Lifford's approval was only an intermittent blessing.

Dan Abernethy was part of the in-crowd in Caharoe and was already on the books of Lalor and Son – as were most of the businesspeople of the town. Robert Lalor was rarely out of Lovett's Hotel in the square. There he slapped backs and bought rounds of drinks for people who could well afford their own, acting the big man courting and keeping the business that his father had built in the previous decades. Meanwhile his father Hugh preferred the salubrious and pastoral surroundings of the Mountainacre Golf Club. He was Captain, Life Captain, and God for all Colm knew or cared less about golf.

Colm had been intrigued when he saw Dan's name in the appointment book. Perhaps there was a fracture in the polite society of Caharoe? Well, the meeting would reveal all.

Dan arrived early for his noon appointment. He had arranged a locum for his surgery at Michaelmas House and was anxious to get his business done as soon as possible. Betty had been a little subdued in the moments before he arrived but Colm realized that she was merely taking a deep breath before she smothered Dr Dan with flirtatiousness. Her deference to the GP was mildly amusing at first but soon Colm began to fear she was going to faint with the excitement. She was all of a flap, taking his coat, making him tea. She would surely offer to polish his shoes next or nip up to the house and do a spot of ironing. How was Alison? How was young Lucy?

'All fine, Betty. Thanks for asking.' Dan stood back from the onslaught of her rampant goodwill with an indulgent smile on his handsome face.

'Relax now, Betty. I am here to see this man, about whom I have heard some very complimentary things. Do you think I am in good hands?'

'Oh yes, Dr Dan, you really are. He is so knowledgeable, so polite. Such a lovely little son too, about the same age as Lucy. Sure they are probably in school together.'

Colm could have done without Betty praising him as if he were her favourite nephew, and the mention of his son to a stranger made him feel uneasy. He brought the conversation to a halt by directing Dan to his office. Hanging back, he popped his head inside Betty's door.

'A few moments of deep breathing now, Betty, and take your tongue off the desk. You are drooling all over important contracts and title papers.'

'Oh God, Colm, I just can't help it. Do you not think he is the spit of John F. Kennedy?'

'He looks a bit more vibrant to me, I have to say, a tad more colour in his cheeks, and his suits are a lot sharper. Kennedy was an awful man for the too-short trouser leg, don't you think?'

As he closed the door he could hear Betty warbling into an incredibly dodgy version of 'I've Got You Under My Skin'. Dear God, it was going to be a long day.

Colm found Dan's behaviour at the beginning of the meeting strangely reticent. Colm felt as if he was being sounded out to see if he was fit to handle whatever business Dan had in mind. Certainly Dan was not a man to get straight down to matters when there was opportunity for the soft-soap approach. In fact it turned out to be a lot like an interview and Colm found himself answering questions – about where he had studied law, who had lectured him and under whom he had first practised as a solicitor – that would normally make his protective barriers slam shut in the face of the would-be intruder. Yet the enquiries were delivered in such a friendly fashion that Colm found himself talking about his past quite readily. There was no doubt that Dan Abernethy possessed an easy way in company and conversation; a charismatic touch, Colm remembered Betty saying dreamily. Whatever Betty's fantasies might be, Colm was disarmed by the charm of his new client. Talk moved to the changes in the town since Dan had moved there in the nineties, how it had once lost its young people to Cork City and Dublin but now they were falling over each other to move back to Caharoe and the hundreds of other small towns like it all over the country. Places that once had been seen as remote backwaters to be fled from, inhabited only by the parents of those who had gone and those too young to go, were now thriving. An unimaginable turnaround it seemed to anyone that had experienced the drab eighties, so utterly devoid of promise or prosperity.

'And what made you come here, Dr Abernethy, when you could have picked a practice in Dublin or somewhere with a bit more going on?' Colm realized he had posed the first question of their half-hour conversation. For a solicitor that was quite a long time to be on the receiving end of an interrogation, amiable though it was.

'Dan. Call me Dan, please. A woman of course. What takes any man anywhere, or drives him away, only matters of the heart? Anything else is just incidental detail.'

Colm was struck by how unusually romantic a statement that was for a man to make when career, wealth and competition were the usual pillars of polite conversation. He had, he realized, put Dr Abernethy in the same box as the Lalors and the Lovetts and all the other old families of Caharoe who drank together, dined out in all the best restaurants in the city and trundled a well-worn path to the clubhouse at the golf course. He had discounted that group because he felt that they tried to keep the ordinary townspeople as well as newcomers like himself at arm's length, holding themselves up as some class of aristocracy that he found laughable. He felt he had been prejudiced, a trait that he detested in anyone. Dan continued unaware that Colm was chiding himself for his misjudgement.

'I met a girl from Caharoe in a coffee shop on Camden Street that I always haunted in between lectures. Sometimes when I was ducking college it was a good place to go to consider not being a doctor at all. It was a million miles away from medicine, though come to think of it I could easily have done all my microbiology experiments in the toilets. Sweet Jesus, they were disgusting.'

Colm smiled and Dan was encouraged to continue.

'It's not there now, of course, not since the street got smartened up and the old traders who kept the place alive could no longer afford the new rents. The Daisy May went the way of the rest of them. Well, anyway, I met Alison Shepherd there. My head was turned and the rest has followed on. Caharoe is my home now more than anywhere else I have ever been. It's not a bad spot and I am fond of it for making me feel like I could stay. It's an incredible gift when a place allows you in and doesn't ask too many questions in the process, don't you think?'

Colm shifted a little uncomfortably. He too had enjoyed the quiet hospitality of this new town, although he didn't doubt that enquiries were made when his back was turned.

Dan moved forward a little in his chair and Colm took the signal from his client that the personal bit, however beguilingly intended, was over and it was on to business. He was wrong. Dan had merely completed the overture; he was just about to disclose the real intention at its heart.

'What about Leda, Colm? Tell me what happened to Leda.'

Outside, Betty's singing subsided and a peaceful hum settled over the offices as she went about her work: answering phones, organizing the diary and seeing to the reams of title-transfer work that had become the backbone of Colm's practice. She momentarily forgot that the object of her infatuation was a mere two doors down the corridor sipping tea from her mug with the red roses. She could not have imagined that Tom's absent mother was the topic of conversation.

Leda. Colm had never even disclosed her name.

Chapter Twenty-Two

The ensuing shocked silence from Colm gave Dan ample opportunity to outline why he needed to know Leda's address, telephone number and any other details that her estranged partner and father of her child might know about her. His father was in danger of public humiliation and he wanted to avert that at all costs. The story rolled from him fluently and he forgot for a moment that none of it interested Colm that much other than what way, if any, it might affect his son or himself.

'How did you know she was Tom's mother? I have told no one here Leda's name. My mother knew of her, and some of the people I worked with in Dublin, but no one else. I need to know who told you.'

'Birth records are not that hard to track down, and your name and profession listed there seemed to be too much of a coincidence. You can rest assured it is of no real interest to me who the mother of your child is and no one will hear the details from me, but I do need to find Leda and let her know that my father is not alone in this. The public shame of this coming out now would destroy him, so I need to contact Leda myself and talk some sense into her. I will make a deal with her because I honestly think she is not without a certain grievance. My father did not treat her well and she was young and deserved better. Although I have to say the experience seems not to have cowed her.'

'So your father is the nameless politician that she had her affair with? I was never that interested in politics, but Betty, your number-one fan out there in the lobby, has filled me in on your illustrious parentage. I just never put two and two together. Didn't want to, I suppose. Nothing that Leda did then or now interests me.' Colm's attempt at nonchalance was lacking conviction. Dan felt sure that the break-up of their relationship was still troubling him in ways he was unprepared to disclose, but Dan was happy to agree that it was none of his business.

'Leda was in an on-off relationship with my father from the time she was about seventeen. I am not sure when it finished, to be honest, but I think a lot of people suspected it around Leachlara, where we come from. They would never say it to me, of course, and that suited me. I found the whole thing revolting and I told my father as much. Politics is full of little scandals threatening to reveal themselves. It seems to be what the whole thing thrives on. Leda has got in on the act and has decided to sink my father's reputation if he doesn't pay her a substantial sum of money.'

'Leda never told me much about herself and I learned that the truth was an entirely optional extra in her account of things. Anything I know about her that I believe to be true I found out from her sister, Ciara. She mentioned a politician but I never pressed her for details.'

It had all been going Dan's way up until now, but the mention of Ciara threatened to throw him off balance. His brief loss of composure did not go unnoticed by Colm but he remained preoccupied by what all this might mean for him and Tom and the life they were slowly but surely building in Caharoe.

'Ciara Clancy was a friend of my wife's in college. They have lost touch somewhat. I had no idea that you would know Ciara too. Leda and Ciara generally didn't keep the same company. As far as I remember they never really got on.'

'I have no direct dealings with Leda any more. Ciara is the only connection between us. You are right, they don't get on, but Ciara makes it her business to keep tabs on Leda's whereabouts. She has been very good to Tom and so I hold her in far higher regard than I do his mother. I will talk to Ciara and see what I can find out.'

'Thanks, Colm. A phone number or an address would be perfect. I hope you don't think that I speak out of turn when I say that you and your boy are a good deal better off without Leda, but that's just my opinion.'

Dan picked up his bag where he had placed it by the side of his chair. An awkward atmosphere hung between them. They were strangers who had exchanged their secrets with none of the comfort of anonymity that make such confessions fluent. Colm had one more question he had to ask.

'If your wife and yourself know Ciara you could have just asked her to put you in touch with Leda. Besides, Ciara would probably have tried to talk some sense into Leda. Why involve me? Why go trawling through where you don't belong? The direct route would surely have been easier for all of us.'

Dan empathized with Colm's distaste for people knowing his business and forgave the edge of annoyance in his voice. 'Just as you want nothing to do with Leda, Colm, we don't really want to get in touch with Ciara again. Perhaps we can respect each other's motives without understanding the reasons behind them. I would be grateful for your assistance and I won't bother you again unless I move the practice business from Lalors – although that is unlikely at this stage. The Lalors have been involved in Michaelmas since Alison's parents started up. As far as I can see they have not put a foot wrong but I wish you well,

Colm. There is lots going on in Caharoe now for the two of you to have plenty to do.'

'The practice is doing just fine. I will be in touch with Leda's details whenever I get hold of them from Ciara.' They shook hands, and Colm regretted the defensive tone in his voice, which he was sure had betrayed his anxiety. By contrast Dan Abernethy left the office relaxed and largely impervious to the swoon of Betty Linehan as she showed him to the door with a theatrical flourish.

'I think he might have found the door unaccompanied, Betty, seeing as we have only the one.' Colm eyed Betty impatiently, but she was in another world and his sarcasm was wasted.

'Oh, I do hope we will be seeing a lot more of him, Colm. You should offer your services at a reduced rate, him being the town GP and all.'

'I think if you want to see Dr Abernethy again you will have to take yourself off to the surgery. We have very little to offer him here.'

Colm tried to concentrate on his work after Dan had left but it was impossible for him to direct his mind elsewhere. He popped off an email to Ciara, as casually as he could manage, asking for Leda's details. He made it clear that he didn't intend to contact her but the family GP had advised him that it would be prudent to have Tom's mother's contact details in case of a medical emergency. He didn't feel a shred of loyalty to Leda as he gave the false reason for his request. Leda had long ago shown that she could look after herself. As he pressed send he wondered if Ciara's reluctance to visit them in Caharoe was linked to her knowing the Abernethys. Ever since they had moved to Cork Ciara had pleaded that work commitments in London prevented her from making a visit, and so he and Tom met her in Dublin for day-long visits after which she flew home and they moved on to spend the night with his mother in

Grosvenor Gardens. He waited for a response for a few minutes and it came, as Ciara was never far from her laptop.

> Hi Colm,
> It's 28 Seabury Crescent, Sandymount, Dublin 4. Apparently she has found the man of her dreams, a stockbroker (rich of course). Bob Cantwell I think his name is. Engaged. Wedding to follow in Mauritius by all accounts. Anyway it looks as if Sis has landed on her feet again, as usual.
> Love to Tom, will ring on Fri as normal,
> C
> PS. How useful do you think Leda would actually be in a medical emergency?!!

Needing to clear his head he rang Mrs Timmons, Tom's childminder, to tell her that he would pick Tom up at the school gate at 2 p.m. and drop him home to her at Lantern Lodge. Distraction, in the person of his five-year-old whirlwind of a son, was exactly what he needed to keep the morning's events from preoccupying him solely for the rest of the day.

Chapter Twenty-Three

Dublin 1999

'It's a boy. Good God, he is tiny.' Colm Lifford was beaming, overjoyed and terrified he was going to cry and make a fool of himself. He thought his heart was going to break open. Leda was lying there stunned and not saying anything at all. 'You did great, pet, absolutely brilliant. I am so proud of you! Wait until you get a proper look at him, he is amazing.' Colm was gushing. He could not help it. He followed the midwife to the resuscitation area at the side of the delivery room. He watched entranced as his little son was checked, weighed and wrapped in a hospital blanket that had swaddled thousands of other babies in their first minutes.

'Six pounds and seven ounces. That's a grand healthy weight,' the midwife said as she plonked the screaming purple baby on Leda's chest.

Leda was exhausted, barely able to focus on the little sparrow-like creature that had somehow attached himself to her. The room began to shudder around her, the bright lights swimming towards her and then away, making her dizzy. The huge metal light fitting over the bed seemed as if it was going to plunge down on top of her. She thought she might pass out or vomit or both. Colm was gazing at her and the baby. She felt his eyes upon her, upon them both, but she did not dare to take them on. She looked straight ahead at the clock on the wall opposite the bed. Quarter past five. Dawn was breaking for the second time without any rest. Not to mention the last six weeks of broken sleep as she rolled her alien, misshapen body around the bed in futile attempts at rest. No wonder I feel like crap, she thought. A day and most of a night filled with instructions, warm and good-natured, but instructions nonetheless: 'Walk it out . . . Change position . . . Try the gas . . . Don't push. Not yet . . . Not until I say so . . . Push now . . . Harder, Leda . . . Push harder . . .'

The midwives had been lovely to them since the first moment they had arrived, breathless, distressed and terrified. Leda was suffocated by a rising panic, an absolutely ridiculous urge to run away. Colm held her hand tightly as if he sensed that she would rather be anywhere else in the world than in the place she would finally meet her baby. It gripped her now again as the unfurling baby lodged on her chest gave voice to another piercing wail. She needed to be alone, badly. She wanted to wash and sleep in darkness and silence. Alone. No Colm. No baby. Leda looked at Polly, the kindest of the midwives, silently begging for her assistance.

Polly perched herself next to Leda on the bed and whispered in soft tones to the baby, trying to calm him down. She often witnessed this, a new mother so overwhelmed by a difficult birth, so shocked by the pain and the intensity of the experience that she was at a loss to respond to her new baby's needs. She nodded to Colm to sit down. When Leda stole a look at him she saw pure delight in all his features. He was thrilled and it showed. She turned to the midwife before he could see that her expression was vacant and wanting. Colm was oblivious.

The ocean in front of him was pure and clear and he had dived straight in.

'Do you want me to help you latch him on? It's a good idea to get this first feed in more or less immediately,' Polly offered as helpfully as she could. Leda didn't answer and Polly took her silence as acquiescence and began to manipulate her breast into the baby's mouth. The baby tugged at her nipple, attempting to feed. It didn't feel anything like Leda had expected. She didn't flood with emotion as the book that Colm had bought said she might. She didn't feel like herself any more. She was rooted to the spot against her will. The need to flee burned itself inside her while simultaneously she reconciled herself to staying put.

Colm raced from the Reilly & Maitland offices on Baggot Street as soon as he could the next evening. The last meeting had dragged on despite his best efforts to wrap it up early. The client was notoriously long-winded and Colm had been fit to strangle him as each convoluted and superfluous point was made. He didn't tell him that he had a baby son and girlfriend to see in the Rotunda because he didn't want to spoil the most amazing thing that had ever happened to him by sharing it with this windbag.

When he finally ushered the client out of the office at quarter to six he paused only to grab his brief bag and lock up the office door. It was pointless hailing a taxi. With the traffic at this hour of the evening he would be quicker walking. He sprinted for a while but then, as he picked up flowers for Leda, a little bear from a newsagent's on Westmoreland Street for the baby and some of Leda's favourite chocolate bars, he slowed down, enjoying the gentle stroll of anticipation. Buses roared over O'Connell Bridge, belching their fumes and noise into the air of a remarkably still and gentle October evening. Colm fell into the swell of people waiting for the pedestrian lights to change at Aston Quay. The rhythm of the crowd suited his mood, the noise, the jostling for better position, the rustle of bags and bodies united by the inexorable pull of home. He covered the last steps of the journey to the Rotunda infused with a settling sense of belonging.

Leda, the pregnancy that she had concealed for so long, and now the baby had all been such a huge shock to his well-ordered and planned life. Since he had left college everything had been about building a career, getting on in life and eventually making a success of his own practice. He would not and could not live in the shadow of his father's business ruin for ever.

'Keep your head high, Colm. Head high,' had been his mother's mantra when Patrick Lifford's hastily built and shoddily run business empire imploded in disgrace in the late eighties. It had all been bluster. Massive deals in the pipeline that had never even been close to being pulled off. Grandiose development plans that looked incredibly impressive on paper in times when everything was decidedly lacklustre but never amounted to anything. Patrick Lifford had charm, brass neck and a barrowful of guts. What he didn't have when it all blew up in his face was a penny of his investors' money. It had all gone on entertaining other potential investors and creating the image of a wealthy property developer on the up. When the house was searched for incriminating papers that would detail secret money trails only cheque stubs and bills were found. There was no secret stash salted away and no assets to confiscate except the house the family had moved to a few months previously.

Colm's memory of his mother's face as her home was raided came back to him as he reached the doors of the Rotunda. Ashen and subdued, she had fought back tears, railing at the impending disaster with every shred of her being but managing only a silent protest. She did not look to her husband for explanation or for protection from the nightmare. Colm had tried to catch his father's eye but to no avail. Skulking by the elegant marble fireplace, puffing on a huge cigar, Patrick Lifford looked brazen and unbowed by the early-morning invasion. He oozed disdain for the legal process that was gathering its preliminary evidence in his family's home. Colm thought much later that his father had surely known for weeks that his game of toss and shuffle with other people's money was coming to an end. Maybe he thought they would be able to keep the house because surely no judge would be so cruel as to toss the deserted wife and dependent son on to the street when it was obvious that she was not complicit in her husband's dishonest business dealings. Perhaps he didn't think of his family at all before he filled his suit pockets with stones and walked into the sea, leaving them both for good.

Colm's own chance at fatherhood was coming absolutely out of the blue. It wouldn't take much effort to outshine Patrick Lifford's paternal record and he willed himself to do better for his son, to be present always, whatever that might entail.

Colm took the three flights of stairs as a gaggle of people had congregated outside the lifts and he wanted to see Leda and the baby as soon as he could. He had been thinking of names. He had made a list to show Leda. They should call him something soon, shouldn't they? He would have to be registered. So much to do, so much to sort out, but even that thought added to rather than detracted from his happiness.

Polly was at the nurse's station when he got to the second floor out of breath from the sprint up the stairs. She was cradling an infant in the crook of her neck while she looked through a patient file with her free hand. She smiled. 'Here's Daddy now.' Colm had pictured his son several times during the day either lying in one of the clear plastic cribs by Leda's bed or wrapped in her arms. Somehow it didn't feel right that he was less than two days old and he was already in the care of a stranger – capable as that stranger undoubtedly was.

'Where's Leda?' Colm asked, more than a little panicked.

'Leda is just a bit overwhelmed. Exhausted really, I suppose, and she was sleeping through today when this little chap was crying so we thought it best to give her a little time to get some energy back. We will just bring him to her when he needs to feed. Luckily enough the wards are quiet tonight. It seems the stork is taking a little bit of a kip so we can have him up here with us.'

'Well, now that I am here can I take him for a while?'

'Absolutely. We were hoping that you would come in tonight but Leda said you were in court all day and could not be contacted.'

'That's ridiculous. I have no court duties this week. She knows that and she knows my mobile number. I could have been here hours ago. I could have arranged things, cancelled appointments or got them covered by one of the others . . .' His voice trailed off in exasperation.

Polly smiled. It seemed daft that Leda would not want to talk to her boyfriend the day after she had given birth to their child. All the older midwives were fond of saying that no two babies were the same. They would repeat it ad nauseam to explain anything that happened in the labour ward. Polly was beginning to think that the babies weren't generally the problem but some of the mothers were a rare bunch indeed.

'Well, maybe Leda got confused,' Polly said, although she doubted that she sounded any more convinced than she felt. He has landed himself a cold fish, she thought as she watched Colm deposit his belongings on the tubular chair across from the nurses' station. The flowers, teddy bear and the massive bars of chocolate, the stock deliveries of the new father, lay with the brief bag in an abandoned heap.

Polly expertly handed her tiny charge to a petrified Colm. He had never held a newborn. Dear God, don't drop him, he counselled himself, but the little bundle appeared to welcome yet another warm-as-toast body to cling to. He snuggled, yawned and settled into the deep natural pillow of flesh on Colm's chest. His father's amateur skills didn't stop him burrowing for comfort. His initial panic laid to rest, Colm flashed a smile of gratitude to Polly.

'We moved Leda into room three to get her off the ward. You can pop your head around the door; if she is awake she might be glad of the company.'

'I think I will let her sleep for the moment. In fairness, I'm tired too, and all I did was watch her giving birth.'

'Well, his crib is here behind me,' Polly said, motioning to the ad hoc nursery in the rear office of the nurses' station. 'He should need feeding in about two hours.'

'How will I know?' Colm's panic started to rise again.

'Oh, you'll know! He might be the size of a stray kitten but his lungs will put a lion to shame when he wants grub.'

Colm relaxed again, confident that he could keep his baby alive and happy until the next feed. Polly watched his solid frame covering the length of the second floor in relaxed strides with his small bundle of a son tucked cosily against him. She saw all types of men in this job but she would be happier if more of them looked like Colm Lifford. He was tall and broad without being too brawny. He looked good in a shirt and tie but Polly thought he would look even better in casual clothes. His dark hair was cut short and his strong features were softened by a smile that lit his entire face. There was something definitely wrong with the girl in room three if she couldn't appreciate the gorgeous man she had landed herself, Polly thought. She managed one more appreciative glance before the ward sister arrived back to the nurses' station intending to stamp out any idle tendencies in her staff.

Colm noticed the other fathers coming and going as visiting hours proceeded, arriving to mothers sleeping alongside, watching or feeding their babies. Older children whooshed up and down the wards carrying balloons, ecstatic at the long-awaited arrival of a new sibling. He paused outside Leda's room as if he was about to go in. The lights off within and the lack of any obvious sign of life gave him second thoughts and he continued his patrol down the overheated corridor.

Polly opened Leda Clancy's file. Day two was ordinarily too early to start thinking about postnatal depression. The expected baby blues, experienced by the vast majority of first mothers as pregnancy hormones crashed out of the system, had yet to play out. Polly overcame her residual reticence and noted on the file that the young mother may well require special attention. She didn't mention postnatal depression but any of the medical staff on the ward would know what she was alluding to. She had seen many mothers scouring the charts hanging from the foot of their beds to see what the doctors and midwives had said about them, their delivery and their babies. Better be safe than sorry, she thought as she closed the file and headed to the canteen for coffee and chips and a swift fag at the back door.

Chapter Twenty-Four

'I was thinking of Thomas, Tom. Tommy even? What do you think, Leda?'

'Haven't really thought. You choose, Colm. He's yours. You choose.'

'For God's sake, he's yours too; you had him, remember? I just thought Tom is a good solid man's man sort of a name. He's not going to be Patrick anyway, that's for sure. What about your Dad, Leda?' Colm enquired, although he secretly wished that this little boy could start with a new name, nothing begged or stolen from the past.

If Leda heard his enquiry about her father's name she made no attempt to answer. Instead she said: 'Tom is grand. Yeah, Tom Lifford sounds about right.' She might as well have been naming a stray dog, but Colm's interest in little Tom was spilling out of him. Its abundance made up for the want in Leda's reaction. He was chuffed that the surname was not going to be an issue. It's not as if they had had a chance to discuss the details since she'd dropped the time bomb of the pregnancy just weeks before.

Colm had brought their little boy to room three when he

started to squall for his feed, just as Polly had said he would. He knocked first and then thought how ridiculous that was. The baby was hungry; Leda would have to wake up.

Listless. That was the word he used afterwards when anyone asked him how Leda had seemed. He knew what they were doing, of course, asking him to point out for them the clues that he had so blatantly missed. The truth was that Leda's interest in her pregnancy had been minimal to begin with. Colm thought she was so relaxed with the idea because she had lived with the knowledge for seven months before she told him and so had done all the thinking, agonizing and deciding before she saw fit to let him in on the secret. The trip to visit her sister in Spain made sense in retrospect. He thought he had been given the brush-off and wasn't particularly upset: even though he had found Leda attractive and had enjoyed their short relationship he'd never seen her as a permanent fixture in his life. She just hadn't seemed interested in anything long term in all the months he had known her: reluctant even to commit to a concert or dinner date that was anything more than days away. So he was taken aback when his apartment intercom had sounded about six weeks before and he'd heard her voice; and even more shocked when her appearance at his front door revealed an unmistakeable roundness and fullness where before had been the slenderest of waists.

The prospect of a baby had changed everything. He didn't have to think: of course he would do the right thing; Leda would have every kind of support that she needed. He thought they might even make the relationship work. A child was bound to bring them together, wasn't it? He never doubted he was the father of the baby she was carrying. Even though it was a thunderbolt, totally unexpected, somehow the shape of the story seemed to fit something that was missing inside him. How long had she known? Why hadn't she told him before now? The questions kept coming, but Leda soon realized they were not fuelled by any sort of recrimination but an appetite for detail that she sated with as many plausible answers as possible. Her older sister Ciara had lived in a small town close to Barcelona for a few years. She had gone to teach English the summer she finished her degree in Trinity and had never come home for long since then.

Colm listened as Leda described the lovely life Ciara had made for herself in Spain: the little seaside bar and restaurant she ran with José Sanchez with whom she had been living for nearly a year, the sunshine and the languid lifestyle. She seemed entirely more animated by her sister's exotic life in Spain than her own incredible news. Her tone was envious and she was covetous of her sister's carefree life. 'Lucky cow, she got away from the lunatics at home. Never looked back.'

He made Leda promise that she would move into his apartment. She had been staying with her friend Siobhan in Glasnevin since she had returned from Spain, but she agreed with Colm that something more comfortable and suitable for when the baby was born was a good idea. Colm started to plan aloud all the things they needed to do to get sorted. Clear all the junk from the spare room for a start: his lecture notes from a decade before, barely looked at for summer exams, were now practically illegible and thoroughly disposable. Colm didn't venture to talk about after the birth – nothing about Leda's demeanour gave him any encouragement, and so he thought best to leave well alone. There would be plenty of time for plans and discussion when their baby was born. He hadn't counted on Leda shutting down on the world, on Colm and on her son.

The next night in hospital Colm found Leda even more withdrawn than the previous evening. He thought that if she was at home in the apartment she might find things a little easier and so he had asked a very dubious Polly about an early discharge. 'I will mark it as a request on her chart, Colm, but it's up to her consultant in the morning to decide if she is well enough equipped to go home.' He knew by her tone that Polly thought that she was far from ready and Leda's surly behaviour was doing nothing to convince him either.

'I'm not going to feed him any more,' Leda announced as casually as if she had asked him to pass the tissues or the water. Colm looked up from the foot of her bed, where he was making a thorough mess of changing his son's nappy. The bed was covered in a mass of wipes, some soiled, some clean. The dirty nappy lay open, a taunt to the new father's inefficiency. Colm thought he must have misheard her, so addled was he by the enormity of the task before him. 'Sure you'll have to feed him. Poor little devil is starving!'

'They have loads of formula. He can have some of that.'

'But I thought you wanted to feed him yourself. The book says—'

Before Colm could repeat what Miriam Stoppard or another of his recently consulted experts had said about the value of breastfeeding Leda caught up the box of breast pads on the bedside locker and flung them at the door, narrowly missing his head. 'Nobody asked me before they shoved his mouth on to me. I am not a dairy cow and I am not going to feed him. They make formula and he can have that.'

'Jesus, Leda, calm down. I thought you wanted to. You never said, so I presumed.'

'Dead fucking right you presumed. Well, presume this from now on. I do not intend to be at your beck and call, or at his either.' She threw a look at their baby that shocked Colm with its coldness. He finished the nappy change as quickly as he could and managed to re-dress the baby in much the same arrangement as he had found him. A few poppers were probably still undone but his son looked fairly content. All the saliva in Colm's mouth had dried and it was an effort for him to find the words to address Leda.

'Look, this little lad is depending on us. I don't suppose it matters what he eats as long as he is not hungry.'

'Exactly what I was saying.'

'I'll find Polly or one of the other nurses and say you've changed your mind.'

'I was never fucking asked in the first place.'

'Jesus, Leda, will you forget about yourself for a minute and concentrate on this little baby? He needs us to think about him.'

Leda resettled the covers around her, straightening out her legs the length of the bed where her baby had just been lying. He chose not to look at her again before he left the room with his son in the crook of his arm. Colm knew his son was too young to look like anybody but he was overwhelmed by the sense of recognition that filled him as he gazed down at the little boy's blue, unfocused eyes. Polly set him up with countless bottles of formula and did the first feed with him until he saw how easy it was and how little there was to be terrified of. She didn't seem too surprised that Leda had forgone her attempts at breastfeeding. 'Maybe it's for the best, especially if she is that tired.'

'Oh, I know he won't be hungry, it's just that she doesn't seem to be responding to him at all. I'm not sure what's normal but her reaction to him feels so wrong. I just want him to be OK, you know.' He paused. He had never felt comfortable communicating his feelings and he felt plain stupid now for opening up to a stranger. He was tired. Tiredness makes you do stupid things, he reasoned. He hadn't counted on Polly's kindness or the fact that her heart went out to him and his little baby.

'Listen, babies want to thrive. It's their nature. You keep doing what you are doing and he will be grand. Leda will come round, you'll see.'

Colm nodded gratefully, afraid his voice would betray him if he attempted to respond.

'Have you thought of a name yet?' Polly asked breezily, changing the topic.

'We've decided on Tom,' Colm said, trading the first secret of his little boy's life with someone he hadn't even met three days ago. The thought made him guilty. It really was time he told his mother that she was a grandmother. Polly was saying how much she liked the name, what a grand solid little name it was. Colm was nodding, pleased that she liked his choice, but really he was thinking of and dreading the phone call to Iris Lifford. Where to begin? How would he field the litany of questions that would roll like unrelenting gunfire down the phone, each one designed to annihilate its target? The mere thought exhausted him. He looked down at Tom dozing after a mammoth feed and decided it was much too late to ring tonight. He would rather spend the next few hours here with his son before he handed him back to Polly. The light in room three remained off and Polly noticed that Colm did not even look in its direction as he gathered his brief bag and coat and wandered out from beneath the harsh lights of the hospital into the open anonymous space of a Dublin night.

Chapter Twenty-Five

The onset of winter irritated every ounce of Iris Lifford's being. All that darkness, cold and rain, not to mention the glare of orange street lamps from early evening, made serious inroads in her otherwise relentlessly optimistic nature. It was impossible to keep the hallway dry and even the simplest trip to the shed for timber to light the living-room fire meant changing into boots and donning a scarf and coat. Her garden, so neatly manicured in spring and summer, and even rather glorious in autumn, lost all its power to please her as leaves shed for the winter descended into damp sludge on her paths and lawn. Colm usually rang from the offices of Reilly & Maitland to check on his mother in between meetings with clients. He was a good and attentive son who made sure that his mother never wanted for anything, financial or practical. If a drain was blocked or a gutter overflowing Colm would make sure that someone came to fix it and Iris never received a bill for any of the work. She was proud that she had raised a kind and gentle son. He was the best thing that she had done in her life. She was grateful that the horrible business with her husband's financial dealings had not sunk them. With the help of a handful of loyal friends and relatives they had picked up the broken pieces and turned their backs on the disgrace of Patrick Lifford's memory. Colm seemed to be doing well at his legal career and though Iris hoped he would make partner at Reilly & Maitland she had stopped mentioning the prospect to Colm. Her ambition on his behalf irritated him so she kept quiet, but she couldn't stop herself willing it to happen.

She was polishing the brass fittings on her hall door when the early-morning phone call came. A grandson? Did Colm just say a grandson? Maybe it was time to take the hearing aid that nice doctor had given her out of the cupboard. There was only so long that she could deny that she was only hearing the odd word here and there and imagining the rest. Colm raised his voice and delivered the message more vehemently.

'I know it's sudden, Mam. To tell you the truth I've only known that Leda was pregnant for about six weeks and then she went into labour early and I just never got the chance . . .' His voice tailed off and, given a modicum of leeway, Iris was like an animal sprung from a trap.

'And just who is Leda, Colm?'

'She is my girlfriend. Well, *was* my girlfriend for a few months at the start of the year. It wasn't serious but she got pregnant and now . . . well, now we have a baby. His name is Tom.'

'Well, I suppose I should be honoured that you got round to telling me at all.'

'I was trying to get my head round it myself, Mam. I didn't mean not to tell you. It wasn't deliberate. He is gorgeous. Just wait until you see him.'

Colm's effort at softening Iris worked somewhat.

'I would quite like to see him if that wouldn't be too much trouble to you and – what did you say her name was? Leda?'

'Come over to the apartment, you can see him now. He is home from hospital. They discharge very quickly these days,'

Colm added, knowing how pathetically inadequate he must sound.

He knew his mother's feelings were hurt but he had bigger problems on his hands. She would have to take her place in the queue for satisfaction behind Harry Reilly of Reilly & Maitland who was already firmly on the warpath. Unsolicited leave was frowned upon. In fact, even leave of the totally above-board kind was considered an absolute nuisance. Harry sounded as if he had adhered himself to the ceiling with disbelieving rage when Colm had rung that morning to announce that he would not be in that day and might not be in all week in fact. A baby son, whom he had neglected to tell anyone about, was the elaborate excuse. Well, you had to hand it to him for originality, Harry thought gruffly as he slammed the phone down on Colm.

An irate boss and a mother whose nose was out of joint were, however, falling down the list of worries occupying Colm. To those minor irritations he could now add the fact that Leda was, to all intents and purposes, missing. She had fled the apartment the very minute Colm had come back from work the evening before.

'I have to get out of here or I will explode. I need air and not to be here listening to him crying,' she said, tossing her head in the direction of Tom's Moses basket.

'When will you be back?' Colm asked, but if Leda answered from beyond the slammed door Tom's cries drowned it out.

Dear Jesus, he didn't even know when she had last fed him. Maybe Tom's cries were hunger but the stench that rose from the basket revealed that a change of nappy might be the best bet. Now some twelve hours later, having changed five nappies, given four bottles and had so little sleep that he thought his eyelids were about to go on strike, Colm was allowing himself to panic. Where was she? What if she didn't come back? How would he and Tom manage? From his perch on the couch he watched his son gurgle contentedly in his sleep and his own body gave in to the pure exhaustion that overwhelmed him.

Iris let herself into Colm's apartment with the key she kept for an emergency. She didn't approve of the area where her son had bought his apartment, thinking it a little rough, even though she had to admit the apartments were in themselves quite beautiful. She had avoided visiting as much as possible, preferring her son to come home to her instead.

Today was different, to say the very least of it. She had spent the duration of the uncomfortable bus journey from the city centre in a heady flux of exasperation and anticipation. Colm had thrown a bombshell and she wasn't sure if her temper or delight was going to win through, but as the bus neared the stop closest to Colm's apartment the butterflies that unsettled her stomach gave some indication of the softness of heart that Iris Lifford had spent years doing her best to hide.

She picked her way through the babycare shop and supermarket shopping bags that littered his hallway. Nappies, babygros still in their packets and baby bottles peeked from their packaging. There was even a clothes airer with some vests and blue baby blankets strewn at random on its rails. She followed the cries to the kitchen and she got the first glimpse of a small red-faced infant squirming and squalling on Colm's shoulder. Her son was struggling with the sterilizer. The steam burned his hands as he wrestled the scalding bottles from their heated cauldron. She dropped her bag and her hands reached instinctively for the brand-new little person that would, she dared to hope, look utterly familiar.

Colm was relieved at the way his mother wrapped herself up in Tom, expertly giving him his bottle and patiently winding him as if she had had recent practice. For her part Iris was glad that Leda had been asleep when she arrived. Good manners may have dictated that she be up to meet her child's grandmother, particularly in these most irregular circumstances, but Iris had to admit that she relished the chance to have Tom to herself. There would be time enough to meet and analyse this Leda woman who had insinuated herself into her son's life and home. Once she had jotted down a feeding schedule from Colm and packed him off to bed to catch up on some missed sleep, Iris turned her attention to the shoddy state of the apartment. She noticed it had gone distinctly downhill since her last visit six or so months before. Colm had always sent his clothes out for laundering and ironing, an extravagance that the extraordinarily houseproud and parsimonious Iris could never condone. She poked her head into the washing machine while Tom slept and found the undisturbed manual and some detergent tablets. Time to put you into active service, she thought as she scoured the apartment, picking up dirty baby vests, bibs, sheets and tea towels that lurked in heaps on every chair and on the table and even on the floor (she discovered with disapproval). With one load washing and another gathered and waiting, Iris went to sort out the assorted babycare debris that she had passed in the hallway.

It became clear that someone without a single clue about what babies needed had gone on some kind of hormonal rampage in Mothercare. She was anxious not to judge Leda before they met but honestly this was insane. Apart from the ridiculous amount, twenty-three to be precise, of newborn babygros and fifteen vests, there were at least another half-dozen bottles, not counting the full set that Iris had just arranged, six ounces of formula apiece, in a neat line on the door of Colm's otherwise empty fridge. She abhorred the waste and the mess, but she had to admit she was relishing the chance to sort it all out.

First she unwrapped from the booty what she thought her grandson might feasibly need. It was a neat pile. Then she put together a bag of returns for Mothercare. She would take them back herself and exchange them for bigger sizes. They were bound to be understanding and probably still amused at the new mother who had bought them out of every tiny infant size that they had in stock. Receipts tumbled out on to the ground. She was puzzled at the fact that it was Colm who had signed for all the purchases. If he was there could he not have talked some common sense into Leda? She was, she had to admit, somewhat disappointed that Colm seemed to have inherited none of her sense of prudence.

The phone ringing jolted her out of her zealous bout of housekeeping. She was annoyed at herself because she had meant to take it off the hook so as not to interrupt the sleeping house. She pounced on its third ring without pausing to allow the caller to greet her.

'Good morning. This is Colm Lifford's phone. I am afraid he is unavailable at the moment but I can take a message.'

The spiky formality, when she had been expecting Colm's calm and understanding voice, made Leda think about hanging up. Had he patched the apartment phone through to Reilly & Maitland? This sounded a bit like one of the nosy crew at the office reception desk, an unfriendly bunch she remembered from the short weeks that she had temped there.

'Who is this?' Leda asked with rising irritation.

'This is Mrs Iris Lifford, Colm's mother, and who may I ask is this?'

'I'm a friend of Colm's and I need to talk to him straight away.'

'Well, that won't be possible, I'm afraid. As I said, he is unavailable.'

'Look, this is Leda Clancy. I need to talk to him about Tom.'

'Did you say Leda? I understood from Colm that you were asleep here in the apartment!'

'I'm staying with a friend for a while, not that it's any of your business. Now *can* I speak to Colm?'

'Listen here. If it has to do with my son and my grandson then it's one hundred per cent my business. I'll thank you not to take that tone with me, young lady.'

'Just get Colm, will you?' Leda snapped.

Iris put the phone down and took a deep breath. It looked as if Colm was still being incredibly tight-fisted with the truth. She knocked on her son's bedroom door and she heard his progress as he shuffled towards the kitchen. His clothes were wrinkled and he looked immeasurably worse than when he had gone to bed some hours before.

'Mam, is it Tom? Is he OK?'

'Tom is fine, Colm. It would appear that the mother of your child is on the other end of the phone and not here in this apartment, recovering from a sleepless night. Perhaps when you have finished speaking to her you might fill your mother in on any details you may have omitted. I do not appreciate being taken for a fool.'

Chapter Twenty-Six

There was only one thing worse than not knowing all the facts of a situation and that, Iris had decided, was discovering the truly unpalatable ones. It had been six weeks since she had received Colm's early-morning phone call. Six weeks since she had clapped eyes on Tom and devoted herself almost entirely to his care. She had of course gone home to sleep in her house at Grosvenor Gardens. She preferred to sleep in her own bed and take the first available bus to Colm's apartment in the morning, gleefully receiving her gurgling grandson swaddled in the warmth of his baby blankets. Her work at the church had been scaled back completely. She had managed only one morning mass in three weeks and had temporarily handed her church-cleaning duties to a kind and unquestioning neighbour. She knew Father Hogan would do anything rather than pry and had done her best to dodge him, but he followed her to her car, which she had parked beneath the whitebeam trees that lined the church car park. She rarely drove any more, preferring to get maximum value from her free travel card, but this morning she had gone to the flower market to collect blooms for the altar display.

'Iris, we are beginning to forget what you look like around here. You haven't defected to another parish after all these years, have you?'

'Oh, don't be daft, Father. Everything is fine but I do hope you will excuse me as I am in a terrible rush.'

'Certainly, Iris. I merely wanted to say if there was anything at all bothering you that you could certainly confide in Father Michael or myself. We would be only too glad to help.'

There was a list of things bothering her. Where would she start? If she told Father Hogan that Colm had a new son he would, naturally enough, want to see him. He would also want to know why she hadn't shared the good news of the child's impending arrival. He might even start planning the christening and expect to officiate at the happy ceremony. Having stood by Iris Lifford through the difficult times of her husband's disgrace, Father Hogan would no doubt be looking forward to meeting Colm's new family. A missing mother was going to be a difficult one to explain. Could you even christen a child without its mother being present? Did Colm actually want Tom christened? No, there was no good place to start this story. This can of worms was definitely too fresh a catch to go opening it up to scrutiny it could not bear.

'Things are absolutely fine, Father,' Iris said with as much conviction as she could muster. She started her car and when she dared to look in the rear-view mirror she saw Father Hogan's vestments flapping like oversize bunting in the breeze.

After Leda's phone call to the apartment Colm had told his mother the scant information he knew about her whereabouts and her intentions. It was a catalogue of grim revelations. Leda, it seemed, had been calm and relaxed in the weeks before Tom's birth. She seemed glad that Colm had taken such a passionate interest in the baby she was carrying.

'And you didn't notice anything strange about her behaviour?' Iris was perplexed and Colm knew that question time had well and truly begun.

'If you are asking me if she littered our conversations with clues that she would reluctantly spend a bare week with her baby son and then decide that she never wanted to see him again then I would have to say no she didn't. She seemed OK while she still had Tom inside her.'

'All I am saying, Colm, is that it is highly unusual behaviour. Did she seem depressed? Were there any clues? The slightest hint—'

'No, there were no clues.' His tone was snappy and silence hung between them awkwardly. Iris was cowed only for a moment.

'So what exactly happens next? What happens to Tom?'

'He stays with me, of course. I will do whatever it takes to mind him.'

'How will you manage?'

'I will cut back on work or I will work from here at night when he is asleep. I will do whatever I have to do.'

'It could have consequences for your career.' The words sounded cold and she regretted them immediately.

'Mam, he has lost something huge already. He will not lose me. I promise him that.'

A blush rose on Iris's face. She should not have doubted her son, but her life had served to make her distrustful of intentions and suspicious of motives. Colm had never done anything to damage her pride or belief in him. She felt ashamed that she had not supported him without question.

'I will help you keep your promise, Colm.'

With her composure cracking a little Iris scurried in response to an imaginary cry from Tom's room. She did not want her son to see the tears that welled in her eyes. It was time for them all to be resilient and do what needed to be done.

'Even you, my little man,' she whispered to the small figure of a soundly sleeping Tom.

The most immediate problem came from an unexpected source. Polly's concerns on Leda's hospital notes had made their inevitable progress to the public health nurse's office. Colm and Iris had covered their tracks well, making sure that Tom was taken for his appointed weigh-ins and check-ups at the public health dispensary and he had his initial weigh-in and the BCG vaccination right on time. Sometimes Colm took the morning off from Reilly & Maitland or manufactured an out-of-office appointment with a client that would give him just enough time to bring Tom and his mother to the health centre. Afterwards Iris would unfurl the buggy and walk back to the apartment with Tom snugly wrapped while Colm returned to work, doing his level best not to be spotted by either of the senior partners when he turned up late. This was relatively easy most days, because their work, and one could only lightly apply the term work to what the senior partners actually spent their time doing, was conducted on the golf course or in the fine restaurants that lined the streets around the offices.

It would be easier to let Iris do the job from beginning to end, but Colm had his lines about Leda and her absence rehearsed as he would the facts of any case he was delivering to a barrister, and he was terrified that Iris would blurt something out to the nurse that would alert suspicion about Leda's whereabouts. She promised she wouldn't, but it was something Colm did not wish to put to the test.

It seemed that fathers of newborn babies were a rarity in the health centre as it was predominantly mothers on maternity leave who brought their babies for vaccinations. His peculiarity made Colm a target for sympathetic glances and lots of 'Aren't you great?' comments. The attention made him uncomfortable and he was terrified of getting engaged in conversation and forgetting to tell the requisite lies. When pushed he said he was giving his wife a rest as she had been up a lot of the night and she needed the extra sleep more than he did. That was usually enough for most women to fall silent as they contemplated their own plight, exhausted, up all night too but still expected to cope the following day with no one to share the load. They slipped into a reverie that Colm guessed involved a comfortable bed, a dark room and complete silence. It was much like the daydream he himself had become prone to over the last few weeks. He had never guessed the torturous consequences of continually interrupted sleep, how a night could last as long as a week but an hour's sleep only ever felt like a scant five minutes.

Colm was always relieved when he got from the confines of the too-small waiting room into the relatively spacious and calm nurse's office. His relief turned to dismay one morning when Tom was just seven weeks old. After introducing herself, Nurse Brid Halloran expressed her disappointment that it was Colm again and not Leda who had brought Tom for his weigh-in and check-up.

'Is there a problem with me bringing him?' Colm asked as lightly as he could.

'No, not at all, Mr Lifford, absolutely not. We love to see dads in here. Sure, you are as rare as hens' teeth. No, it's not that, it's just that Leda's file has come through from the Rotunda and some cause for concern about Leda's behaviour and mood have been noted by the midwifery team in the postnatal ward. We like to follow these cases up, just because some new mothers need more emotional support than others, and it would seem Leda might be one of those that need a helping hand.'

Colm knew he should be saying something to refute the suggestion or reassure the nurse that while Leda had had initial problems everything was fine now, but he was caught off balance. That annoyed him because for the last few weeks he had been rehearsing in his head the moment the subject would be broached. Maybe he should have left his mother to handle this situation after all. Iris Lifford would have wiped the floor with this woman – in the politest of ways, naturally.

Brid Halloran continued to enter Tom's details into the computer. Colm looked at the Post-its that framed her monitor filled with names, dates and phone numbers. Little sketches of other lives which meant nothing to him, but reading them gave him something to do in this long and awkward silence.

When Brid had completed Tom's data entry she turned to look at his father for some form of response. He was the thoughtful type, she decided, one who considered everything, someone whom she just didn't really have the time for today. She cleared her throat to break the silence, which was enough to spur Colm into opening his mouth.

'Well, Leda did have a hard time in the Rotunda. The labour was long and she was exhausted and then the breastfeeding didn't go smoothly. She just got overwhelmed, but she is well on her way now. That's why I do these appointments, because it's the least I can do when she is up several times a night with Tom. If I look after Tom for a few hours she gets to catch up on a bit of sleep.' Colm didn't want to overcook his explanation so he stopped to see if Nurse Halloran was buying his story.

'Well, sharing the load is the only way to get through these first weeks. It's too much for any one person on their own, dealing with demanding little mites like you, Tom Lifford.' She took Tom from Colm and gave him a nose rub. Tom made a contented gurgle and resigned himself happily to the measuring and weighing process.

Colm was relieved, but he would not really relax until he had Tom dressed and back outside in the world, where he could protect them both from the prods and the questions of well-meaning people who had not got a clue. He dressed Tom quickly. Nearly two months of practice had made him efficient and calm in the way he went about the task. Of all mornings he prayed that Tom would not wriggle too much and they could get out of the health centre and back to Iris as quickly as possible. His escape was nearly complete and his panicked breathing was returning to normal as he listened to the nurse tap more details into the computer. Tom had put on a suitable amount of weight and his progress was totally in line with other babies of his age. His son was gurgling as if he knew he had done well. Colm lifted him up and cradled him against his neck for a hug, soothing himself by rubbing his son's back.

'Any particular afternoon suit Leda for a home visit?'

Colm thought he might choke. 'A home visit? You do home visits?'

'Yes. The team here spend mornings in the centre and then afternoons visiting new parents. It's all part of our community service. The only reason Leda has slipped through the net is that we had two nurses out on sick leave the week Tom here was born so we had to postpone the visits to some of that week's babies rather than create an ongoing backlog. We are fitting in everybody now as best we can. So what day would suit? I'm afraid Wednesday is difficult for me because I have a meeting at two and, going on previous experience, it tends to run late.'

'What about this day week?' Colm asked with as much assurance as he could muster. He knew there was no point in trying to dodge the issue because that would alert more suspicion. He had no idea how he was going to persuade Leda to be present for the public health nurse's visit, but one of the most basic tenets of his legal training was never to reveal that you were unsure of your next move, so he ploughed on as if he knew what he was doing.

'Will we say Monday at two? Just let me check the address and get directions from you. Twenty-one, The Malt Store, Claddagh Road: is that correct?'

'That's us. Our building is in the grounds of the old distillery that runs along by Velvet Lane.'

'Oh, I know – the place with the huge wrought-iron gates. I thought that would be strictly a child-free zone, way too exclusive for a buggy and a swing. Then again I've only seen it when I'm whizzing by on the bus. Shows you how wrong first impressions can be.'

'I think Tom is the first baby all right, but nobody has reported us for night-time disturbance – yet anyway.' Colm attempted a smile. He hoped it didn't look as mangled as he felt inside.

He picked up Tom's changing bag and coat, which he had put on a side table when he came in. 'See you this day week so at two.'

'Looking forward to it, and tell Leda we are not the secret police. We are here to help if we are needed.'

'I'll tell her that. She will be glad of the visit.'

Iris was not impressed. 'How on earth do you think you are going to magic Leda out of thin air in time for this nurse's visit? She hasn't made contact in almost two months, you don't even know if she is still in the country, Colm!'

'What would you suggest I said? If I tell them the truth about Leda I could have social services and all sorts down my back. We're not married so I don't have as many rights as I should have. I bought myself as much time as I could so I could sort something out. God knows what though.'

'That girl has a lot to answer for. Off she goes without a care in the world and no idea of the trail of trouble in her wake.'

'Nothing except for the fact that she has abandoned her son and that must bother her.'

'I wouldn't bank on it,' Iris said waspishly.

Colm watched as his mother pushed Tom's buggy in the direction of home. She would complete the journey in a brisk thirty minutes and her pace would never flag. She prided herself on her fitness and triumph over old age's attempts to undo the benefits of a lifetime of healthy living. He was putting off getting into the car and driving back to work because he knew that concentrating on any case today was going to be an impossible task. Going home and spending the day with Tom was what he really wanted to do, but another day's absence from Reilly & Maitland was not going to solve anything. He would go to work and bury himself in some case and drink as much coffee as would see him through the day. He waited until his mother turned the corner on to Hayden Row and disappeared from view. He would find Leda and persuade her to come back and act motherly for an afternoon. She owed them both that.

Chapter Twenty-Seven

London and Dublin 1999

Lunchtime trade at Georgia Baxter's City Tearooms was busier than Ciara had imagined it would be and she was getting ever more irritated that the staff seemed intent on ignoring her table. Patience had never been her strong suit and her lunch companion was comforted to see nothing had changed.

'Five more minutes, Leda. I swear to God, do they think we have all day?'

'I'm not even hungry, Ciara. A cup of coffee would do me fine. We passed a coffee shop on the corner. Why don't we go there?'

'I could eat a small suckling pig, and a cup of coffee is not going to bridge the gap, I'm afraid. You look even more skinny than normal. Are you taking this slimming racket to extremes?'

'No I'm not. It's just that I got fairly tubby last summer, too many takeaways and too many dinners out. Had to sort myself out, that's all.'

'Was it that cute solicitor, the one you were telling me about in Spain, that had you out on these appetite-enhancing dates?

Mind you, I thought you looked gorgeous. You had a bit of colour in your face for the first time in ages.'

'No, it wasn't Colm; it wasn't his fault at all. I was just extra hungry, that's all, but I've sorted it out now.'

The waiter had risked showing his face at Ciara's table and had asked if they'd had time enough to decide on what they wanted to order.

'I think we have had sufficient time to raise a free-range chicken for ourselves actually. We've been sitting here for half an hour,' Ciara said sarcastically.

'Apologies for that, it's just that we are very busy today. What can I get you both?'

'I'll have the crab cakes, green salad and a glass of house white please and my little sister here will have exactly the same. With chips.'

Leda protested, but Ciara was having none of it. She had got such a fright from Leda's appearance when she had met her at Gatwick that morning. She looked pale and drawn, so very unlike the sister who had come on a surprise visit to her Spanish hideout last summer. Mind you, six months could change a lot of things, as Ciara well knew. You could be forgiven for thinking that you have found the love of your life during the course of a long hot summer and then realize when the quiet season comes that your lover wants to shut up shop and head for his home town and no he doesn't want you to come with him and no he isn't interested in paying back the loan you gave him for the first month's rental either. It had been a bruising experience but Ciara had to admit that she had yet again broken the first rule of Ciara Clancy's guide to life and was now suffering the consequences. Rule number one: never trust a man under any circumstances. Ever.

The food arrived, but its delicious smells did nothing to tempt Leda. She stared at it as if it was some alien substance she had not seen before while she fingered the stem of her wine glass.

'I take it there is something up at home, Leda. Something had to prompt you to visit at such short notice. Who has the biggest grievance in the Clancy household at the moment?'

'It's not home. Sure you keep in more contact with them than I do, although Mam complains that you haven't visited in ages.'

'Going back as seldom as I can is the only way I know how to survive. Every time I go in that door in Leachlara I feel any spirit I have drain out of me. If I had stayed I would be just as miserable as Mam. I can do nothing about the life she has had but I can't partake of it either, pretend it's OK or normal, because I would crack up myself if I did that.'

'You're right about that, Ciara, and at this stage I don't think Mam wants it to change. She is not happy but she is comfortable, and Dad is never going to change either. As long as he has the pubs of Leachlara within walking distance his life is complete. Anyway, I haven't been home for months. I just ring so they don't think I am missing or dead or something.'

Ciara had finished her own crab cakes and had now speared one of Leda's with her fork and dragged it across the table in full sight of the disapproving waiter. 'So are you going to tell me what has you looking like such a scrawny bird? No offence, but you look like shite.'

'Gee, thanks, Sis.'

'You know me. I tell it like I see it. So spit it out. Did this Colm guy treat you bad or what? 'Cause I'll go and beat him up if he has. I have some vengeance of my own that I could take out on him.'

'No, not Colm. He wouldn't do that. The thing is, I had a baby boy seven weeks ago.'

Ciara had just downed a huge mouthful of her lunch, and the shock of what she just thought she heard her sister say made her gag. She ditched what was left of the mouthful into her cloth napkin. 'What did you just say?'

'I said I had a baby. Seven weeks ago. It's a boy.'

'Am I raving here or something? This means you were pregnant when you were in Spain. Why didn't you tell me? What's his name? Where is he?'

Believing that his customer was choking on something in her lunch, the waiter rushed to Ciara's aid with a tumbler of water. She gulped it down in one go while staring at her younger sister in disbelief.

'Couldn't get my head around it myself. Came to see you out of shock really when I found out for definite. My periods are always all over the place so I take no notice when I miss one or two. Then you kept going on about how well and healthy I looked, and you and José seemed to have such a perfect thing going. So I pretended it wasn't happening, which was quite easy because I was a lot happier not thinking about it.'

'I take it this Colm guy is the father and the baby is with him. Why didn't you bring him over? You should have known I would want to see him, see them both for that matter. Are you living together now?' Questions tumbled out of Ciara. She had expected her sister to come bearing news of some disaster, some predicament that would be difficult to solve, but she never expected this. How could she have missed the clues in Spain and how could Leda have spent four days with her and never divulge a thing?

Leda took a generous sip from her wine to steel herself for the next bit. 'The thing is, I'm not really cut out for motherhood. It's not as if I planned it. Colm seems really into it, so I have left Tom with him indefinitely, permanently probably.'

'How could you give your own baby away? What has come over you that you think that is an OK thing to do?'

'You know as well as I do that we lived in a house with two people who happened to be our parents but neither were cut out for the job. All I have done is save Tom finding that out about me. Colm is a good person. He takes care of things and he is brilliant in a crisis. He will do everything for Tom and he will never even miss me. I haven't given him away as such. I've just left his father in charge of him.'

Ciara pushed her plate away from her and downed her wine in one furious gulp. She was stunned, disappointed and incredibly angry. 'I have never understood you, Leda. Yes, you are right: we had a shit upbringing by two people who couldn't even look after themselves, but you know what?'

'What?' Leda asked sharply, ready to dismiss whatever wisdom was to come.

'They might have been useless but we knew their names. We knew which door to knock on if we needed to go home. We knew they would never close the door in our faces. How can you seriously say that you gave your son away because you are not really into motherhood? It's not a lifestyle, Leda, it's a responsibility, and I will not let you get away with turning your back on it.'

Leda's face flushed. Ciara had never lost her ability to cut somebody down to size.

'I'm too young for this. This is not what I want for my life. Colm is OK but it was just a bit of fun. I never wanted it to last.'

'Don't tell me you still think you have a future with that ratbag Abernethy. No matter how many times he walks on you, you always come back for more. His wife died but you still weren't good enough to be anything but a dirty little secret. He has treated you like something he brought in on his shoe, a problem to be disposed of, but you still think he will change.' Disdain melted from Ciara's every word. As she berated her sister the thought niggled at her that if Leda was still sleeping with Con there was a chance that this baby was his and not this Colm guy's at all. 'Are you sure the baby is Colm's and not Con's?' she asked as calmly and coolly as she could manage.

'The baby's got nothing to do with Con, OK, so don't get your knickers in a twist.' Leda was sorry that she had ever told her sister a thing. A moment of weakness and doubt had brought her here to London to confide in her sister and she was mad at herself for not keeping quiet.

'So you have stopped sleeping with Con Abernethy. Is that what you are telling me?' Ciara asked stubbornly, holding back the doubts that were making her head swim.

'Yes, Con and I are finished. We have been for a while. Not that it's any of your business who I sleep with, is it?'

'It becomes my business when I have a nephew in Ireland that you have abandoned because you are such a selfish little git.'

'Who do you think you are to lecture me on the right thing to do?' Leda barked.

'What do you mean? I'm not the one who has left my baby behind me like a piece of lost luggage. I wouldn't do that.'

'No, but you would try to shag your best friend's boyfriend the night of his mother's funeral. You always criticize me for sleeping with Con, when you couldn't keep your hands off Dan Abernethy even if it meant losing your best friend in the whole world. Go and lecture someone else, Ciara, who doesn't know the things that you have done.'

Chapter Twenty-Eight

The offices of Reilly & Maitland quietened down quite suddenly once 5 p.m. came. The phones were switched to the answering service and all of the front-office staff departed immediately, pausing only to grab coats and a handful of groceries bought at lunchtime, the stock baggage of the city-centre worker. Colm waited until a decent amount of time had elapsed before he too legged it to the door and to his new life beyond. He had done his best to answer all his colleagues' questions about Tom as honestly as he could. They all knew Leda was the mother of his baby and they knew she wasn't handling motherhood with any degree of ease. Only a handful of people knew that she was on a permanent discharge from her duty authorized by no one but herself.

He knew opinion in the office was firmly divided about the situation he had found himself in. There were those who made a fuss over the photo he had of Tom on his desk and asked regularly how he was doing and was he sleeping? How was Colm coping and did he need anything at all? They were the ones who pressed brightly coloured packages with vests and rattles and babygros into his hands along with cards that said:

'Congratulations, Colm and Leda.' The others made polite enquiries but after the initial days stayed mostly silent. They made no fuss and if Colm was in any doubt about how they really felt, his best friend in the office, Rory McHugh, had put pictures to their thoughts admirably earlier on that afternoon.

'They think, Colm, that it's some achievement to be landed with a surprise pregnancy and end up losing the woman but keeping the baby.'

'What do you think? Do you think I am mad?'

'Well, it wouldn't be my choice, but I will tell you this much: that little lad there in that photo seems to have brought a smile to your face. You look knackered. You look, if you don't mind me saying, like you have cycled a long distance behind a car with no exhaust, but despite that you look happier than I have ever seen you. So I think young Tom there is an all-round good thing.'

'I think he is, yeah,' Colm agreed with an appreciative smile, unable to take his eyes off the photo of his infant son.

'Jesus, Lifford, I always knew you were soft in the head but you really have lost it now. And before you ask, no I do not want to check out the range of products at Mothercare after work, OK? Not unless they have started serving pints for men like me at sea amid the merchandise.'

He had given Colm a friendly thump on the shoulder. It was the most physical affection they had ever shown each other but today Colm appreciated it. It was enough to reassure him that he was doing the right thing. As Rory left Colm's office he shook his head and said quietly to nobody in particular, 'There but for the grace of God and the reliability of Durex go I.'

Colm looked at the list of phone numbers that he had jotted on his pad this morning. The first was Leda's mobile number. What were the chances she was going to answer that all of a sudden when she had failed to do so over the last several weeks? He had the phone number of the last place that he knew Leda had spent time, her friend Siobhan's house in Glasnevin. He had the contact name and phone number of the employment agency that had matched Leda's skills with the temporary vacancy at Reilly & Maitland, where they had first met. She had made an attractive addition to the array of bored faces in the front office. The agency, he knew, was duty bound not to release personal details of their clients but Colm thought it would help to find out if her name was still on their books and if she was listed as available for work. Lastly he had trawled the phone directory and come up with a number for the only Clancy family in Leachlara. Ted and Agnes Clancy, Briartullog, Leachlara, Co. Tipperary, most likely Tom's grandparents and they probably didn't even know he existed. Leachlara would be the last pit stop and only if he drew a blank everywhere else. He doubted that she would take refuge there, and if they took their family ties more seriously than Leda did where would that leave Tom and himself?

Ciara hadn't murdered Leda yet but then a bare twelve hours had passed since she had picked her up at the airport, so anything was possible. They hadn't spoken all the way home from Georgia Baxter's. Ciara was fuming that Leda had had the nerve to bring up Dan Abernethy when she herself had abandoned her child with a man whom she would not contemplate staying with herself. Ciara had long ago decided to put the heartbreak of losing Alison's friendship behind her. She had made the mistake of thinking their friendship could survive anything, even her own desperately bad judgement, but Alison had never allowed her to make amends. Perhaps Dan had insisted she break off contact. Maybe that was the only way that he could assuage his own guilt. If he had, Ciara was disappointed that her friend would have allowed herself to be dictated to in such a manner. She had subconsciously used it as a yardstick in the relationships she had had for the last decade:

none had ever been worth jettisoning a friend for. Maybe Ciara had decided she wouldn't let herself love someone that much.

Leda had been in the bath for an hour and the chicken stir-fry that Ciara had prepared for dinner was turning into a slow and watery stew on the hob. 'Damn her anyway, she'll eat it if she's hungry,' she said angrily as she reached into the bottom of the fridge for a mercifully cold bottle of beer. She was cursing her bottle-opener for being the most useless man-made implement in the whole wide and annoying world when Leda's mobile phone started to ring. Its vibrating motion sent it spinning across the kitchen worktop in Ciara's direction. The screen displayed its short message: 'COLM calling'. Ciara didn't waste any time. She would have to believe Leda when she said she was finished with Con and begin to unravel the complicated situation her sister had left behind her in Ireland.

'Hello, Colm, this is Ciara Clancy, Leda's sister, and I am very glad you called.'

Chapter Twenty-Nine

'I thought you didn't travel Ryanair on principle. Mind you, principles come and go with you, don't they?' Leda was picking a fight with Ciara but her sister simply would not take the bait. She was pretty sure that up as far as last night Ciara was an absolute supporter of the right to privacy but all that had been cast aside when the chance to talk to Colm Lifford presented itself. Since that conversation Ciara had been a woman on a mission. When she finished talking to Colm she went on to her work laptop (it was absolutely the best thing about an otherwise boring job she had landed herself in at a language school in Islington) and booked airline tickets for herself and Leda out of Gatwick the next morning. She half expected her laptop to flash a 'You are joking, Ms Clancy' message on the screen when she entered her highly abused credit-card details but the booking went through without a hitch. She would worry about her mounting credit-card debt some day soon.

They would have to be at Victoria Station to get the train at about six thirty, but that shouldn't be a problem, she decided as she made a mental note to put the louder of the two alarm clocks that she possessed under Leda's bed. Getting up early in the morning was not a skill native to the Clancy family, but years away from Leachlara had made Ciara an expert in punctuality. Next she composed the most pity-inducing yet plausible email she could manage to her boss at the language school. She outlined a family crisis, not so tragic that it would require too much explanation when she came back from Ireland, but still grave enough that her presence was required at home urgently. She expressed regret at the short notice and disappointment at letting down her Spanish-language students and vowed to make up the lost tuition time when she returned. She ended the email with a promise to ring in the morning from the airport. She pressed the send button, more confident than she had ever been that she was doing the right thing.

The check-in queue at Gatwick was agonizingly long. When her baiting of Ciara had failed to garner a response Leda switched into her default uncommunicative mode, accompanied by her best surly expression, which came to her with the greatest of ease. She had come to London to escape the suffocation of home. Even her friend Siobhan, whom she had thought she could rely on thoroughly, seemed appalled at her leaving Colm alone to care for Tom. It wouldn't be fair if he had done it to her, Siobhan had argued, and it wasn't fair the other way round either. She was her friend but she could not approve of what she had done. Leda had tried to fight her corner with Siobhan and now Ciara also but no one was listening to her – as usual. At the rate the queue was moving it looked as if they would be here for thirty minutes at least before boarding a plane back to a son she didn't want to see. When she looked at Tom she saw something of her own needy and smaller self and that was what had made her want to run in the first place.

Finally Ciara was at the head of the queue. It had taken an hour and fifteen minutes, which seemed all the longer for more than half of it having passed with no communication, barbed or otherwise, from Leda. She slammed the reservation-number page that she had printed off the Ryanair website the night before on to the check-in desk. It wasn't until she turned back to Leda to produce the second piece of luggage for the hold that she realized her sister had gone.

'She must be gone to buy a paper or something. Can I check her in and go after her? I will bring her back here to the desk when I find her.'

'I'm afraid that's totally impossible. You cannot check in for somebody else. It's just not the way we operate. I suggest you find your travelling companion and rejoin the queue. Has she got a mobile? Maybe you could try that. You really need to move aside now. The gate closes in forty minutes and we need to process all these people,' the clerk said as she waved her hand at the queue that snaked its way, two to three people wide, all the way back to the opposite bank of check-in desks.

Ciara gathered her computer printout and her battered trolley case and made her way to the rows of seats in the middle of the departure hall. She couldn't quite believe what her sister had just done but she knew it was no accident – and if she had been in any doubt there was a text message on her mobile, a beep she had not heard while standing in the queue, confirming that Leda had indeed done a runner.

> I know you mean well but I can't go back. I need space. Sorry you had to pay for flight but at least it was a cheap one, L

Ciara dialled the number, but she already knew her sister would not answer. Leda was sipping a coffee while waiting to board the Gatwick Express. She had turned down the ringer on her phone but she still felt its familiar vibrating pulse against her thigh as it languished unanswered in her coat pocket. She needed a new number. The first thing she would do when she got off the train was to buy a new SIM card. As she had said to

Ciara, she needed some space. The platform display announced a train to Victoria leaving in 1 minute 56 seconds. London stretched out wide and promising in front of her. It would do for the moment.

Posters of the great Irish writers lined the walls of the travelator corridor to baggage reclaim at Dublin airport. All grey, nearly all wearing glasses and mostly men, it had to be said. It reminded Ciara of the poster that she and Alison had hung over the mantelpiece in their Ranelagh flat. They had bought it in one of the tourist shops on Nassau Street. It was a perfect fit because it covered the horrible dark patch of smoke that had lingered when they had taken down Jean McDermott's choice of artwork, a totally bizarre and lurid pink and orange print of a fish eating a girl. They had hidden it behind the sofa in case dumping it counted against their deposit. To tell the truth, they had become used to its kitsch until Dan started to comment on it every time he came in. 'Ah now, girls, I know you arts students like to show how multi-talented you all are, but displaying your school art project? Have you no shame?'

Ciara was in danger of lapsing into a bout of nostalgia. Her memories of college, of first living away from home and of Dublin were absolutely bound up in her friendship with Alison and the effect Dan Abernethy had had on both their lives. She had let a few days elapse before she attempted to ring Alison after the night in Aughasallagh. Dan was due back in Dublin for his final exams on the Monday. She rang the Shepherds' private phone line several times that morning but there was no answer. As a last resort she rang the surgery number and the phone was answered by Cathy Shepherd, whose tone turned decidedly frosty when she realized she was talking to Ciara. Obviously Alison had filled her mother in on what had happened between her and Dan.

'This is the surgery line, Ciara,' Cathy said curtly.

'I know that, Mrs Shepherd, but I have tried the house number and there is no answer. I need to talk to Alison and explain things.'

'Look, I know Alison is down there but she is very upset and might not want to talk to you. I will tell her you are looking for her but I can't promise anything. She is very hurt.'

Ciara felt bad enough already and talking to Cathy didn't make her feel any better. In the following weeks she continued to call the surgery every few days. Cathy insisted she was giving the messages to Alison but none of her calls was returned so Ciara gradually gave up. As a last resort she wrote a letter to Alison, trying to excuse her stupidity and beg her forgiveness, but the letter was returned unopened to the house in Leachlara. Alison had readdressed the letter and the sight of her friend's handwriting on the envelope was the final act of rejection. Ciara abandoned hope that their friendship could be restored.

She wrestled her thoughts back to the present while she waited for her bag. Delving into the past was too painful. As soon as she had got her trolley case from the carousel she headed out to find a bus or a taxi that would take her to Colm's apartment to meet her nephew. Despite her mounting credit-card debt she opted for the luxury of a taxi, to avoid scrimping for the exact change for a bus. It used to cost fifty-five pence from Nassau Street to the Northbrook Road stop and she would happily walk the last ten minutes, nipping into Spar for a bar of chocolate or a pint of milk and a sliced pan if she was ravenous for supper. As she waited in the taxi rank she wondered how much it cost now.

The upbeat humour of the taxi driver suited her. She could do with a bit of jovial conversation with somebody before she landed on top of Colm and Tom. She would need to muster any charm and warmth she had left after what had happened with Leda that morning. Colm must already think the worst of her because she would be linked in his head with Leda but at least he had told her she was still welcome when she had phoned him to say that Leda had done a runner. Again. He didn't seem shocked. Perhaps Leda's behaviour had already exhausted his capacity for surprise.

She marvelled at how different the roads around the airport looked since the last time she had seen them. It was so much more built up; roads were clogged with traffic and everywhere held the fragile promise of unfinished newness. She had heard of the Celtic Tiger of course. Every Irish person she had met in Spain and England felt duty bound to tell her about the miracle of economics that had swept all before it at home. Thinking she had fled unemployment, they were only too keen to tell her now that they were giving jobs away but that you might need three of them to find a house to call your own. Ciara never admitted that she was fleeing something that a job or the celebrated Tiger couldn't cure. She had heard the phrase so many times that she thought her head might implode if she heard it once more. As it happened, it didn't, because the taxi man had used it twice before they had even reached the M50, rolling the 'r' of Tiger for dramatic effect.

'So tell me, love, are you here for business or pleasure?' he enquired as he cruised down the bus lane towards Drumcondra and the older Dublin she hoped she might yet recognize.

'A bit of both maybe, but mostly pleasure I hope,' she answered quietly as she gazed out of the window. She couldn't match the place she was seeing now with the place she had left years before. Dublin didn't have this much traffic the last time she was here and there were new apartment blocks everywhere. It seemed as if it had turned into a city of apartment-dwellers, the newest of them her nephew Tom and his father, Colm. 'Twenty One, The Malt Store, Claddagh Road. It's off the South Circular,' she announced to the driver confidently as if she knew exactly where she was going and whom she would find there.

Chapter Thirty

No stone had been left unturned to make Colm's apartment look like a grotto to healthy and normal family life. This whole procedure was not going to flounder on Iris Lifford's lack of effort. The place had been vacuumed to within an inch of its life. The sterilizer had sterilized everything she could lay her hands on. Tom was pristine in his green and blue sleepsuit. If he smelt divine of baby lotion and as if he had been bathed just before Nurse Halloran arrived, it was because he had been. Colm did his best not to screw up anything that his mother had neatly arranged because he knew that however co-operative she was being they were very close to the flip side of her industry, which was an outright explosion. That they must avoid at all costs. He had had some photos of Tom developed and he had stuck them into frames that he'd had stashed in the drawer of his desk. He put them in a few visible places around the living room. In the drawer he also found a photo of himself and Leda that Rory had taken of them at the Reilly & Maitland St Patrick's Day Lunch. It was a day when he had realized that it was entirely possible to spend an unspeakably awful day with a beautiful girl if she decided that there was no real reason to talk to their colleagues or to him. The photo looked convincing enough, because Leda always looked gorgeous no matter what her mood. He could say that now even after all that had happened and all that she had done. Colm himself was smiling too, because just as he was taking the photo Rory had dropped the punchline to a joke he had been telling him piecemeal throughout the otherwise depressing lunch. It was to all intents and purposes a heart-warming photo of a couple in love, a couple expecting their first child, except one of them didn't know and one of them seemed not to care, either then or now. Colm resisted the urge to tear it to pieces and placed it back in the drawer face down. He would deal with it another day.

Ciara had said that she would turn up about an hour before the appointment and Colm secretly hoped that his mother would make herself scarce so that they could put on a convincing act of young parents struggling with, but ultimately managing, the difficulties of being new parents. It was not as if he was breaking the law wanting to raise his own child but he did feel that he needed the nurse to think that all was well so that she would sign off on the Leda Clancy file and be happy to see a happy and healthy Tom for the remainder of his vaccinations. The initial meeting with Ciara had been uneasy because Colm had been beset with worry that she would have plans for Tom that involved more time with the Clancy family, or that she would want to take Tom to Leda. As far as he was concerned Leda could be with Tom if she would agree to move back into the apartment, but his son was not going anywhere out of his sight. He was deeply relieved that Ciara, who professed herself devoid of anything one might mistake for maternal instinct, had no notion of playing happy Clancy families. She wanted the best for Tom and she wanted to meet Colm herself to see what he was made of, but her role in Tom's life was going to be that of a devoted aunty – if that was OK with Colm.

'God yeah, it is. I have to say I am relieved.' His sharp exhalation of breath gave Ciara some idea of how worried he had been about meeting her. 'I am not at all sure that your parents know of their grandchild's existence. In fact I am almost certain that they don't, as they didn't visit the hospital or even telephone while Leda was staying with me. If it's all right with you I would like to keep things that way for the moment – just until I feel I have Tom totally settled and on an even keel.'

Ciara knew he was worried that even if Leda didn't want Tom her parents might, so she let him know that the Leachlara contingent would not descend on him.

'Listen, Colm, I wouldn't leave my pet cat, if I had one, with my folks for the weekend. They would mean well but it wouldn't be a good idea so I think we will keep Tom to ourselves for the moment. Besides, the last thing Leda needs is the whole of Leachlara discussing her baby in the pubs. Dad is out there most nights and he cannot hold water.'

'She was never that keen on going home or talking about it. I never pushed the issue because I didn't want to be crowding her and anyway our relationship didn't last long enough for us to get down to the nitty gritty of finding out about each other's families. She only ever talked to Mam after Tom was born and she had left at that stage so they didn't exactly hit it off. Tell me to mind my own business, but did she fall out with your folks or what? I know families can be hard. Believe me.'

Ciara took a deep breath. She could just be evasive but that wasn't really fair, was it? She could give Colm the sketch of the truth without revealing details. It might go some way to explaining the way that Leda had behaved, although Ciara would be the first to admit that nothing could excuse her latest trick. 'When Leda was younger she had a relationship with a man from Leachlara who was much older than her, forty years older than her actually. He was married and she thought she was in love with him. Maybe she was. He was just a scumbag who took advantage of the fact that Leda was innocent and unhappy at home.'

Ciara made it sound like a distant memory. There was no way she was going to admit that Leda might still be involved with Con Abernethy and that it could well explain her strange behaviour about her pregnancy and her son's birth. It was good to be honest but only to the point that served one's purpose best.

'And your parents naturally enough did not approve, I presume.' Colm thought he was beginning to understand Leda's evasiveness about home.

'Not quite as simple as that, I am afraid. The man was, still is in fact, prominent and well known, and so it was let go much further and longer than it should have been. He was a drinking mate of Dad's and Dad chose not to pull his friend up about his involvement with his daughter. Mam is not the best at seeing what's in front of her nose so nothing helpful came from there either. I tried to keep her away from him but she always went to him behind my back because presumably he made promises that she never learned he wouldn't keep. I gave up in the end because life threw its own crap my way and, as they do say, the best thing about banging your head off a brick wall is that it feels fantastic when you stop. Pretty pathetic, but there you have it. Anyway, I reckon it has properly screwed up Leda so she doesn't know how to recognize or appreciate decency and kindness. I could tell you who this man is but I'm not sure what good it would do.'

'No, I don't really want to know, to be honest, but thanks for telling me that much.' Ciara's rundown of the balls-up the Clancy family seemed to have made of Leda put Colm in mind of his own family's shortcomings. Family misfortune was all cut from the same material. The only variety was in the detail.

He could tell Ciara all about the disgrace and hardship that Patrick Lifford's shamefully dishonest business dealings had caused his mother and himself, but he wasn't sure that she would learn anything real or helpful about him in the process. In the same way, knowing the identity of some two-bit dodgy county councillor from Tipperary who abused the innocence of a teenage girl under the eyes of her parents was not going to help him or Tom now.

He wasn't sure how exactly he decided to ask Ciara to impersonate Leda at the public health nurse's visit but he was taken aback by how readily she agreed. He expected some words about deceit, being caught out in the lie or some reticence, but Ciara was up for it at once. Colm doubted if they could pull it off but it seemed she was not afflicted by a single reservation. She didn't doubt her ability to be convincing and her faith buoyed Colm's confidence. Iris was appalled but, always a pragmatist, she decided to keep her disapproval to herself for the moment. At least Ciara had shown some gumption by turning up, which when compared to what Iris saw as cowardice in Leda was to be applauded.

As a gesture of her good will she invited Colm, Tom and Ciara to her house on Grosvenor Gardens for Sunday lunch the day before the appointment. There was no point in them all sitting down for the first time on Monday and hoping to pull off this stunt. Iris thought that because she had never met Leda, only dealing with her rudeness and aggression with some success on the phone, she might find it easy enough to think of Ciara as actually being Leda. She was more than a little inquisitive to see from what and where exactly this Leda creature had sprung.

Ciara had accepted the invitation with relish. Turning down a chance to look inside one of the houses in Grosvenor Gardens was not an option. She had gazed at the beautifully lit windows of that type of house when she had walked home from college years before. She adored the elegant steps up to the front doors and the gravel crunching beneath the feet announcing any visitor before they had a chance to chime the doorbell or clutch in their hand the polished brass knocker. The plants and the neat squares of front gardens were always immaculate and it was easy to spot the houses whose inhabitants took pride in their appearance and the others that had been carelessly and crudely divided into flats. Curtains were a dead giveaway. In the flats dirty nets usually served as the only screen from passing traffic and they were hung haphazardly, a single packet of hooks split it seemed between every dismal window in the house. The grand houses had luxuriously heavy, well-lined drapes to keep out the world and its coldness but mostly left open to show the attractions that lay inside. Ciara had imagined life to be more beautiful, more gentle when lived in such attractive surroundings. She had thought back then she would definitely be different if she had come from a house like that. Leachlara left a different sort of mark and one that was hard to wipe away. Ciara was enthralled at the prospect of having a good look from the inside out.

She brought flowers to Iris. They weren't a cheap supermarket bouquet but some grasses and gerberas wrapped in wax paper and tied with bamboo from a classy florist that had replaced a kebab shop where the long, loping curve of Ranelagh Road turned into the elegant straight that marked the start of the village proper. Leda had told her that Colm's mother was a boot so she was prepared for the worst, notwithstanding her sister's leaning towards exaggeration and negativity. It was hardly likely that Iris Lifford would think well of Leda. Ciara was Leda's only sister and right at this moment not even she could think of a good word to say about the girl. Colm talked about Iris with gratitude and respect but with little fondness that Ciara could detect, but then again she had only known him for a couple of days. He was unlikely to open up unnecessarily or tell her anything beyond the barest bones of his story. Circumstances had thrown them together. He needed her. A little baby needed her. It felt good to help and it felt right. Ciara hadn't felt much of either in a long time.

Chapter Thirty-One

When it came to the appointed time Iris Lifford could not bring herself to be present to watch her son partake in a deception. She considered it a benign enough adjustment of the true facts but she didn't want to witness Colm being dishonest. What if it came naturally to him and lies fell from his mouth with the greatest of ease? Then Iris Lifford would have to admit that he was a Lifford in more than name. She had been ashamed of one man for most of her life; she could not accept that she would have to think badly of another. She took herself home to make a Christmas wreath for Father Hogan's front door from the greens and berries that were abundant in the garden. She would make an extra special one to make up for the fact that she had neglected some of her church duties for the last number of weeks. She constructed it carefully, securing each stem to the next and to the central frame. It took her mind off what was happening at Colm's apartment, but as the clock moved toward 3 p.m. she couldn't help thinking that it should be finished by now.

Over at Claddagh Road Ciara was playing a blinder. Tom had taken to her like a duck to water. She sang to him all sorts of songs and none of the usual nursery rhymes that most people feel compelled to babble in a dopey, gormless sort of voice to young babies. His aunt treated Tom to what Colm had to admit was a fairly feisty rendition of 'Fever' and a gorgeous version of Kate Bush's 'Running Up That Hill'. Listening to her voice echo around the apartment made him a bit depressed. He didn't miss Leda for himself but he missed her on Tom's behalf. This is what it should be like, shouldn't it? A mother singing to her new baby and the baby dozing appreciatively in her arms. Tom was being deprived of that. As heart-warming as the scene with Tom and Ciara was to watch, at best his aunt would only be an intermittent presence in his life. At worst she would personify all that he had lost.

Colm waited in the hallway for the doorbell to ring but Brid Halloran was late, fifteen minutes late, and when she finally arrived she spent another five minutes telling them about the traffic-light sequence on Harcourt Road that had broken her heart. 'Ten seconds of green light, did you ever hear the like of it?'

Colm and Ciara agreed that it was a scandal and the sense of nervousness that had enveloped them began to lift a little, which was exactly what Brid had planned so she would see these parents at their relaxed best. Colm offered to make tea or coffee and while he busied himself with that Brid launched into the business at hand. She had to say this new mother was looking brilliant and not at all down in her form as she had imagined would be the case. She thought it remarkably unfair the way that some mothers resumed their figures within a matter of weeks as if pregnancy was some sort of outer-body Ziploc experience that could be peeled off, while others (and she had to include herself sorrowfully in this lot) wore the body print of their pregnancy for years after their baby's delivery. Leda was glowing. If anything it was Colm who seemed to be bearing the brunt of new parenthood, Brid decided. He was a very handsome man and quite young, she thought, but he looked worn to a thread of life, with dark circles threatening to blot over his eyes. He was obviously doing more than his fair share and that was helping his partner get the better of a difficult start at motherhood.

'Well now, Leda, tell me how you are feeling, and don't just say tired because I know you are thoroughly exhausted, that goes with your new job description, I'm afraid, and tell me about the birth.'

'Oh, Brid, I was shell-shocked in the hospital. I had read all the books, hadn't I, Colm?'

Colm nodded, relieved that the onus had shifted from him, however temporarily, for once in his son's life. Tom was curled asleep on Ciara's lap, lulled by her voice as she fluently explained her feelings, her initial withdrawal from Tom at the hospital and how Colm had helped her to get through it by being patient and kind. She was quietly persuasive without being overpowering and Brid seemed genuinely touched by her willingness to be honest. Colm was terrified he would call her Ciara, so he restricted his input to the odd nod of the head and smile at the funny, self-deprecating comments that Ciara scattered like favours in her conversation.

'God, that was easier than I thought!' Ciara was on a high at her own performance when Brid Halloran had left them, rushing to another appointment. 'I half expected she would want me to sign up for counselling or something, but she seemed convinced. And as for you, Mr Tom Lifford, weren't you the great man snoring your way through the whole ordeal?'

'You were brilliant, Ciara. Sorry I wasn't a bit more helpful. I was just terrified we would confuse each other and say something that would make her suspicious.'

'Take a chill pill, for God's sake. She wasn't suspicious. She was concerned about how Leda was coping, that's all, and we put her mind at rest. From now on it's plain sailing for you and

Tom. Leda is out of the picture and I wouldn't worry about her coming back either. My sister seems to specialize in running away.'

'Yes, I am beginning to doubt she will be challenging for custody by all you have told me.'

'You have nothing to fear from Leda, Colm, except her indifference. If you are prepared for that you and Tom here will be fine. At some stage she will ring me or home just to tell us she is still alive. She's very thoughtful, is my little sister.'

Ciara's sarcasm was tangible and Colm allowed himself to laugh. He had to admit that Tom had drawn a dodgy straw with his mother but it did look as if he had the devotion of his loving aunt. Colm, after all they had been through, took some small comfort in that fact.

Chapter Thirty-Two

Dublin and Caharoe 2005

There was no right way to go about what Dan Abernethy was planning but he knew he had to give it his best attempt. He had told Alison about Colm Lifford's relationship with Leda and sworn her to secrecy. He had told Colm that not another soul would hear it, but he counted Alison and himself as one and the same. Alison had offered to come with him to meet Leda but he really didn't want to expose her to any of the vitriol that he feared she might spout. 'I'll do it alone, Ali. It's better that way and I'll ring you the minute I get out. It shouldn't take long and hopefully I will be home before midnight.'

'OK, but take no crap from her. Treat her like an enemy, because that's what she is. Don't be afraid to put her in her place.'

He was about to test Alison's aggressive strategy by arriving on Leda Clancy's doorstep unannounced on a rainy Monday night, attempting to cut a deal on his father's behalf. When Con found out that Dan had Leda's address he half-heartedly offered to take the issue from there, but Dan knew that his father did not have the stomach for a showdown with anyone, let alone Leda, who had shown her talent for outwitting him. There was not much that Con Abernethy would admit to being unable to handle but this was a mess that he was very glad that Dan had offered to clean up. One hundred thousand euros was the initial payment that Leda had asked for and Dan knew that Con had funds for many multiples of that, but he was hoping that Leda would prove malleable if Dan threatened to reveal her past indiscretions to Bob Cantwell, the new man in her life. One payment and her subsequent silence on the matter was the outcome he hoped to bring about.

Colm had shown him the email from Ciara so he knew that she lived with her fiancé, who most likely knew nothing of her past. Some of it might stain the sheen of his bride-to-be and hopefully Leda would accept a sensible amount in return for Dan's guarantee of silence. He didn't want to have to blackmail her as such. He didn't really have the first clue about how to be menacing, but it was a long time since he had seen Leda Clancy and maybe she would take a phantom threat seriously. It was surely better than sending his father into the fray, who might just collapse under the heat of Leda's first flirtatious comment.

There were two cars parked in the driveway, a new black Audi and a rather battered-looking gold Punto, so it seemed they were both at home. A stroke of luck, Dan hoped, while his heart pounded in his chest. Leda answered the door on the fourth ring. She broke into a grin almost immediately.

'Well my oh my, if it isn't Dan Abernethy? I was expecting to hear from your father or maybe Columbo. Didn't think he would allow you to become shop-soiled by dealing with the likes of me – or is the tail wagging the dog these days?'

'We need to talk, Leda, privately if that's possible.' Dan nodded beyond the hall door where they were standing as if he understood that someone else was at home.

'Come on in. My fiancé is away on business. We have the

place to ourselves.' She clocked his disappointment that his unexpected arrival was not more awkward for her and she smiled languorously at him. She closed the hall door as Dan stepped inside, pinning his tall frame against the opposite wall of the narrow hallway. 'How did you find me? Of course, I don't need to ask. Columbo knows where the dogs on the street are mating.'

Dan didn't tell her that his father could not bear to tell Columbo about Leda's demand for money. It would take too much swallowing of pride for him to admit that Columbo had been right that he should have left his brain to do the thinking for him. Besides, Columbo had moved on to the next candidate as the memory of the Abernethy era faded with every passing day.

She led the way to the back of the house where the deceptively narrow entrance hall opened out to a glass-walled room looking out on to an expensively landscaped back garden. Money had been recently spent here and it was clear that Ciara was right. Leda Clancy had landed dead on her feet. She gestured at the dining table, where magazines and papers were strewn about. Gossip magazines lay open, resting on the telltale colour of the financial papers. Dan sat down, not really knowing how to start. Leda filled the pause in proceedings enthusiastically. She was willing to whittle whatever satisfaction she could out of Dan Abernethy, and it helped that he was even more gorgeous than the last time she had seen him in the pub in Leachlara the night they had buried the witch. Ageing obviously treated the Abernethy men well.

'I'm sure I can arrange for you to meet Bob another time if you really want to although he is very busy, poor pet. To and fro to London on a weekly basis. In fact I met him in London but he enticed me back here. It wasn't difficult, I have to say. I've always been a bit of a home bird.'

'I'd say Ted and Aggie haven't seen you in a while. You

outgrew Leachlara fairly rapidly.' Dan wanted to make it clear to Leda that he didn't believe a word she said but it was a topic about which her feelings were unable to be hurt.

'Dan, you can hardly talk. Everyone around Leachlara knows that the night your mother was buried was the last night you spent in that house. People think you took the death of your mother so unbelievably hard that you couldn't stand to be in the house without her. Of course we both know that's not what happened really, don't we? Compromising positions with my big sister while your lovely wee girlfriend had her innocent back turned. Tell me now, while I have you here with me, did you jump on her or did my trollop of a sister make the first move?'

'I didn't come here to talk about Ciara or Alison so kindly leave them out of the conversation. You have caused enough trouble so let's see if we can sort something out so that my family never have to see or hear from you again.'

'Oh, it suits me not to talk about either of them. I stay well clear of my darling sister because she never tires of lecturing me, as if her life can be held up as some sort of exemplary model of behaviour that I should try to emulate. As for your dowdy little Alison, that pot plant over there has more personality so no quarrel there either. I have to say though that you are looking incredibly well after years with that vapid little dishcloth. Either you thrive on the boring or else she is a little belter behind that curtain of blandness. Though I doubt it somehow.'

Rage was simmering inside Dan's head but he knew that a furious argument with Leda would solve nothing at all. Tell her what he knew, cut a deal with her and get home.

'Let's cut to the chase, Leda. How much do you want to give me back every piece of paperwork belonging to my father that you stole and get out of our lives for good?'

'I'm not greedy, honestly, I just feel that I'm entitled to a little something for all the times I made your father a happy man. At his age it nearly qualifies as home help, doesn't it?' She laughed gleefully, enjoying her own little joke even if Dan obviously did not.

'How much, Leda?'

'I told your father. A hundred grand, and I have debts I need clearing that he didn't give me a chance to mention. He really was quite rude on the phone and I hardly deserve that after all these years. It's credit cards mostly. Amazing how many of those you can actually get your hands on and you never have to stop until you hit the limit and then, bang, there's another one all fresh and green in your wallet panting for a bit of action.'

'How much does it all come to?' Dan had taken a pen from his inside pocket and he was tapping it relentlessly against the folder he had carried in under his arm.

'My head started to pain me a bit when I got as far as adding up to thirty thousand so I stopped, but I'd say forty should cover it. Tell you what, one hundred and fifty grand and I start with a clean slate and a nice little stash. Every girl needs a running-away fund, don't you think?'

Dan opened the folder and produced three bank drafts payable to Leda, each to the value of fifty thousand euros. He had brought a fourth but it remained folded in his inside pocket. The prospect of ready cash was enough to persuade Leda not to push her luck further. One hundred and fifty thousand would do very nicely indeed.

'No paper trail, Dan, I like your style. I'd say Con came up with that little manoeuvre.' She rose from her chair and took a battered pink girly school folder from the top drawer of the chest of drawers. When she extended it open above the table stacks of photocopied credit-card statements tumbled in front of where Dan was sitting.

'It's all there. I'm too honest for my own good.' Leda sat down with a thump and pulled the bank drafts to herself. Across the table Dan gathered the photocopies into a neat pile. How many credit card accounts could his father possibly have? His mind boggled at the extent of what he didn't know about the man. He rose from the table. He would look at it all later. First he needed to dispatch Leda for good.

'I wouldn't come knocking for another instalment, Leda, unless you want your new fiancé to know that you have a son that you left the week you gave birth to him. He might look at you a little differently if he knew that. Might be a bit of a deal-breaker if he knew what you were really capable of, don't you think?'

Dan was quite proud of how coolly he delivered the statement and satisfied that Leda was visibly shocked that he knew about Colm and Tom. Her neck reddened and the blush moved vigorously up her face. She seemed embarrassed and unnerved, thrown off balance for the first time in their conversation.

'You have done your homework, I'll give you that,' was the weak retort she managed as she tried to think what this might mean for herself. She didn't think of Tom or Colm as a rule. That chapter was well and truly closed.

'I just don't ever want to have to clap eyes on you again, so bear in mind I know things that can damage your perfect little set-up.' He gestured around the room. She believed him when he said he would tell Bob. There was of course one way she could avoid that. Left stranded with a single ace in her hand she only had one option – to play it.

'I told you I wasn't greedy, Dan. Anyway, you know what they say: you should always leave something in the pot for the next man. It wouldn't be right to clear him out. What if his son should fall on hard times and need a bit of a dig-out?'

'Don't worry, I don't intend going bankrupt. My father's money won't be plundered by me.' Even now her cheek appalled him. Why could she not have the decency to take the cash and shut her mouth?

'I wasn't talking about you. You'll never take any risks. You showed that when you plumped for Alison, who came free with a GP practice stuck to her arse. I was talking about Tom Lifford – or should I say more correctly Tom Abernethy. It's the least I can do to make sure Con is not cleared out in case his youngest boy should ever come knocking on Daddy's door.'

'You are pure poison, Leda. Is there no depth you won't stoop to? Involving an innocent little boy – your son, I might remind you – and his father in your little scam. Colm Lifford is a lovely man and—'

Leda cut in. 'Yeah, lovely and downright gullible. He had a big gaping hole in his life and I offered him a baby-shaped Band-Aid to plug the gap. He fell for it hook, line and sinker. Think about it. I slept with your father for years and I slept with Colm a handful of times. Which of them is more likely to be the father? I had an abortion the year your mother died, forgot to take the pill and got caught. I didn't bother Con with the details, I just charged the flights and the clinic fee to one of my credit cards that he settled every month. Since that abortion my periods have been all over the place so when I got pregnant on Tom I didn't even realize until it was too late to take care of it.'

Dan was ashen-faced and Leda couldn't resist another dig now that she had the advantage again. Dan could find no words to respond to anything she was saying.

'Do you not like me talking about my periods, Dan? I thought you being a family GP you would be listening to stories like mine all day. Anyway, there was no point in upsetting the little arrangement that I had with Con for the sake of a baby that I didn't want or that he sure as hell wouldn't want. Enter Colm looking for a life and I gratefully hand him the child. He is a brilliant father, luckily enough, although that's according to my sister dearest and we both know she is prone to strange fits of lack of judgement, don't we? But I am willing to believe that in this instance she is telling the truth. It helps my conscience if it ever troubles me – although thankfully that's rarely.'

'How do I know you are telling the truth?' Dan asked weakly.

In his heart he knew this could well be true and he felt his legs had been cut from under him.

'Why would I lie, Dan? I have my money,' Leda said, raising her bank drafts like prized trophies in his face. 'But I will not have you threaten what I have with Bob because I will sink your cosy little world without trace if you push me. I'm not sure how Con Abernethy would feel if he knew his son was growing up in Caharoe but I look forward to finding out if you so much as lay a fingerprint on my life.'

'Don't you think Colm should know that he is raising a child that isn't his own?'

'Fuck no. Spare me the Mother Teresa bit. The arrangement suits everyone. Tom would be richer if he was an Abernethy but he will probably be less fucked up as a Lifford. Con doesn't want a child. Colm was gagging for one. You don't want a little brother and what would your squeaky clean Alison make of everything? I know when to leave well enough alone. I sincerely hope you do too.'

Dan didn't remember much about leaving Leda's house except how cheerfully she bade him farewell, as if she had already forgotten the gravity of what they had spoken about. He went in a daze to the car that he had parked a street away. Instead of clearing his head the walk made him even more confused. When he reached the car he found his mobile phone, which he had left there, showed two missed calls, one from Leachlara and one from Michaelmas. He rang his father first because whatever energy he possessed he wanted to save to talk to Alison. He could fake it with his father. It seemed much of what he knew about Con was no more than half the truth anyway. Con answered the phone immediately, as if he had been sitting on it waiting for a call. He listened to the bare bones as Dan laid them out. She had taken the money and probably wouldn't trouble them again. Dan had received a bundle of paperwork in return that he would pass on to the Lalors to see if some kind of settlement with the Revenue could be stealthily agreed. Dan listened as his father congratulated him on a job well done. 'I'm grateful to you for looking after this mess for me. I should never have got involved with her. Nothing good came out of it. I promise you, son, it's a clean slate from here and now.'

'OK. Look, Dad, it's a long way back to Caharoe. I'll talk to you tomorrow.'

'You could break the trip by spending the night here,' Con ventured gently.

'No I couldn't. I want to go home.' His son's reply was definite.

'Well, goodnight and thanks.'

Alison sent questions down the phone like wildfire. Yes he had put Leda in her place. She had settled quickly enough and there were other bits of news. He would tell her when he got home. He asked her to wait up. He would get there as soon as he could.

The traffic was mercifully light and Dan made good time out of Dublin, coming through Abbeyleix a full forty minutes earlier than he expected. He listened to the radio to drown out his thoughts but Leda's face and all she had told him crowded his mind, giving him no respite. He imagined what Tom Lifford might look like. If he saw him would he know if Leda were telling the truth? He thought of Lucy maybe having an uncle younger than her (was that what Tom was?) and of himself having a brother of sorts. Tom must be in the same school as Lucy. Maybe Dan had seen him. Scalding tears trickled down his face while he tried to concentrate on the road in front of him, at once familiar but now rather alien – like everything else. He tried to think of home and his family there, a foil to everything that had happened since he left Caharoe that afternoon. Alison would know what to do. If he could just get home he would tell her everything. Images of her and Lucy swam in and out of focus. Only when his eyes closed did peace wash over him.

* * *

Garda records would show that no other vehicle was involved. Daniel William Abernethy GP, aged 38, of Michaelmas House, Caharoe, Co. Cork, had momentarily lost concentration and control of his car as he travelled the dead-straight, tree-lined road that would lead him from the edges of his native Tipperary into Cork. He had made an eight-hour round trip to Dublin and exhaustion was cited as the most likely cause of the accident. He was within twenty miles of home when his car careered off the road at around 11.30 p.m., upturning into the low-lying land below the road and causing him fatal injuries. A passing motorist alerted the emergency services but Dan was already dead when their help arrived. Alison was nudging life into the open fire when the doorbell of Michaelmas House rang at two minutes past midnight.

Chapter Thirty-Three

People meant well and Alison knew that, but the constant company of her parents, relatives and friends around Caharoe that she had clung to for survival in the first days and weeks after Dan had died had now become suffocating. She was having no time alone with Lucy and she was finding it difficult to know how her little girl was coping with the loss of her father. She seemed to be getting a little better as every day passed, but with people around all the time fussing about everything from what she was eating to the toys she was playing with they were inhabiting an unreal world. Alison knew she would have to pluck them from these false surroundings and see if the two of them could build something from the fragments they had been left. She knew it would take courage that she didn't know if she possessed for the two of them to set off alone, a pair where once there had been three. Dan had wanted more children, he used to joke that he would settle for five, but Alison had delayed, hoping to get the post of Assistant Principal in the school. Maternity leave would not have helped her cause, she felt, and she persuaded Dan that they had plenty of time because she was only thirty-three. 'We have years left,' was her standard response when he raised the issue of not wanting Lucy to be an only child as they themselves had been. He agreed because of course they had, and then he would ask her a few short weeks later if she had changed her mind. Now she had taken extended leave from her teaching post and wasn't even sure if she could ever go back. Going out to work had always been followed by coming home to Dan. It had been the rhythm of her life and she was at a loss without its comforting pattern. Michaelmas, full of people all the time, only echoed with reminders of what was missing: with his empty chair, the surgery running without him, rows of suits hanging in the wardrobe and the vacant space beside her in their bed. She thought of Lucy, who loved to walk between them, holding each of their hands, when they went on their walks through Bracken Woods at the weekend. It cut her right to the bone that her little girl would never again experience the absolute security of a parent at either hand, listening to every word and sharing every step.

First she would tackle her father-in-law, who had more or less taken up residence in Lovett's Hotel, hoping to find something in his daily visits to Michaelmas that would mend what had been broken the night he lost his son. He broke down every time he was with Lucy so on top of losing her father she had to cope with a grandfather who couldn't stop crying when faced with the fact that she was the only precious remnant of his dead son. When he returned to Lovett's at night he drank whiskey in his room until he fell asleep or passed out; whichever happened first. His face had aged dramatically and his features struggled against the dead weight of unimaginable heartache. His suits hung from his frame loosely and tauntingly as if pain would soon hollow him out completely and leave only a shell ruined by loss. He blamed himself for sending Dan on a journey when he should have gone himself and he felt sure Alison blamed him too, or if she didn't she had every right to do so. He hung around Caharoe thinking that if anything were to change the way he was feeling it would surely happen here where Dan had called home.

Three months after Dan's death Alison found herself alone with Con in the kitchen at Michaelmas. Her mother had taken Lucy for a day out at Fota and her father had resumed his old role as the town GP. Alison knew that his heart was no longer in the job. The break in France and the fact that he no longer had Dan to pass the practice on to had shaken his devotion to medicine totally. He was doing it now just to keep himself busy and to stop himself thinking. Her mother had admitted as much to her. She would have to get her parents to resume their life too but that was another day's work. Firstly she felt responsibility to put her father-in-law back on an even keel.

'You know, Con, we can't really go on like this, you living in Lovett's and being here every day. Don't get me wrong. I wouldn't mind you being here if I thought it was doing you any good, but you seem to be getting worse with every passing minute. Don't you miss Leachlara, your home, your friends, people like Columbo?'

'I miss Dan, Alison, that's what I miss.' He bowed his head and she felt bad for talking to him when he clearly wasn't ready. Yet there was nothing to be gained from him sulking around the house drunk or well on his way to getting there. Moving on was imperative for all of them.

'We all miss him. Dan was at the heart of everything for all of us.' Alison fought back the tears that were gathering at the corners of her eyes. She knew she had to be strong for her own sake and for Con's too. 'Why don't you go home to Leachlara every few days and then come back here to spend some time with Lucy and myself? You have such a lot of people there that care for you. People who would look out for you. Sure there is no one in Lovett's that you know really. It's miserable to be in that place drinking on your own when you could be in Shanahan's with a few people to talk to while you had your pint.'

'I didn't realize I wasn't wanted. I'll go tonight.' His tone was one of petulant self-pity and because the gentle approach hadn't worked Alison had no alternative but to deliver a few home truths.

'Listen, Con, you are not being fair. I have made it abundantly plain that you are welcome in this house but what kind of example are you setting for Lucy? She has been through things a little girl should not have to see and I won't have her look at you rot over in Lovett's and turn into someone she doesn't even recognize. We are all she has left, you and me and my mam and dad. We have to keep things together and you are not doing that right now. That has to change.' She was winded after her spiel and she hoped she wasn't being too cruel but her well of mothering had enough calls on it minding Lucy. It did not have reserves to protect Con from himself too.

'OK. I will go back to Leachlara during the week and maybe call to you and Lucy each weekend. Is that all right with you?' He eyed her uncertainly, unsure of his ground. In his heart and soul he knew he needed a good shake-up but he didn't feel able to resume normal life. Nothing would be the same without Dan – but he would have to try. He couldn't hide out in Caharoe any longer.

'We would look forward to that, Con. We really would. I've been thinking about moving out of Michaelmas. There doesn't seem to be much point in staying here without Dan. To be honest I am fairly sure that my father has lost interest in the practice and there is no point in me living here when a GP and his family could take over the place on a lease. I can let the decision of what to do with Michaelmas in the long term wait for a while. I won't move far though. Just a few miles out the road because I want Lucy to stay in Caharoe School with her friends. Nor would I want to live in another house in the town because not one of them could compare to Michaelmas.' She looked around the kitchen as she spoke. Something in the place had died with Dan and she knew she could not stay here. 'But wherever we go, Con, there will always be a bed for you and I mean that with all my heart.'

Con reached his hand to her across the table where they had shared a pot of tea. He had so many things he needed to say, mostly about the guilt that racked him because Dan had died on his way back from Dublin after seeing Leda on his account. He needed Alison to absolve him of some of the responsibility because he couldn't bear its weight much longer. He gripped her hand tightly but words had a habit of failing him since all this had happened. Alison knew pretty much what he was thinking.

'You know, Con, I tried to persuade Dan to stay the night in Dublin. We have plenty of friends that he could have called in on and stayed over or he could have booked a hotel. I told him he could ring a locum agency and get someone to stand in for him on the Tuesday morning surgery but he was having none of it. He wanted to be home here with us. What happened is one of those awful tragic things that happen every day to other families. I just never thought it would happen to us or to Dan. He was such a careful driver, too. I always loved travelling with him. I felt so safe whenever I was with him. I don't feel safe any more. I think now anything can happen.' She looked at Con, who seemed more depressed than ever listening to her. 'God, listen to me. I will have us both in floods of tears if I don't stop and we both know Dan would have wanted us to buck up and be strong for Lucy.'

'He would. He wanted everything for you and Lucy. He was so proud of you both. I think he was a bit ashamed of me, and who could blame him? I handed over that folder of stuff from Leda to Robert Lalor a few nights ago in Lovett's. I could tell that he was shocked at the extent of the mess I had gotten myself into. To be honest, I couldn't recall some of the stuff myself. I ignored it while it all simmered away in the background.'

'What did he advise you to do next?'

'I don't have to do a thing. He is going to approach the Revenue on my behalf and say I want to make a full settlement of everything I owe. He has an accountant attached to the firm who will estimate the final total for me. There will be fines and all sorts of penalties of course but there's plenty of property to sell, so even if it takes every cent then so be it. My name will be in the paper of course as a tax dodger but I couldn't give a damn now. The party will distance itself from me but sure they have done that already. Counted votes are soon forgotten and I mean nothing to them any more. I was important once but I don't matter an iota in the end.'

'It will be good to get it sorted once and for all. It's what Dan would have wanted you to do.'

'Yes. Dan was always strictly honest and maybe I made him that way with all my crooked little schemes. The only good thing about all of this is there won't be a bit left for Leda Clancy if she decides to come calling for more. She has nothing on me now and there's a small bit of comfort in that. I'll get my stuff together in Lovett's and I will tip off back to Leachlara. Will you tell Lucy that I will see her in a few days?'

She saw Con to the front door of Michaelmas and watched him as he gingerly picked his steps across the square. She hoped he wouldn't knock back a whiskey for the road but she couldn't stop him. It was the first break she was consciously making with the past. Dan was gone. Every day from here on in would be spent coping with that heartbreaking fact.

Ann Baxter, a neighbour and good friend from two doors up, was passing by the door and greeted Alison with a smile whose meaning she had come to decipher over the past number of months. It was part pity mixed with several parts of not having a clue what the best thing was to say.

'How are you, Ann?' offered Alison in order to bypass the awful awkwardness she felt when people treated her as if she might shatter into a million fine pieces under their gaze.

'Oh, everything's grand with us, but tell me how are you feeling? We all find it so hard to think Dan is gone.' She bit her lip then, thinking that she shouldn't have mentioned Dan's name, and her face flushed at her slip-up.

'I'm not great, to be honest. It's very hard but for Lucy's sake I will have to manage it somehow. I have no choice. I miss him terribly and there is not a minute of the day that I don't think of him and I'm not sure I want that to stop. What if I start forgetting him, Ann? What will I do then?'

Ann stepped up to where Alison was standing and wrapped her in a solid hug. 'Everyone on this street cares about you and we all cared about Dan. We will pull you through all of this if you let us.'

Alison was at once grateful and overwhelmed by all the kindness she had been offered. She and Dan had led a very private life and now everything from her tears to her and her daughter's future was a public commodity. She felt, in spite of all the kindness, as if she were thoroughly unprotected, that she had been skinned alive and every contact was sharper and deeper than she could cope with.

Ann made her promise to call in for a cup of coffee some morning and to talk if she wanted. When she was gone Alison closed the front door of Michaelmas behind her. She leaned against its solidness for support. Tears fell, as they did every day. 'I miss you, Dan,' she said aloud in the empty hallway and for a moment she imagined she could see him smiling and walking towards her. When she wiped away the tears he was gone.

Lucy and Alison's mother would be home soon and her father would be finished in the surgery. Maybe she would fix something for them all to eat. It had been ages since she had attempted even the smallest task for herself and Lucy. Making dinner would only be a small attempt at normality, but she had to start somewhere.

Chapter Thirty-Four

'I think, Mam, that you and Dad should go back to France so that Lucy and I have somewhere to go on holidays. It is senseless you both staying on here running a surgery that neither of you are the slightest bit interested in any more.'

Alison had brought her mother out for an early-evening walk while Richard Shepherd had looked after seeing Lucy to bed and reading her a bedtime story. Caharoe was quiet at that hour of the evening. Shoppers had gone home, schoolchildren had retreated to dinners and attempts to unravel homework and the pubs had yet to empty of the after-work drinkers. They headed for the Bracken river walk that would bring them out on the Mountainacre Road; from there they would trace the loop home that would bring them down the lane that linked Earl Street with the main street in Caharoe. It would take them a good forty minutes, time, Alison hoped, to get everything she was struggling with off her chest. She knew that approaching her mother and not her father was the best way to get them to reconsider their decision to stay in Caharoe indefinitely.

'I mean, Dad got back up on the surgery treadmill because he feels it is the most practical thing he could be doing. But he has not stopped to think that the surgery means nothing to me now that Dan is gone. If you are not running it for yourselves, which I think you most definitely are not, please, please, Mam, don't be doing it on my account.'

Cathy Shepherd was taken aback. She had to admit that they had thrown themselves into running the surgery automatically after Dan had died so that Alison would not have to worry about it. It had not occurred to her or to Richard that their daughter had already finished with the Michaelmas family practice.

'Do you not think it a bit soon, Alison? I mean too soon after Dan for you and Lucy to be alone? I understand why you had to see off Con. The man was going to drink himself to death outside your door if you didn't take him in hand, but Dad and myself are different, surely? We are trying to help even if we are making a bags of it.'

'Oh, Mam, I don't mean to be thankless and I am sorry if I came across that way but alone is exactly what Lucy and I will be. I have to see if we can find our feet without being propped up at every turn. I know you and Dad mean well and, believe me, a huge part of me wants you both to stay here for ever, standing between me and everything difficult that will come up. That won't solve anything in the long run though. I owe it to Lucy to make things work out all right for the two of us. I owe it to Dan, because he would do the same for her if I was gone.'

Cathy was not convinced that her daughter knew what was good for her on this occasion. It had been such a short time since her son-in-law had died and although she took her daughter's attempt at bravery as an encouraging sign that she was making progress in dealing with her grief, she couldn't help but think that it was too much too soon. She waited until they were out of earshot of Betty Linehan, who was walking her dog. Betty had greeted them warmly and yet again Alison felt the X-ray gaze that attempted to work out exactly how she was doing. Betty was a lovely woman but she was a vessel made for news and Cathy didn't want her knowing any of her family's business.

'We want to help, Alison. We want to deal with the difficult things that will arise so that you don't have to. Running the surgery is one less thing for you to worry about, no?'

Alison was close to total exasperation. She felt strangled by all the help; her parents convinced that even in her thirties she was next to incapable of doing anything for herself. 'Mam, just think about what you have just said for a minute. Dan is gone. Running the surgery for me is a waste of your time and you said yourself it is driving Dad up the wall—'

'No, what I said was that he is finding it difficult to adjust to the workload after all the relaxation in France, but it's nothing he can't get used to, honestly.'

'Dad is burnt out, Mam. Can't you see? The place needs a young GP to cope with all the new patients. Dan was even thinking of taking on a junior partner because the patient list had almost doubled in a couple of years. Dad and yourself are struggling and for what?'

Cathy was having difficulty imagining another GP in Michaelmas House. She still thought of the place as home even though she hadn't lived in it for more than a decade.

'I don't think it would be very pleasant for you and Lucy to have tenants on the middle floor. It would break up the house entirely. It's not a good idea to have strangers sharing your home.'

Alison took a deep breath and ploughed on. 'That's the other thing. I don't really want to live in Michaelmas any longer. The big gap that Dan has left there is too painful for me. Without him the place doesn't feel like home and if I am not happy there I won't be able to make Lucy happy either. We could lease the place to a GP and his or her family. I have enough money set aside that I can buy another smaller house for myself and Lucy, and in the future you, me and Dad can decide what should be done with Michaelmas in the long run.'

The colour had drained from her mother's face and Alison was genuinely sorry that she had to upset her parents in order to move on herself.

'I had no idea that you felt that way about Michaelmas. I somehow thought you would always be there, but with Dan gone things have changed, I know that. Your dad had said to me that maybe you would want to move but I told him he was talking nonsense. I will have to go back with my tail between my legs on that front. It's not like your father to be so prescient. Maybe living in France has done him the world of good.' Cathy managed a smile that relieved a little of her daughter's guilt. The fall of summer darkness was still some way off, but they picked up their pace a little so that they would have negotiated the more dangerous bends of the road while there was still some brightness to light their way.

'I was thinking of moving a little bit out of town. Everyone in Caharoe has been so good to me but I feel as if I have been stuck in the same place all my life. That's not necessarily a bad thing but right now it all feels claustrophobic. I want Lucy to keep her friends in school, so only a few miles out. There are houses being built and for sale everywhere so it shouldn't be that difficult to find something.'

'Why don't I get your father to talk to Robert Lalor? He would have you fixed up with a place in no time. He has contacts—'

'Mam, do you remember what I said? I need to be able to handle things for myself. I know you are trying to help but—'

'But I am going feet first into what is essentially your own business again. OK, I am getting the message.'

Alison had already decided that she would ask Colm Lifford to help her with the legal elements of the purchase of a house. Dan had been really impressed with him and had told Alison that he was a thoroughly nice and sound sort of a man. Alison had always found the Lalor men a bit creepy so it seemed a good move to change her own private legal affairs to someone who didn't know her seed, breed and generation inside out. Besides, she had other reasons for wanting to meet Colm Lifford and she was about to test one of them out on her mother, who now seemed lost in her melancholy thoughts.

'Do you remember Ciara and Leda Clancy, Mam?' Alison had not told her parents that Dan had been visiting Leda in Dublin the night he had died. She made up some function that he could have feasibly wanted to attend and left it at that. It seemed pointless to add another layer of heartache to what had already happened and her parents would never have forgiven Con Abernethy for Dan dying while on a mercy mission on his behalf. Alison felt that Con had enough to contend with without taking on the Shepherds' angry disapproval.

'Oh, Alison, what a silly question. How could I forget them? I can still remember the day that you and Dan arrived back from Aughasallagh looking so distraught and all because of that little rip who couldn't keep her hands to herself. I was glad you dealt with her so well, showed her you wouldn't tolerate that sort of behaviour in a friend. I did think the two of you would make up eventually though. I was a bit sorry that you didn't.'

In the weeks after Aughasallagh Cathy had reported every time Ciara rang the surgery, but she could never get any positive reaction from her daughter. Alison's position on Ciara refused to soften even when it became clear that her relationship with Dan would weather the storm. Ciara gave up her attempts to get back in touch when her efforts were continually ignored. Even when they drew up the wedding-invitation list Ciara's name did not feature and Cathy decided to let the issue lie. Her daughter was quiet but stubborn too.

Dan had kept his word to Alison and until the day he had found out about Colm Lifford knowing Ciara he had not mentioned her name, sticking faithfully to the promise he made the night he thought he might lose her for good. It all felt so over the top to Alison now and she was ashamed of her behaviour. She was ready to admit that she had missed Ciara's friendship keenly in the months since Dan's death. Every time her mind had gone back over their early months and years together, Ciara's presence overwhelmed her memories. It seemed as if she couldn't picture Dan without seeing also the face of her lost friend.

'I had no right to banish her for good or make Dan promise never to mention her name again. It all seems so juvenile, looking back. He was upset and they were drunk. They acted foolishly and I made the two of them suffer for over ten years. I can honestly say that I have never had more than two glasses of wine at any one time in my life. How can I know what I would do if I were that drunk and that upset? I shouldn't have judged them so harshly and I should have trusted what I had with Dan was strong enough to withstand a stupid slip-up and not behaved like a little girl when her favourite toy is snatched from her. I've made friends since, plenty of them, through teaching and through my life with Dan, and they have been really brilliant to me, but being with her was how I imagined it would be to have a sister. I should have just been a bit more grown up.'

Alison thought about her closest friend, Ellen, a teacher in the school, who had minded her so well since Dan had died. Calling to the house every day after school, bringing dishes of food that their diminished appetites could not possibly do justice to and ringing her every night around bedtime to make sure she was doing OK. She knew that was real friendship but she couldn't help being haunted by the way she had cut ties with Ciara, pulling out the tender roots of something that could have been with her for a lifetime.

'Well, it did seem a little over the top at the time, but you were so certain that I gave up trying to talk you out of it. Have you thought of getting in touch with her since Dan died? People change though, so if you do contact her be prepared for her to be different than you remember. Ten years is a long time.'

'I really thought she would turn up at Dan's funeral if she heard – and she must have heard. It was big news in Leachlara and her folks still live there. How silly is that? After cutting her out like a bit of disease I still thought she would come to my rescue. I even wrote her a letter the night of Dan's funeral, when the house was full downstairs and I thought I couldn't breathe with all the people around me. I didn't post it of course because I was too chicken shit to follow through on it.'

'You could find out where to get hold of her, couldn't you? A phone call to the Clancys in Leachlara should get you her address or her phone number.'

'I don't think I will have to go as far as that. Dan had a meeting with the new solicitor on Bridge Street a week or so before he died. Turns out he has a son about the same age as Lucy, a bit younger I think, and Leda Clancy is the child's mother. Leda abandoned the two of them a few days after the child was born, but he is still in touch with Ciara. I can ask him.'

'I would believe anything about Leda Clancy, I really would. I wonder was she still carrying on with Con while she was letting her child to fend for itself?'

'Well, she left it with its father. That's not fending for itself, I guess.'

Cathy took that as a cue from her daughter to stop gossiping about Leda. 'Why didn't you tell me any of this before if it was bothering you?'

'The truth of it is that I don't really know if contacting Ciara will do any good, but it's something I know I must do. Even if she slaps me in the face I have to take that too. It's part of the whole growing-up thing and I have left it way too late on a lot of fronts. As for leaving Michaelmas, well, don't you think it's about time I left home?' Alison smiled at her mother who had been there for her through everything, who knew every single one of her faults and loved her anyway.

'Don't be hard on yourself, love. We all have things we wish we could have done differently. It's part of being alive. Without the mistakes we would not have experienced anything worthwhile.'

'Were you always so wise?' Alison attempted to lighten the atmosphere as they turned the corner of Earl Street on to the square in Caharoe.

'I will have punctures put in my wisdom now when I tell your father I am taking him across to Lovett's for a drink. He will be settled in watching the news and he will be like a grumpy old hen, scratching and pecking and not wanting to be moved off her perch. Still, a drink in his hand will come in handy when I tell him everything you have told me tonight.'

'Thanks. I appreciate you doing the referee bit. Dad and I have always needed you in the middle to translate.'

'Hurry up before he falls asleep at the fire, because then there will be no moving him.'

Cathy Shepherd watched as her daughter turned the key in the door of Michaelmas. She didn't look at the plaque on the wall that had marked this place as her home. She knew only too well that staring sadness down never made it a shred easier to bear.

Chapter Thirty-Five

It took almost six weeks of fussing and packing and incessant reconsidering of their decision before Cathy and Richard Shepherd finally made it to the ferry port in Ringaskiddy to bring them back to France. Richard had booked flights for Alison and Lucy into Poitiers airport for two months later, feeling he could only relax in France if he knew when exactly to the minute and the hour he would see his daughter and granddaughter again. He was sad that the next time he and Cathy would come home, most likely at Christmas, they would not be staying in Michaelmas, but he knew that they could not tie Alison to a house that she had decided she couldn't settle in any more. Not after all that had happened. It would be a bit rich to be churlish about her leaving when he and Cathy had already decided that a little run-down villa outside Saumur was an infinitely more attractive prospect for them. Pursuit of the sun had driven them further south to find a permanent base and the châteaux of the Loire had completed the seduction. Missing being a doctor was not an issue. He wasn't quite sure when he had reached the patient-overload stage but he had found it hard to listen intently or sincerely as yet another tale of woe was set out before him. Since Dan's death he had felt like an alien in a world of his own making. The new computer system that his son-in-law had put in to modernize the place (only moments, it would seem, after he had left for France) was a devil to negotiate and the simple act of writing a prescription had turned into a palaver that threatened to undo him every time. Out of a list of possible prescription drugs he had on occasion selected the wrong one and was lucky enough that the staff at Esther Quinn's chemist shop were sharp and knew their customers and their attendant ailments well. He had interviewed a number of GPs who were interested in leasing the house and practice at Michaelmas and had settled on a husband and wife team, Helen and Michael Dowling, GPs of six years' experience in a Dublin practice, who wanted to move with their young family back to their native Munster. They seemed warm, enthusiastic and keen; the traits that Richard Shepherd felt had lately deserted him. He thought of them as two safe pairs of hands and that was what the practice and Caharoe needed. They agreed on an initial three-year lease, time enough, Richard hoped, for Alison and Lucy to be settled in their new house and willing to make permanent the leaving of Michaelmas.

'I think you are going to like this one, Alison, and I say that while bearing in mind how cruelly you have dismissed some of the properties I have already shown you.'

There was an air of mischief in Colm Lifford's voice, and she knew she had been a little bit cutting about one house in particular that he had given her the keys of to look around. He had a pretty good relationship with Sean O'Connor, an auctioneer a few doors up from him on Bridge Street, and he had been able to secure private viewings for Alison of houses up for sale around Caharoe.

'You're not still smarting over that monstrosity with pillars that you showed me out on the Mountainacre Road, are you?' Alison chipped.

'I would say "monstrosity" is a touch strong but how was I to know that you had a thing against pillars?'

'I don't have a thing against real pillars that are fundamental to the construction of a house but I do hate the ones that look as if they have been purloined from a child's Lego set to be tacked on and spray painted, in this case a brutal shade of peach.'

'OK, I get the message. No pillars, ever again. Do you want to hear about this dinky little house that has just come up for sale? I think our search might be over.'

'Whereabouts is it?'

'Well, if you and Lucy fancy a bit of a mystery tour with myself and Tom on Saturday morning I will get the keys from Sean O'Connor and take you up there.'

'That sounds like a brilliant idea. I think it's really important for Lucy to see the houses we might move to but to be honest I think she is losing the will to live watching me go in and out of rooms as if all will be revealed by one more open door. She would love to have Tom there to mess around with and I would like to have your opinion on the place too.'

'That's a plan so. We will pick you both up at about eleven. Now, do you remember I said that Ciara was off in India on some kind of trekking holiday? Well, she's back as of last night.'

'Have you managed to talk to her about me?' Alison's heart pounded. Her head told her that it didn't matter what Ciara said. Yes, she would be disappointed if Ciara was not interested, but it had been ten years, after all, and as her mother had warned her, people do change – but her heart still raced.

'Yes, I talked to her this morning. She was a bit shocked that I knew you and admitted she had been avoiding coming to see Tom and me here because she didn't want to run into you by accident in Caharoe. Says she nearly died when I told her we were moving here. Of all the towns in all the world and all of that. Anyway, if you are willing she says she would love to see you and she has agreed to come to Tom's birthday party in October so you could maybe meet her there. But a chance to talk on your own before then might be easier. I can arrange it, or do you want to call her yourself?'

Alison allowed herself to breathe again. 'I really appreciate all your help, I really do, but I should take it from here. If it goes badly, I don't want it to spoil Tom's party. Besides, I have wasted enough time already. If you give me her details I will call or email her.'

'She asked me to tell you how absolutely sorry she was about what happened to Dan and wanted to know all about Lucy, so I filled her in as best I could.'

Colm was hoping that the mentioning of Dan's name wouldn't upset Alison too much. He knew how raw she must still feel.

'That was nice of her. Maybe if he hadn't died I wouldn't have thought to make contact with her again. Who knows? Thank you again, Colm, because I am not sure I would have known how to make the first move. I look forward to Saturday.' Alison hung up the phone as emotions of all colours washed over her. She had expected rejection from Ciara, had felt on some level that she probably deserved it, so Colm's news of her reaction was a welcome but overwhelming relief.

Colm put down the phone too and enjoyed the blissful silence of the office on Betty's day off. He couldn't help smiling. She wanted his opinion about her house and she appreciated his help with Ciara, although in truth that was not a difficult task as Ciara had jumped at the offer. She had even given him the bones of their falling-out. Ciara admitted that she had developed a bit of a crush on Dan the summer of their final exams and when left alone with him the night of his mother's funeral she had encouraged his drunken kisses and was hurt when he pulled away disgustedly from her. 'Of course, me being me, I couldn't help making the mess bigger by trying it on again a few weeks later. Dan was having none of it, which was bad enough for my ego but that would have been the end of it only this time Alison caught me in the act.' Ciara told Colm that she had tried to make amends with Alison but her friend had remained stubborn and had ignored her until now. 'Sometimes I blamed Dan, thinking he must have forced her to cut me off, but I can't be sure. Maybe I will get to ask her now.'

Colm thought it seemed kind of old-fashioned to fall out with your best friend for over a decade for something that was ultimately so harmless. There were so many bigger betrayals possible in life, but then he had to remember not everyone had had a life that taught them that trust was an affliction suffered only by the inexperienced. He had to chide himself for being a cynical old misery when he started thinking like that and he had to admit that meeting and spending time with Alison had awakened something in him that he thought his bruising experience with Leda had ruined for good. He found it hard to stop picturing her face and he loved the sound of her voice, soft, lilting and a little playful. Maybe, just maybe there could be something there. Time, and he was prepared to devote plenty of it, would tell. He had come to enjoy his conversations with Alison Abernethy once they had got over any initial awkwardness of both knowing far too much about each other's business without having ever met properly. Alison had made it plain that anything she knew from Dan would remain confidential between them (she had sworn her mother to secrecy) and Colm obviously had no interest in delving more deeply into the relationship between her father-in-law and the mother of his child. He told her that he wished he had been kinder to Dan on the one occasion they had met but he was knocked sideways by how much Dan had known about his life, when Colm had thought that Caharoe could be a fresh start. Alison reassured him that he couldn't have been too off-putting because Dan had told her that Colm Lifford seemed way too straight and decent a man to be a solicitor. Colm laughed and said he would take the sideways swipe of her late husband as a compliment.

He had been living in Caharoe for twelve months without so much as thinking about a woman (if you didn't count how to throttle Betty Linehan) and he knew his stifled-up desire was bound to catch up with him eventually. He had gone out with a handful of women in Dublin since Tom had been born. He had never found it difficult to get dates for work functions or weddings, but he had never let himself get more than superficially involved with anyone since Leda. He and Tom had way too much to lose if he got close to someone and it didn't work out. He had decided, until he met Alison Abernethy that is, to steer clear of anything serious. He was acutely aware that his judgement had let him down before and he was sensitive to the fact that it was only months since she had lost her husband. Alison had come to him for his professional help and he would keep it strictly professional as long as that was what she wanted, but at the first sign that she wanted more, he would be only too happy to admit how he felt himself.

Chapter Thirty-Six

Alison was doing her best to prepare herself for the expected ring of the doorbell, but she was overcome with nerves as she made her way from the kitchen of her new house to the front door. Colm had taken Lucy and Tom to see a film in Cork and had promised them treats afterwards so Alison knew that she had plenty of time with Ciara. It had been a risk suggesting Ciara come to Cork but she had readily agreed. She had flown in to Cork airport from London that morning, where Colm and an overexcited Tom had picked her up. They had left her bags at Lantern Lodge and Colm gave her the keys to an old car that he hadn't yet got round to selling. He was glad he had kept the insurance up and Ciara too was happy to be able to arrive at Alison's house under her own steam. Colm wished her good luck before he and Tom left to collect Lucy. Iris Lifford was due for one of her flying visits, and he counselled Ciara to be gone before his whirlwind mother roped her into redecorating or making dinner enough to feed twenty, which were her favourite occupations when she visited her son and grandson. It didn't matter that Colm told her every time she came to Lantern Lodge that she was to relax and take it easy and that he had come to enjoy cooking so she wouldn't starve if she would just wait for him to make dinner. She couldn't help herself and seeing as he couldn't stop her he'd given up trying. Ciara had only upped her domesticity a notch or two, from nonexistent to passable, so she was in no real mood to tussle with Granny Lifford over the Marigolds or the bleach. Better to pour Colm's mother a glass of wine before dinner and congratulate her on a job expertly completed. Before she could get to that glass of wine, however, she had to survive a visit with her friend whom she hadn't seen for eleven years. When Ciara came to think about it, Iris Lifford might be very lucky indeed to get anything from the first bottle if today went badly.

Nothing much fazed Ciara any more. She was good at her job at the language school despite the fact that teaching bored her rigid. She had travelled a bit and shaken off the Leachlara birthmark that she felt as a handicap when she had first left, young and innocent but energized by a compulsion to flee at all costs. Still, on the point of confronting Alison, her first true adult friend, whatever composed confidence she had managed to cultivate in the intervening years seemed to fracture as lunchtime grew closer. Colm had carefully written out directions to Alison's house, which turned out to be only a few miles of convoluted country lanes away from Lantern Lodge.

Colm said she would spot Alison's home immediately. Her new stone house stood out in the sea of identikit bungalows that trimmed the road like braid. To the side was a room almost entirely of glass reflecting the rich colours of the garden. The house was the first thing they spoke about when Ciara arrived on the dot of one o'clock. It seemed an easy and neutral topic, unlike much of what else they might have to discuss.

'It really is beautiful, Alison, really smart and yet cosy-looking. How did you find it or did you have it built?'

'Colm found it for me. He knew I wanted to move out of Michaelmas and when he saw this was for sale he brought me up here to see it. I put an offer in before we even left that first day. An American writer had it built as her retreat, but when it came to it she found Caharoe just too small and quiet. She still calls from time to time. It seemed to matter to her that I fell in love with the place. I think it compensates for the fact that she didn't go through with her plan to base herself here. She's very New York though. Caharoe must have seemed like the end of the world.'

'It's pretty different from Michaelmas. Do you miss living in the town?' Ciara was looking at the house and, while she could appreciate the fact that it was beautiful, she knew she could never live in the middle of nowhere again. Leachlara had cured her of that. From the minute she left she hankered after the city, with all its attendant buzz and promise. Noise and distraction remained her salvation.

'It's different to Michaelmas, that's for sure, with none of the nooks and crannies and the crooked walls, but I knew I could make it my own. Apart from the time I spent with you in Dublin I lived my entire life in that house and I most likely would have been happy to stay there except for what happened. I needed to start again and I couldn't do that in Michaelmas. I still see all the friends and neighbours that I had in town. They sometimes come out here, braving the absence of street lights, but they prefer me to come into town, convincing themselves that my trip in there is less of a distance than the haul out here! I had been looking, wondering if I would even know the right house if it came up, and the minute we saw this both Lucy and I thought it was just perfect. Or "deadly", as Lucy would say. It's her new word. "Cool" is just so last year, you know.'

Ciara laughed and welcoming the opening in the conversation she asked if she could see photos of Lucy. Alison reached to a shelf by the fireplace and took down a bulging photo album, the sight of which made Ciara gulp, though she hoped not audibly.

'Here, look at this and while I get our lunch together you can pretend you looked at all of them.'

'What makes you think that I won't look at every single one?' Ciara said, annoyed at herself for messing up before they had barely begun.

'Oh, I don't know. Maybe because you always had the attention span of a gnat and I guess I am hoping you haven't changed too much.' Alison smiled, hoping that a little humour might smooth the way for them to open up with one another.

'Well, as it happens my attention span is as crippled as it always was but I did think I had got a little bit more skilful at covering my shortcomings.'

Alison disappeared into the kitchen and from the living room Ciara could hear the kettle boiling and the low hum of the radio. It seemed that Alison was still addicted to it. The butterflies in Ciara's stomach relaxed a little and she looked at the photos of Lucy, the green eyes of Dan and, with them, the echoes of the past looking back at her from every one.

They picked over a lunch that neither had any real appetite for while both tried to work up the courage to talk about Dan. Accustomed to her role by now as his memory-keeper, it was Alison who mentioned him first.

'I half expected you to come to Dan's funeral. I knew you would have heard if you were in any contact with your parents. It was big news in Leachlara because of Con and everything.'

Try as she might, Ciara could not get herself to come up with a suitable response so Alison continued, determined for them to discuss what had torn them apart.

'Without Dan I felt I would hardly be able to stand upright, and for the first time I allowed myself to miss you. I feel so ashamed that we lost contact because of me. It seems such a waste, doesn't it? I wrote you a letter but I didn't know where to send it. To be honest, I am not sure I would have posted it even if I had known. Too afraid you might not respond, that you would say my getting in contact was too little too late. I know I don't deserve much after rejecting all your attempts to make things up.'

'I would have come, but I had no idea that you would have wanted me there. You made it pretty plain that you never wanted to see me again that night in Aughasallagh and when you wouldn't take my calls and sent back my letter I gave up. You are right, it is a waste, all this lost time, but you shouldn't blame yourself about what happened. I drank too much at Mary Abernethy's funeral and I lost myself in some sort of reverie over the perfect life that you and Dan had. Leda turned up hunting Con and I was reminded once again of how absolutely mental the entire Clancy household was. I wanted to be normal. I wanted some of what looked to be your perfect life and I tried to help myself. I am sorry, I really am. I'm not sparing Dan because he isn't here to defend himself: it was mostly my fault. He kissed me but I was the one that made the move on him really. Even though he was upset and drunk he still told me to cop on. I took advantage of you not being there and of him being in such a state. He must have told you how it happened. Then I made things worse that night on the beach. My pride was hurt that he had rejected me and so I tried it on again. I wanted to prove to myself that I could have him if I wanted to. It was drink, stupidity and a crush that had run a bit mad in my head.' Ciara was on a roll now. Her initial fear of being unable to speak about Dan was now being replaced by a growing panic that she would say too much and offend where she meant only to explain.

'We didn't really talk about it. Once I had forgiven him, and I forgave him because I wanted him more than anything, we never really spoke about it again. He never went back to Leachlara, or Aughasallagh either, not for a single night after that, and that put Con's nose seriously out of joint, but he had to learn to live with it or else never see us at all. When we settled here it was easy not to talk about it because it all seemed so distant. Dublin seemed like another life, as if it had happened to someone else.' Alison's expression was lonesome and it seemed to Ciara that she regretted how firmly she had closed the door on that previous life.

'We were so green, but at least you were always just yourself, Alison, whereas I was going around furiously trying to pretend I was more sophisticated than I actually was. All that gear from the charity shops was my way of trying to create another Ciara, someone who could give a good old lash to the world. Still trying to give a good old lash to the world – with mixed results.'

Alison listened as Ciara unravelled the uncertainty at the heart of all her attempts at bravado.

'You had me fooled. All I ever wanted was to have a fraction of your confidence, Ciara. In the beginning I never thought I deserved Dan. I thought he was so handsome and gorgeous that he was definitely going to get snatched away from me by someone better-looking or cleverer. You were the only one that buoyed my confidence and self-esteem about him. You kept telling me that he was the lucky one and I was so unsure of myself that I needed to hear that from you. That's why I couldn't bear it when you were the better-looking, clever one that I might have lost him to. I couldn't think straight. I just knew that if I could banish you we might have a chance. I should have given him credit for loving me as I know now that he did. He never wanted anyone else. I found that out in the time we had together.'

Ciara moved from where she sat at the table to the vacant chair at Alison's side. She felt like giving her shoulder a squeeze but thought some comforting words might be more appropriate. An awkward attempt at affection might ruin the shaky communication that they had just managed to open again. Besides, Alison wasn't finished talking and Ciara was hungry for her conversation.

'Do you ever see Leda now? Colm says you are in touch but wasn't sure to what extent.' Alison had thought about withholding the information of Dan's trip to Leda, but if they were to attempt a reconciliation she knew that it was better to have everything out in the open.

'I know where she lives and I know she is OK. I email sometimes just to check in with her but to be honest I absolved myself of guilt about her wayward behaviour a long time ago. I had to, because every stunt she pulled seemed to outdo the last and I had to admit that, try as I might, I had no control over her. What she did to Colm and to Tom was the last straw, walking away from them like they were of no concern. I told Colm that he was better off without her but that doesn't change the fact that what she did was unforgivable. She seems to have settled a bit, met this rich banking guy in England and they got married in Mauritius a few weeks ago. Never met him but he sounds impressive – or should I say the width of his wallet does? Leachlara was deprived of a good gawk at a Clancy family wedding and I guess she was thoughtful in that regard, because I don't think the Clancys are capable of squeezing out a respectable family occasion. The wedding feast of Cana wouldn't be in it with the need for miracles to keep the drink flowing with my dad on the premises. I don't intend testing them on it anyway, if I ever do take the plunge over that unlikely cliff.'

Alison got up and pulled two glasses from the painted dresser next to where they were sitting. She took a corkscrew from the drawer and a bottle of red from the racks that lined the side of a kitchen cupboard.

'I suppose this should have been breathing, but I think a glass or two might help for the next thing I have to tell you.' She poured a generous glass for Ciara and a meaner portion for herself. She still didn't drink much, had never found the taste for it, though she had tried when an anaesthetic against heartache would have been a valuable discovery. Ciara listened rapt as Alison explained about Leda's attempt to blackmail Con and how it had led to him being close to bankruptcy. She told her that was where Dan had been the night he had died, delivering money to her sister, attempting to buy her future silence.

'Oh, sweet divine Alison, I am so dreadfully sorry. I had no idea. How much did she take him for?' Ciara gulped the red wine that Alison had poured, grateful for its warmth, washing away the grit that seemed to have lodged in her throat.

'Not much really in the scheme of things, one hundred and fifty thousand euros, but he is in the middle of a very large settlement with the Revenue for tax evasion, which includes massive penalties and fines that will see most of what he had disappear. He doesn't seem to care, to be honest. He still has his TD's pension – not sure what you would have to do to be stripped of that – so he is not exactly destitute, but he does worry that Leda will come calling again when this money runs out. Could you talk to her? It might make a difference if she knew you know everything. Whatever you think, it was plain she was always fairly terrified of you.'

Ciara promised to talk to Leda and threaten with every ounce of menace that she could muster to throttle her if she so much as picked up the phone to Con Abernethy again. She could still remember how much she hated the man, but Leda was now no better than him. Whatever high moral ground she once occupied as the wronged party had been levelled by her own bad behaviour, her willingness to sink to any depths to get her hands on some cash.

They talked while dusk fell stealthily outside, never bothering to switch on the kitchen lights. A lit lamp from the sitting room cast enough glow through the open door for them to see each other where they sat at the kitchen table. When hunger struck they plundered the well-stocked snack tin, with Ciara going into paroxysms of delight when she spotted Lucy's favourite Macaroon bars in the bottom. 'Jesus, I used to eat these by the lorryload in Leachlara. Let me see if they are still as good.'

She filled Alison in on a decade spent mostly outside of Ireland on the run from home, from boredom and from settling down. Her job at the language school was frustrating her and she was thinking seriously of setting up on her own, finding a premises and doing up a website to canvas for foreign students.

'To be honest, the teaching end of it is doing my head in. I'm not sure how much longer I can feign delight and pride when someone manages to conjugate a verb properly after months of trying. My patience, as you well know, has always let me down. I fancy a stab at running the show, and I'm sure I could get a loan to cover the rent of the premises if I do some creative accounting and perhaps change my name by deed poll. It's worth a shot, and if I got good teachers, word of mouth would have the place up and running after the first batch of students.'

'Sounds great, Ciara, and I know you would be brilliant at heading up your own business. You've got balls and even when you are terrified you still put on a brave front. You should go for it. If the name change and the creative accounting don't come through for you, give me a call. I could help you out with some start-up money, maybe not all of it but some at least.'

'Oh, there is no need for that! I really should be able to round it up myself. Thanks for the confidence boost though. I need a good kick to get me going.'

'So any interesting men on your travels then? All you have talked about is work. Is there a special someone that keeps you in London?'

Alison knew it was a bit rude to ask such a direct question when Ciara had not volunteered any information about her personal life, but they had an abundance of time to make up for that bypassed the need for good manners.

'No one at the moment and I have partially given up on men because I have such lousy luck with them. If I had met you six years ago I would have sworn on my life that I would be settled in Spain by now with this guy José that I spent nearly a year with there. He was gorgeous, sensitive and we got on great but at the end of the summer season he hightailed it back to his home village. Apparently I scared him. That was one amongst a veritable fucking bouquet of his reasons anyway. So I left Spain for London and have been over there since without anything much better happening to me. Maybe I *am* scary. What do you think?'

'No, I don't think you are scary. Formidable maybe, but not scary. I bet you someone will come along when you least expect them.'

'I have been least expecting it for about five years now and, by the way, "formidable" is just the politically correct way of saying I'm scary as hell, but thanks for putting it so nicely. You were so very well brought up always.'

Just then the headlights of Colm's car flooded the darkness of the kitchen. It was past seven and the movie would have been finished for hours. He had given them as much time as he could before interrupting their delicate reunion. He had rung Iris at Lantern Lodge to check if Ciara had arrived back there but she was alone fussing over what to make Tom and himself to eat when they returned.

'Tell you what, Mam, push the boat out. Roast the chicken we were going to have tomorrow and throw on a heap of roast potatoes and your killer gravy. I'll pick up Ciara and Alison on the way and we will have one of your feasts.'

'God, you are not giving me much notice, Colm. Really, a phone call earlier in the day would have been polite.' Iris's tone was perfunctory but not brittle. She wasn't really annoyed and Colm knew her well enough to know that.

'I didn't know earlier in the day and stop pretending you

don't like a culinary challenge because there is nothing you like more. We will be there in an hour or so. I'll pick up some ice cream for dessert.'

Lucy and Tom were asleep in the back of the car, finally worn out from inhaling industrial amounts of popcorn and talking like lunatics through the film and after it. Just as well Colm had not been interested in the movie because he had barely heard a word of it, so overwhelming were the voices of his company.

He delivered the invitation to dinner to Alison and Ciara while he left the engine running to keep his young charges asleep. They seemed happy enough to fall in with his plans and he interpreted this as a sign that their day had gone well. Alison had a moment of conscience trouble.

'Are you sure your mother won't mind us all traipsing in looking for dinner, Colm? It's hardly fair.'

'She is out in the fields rounding up the fatted calf as we speak. She loves to cook and she loves to feed people. Not much call for it in her house any more so she will relish the chance to do it in mine. Pack a pair of pyjamas for Lucy in case she gets too tired. We can put her to bed in the lodge and I will drop her back first thing in the morning. Now, are we ready to hit the road? Because I am causing a hell of a lot of pollution out there with my engine running.'

Ciara was delighted that the invitation for dinner had withstood Alison's good manners. She was ravenous because slim pickings from a lunch her nerves would not allow her to eat and a Macaroon had not filled her. Alison locked the house and they packed into the warm-as-toast car and straight into the arms of Iris Lifford's feverish hospitality.

Chapter Thirty-Seven

Caharoe train station was busy, with people milling around, leaving and being left. There had been talk of its closure or scaling down the decade before but its hinterland had prospered and its future had been secured for another generation. Goods moved in and out of town and people went on all sorts of trips from here that they'd never had money for before. They had all loaded into Colm's car to bring Ciara to her evening train. She would be in Cork by about eight and on the last flight out of the airport headed for a London she had begun to think of as home and all she imagined that might be.

Colm took Tom and Lucy to get a parking-permit ticket in the station kiosk and to load up on the sweets they had been promised. He thought Ciara and Alison might need a moment alone as the house had been full all day and his mother hadn't left until teatime. Iris Lifford had lost none of her ability to sway a conversation or steer a houseful of people in what she thought of as a proper direction. It left little time for silence or relaxation but her frantic need to control the proceedings was a habit she was unlikely to break now. It was one of the things he loved her for but also one of the reasons he was glad he lived in Cork and that she could not bring herself to leave Dublin to join them.

Ciara took advantage of the few short minutes she had with Alison to say some things that might cement their attempts at reconciliation. 'You know where I am now and I am always there if you need me.'

'We'll be in touch, Ciara. Tom thinks you are the coolest aunty on the planet and he's probably right.'

'Well, he got the mammy short straw so I have a bit of compensating to do, I suppose. Seriously though, you know, I'll never forget the years holed up in Jean McDermott's upstairs in Ranelagh, much to our host's constant drunken surprise.'

'It was a pretty unforgettable time all right. I wonder if she is still there or is she dead by now. God knows she drank enough.'

'She's probably still there. You know these ones that pickle themselves in gin, they just go on for ever and a day. I mean it though, Alison. I haven't forgotten it, because you meant so much to me. You were my family when I had none to speak of.' She fought back tears she didn't want to shed. This was the first time in a long time that she had allowed herself to think freely about what she had risked and lost when she had betrayed her friend. All the other times she had let herself off the hook by saying to herself that these things happened but, if she were honest, she knew they didn't just happen. You have to choose and she had chosen badly. 'Thank you, Alison, it's a pity it had to take us so long to try to work this out. I'm a better person now, you know. Different anyway.'

'We're all different and maybe that's no bad thing.'

Ciara moved towards the best friend she had never attempted to replace. She wanted a hug but knew enough not to expect one. Alison held out her hand to Ciara and she grasped it in both of her own, glad of the hint of forgiveness it might imply. It would do to be going on with. They had a lifetime to get close to where they once were.

Glancing at Colm, she tried to lighten the conversation a little, thinking that her feelings had had enough airing for now. 'Keep your man there on the straight and narrow. He has a tendency to fuss and I want young Tom to turn into a well-rounded sort of a person, not a Clancy under any circumstances but not one hundred per cent Lifford either. Oh, and for what it's worth, Iris Lifford is a weapon, safe enough as long as you keep her trained on someone else.'

'I'm not sure he needs much guidance from me but I will help him in any way I can, I promise. As for Iris, she scares the living daylights out of me but I will do my best to stay on her right side. Now go or you will miss the train.'

Lucy had trotted back to where her mother was standing, her teeth glued by some pink concoction that had her almost foaming at the mouth.

'Yes, boss.' Ciara picked up her packed bag from the station platform, gave Lucy's hair a playful tousle and went to say a brief goodbye to Colm, who was talking to a man in uniform who his son had decided was the human embodiment of the Fat Controller from his Thomas the Tank Engine books.

'You know I told you I am going off to see the pyramids, Tom, so I will see you straight after I come back. I suppose you won't be expecting a present from my travels or anything,' Ciara added mischievously.

'I want a mummy suit, like the one you showed us in the brochure, and will you bring one for Lucy too?' And he was gone to where Lucy and Alison were standing looking at the loading of a freight train in the station yard.

'Good God, whatever happened to wanting a stick of rock?'

Colm looked at her in puzzlement. 'I never did get a stick of rock from anywhere. Mam used to call them teeth-rot sticks for the unenlightened.'

Ciara laughed. 'I should have known a well-brought-up urbane young man like you would not have been exposed to such DayGlo teeth-rotting stuff that was the highlight of a day out in Ballybunion for us rural types. You never see them these days. We're all gone too classy for that. Now, while I have you, Colm, can I just say that you shouldn't let the grass grow under your feet? Alison is a great girl—'

'Listen, would you stop with the rural matchmaking act? Let us be and we will see how we get on. She has just lost her husband. Above all, she needs time and I intend to give her that. I know a good thing when I see it or don't you trust my judgement?'

'What can I say? You hooked up with Leda, not exactly the brightest move of your life to date.'

'No, you're right, that was a prize blunder, but I got Tom and for that I would go through every minute of it ten times over.'

'Don't get me started on the weeping. I have hours of travel in front of me: I could do without my mascara tracing a map down my face before I have even left Munster.'

Colm wrapped her in a hug and when she turned to board the train she left behind a team of faces sorry to see her go. She kept her eyes forward on her next step as she had always done. Looking back had never been her strong point.

Ciara waited until she was back in London before she tried to contact Leda. It took more than a half-dozen unanswered phone calls before Ciara finally got hold of her sister. She was in the language-school staffroom when Leda answered her phone. Small talk had never been a sisterly habit of theirs so Ciara cut straight to the matter at hand.

'I'll skin you alive, Leda Clancy, if you so much as pick up the phone to Con or Alison Abernethy ever again, do you hear me?'

'It's Cantwell, Ciara. My name, in case you have forgotten, is Leda Cantwell. A much more attractive surname than Clancy, don't you think? Mind you, deed poll is about your best chance of changing your name. Mauritius was fabulous, thanks for asking. Too bad your invitation got lost in the post – not that a confirmed spinster like yourself would have appreciated the sheer romance of it all.'

Ciara had come to expect the barbed exchanges that littered her now infrequent conversations with Leda. She recognized the familiar quality of the compulsion to hurt with words. It was the pitiful bequest of a childhood riddled with unease and powerlessness.

'I'm delighted for you that your wedding was such a success, Leda, and I'm sure that you and Bob will be very happy – at least until he starts to bore you – but I will crown you if I hear that you have gone anywhere near the Abernethys. You got your paws on some of Con's cash, now drum up a bit of decency and stay away.'

'I was entitled to at least that from the scumbag – or has your friend in her widow's weeds made you forget that? I think he got off lightly under the circumstances. Shame about Dan, but I never asked for a personal delivery of cash. A nice fat anonymous deposit in my account would have suited me fine, but that would have left a paper trail and there is nothing a crooked politician fears more than a paper trail. He was too lazy to get off his arthritic arse and do his own dirty work. Would have been a bit of a result if he'd died in the car crash instead of Dan, who looked like a total babe that night by the way. How's the widow anyway? Bereavement would suit her little pinched face very well, I'd say.'

'Enjoy the blasted money and when it's all gone don't even think of coming for more, do you hear me?' The pencil that Ciara was moving between her finger and thumb snapped under the stress of talking to Leda. Exasperation complicated by a nagging sense of responsibility to her younger sibling guaranteed that she always felt bad after their conversations.

Leda on the other hand seemed not to be equipped with any moral compass. She said and did what she liked.

'Yeah yeah, Ciara, go easy on the sermons. You'll give yourself a heart attack stressing about the likes of Con Abernethy. I'm all set up with Bob because he has the old Midas touch when it comes to cash. It just follows him. And to think I could have settled for someone like Colm Lifford with his poxy provincial practice. I won't need to call on the Bank of Abernethy again. I closed my account the night Dan came to visit. I gave him something to think about on the drive home though, I'd say. I hope dropping my little bombshell didn't make him drive erratically or anything. That would be a shame.'

'What are you talking about? What did you say to him?'

'Well, it was all going well and we were being perfectly civil to each other until he started firing threats at me. He told me he would ruin things between Bob and myself if I ever rang Con again. Well, cute and all as he looked, I wasn't going to let another Abernethy start dictating to me so I told him that Tom Lifford was actually Con's son and nothing to do with Colm at all. That quietened him, I have to say. Poor pet went off in a bit of a daze.'

'You promised me that wasn't the case. You said that Tom was definitely Colm's son.' Ciara thought her head might split open. This was a bridge too far for her to contemplate.

'Ah, I am pretty sure he is Colm's but, you know, sleeping with Con was never an entirely memorable event and as time went on it became more and more forgettable so I couldn't swear on the Bible. But I'm fairly certain. Anyway it doesn't matter now. Tom is settled with Colm and Con isn't destitute enough to need the children's allowance so it's best to leave well enough alone, don't you think? Tell your little addled friend that she can count Con's euros all by herself when he finally croaks it.'

Ciara hung up first, without saying goodbye. Such niceties were thoroughly wasted on her sister. Neither of them had returned to Leachlara in ages and Ciara knew it might be months or even years before they saw each other again. So much for having a sister, she thought as she threw the broken pencil at the waste-paper basket and managed a spectacular over-hit. She went to her laptop and emailed Alison. Between text messages and emails they were managing to build up some regular contact. At the end of her mail she mentioned that Con didn't have to worry about Leda in the future. Her sister had moved on and was out of the picture. It was good news for the Abernethys, and for Colm and Tom too, but Ciara realized that banishing your flesh and blood, even for good reason, was a thoroughly heart-sickening task.

She would never know for sure whether Leda was telling her the truth about Tom, or even if her sister knew what the real truth was, but Ciara was choosing to believe that her nephew was Colm Lifford's son. Anything else was too unnatural and too cruel for everyone involved.

At Lantern Lodge, fussing over Tom's bath and getting him ready for bed was Iris Lifford's favourite task of the day when she was staying with her son and grandson. It reminded her of a lifetime ago when the child was Colm and her life stretched without complication before her. She had learned not to plan but she had always looked on Tom as an unexpected salve for past disappointments. She kissed the top of his head as she settled him into bed. The perfume of his freshly washed hair promised to linger with her.

'Are you happy living in Cork, Tom, or do you miss Dublin?' she asked gently.

'I love it here, Granny. Don't remember much about living in Dublin. I was only young when we moved, you know,' he added with all the full sure knowledge of a six-year-old. 'I miss you though and I love that you visit all the time. I like that.'

Iris hugged him to her. 'I like it too, Tom. I look forward to my next visit all the time. Tell me now who is coming to your birthday party?'

Tom gulped with excitement. 'Well, Dad says I can invite all the boys in my class. There are ten of them and I can get a bouncy castle and we can play football in the field 'cause I am getting goalposts for my birthday. It will be deadly.'

Iris smiled. His enthusiasm was infectious. 'Can I come or will your gran be in the way of all the boys?'

'Of course you can, Granny. You won't be lonely. There will be other girls too.' Fifty years had passed since Iris had thought of herself as a girl and it was refreshing to be addressed as such. Tom continued: 'Aunty Ciara is coming and so is Dad's friend Alison, and Lucy. Lucy is cool. I really like her. She's eight now. She knows loads even though she's a girl. She has a Nintendo and she lets me play with it all the time. Dad is always really happy when Alison is here.'

Iris set aside the bedtime story. She was going to learn a lot more here than she ever would downstairs.

Colm opened a bottle of wine while he waited for his mother to come and join him for dinner. He could hear the soft murmur of chat from upstairs punctuated by Tom's squeals of delight and his mother's familiar laugh. Tom would be wrecked if she didn't let him fall asleep, but he knew better than to disturb his mother in full flight in her favourite role. He poured himself a glass of red and turned the oven down to a whispering heat. He reached for the phone to call Alison. He hadn't talked to her all day and he craved some moments' conversation with her, albeit divided by a few miles of country roads, every twist and turn of which he had committed to memory in the last couple of months.

When Iris eventually came downstairs she moved her dinner around the plate in a way Colm knew she would find utterly irritating if someone did it to a meal that she had prepared. It was obvious she was rippling with inquisitiveness and it had dampened her usually healthy appetite.

'Are you not hungry, Mam?' Colm was toying with her a little before he gave in to the inevitable. The long conversation with Tom had obviously yielded information that Iris was still processing. The questions would come. This was merely the pause before Iris gave them her considerable voice.

'Tom tells me that you and he are spending a lot of time with Alison Abernethy and Lucy, who I now know is the coolest girl alive in your son's estimation. In fact he says this is the first Saturday in ages that all of you haven't been away on a trip somewhere. I'm very sorry that you have had to take today off to spend with your mother. It must be a bit of a drag, as Tom would so neatly put it.'

'Oh, Mam, calm down. Get off your little pulpit. Of course I would tell you about Alison if there were anything new to tell. Yes, we are spending time together but you knew that. Lucy and Tom get on really well and I am stone mad about Alison, so mad that I am terrified of losing her if I admit to her how I really feel. She has been through so much and for all our sakes I cannot afford to mess this one up. So you haven't been excluded from anything massive. The truth is we see each other but Tom and Lucy are always with us and our days together are much more about them having a good time than about us. Timing is everything and I am just not sure that this is the right time for Alison.'

Iris sighed. She had always felt caution was useful to prevent you doing the wrong thing but that it should never stop you doing the right thing. 'You know I think Alison is lovely. I told you she was an absolute lady the first night that she came here with Ciara. Hang the timing and tell her how you feel. If there is anything a woman truly values in a man's character it is a backbone. Believe me, I have suffered at the hands of the spineless variety and it is not to be recommended.' Memories of Patrick Lifford hung between them, as real as if he had lately stood in the kitchen where the remnants of his family now shared supper. 'Be a man, Colm. She will thank you for it and you and Tom will be far the happier for it. He talks about the four of you like you are a single unit. He has already made the leap of faith and you must follow.'

Iris raised her glass and Colm followed her lead and they touched with a satisfying clink.

'You are always right, Mam. It's totally insufferable really,' he added mischievously.

'Of course I am right. I'm your mother. It's my prerogative. God charges us mothers with plenty of monotony in life, but he blesses us with spades of intuition. Something men lack, if you don't mind me saying.'

Colm wasn't hungry any more. He pushed his plate away from him, unwilling to lose any more time. 'I'll go and talk to Alison tonight, Mam. Will you sit with Tom?'

'It would be my pleasure.'

Alison answered the call from his mobile on the second ring.

'Is it all right if I come over?' he asked tentatively, trying to conceal his nerves.

'Of course it is. I'd love to see you. Has your mother's fussing driven you out?'

'Well, sort of,' he answered. 'I'll see you in a few minutes.'

Alison raced upstairs. At most she had about ten minutes before his car would pull in the gate. She was just out of a long, luxurious soak in the bath and she wanted to brush her hair, spray on some perfume and put on the nice dressing gown and not the towelling nightmare she had chosen for pure comfort. She opened the door as soon as her low-lit living room was flooded by his car lights and waited to welcome him into the warmth of the house.

'I had to come,' he blurted out nervously. 'I can't hide how I feel about you any longer. I'm sorry for barging in but—'

Alison held out her hand and brought him inside, closing

the door behind them. They made it to the couch in the living room lost in feverish kissing, touching each other hungrily and willing their bodies to communicate feelings that both had been afraid to give their voices to. They made love wallowing in the passion hidden for so long. They huddled under a few blankets from the couch until cold drove them to Alison's bed in the early hours. They tiptoed past Lucy's bedroom door which was always slightly ajar. There they made love again, more slowly this time, savouring every touch. At dawn Colm nuzzled Alison awake with a kiss.

'I had better get home,' he whispered, though it was the last thing he wanted to do.

'What's the matter? Is Iris withdrawing her Cinderella pass at first light?' Alison teased.

'No, it's not that.' Colm laughed. 'I just want to be there when Tom wakes up. You understand, don't you?'

'Absolutely,' she replied, pulling him to her for one last delicious embrace.

'My mother is getting the early train back to Dublin. Some church function she wants to go to, so the coast will be clear. Will you and Lucy come over to the lodge for lunch with Tom and myself?' Colm asked, desperately wanting to know when he could see her again.

'Try keeping us away.'

She heard her front door close and his car leave before falling into a deliciously contented sleep.

Chapter Thirty-Eight

The next day Alison heard Colm kick his boots off at the back door of Lantern Lodge. He strode in and parked himself next to where she was crouching down over the lacklustre fire that refused to catch properly. His closeness made her feel self-conscious, so she stoked a bit more until finally Colm broke the silence.

'Alison, it's always slow to take off when the wind is blowing up this way from the river. Give it a chance and it will get going.'

Her hair was damp. So much for being back at four, she thought. Ten minutes earlier he would have caught her at the kitchen sink scrubbing honey and oatmeal gunge from her face, trying to freshen her complexion a bit. Small mercies, she thought, extremely small mercies.

'Are Tom and Lucy not with you?'

'We were at the river building a dam. They are tormenting poor old Moll out there in the back yard. I think Lucy is going to ask you for a dog now. Sorry about that!'

'I've told her before she can get a dog when I get the back

garden sorted and a proper kennel put in, but patience is not one of Lucy's best traits.'

'I told them you would join me on quality control after they had finished the finer points of the dam. They have it decorated with weeds and everything. Are you up for a bit of judging? They are getting pizza in town and proper chips if they do well.'

'Ah yeah, why not? Sounds like they are having a great time.' The fire caught with an uproariously loud belch behind her. If she stayed there any longer she would lose the hem of her skirt to the inferno. She stood up, summoning the courage to look at him at last.

'You've got something stuck on your face, Alison. Is it porridge?' He peered closer at her. 'Yup, it's definitely porridge. Did you sneak some of this morning's leftovers from the pot?' His tone was playful, enjoying her mortification just a little too much.

'It's a face mask – was a face mask . . . supposed to be very invigorating . . .' She trailed off, her voice deserting her.

Colm's hand moved to stroke her cheek. He flicked the offending piece of porridge into the fire. The heat of his fingers startled her. Once more she was scorched by his touch. It had lost none of its power despite being imagined a thousand times in her head.

'They do say porridge is wonderful, but I think you have to eat it rather than plaster it on your face to get the benefit. I'm no expert, but that is what I have heard.'

He cupped her face in his hands and brought his lips slowly to hers. Her kiss was hot and gorgeous, just as he remembered their first kisses the night before. It had been such a relief that she had wanted his touch as much as he had wanted her from the first moment he had seen her. They settled into a lingering embrace, losing themselves in each other's arms. They might not have heard the upward latch of the hall door as it clinked open but there was no mistaking Tom and Lucy's presence as their excited voices hollered through the echoing house, thundering up the hallway to where their parents clung together.

'Mam! Colm! Wait until you see this.' Colm stepped backwards from her just in time to beam at the overexcited children who had hauled themselves back from the river. Their clothes were covered in mud and their faces smeared like child warriors. They were unrecognizable as the clean-cut children who had left the lunch table a few hours before.

'Out you both go before you destroy the house,' chided Colm. 'We will catch you up. Are you coming, Ali?'

'You go on with them. I will have to root out a pair of boots in the back kitchen. I'll follow you.'

They kissed again. His hands rested snugly on the small hollow of her back.

She was first to break away. 'Go on, they're waiting.'

Iris's wellington boots were standing to attention under the stray coats in the back kitchen. She knew they belonged to Iris because they were in sterile condition, smelling strongly of all-killing bleach. Oh yeah, and the name label on the inside was a bit of a giveaway. Who in the name of God labels their wellingtons? 'IRIS LIFFORD' in bold block capitals and the date as if they would some day be of historic significance. They pinched Alison as she pulled them on. The grand matriarch's revenge, she thought, for helping herself to what didn't belong to her. She couldn't help but laugh to herself. An oversized knitted cap completed her agricultural look.

* * *

In front of me on the damp and mossy path to the Bracken I could see Colm with his arm looped loosely around his son's shoulder. Moll yapped excitedly as she rattled an awkward dance between their feet. Lucy ran ahead of them, buoyed up by a rampant sense of adventure. At first after Dan had gone I wondered if I would ever have the strength to make my daughter happy again. With what would I fill the void that his death had left in our lives? I hoped that if I could set aside my own sense of heartache and loss and just pretend, that might work. I would never have imagined that Lucy and I would survive simply because Lucy expected us to do just that. My daughter's instinct had no concept of giving in to despair. Children think things will get better because they trust the adults they love will kiss the bruise and make it right. They set aside the bad and seek out the good bits, clinging to little parcels of happiness that they recall from other days, and they survive. As I watched the lively crew weave noisily in front of me, I dared to think I could find a way to trust myself too and that my own happiness might just be there for the taking.

The path to the fields curled down to the river bank. I quickened my step so that we might all arrive together.

ACKNOWLEDGEMENTS

Many thanks to my editor Francesca Liversidge for the enthusiasm and warmth she has shown to me and to *Barefoot over Stones*, and to Jessica Broughton for all her help. Thanks to Eoin McHugh and all at Transworld Ireland for welcoming me to their exciting new imprint. I wish to acknowledge the kindness of Donagh Long, who gave me permission to use the lyrics of his song, 'Never Be The Sun'. Thank you to friends and family who read bits or all of the manuscript at various times and offered their encouragement. Particular thanks to close friends who offered practical support, you know who you are! Thanks to Joan Gough for childminding and for offering me time to work. Love and gratitude are due to my children for being as patient as they could be when their mother was distracted. I want to thank Mary Lyons sincerely for her support. Finally, a special thanks to Noel Gough for believing in me and holding us all together.